Something in Common

Roisin Meaney

W F HOWES LTD

This large print edition published in 2014 by
W F Howes Ltd
Unit 4, Rearsby Business Park, Gaddesby Lane,
Rearsby, Leicester LE7 4YH

1 3 5 7 9 10 8 6 4 2

First published in the United Kingdom in 2013
by Hachette Books Ireland

A CIP catalogue record for this book is available
from the British Library

ISBN 978 1 47125 069 9

Typeset by Palimpsest Book Production Limited,
Falkirk, Stirlingshire
Printed and bound by
www.printondemand-worldwide.com of Peterborough, England

For Treas, for her unstinting support

Our lives are written by other people. Some are with us from the start: parents, siblings, first friends, each adding a chapter to our stories as the years go by. Others find us later – teachers, work colleagues, romantic partners, new friends – and these more mature relationships bring further twists to our plots, at times leading us down paths we might not otherwise have chosen, turning new pages and ushering us along.

Of course, many more whose orbits briefly intersect ours leave little or no legacy. The gruff sweet-shop owner who relieves us of our pocket money each Friday, the smiling dentist who subsequently drills and fills our childhood teeth, the librarian who silently stamps our fortnightly teenage borrowings, the boy with the woolly hat pulled over his ginger hair who pushes the newspaper through our first very own letterbox every morning for a year – these minor characters leave us largely unaltered, and are quickly forgotten.

And then occasionally there are others, not looked-for, not anticipated. They are the ones presented to us almost as an afterthought, whose paths cross ours in unexpected ways, and who are destined, whether we like it or not, to change us profoundly.

This is the story of such a relationship. It is the story of the unlikeliest of friendships and its effect on the two women involved, from its traumatic beginning to its most unforeseen end.

This is the story of Helen and Sarah.

1975

SARAH

If it hadn't been for the scarf she'd have kept going. She'd noticed the maroon Beetle, of course, as soon as she'd turned onto the bridge – impossible to miss it, so carelessly positioned, front wheels skewed, bonnet poking right out, as if it had been flung there in a temper rather than deliberately parked – but with her mind still picking its way through the interview, the image of the car did little more than skitter across the edges of her vision, gone the minute she'd pedalled past it.

What had they thought of her, the three people who'd just spent forty-five minutes picking their way through her background? She had no idea. There'd been no frowns, no indication of dissatisfaction at anything she'd said, but she'd seen no sign that they'd approved of her either, as they'd scribbled God knows what into their identical navy hard-backed notebooks.

At least she was female, and everyone knew that women made better cooks. But maybe they'd been hoping for someone a bit older than twenty-four, someone with a bit more experience: all she'd done

5

since her Leaving Cert was work, with varying degrees of responsibility, in the kitchen of her uncle's small country hotel.

Not that she hadn't been grateful to Uncle John for taking her in – with her mediocre Leaving Cert there hadn't been a lot of choice. Jobs were scarce, and a lot of businesses preferred to employ a man, who wouldn't leave the minute he got married, or became a parent. Small wonder so many of her friends had emigrated the minute they'd left school, or found husbands as soon as they could.

But emigration hadn't appealed to Sarah, and no man had offered to marry her, so she'd made the most of her time in the hotel. She'd watched others and learnt from them, and she'd devoured cookery books in her spare time. She understood food, she respected it – and she felt she was ready for bigger things. She liked the idea of being head cook, even if it was only in a smallish County Kildare nursing home, forty-odd miles from Dublin. It was a perfectly respectable job, and she'd be doing pretty well to get it.

Christine didn't agree.

'Why you want to work in St Sebastian's is beyond me,' she'd said, drawing her kohl pen in a slow black arc beneath her left eye.

'What's wrong with it?' They'd grown up three miles from the nursing home; it was down the road from their old primary school.

'Nothing as such – well, I presume it's decent

enough, as nursing homes go – but, honestly, who are you going to meet there under seventy-five? What hope have you got of finding anyone if you're stuck in some kitchen surrounded by old-age pensioners?'

'I'm not looking for a job just to find a husband,' Sarah had protested. 'I can meet men socially.'

But her sister's words had struck a nerve. Impossible, unbearable scenario, never to walk down the aisle on someone's arm, never to become a wife and a mother – and it was a fact that a lot of women met their future husbands in the work-place. What hope did Sarah have of finding anyone in a nursing home?

It had been so easy for Christine, paired up with Brian since their early teens, engaged to him now at twenty-three, getting married the year after next. All set to give up her part-time job in the library whenever the first baby was on the way. Ready to be supported by her husband as she cooked his dinners and ironed his shirts for the rest of her life.

And look at Sarah, a year older and currently unattached, and still living at home. Still sleeping in the single bed she'd had since childhood, her Beatles and Dickie Rock and Joe Dolan posters covering the flowery wallpaper her mother had chosen. And two of Sarah's friends were already mothers themselves: Goretti Tobin had two little boys and Avril Delaney had had a baby girl just after Christmas. Where was the man Sarah was destined – must be destined – to marry?

But she had to work, and she loved working with food, which was why she'd answered the St Sebastian's ad. If she got the job she'd take it, whatever about Christine's reservations, and hope for the best.

She wondered if the green trouser suit had made any difference in the end, or if she should have gone with her pink dress, like she'd wanted to. Her mother, not surprisingly, had favoured the suit.

'The colour is better on you,' she'd said, drawing her darning needle through the heel of one of her husband's many dark grey socks. 'And you look much more professional in it.'

'I'm interviewing for a cook's job,' Sarah had pointed out. 'I won't need to look professional when I'm chopping onions or peeling spuds.'

But she knew, of course, that the real objection to the dress was that it was too short. Sarah didn't think it was that short, not compared to some of the ones she saw on *Top of the Pops* every week. Minis were in, everyone was wearing them – and her legs weren't bad, if she said so herself.

Mind you, that woman on the interview panel, the one from the nursing home's board of management – Bernice? Beatrice? – with her blue rinse and lavender cardigan buttoned all the way up, would probably have found fault with anything above the knee, and of course it was a lot easier to cycle in trousers.

She'd be glad when she got home though, already

caught in a small shower and by the look of it, a lot more on—

And there was the scarf, spread like a puddle on the wooden surface of the bridge, nearly under Sarah's wheels before she spotted it. She swerved and pulled on the brakes, and doubled back for a closer look.

It weighed nothing, a wisp of a thing – *100% wild silk*, the label said – in gorgeous swirly blues and turquoises and lilacs. She held it by the ends and opened it out, and found a rectangle about the size of a bath towel. She brought it to her nose and smelt sweetish perfume, and cigarettes.

Where had it come from? It couldn't have been here long – no tyre marks on it that she could see, no sign that anything had disturbed it since its arrival. Perfectly dry, although the bridge itself was damp from the short shower Sarah had cycled through not ten minutes before – and surely such a feathery thing would have been blown away on the tiniest breeze, whisked up and carried off?

She imagined it billowing upwards, skirting the treetops, wrapping itself eventually around a church steeple, to the bemusement of the parishioners below. Or maybe swooping gently into the river and floating away to sea, like the Owl and Pussycat, catching the attention maybe of a passing fisherman, who might scoop it up and take it home to his wife.

She glanced behind her and saw again the carelessly parked car – and only then did she notice a figure standing on its far side, between the car and the waist-high metal railing that spanned the bridge on either side, thirty yards or so from where Sarah stood.

She squinted to get a better view of the person she was looking at. As far as she could see, whoever it was wore a dark coat, brown or black. Big hair, also dark, above it – or maybe a hat, one of those furry ones that Russian secret agents wore in James Bond films.

She got off her bike and wheeled it over to lean it against the railing. As she covered the short distance back towards the car, rubbing her hands to get some warmth into them, the narrow heels of the only presentable shoes she owned made a loud clacking sound on the wooden surface that reminded her, for some reason, of a teacher she'd had in second or third class – Sister Mary Assumpta, or was it Attracta?

Brought a ruler down hard three times on Sarah's palm once when she hadn't known the Irish for something. Gave her such a fright she'd wet her pants. Sister Mary Whatever-her-name-was, everyone terrified of her, slap you soon as look at you. Dead now, died not long after Sarah had moved on to secondary school, keeled over with a brain haemorrhage, or a massive stroke or something. Poor creature, you couldn't hold a grudge when you heard something like that.

As she drew nearer to the other figure, she saw that it wasn't a hat: it was hair with the glossy red-brown richness of a just-hatched conker. It was masses of glorious Shirley Temple curls that Sarah would have traded her boring straw-coloured bob for in an instant. They tumbled down the back of the woman's black sheepskin coat, shielding her face completely as Sarah approached.

She must have heard the ridiculous clippity-clop of Sarah's shoes, but she didn't look around. Her palms were braced against the metal railing – no gloves, she must be cold – the too-long sleeves of her coat, miles too big for her, almost covering her hands, the furry cuff of the left one danger-ously close to the tip of the half-smoked cigarette that was clamped between her first and second fingers. The smoke from it drifted straight upwards, no breeze to push it sideways.

Sarah stopped about six feet away. No movement from the other woman, apart from a tiny, rapidly vanishing puff of steam around her face each time her warm breath met the January air. Would she appreciate an interruption? But if it was her scarf, and surely it was, she'd be glad to have it returned to her, wouldn't she?

'Excuse me.'

No response. No reaction, no sign at all that she'd heard.

'Excuse me.' A little louder.

Still nothing. Didn't she want her scarf back? Sarah held it out. 'I found this lying on the bridge up ahead, and I wondered if it was yours.'

The woman continued to ignore her. This was getting ridiculous. Maybe she was deaf.

Sarah stepped closer. 'Excuse me, I just wanted to—'

'Go away.'

Softly said, the words practically inaudible, the head still turned away. Ash dropped off the end of her cigarette and tumbled towards the water.

'Pardon? I didn't quite catch—'

'Leave me alone.'

Sarah was thrown. Maybe she'd missed the mention of the scarf. 'Oh, well . . . but I found this—'

'Just go away, would you?' Louder, sharper, the voice quite deep for a woman. 'Leave me alone.'

'But your scarf—'

'Keep it.'

Keep it? She was giving her beautiful, and probably very expensive, scarf to a stranger, just like that? Why on earth would anyone just hand over—

The thought stopped short in Sarah's head, snagged on a new and disturbing one. Clearly, the woman was in a distressed state. She was standing on a bridge, and she wasn't interested in having her scarf returned to her. Why wouldn't she want it back, unless she was planning never to wear it again?

A green car drove onto the bridge from the opposite direction. The driver, an elderly man, glanced at the two of them as he passed. Too late, as he reached the far end of the bridge, for Sarah to be wondering if she should have flagged him down.

No, of course she shouldn't have: that would have been overreacting. The woman was upset about something, that was all. She needed a shoulder to cry on, some words of comfort.

'Look,' Sarah said, 'is everything OK? I mean, you seem a little . . . I don't know. I mean, are you all right? Can I help at all?'

A long, slow sigh came from the other woman. She flicked what was left of the cigarette into the river and turned finally to look at Sarah. A few years older, somewhere into her thirties. Not beautiful as much as striking. Eyes so very dark brown they might have been black, deeply sha-dowed beneath, nose large and slightly hooked, bottom lip full and wide. Skin the soft colour of coffee with cream in it, cheekbones high and sharply defined.

But there was a curious blankness in the expres-sion, an emptiness in the dark eyes that caused a fresh flick of uneasiness in Sarah.

'Would you just go away?' the woman said, emphasising each word. 'Would you leave me alone and go away, and just keep the fucking scarf, or dump it, I really don't care.'

The swear word, uttered so quietly and with so little feeling, was shocking in its unexpectedness. Sarah's anxiety increased as the woman turned back to face the river. The two of them stood there as the seconds ticked on, Sarah's mind tumbling about, searching for the right course of action. She couldn't possibly leave her – but what on earth was she to do?

A little brown bird swooped towards the water before lifting off again. The sun, well hidden all day behind the clouds, slid past a particularly dense one, washing the afternoon in a slightly darker shade of grey and causing Sarah to pull the front edges of her jacket more tightly closed. Not long till twilight, and a further drop in temperature. She thought longingly of a hot bath, of her mother's rich, beefy stew.

A sudden burst of birdsong came from a copse a few feet from the bank. It sounded unnervingly out of place in the still, cold January afternoon.

Sarah's stomach rumbled, almost three hours since she'd chopped a hardboiled egg into slices and added it to a handful of raw mushrooms. Much less than she normally ate for lunch, but all she'd been able to face with the interview looming.

She had to say something: they couldn't go on standing here in silence all afternoon. She might be blowing this whole thing out of all proportion, it might still be a case of some sad person simply wanting to be alone for a while. But what if it wasn't?

She had to speak, even if she made an utter fool of herself. Better say it and be wrong than be left wondering. As she opened her mouth, the woman looked around again, and this time the dark eyes were narrowed, the lips pressed together, a frown lodged between her eyebrows.

'Sorry,' Sarah said quickly, 'I know you want me to go, but I can't. Not until I know you're not going to . . .' she faltered, searching for the right words '. . . I'm just afraid you might be thinking of . . .'

She came to a stop again, the words refusing to come out – but surely it must be obvious what she meant. She waited for the woman to protest, to tell Sarah she was being stupid, to laugh at her, even – but there was no protestation, no sign that what was lying unspoken between them surprised her in the least. No indication at all that Sarah had come to the wrong conclusion.

God, she wasn't wrong, she knew that now. Her palms prickled with nervousness. Why did she have to be the one to come on this situation? Why hadn't she cycled on and ignored the damn scarf? No, she didn't mean that; she wanted to help, but she hadn't a clue what to do, not a clue.

'It's none of your business,' the woman snapped. 'You know nothing about me, you've no right to butt in. Just leave me alone, for Christ's sake.'

'I can't,' Sarah insisted, 'not when I know what you want to do. I can't leave you – how can I? How could anyone walk away from this? I'd never be able to live with myself if – I mean, I just can't leave you on your own to—'

Again she stuttered to a standstill, praying for another car to appear. Anyone would do – she'd

15

run out and flag them down, make them stop and help – but no car came. She was alone with a suicidal woman: it was down to her.

'Please don't,' she went on, putting a hand on the sleeve of the too-big coat, feeling the heat of incipient tears behind her eyes. 'You can't do this – things can't be that bad. There must be—'

'How the *fuck* would you know how bad they are?' the woman demanded angrily, snatching her arm away. 'Who the fuck do you think you are, to tell me what I can and can't do? Go away, leave me alone – this has nothing to do with you.'

'I can't go away,' Sarah repeated, eyes burning, voice trembling. 'Look,' she said urgently, blinking hard to keep the tears at bay, 'I have to try to help you, whether you want it or not. I can't just walk away from you – even if I wanted to, I couldn't. You must understand that.' Tears spilled out then and rolled down her face, and without thinking she pressed the scarf to her eyes, smelling again the perfume, the tobacco.

'*Jesus!*' The woman slammed both her hands hard onto the top of the railing, making Sarah's heart jump, making her jerk the scarf away from her face. 'What the hell are *you* crying for? You know *nothing* about me. If you had any fucking *idea* what I'm going through—'

'Tell me,' Sarah cried, rummaging in her jacket pockets for a tissue, remembering that they were in her bag, which was sitting in the bike's basket. 'Tell me what's wrong – maybe it'll help.'

16

Wasn't that what everyone said, that you had to talk about your problems? Never mind that Sarah wouldn't have an idea what to say in response: maybe the act of talking would be enough.

But the woman shook her head violently. '*Jesus Christ!*' she cried. 'You really think you can make all this go away? You think I'll tell you what's wrong and you'll, what, wave your little magic wand and make it all better?' Her eyes were flashing, and bright with tears too now. 'Would you ever just go and leave me to it? Just walk on, pretend you never saw me. Would you just do that? If you want to make anything better, that's what you can do.' She pressed her mouth shut and swung her head away to look out at the river again.

'I can't,' Sarah wept, 'I can't do that. I'm sorry, I can't walk away. Please don't ask me to.' She searched for the right words, anything that might help. 'There must be someone,' she said urgently, dabbing again at her wet face with the scarf, 'you must have some family – think what this would do to them, think how much it would hurt them.'

She had to keep talking, had to keep trying to stop this. 'You don't want to cause more hurt, do you? Because that's all this will do. You'll escape whatever you're running away from, but you'll be leaving more heartache behind you, and where's the good in that?'

She was dimly aware, as she talked, that maybe her words were all wrong. Maybe there was no family – maybe they'd all been wiped out in a terrible car crash, or a house fire. Maybe that was why the woman was here now, planning to end it all. Sarah watched her hands, still planted on the railing. She waited in dread for any sudden movement.

But the woman remained motionless. Sarah glanced up to her face, but the little she could see of it gave nothing away. Was she listening, or had she shifted her awareness somewhere else? No matter: the longer she didn't haul herself upwards onto the railings, the better.

'I just think,' Sarah went on, afraid to let the silence grow, 'that maybe if you got some help or, I don't know, if you had someone to talk to – oh, not me, I don't mean me. Like you said, we don't know each other at all, and of course you're right, I have no idea what's brought you to this state, but I really truly feel that this isn't the answer. Maybe if you spoke to a doctor or . . .' not a psychiatrist, she'd better not say that, it mightn't go down well '. . . or a counsellor, someone professional, they might be able to help you.'

She stopped, drained, finally out of inspiration. A small breeze was cold on her damp cheeks. Her eyes still stung: more tears weren't far away, wouldn't need much encouragement to fall. She'd always been quick to cry, regularly bawled her eyes out at the cinema.

There was silence for a few seconds. Another car drove onto the bridge then, but Sarah didn't turn towards it, made no move to intercept it. She remained standing where she was, her eyes still fixed on the woman's face, every sense alert to the possibility of any sudden movement – though what she could do in that eventuality was beyond her. Grab on, and maybe get pulled over the railing herself? She imagined the two of them spinning through the air like a pair of circus acrobats, whirling and flailing as they plunged towards the water. The thought was horrifying: she shook her head to dislodge it.

Finally, the other woman moved. She lifted an arm and brought the sleeve of her sheepskin coat once across her eyes, and Sarah realised she was wiping away silent tears of her own. Then, without looking in Sarah's direction she turned away abruptly, drawing keys from her coat pocket. Sarah watched as she walked around the Beetle and opened the driver's door.

'Are you OK to drive?' she asked. 'I can stay a bit longer if you want.'

The woman ignored her. She got into the car and switched on the ignition as she banged the door closed. Sarah stood and watched as the Beetle pulled away too fast, causing the tyres to screech loudly for an instant. She waited until it turned off the bridge and disappeared.

They hadn't exchanged names. They would probably never lay eyes on one other again. For all Sarah knew, the woman was going to drive to the next bridge and throw herself off it, uninterrupted by a babbling, tearful cyclist. Sarah might read about it in tomorrow's paper: *Volkswagen Beetle found abandoned by river, fears for driver's safety.*

Had she made a difference? Had anything she'd said struck a chord? She'd never know – but if she read nothing over the next few days, if there was no report of a missing woman on the radio, she'd tell herself that maybe she'd been of some help. She'd let herself believe that she'd saved a life, and hope she was right.

She leant against the railing, trailing the scarf over it and pressing her hands against its cold metal, just as the woman had done. She drew in the dank scent that came up from the river beneath her. Imagine wanting to throw yourself into that freezing water, imagine how desperate you'd have to be, how low you must have fallen to want that.

She pressed her icy palms against her cheeks and eyed the scarf, lying limply there. Should she tie it onto the railings in case the woman came back for it? But that seemed unlikely: the scarf was probably the last thing on her mind right now. Sarah might as well keep it, although she couldn't imagine ever wanting to wear it, pretty as it was. Maybe she'd wash it and add it to her next charity shop round-up.

She retraced her steps to where she'd left the bike, her legs unexpectedly shaky. She pushed the scarf into her handbag, beside the envelope of references she'd brought along to the interview. So unimportant it seemed now, whether or not she was offered the cook's job. She remembered her nervousness as she'd cycled to the nursing home just a couple of hours earlier, not knowing that the real challenge would come on the way home.

As she cycled off, none too steadily, the rain returned in earnest, stabbing into her back, her shoulders, her head. She hardly noticed it.

HELEN

All the way back to Dublin she shivered violently, despite the heavy coat and the relative warmth of the car. Driving through the outskirts of the city, wipers slicing away the rain, she noticed that she was almost out of petrol. Dusk was falling, headlights were being switched on in other cars, streetlights were winking into life. Lights appearing all around her, the whole world lighting up, and nothing but darkness inside her, nothing but a black gaping hole where her heart, or her soul, or her entire being, used to be.

She tried not to think, she tried to keep her head empty. She pulled into a petrol station and rubbed her numb hands together for several minutes before getting out. She pumped fuel into the tank she'd deliberately ignored all week, certain that whoever filled it again wouldn't be her.

A line from a song floated unbidden into in her head, something about learning the truth at seventeen, as she stood by the car, watching the money gauge as it climbed to five pounds. Janis Ian's dreary, angst-ridden song had come on the radio as she'd fed Alice her breakfast that morning, and now it returned, spinning on its imaginary turn-table in her head, spewing out its woebegone lyrics.

It wasn't about learning the truth, it was about recognising the lies. Helen had known it all at seventeen: she'd been wild and hungry and impatient to turn the next page of her life and meet head-on whatever and whoever was waiting there. It had taken her almost another seventeen years to understand that happiness never lasted, that good didn't triumph, that love only laid you bare for the pain that was waiting.

You must have family, the woman on the bridge had said, butting in where she wasn't wanted. Forcing Helen to remember Alice, who smelt of wet grass and pepper, who couldn't sleep without her thumb tucked into her cheek, who screamed if the landing light was turned off, whose chubby little wrists poked from the horrible pastel-coloured cardigans that Helen's mother insisted on knitting.

Alice, the reason Helen hadn't been with Cormac at the end, hadn't held his hand as he'd slipped away. Alice, whom Helen wanted to hate for that but couldn't, because Alice was part of Cormac. She was all he'd left behind.

But the timing, the cruel timing of the rash that had prompted Alice's babysitter Anna to phone Helen, the rash that had forced Helen to leave her dying husband's bedside and attend to Alice, who, it turned out, didn't have meningitis after all, just an outbreak of psoriasis – and by the time Helen had got back to Cormac, it had been too late.

She felt the rumble of the petrol through the nozzle she held, heard its gush into the tank, smelt its acrid tang. She would have done it. She would have climbed onto the railing. She would have jumped out of this putrid life without a backward glance, without a second's hesitation, once she'd keyed herself up enough. She would have done it, if it hadn't been for the interfering woman on the bridge, the crying stranger, with hair the colour of crispbread, in a hideous green trouser suit.

She pulled the nozzle from the tank and hooked it into its cradle. She screwed the petrol cap back on – and then she slammed both of her palms hard on the roof of the car, causing a man at the next pump to look across, startled. She ignored him, feeling the sting of the blow, doing nothing to lessen the sharp heat of it.

Enough lies: of course she wouldn't have done it, because she was a fucking coward. The other woman had had nothing to do with it: all she'd given Helen was an excuse to walk away.

She leant against the car and wrapped the sheepskin coat more tightly around her. She closed her eyes and saw herself standing by the railing, looking down at the rushing water. She remembered taking a deep breath and preparing herself to do it – and her body had refused to move, refused to obey her mind's command.

She'd lit a cigarette and drawn furiously on it, still determined to carry out what she'd come to do. She'd cursed her stubborn, traitorous limbs,

24

willing them to move, but the more she'd thought about it, and pictured herself doing it, the more terrifying the prospect had become.

And out of nowhere she'd heard the soft whirr of bicycle wheels going past. She hadn't looked around, had kept stock still and waited for whoever it was to disappear again, but then she'd heard the wheeze of brakes being pulled, and a few seconds later the clack of approaching footsteps. Female footsteps.

The best of it was, the *killer* was, the woman probably thought she'd saved Helen's life. She'd probably congratulated herself all the way home because she'd rescued someone who was about to jump off a bridge. She'd never know the truth, never know that Helen had already been saved – or damned – by lack of courage.

And her beautiful scarf was gone. Serve her right, too proud to take it back from the woman she'd told to keep it. The ridiculously expensive scarf Cormac had bought her for their first anniversary was gone to a stranger. One more layer to press onto the slab of her grief.

In the small shop beside the petrol station she bought two atrociously priced bananas and a bag of jelly babies. She ate the bananas driving through the wet streets to her parents' house. She slicked on more lipstick as she sat in the parked car outside their wrought-iron gates, listening to the engine ticking itself to sleep.

She wouldn't try it again, she knew that. She'd gone to the edge and pulled herself back, and now there was no edge any more. She couldn't do it: the will required for such an act wasn't in her. The knowledge brought no relief, made her no happier; on the contrary, she now had the added torment of the realisation that there was no escape.

She wondered suddenly if Alice could possibly have been the reason for her failure today. Maybe, despite her conflicted feelings about her daughter, there was some unacknowledged umbilical connection to Alice that had prevented Helen from climbing onto the railing and letting go. It sure as hell hadn't been the thought of never seeing her parents again.

She pulled the key from the ignition – forget it, it was over now – and got out, wrapping Cormac's coat tighter around her as she hurried through the petering-off rain up the driveway.

'What kept you?' her mother said, opening the door. 'You said you'd be back by five. We had to put Alice to bed.'

'I ran out of petrol,' Helen replied, walking around her into the hall, continuing past the giant walnut hallstand, past the marble-topped side table, home to an elegant white telephone and the key to her father's Rolls-Royce, which sat as always on top of his leather driving gloves.

'Really,' her mother said, a hand to the string of small, perfect pearls around her neck, 'I have to say that coat looks ridiculous on you.'

Helen began to climb the stairs. 'Is she in my room?'

'Helen, she's *asleep*, you can't wake her. You can't take her out in the cold – it's not fair to the child.'

It wasn't fair to the child that she had to grow up without a father. It wasn't fair that the child's mother wondered, every now and again, what it would be like to smother her with a pillow. 'She'll be fine, she'll go back to sleep in the car. And I have jelly babies if she doesn't.'

Her mother's exasperated sigh, which she knew intimately, followed her all the way up the stairs, but there was no further argument. The only good thing, if you could call it that, about your husband dying, about being widowed at thirty-two, was that people were forced to make allowances for you – for a while anyway.

She pushed open the door of her old bedroom and walked across the thick wool carpet towards the little hump of her sleeping daughter. Alice lay on her back, her face turned slightly in the direction of the window at which Helen had often stood as a teenager, blowing out the smoke of her illicit cigarettes.

She reached for the small black-patent buckled shoes set neatly by the bed before scooping Alice and the blanket that covered her into her arms. Alice made a sleepy, protesting sound which Helen ignored as she hefted her onto her shoulder and left the room.

Her father stood at the bottom of the stairs, arms outstretched. 'I'll take her.' There was no sign of her mother – sulking, no doubt, in the sitting room.

Helen surrendered her load, grateful that he wasn't putting up a fresh argument, and led the way to the car. Alice was manoeuvred onto the back seat and the blanket wrapped around her. Helen's father closed the passenger door softly and walked around to the driver's side.

'Have you thought at all about what you want to do?' he asked, his hand on the door to prevent it closing, and Helen guessed that he'd been instructed to bring it up. Three fucking weeks, that was all they'd given her to mourn.

She looked at him. 'Do?'

He had the grace to look discomfited. 'About a job, I mean. How you're going to support Alice.'

'Not yet,' she said steadily. 'I've been a bit preoccupied.'

He put his free hand up, warding her off. She imagined him sitting on the bench in his wig and gown, cutting short barristers and criminals alike with just such a gesture. 'I'm not saying you have to decide right away,' he said. 'It's just . . . your mother and I want to help any way we can, you know that.'

'Yes.'

'We'd look after Alice, we'd be happy to, if you wanted to look for work. We'd love to see more of her.'

'I know.'

'Or if it was a question of money, if you wanted to study for—'

'No. Look, I have to get Alice to bed.' She turned

the key, forcing him to release the door. 'I'll give you a ring,' she said, pulling it closed and driving off without looking at him again. She got to the end of the road and turned left, shoving her hair angrily away from her face. Three fucking weeks.

From the back seat came a whimper. Helen said, 'Ssh,' and kept on driving. The trouble was, she *did* need money, or she soon would. Cormac had been useless with it, living from one engagement to the next, he and the lads doing the same dance-hall circuit as The Clipper Carltons and The Dixies and all the other showbands, with no thought for the future – and Helen hadn't been much better. One week they'd be drinking whiskey and eating fillet steak, the next they'd be pulling the sofa apart to find enough change for a pint of milk. There had been no life insurance, no talk of savings.

Alice's arrival had prompted them to become somewhat more responsible, and for a while they'd budgeted for more balanced spending periods. Fillet steak was replaced with pork chops and chicken, and there was generally enough milk in the fridge. Cormac even opened a savings account in Alice's name, and arranged for small monthly payments to be made into it. They still had their moments, of course, when a larger than usual cheque arrived, or when the band was booked to play the Hibernian Ballroom every Thursday night over the summer – although they realised fairly quickly that hangovers and small babies were pretty much incompatible.

And then the unthinkable had happened, and Cormac had been diagnosed and money, or lack of it, had become the least of their worries. During the months of his illness Helen had lived from day to day, eking out the fivers that arrived in mass bouquet cards from relatives on hearing the news, drawing funds when she had to from their miserable joint account, trying to avoid the savings, still tragically small, that had been intended to put Alice through university.

She'd also sold, one bleak afternoon, the pitifully few pieces of decent jewellery she possessed to the only pawnbroker who'd consider taking them. Her wedding and engagement rings, an amethyst necklace she'd inherited from her grandmother, the gold stud earrings Cormac's mother had given her the night before her wedding, a silver locket on a heavy chain from a man who'd wanted to marry her once.

And much as she hated to admit it, they'd hardly have survived without the purplish-blue fifty-pound notes her father slipped her now and again, not thinking, or not caring, that precious few shops were willing to let her break fifty pounds – ridiculous denomination, the price of a half-decent sofa – in return for a thirty-pence loaf of bread. She'd accepted the money with muttered thanks each time and made it last as long as she could.

And then, a week before Cormac's death at the beginning of January, Rick, the band's saxophonist, had slipped her an envelope during what turned out to be his last visit to Cormac in hospital. 'It's from all of us, just to help out,' he'd murmured. Its contents, ten tatty twenty-pound notes, had caused Helen to burst into tears when she'd opened it, to poor Rick's discomfiture.

She drove through Stoneybatter and pulled up in front of the little terraced house Cormac had inherited from his paternal grandmother. 'We got on brilliantly,' he'd told Helen. 'She always said she'd leave me the house. I thought she was joking, but she wasn't.'

The neighbourhood was what Helen's mother would call *decidedly working class*. The houses on Helen's road were old, the dividing walls thin, the rooms – mostly two up, two down – cramped and low-ceilinged, the stairs horribly steep, the gardens tiny. The storage heaters that Cormac had installed were expensive to run and of limited efficiency. But the house was paid for and it belonged to Helen now, and it was the only place that had ever felt like home to her.

She carried a whining, half-awake Alice inside and hauled her upstairs. 'Shush,' she told her, kicking open the door to the second bedroom.

'But I'm *cold*.'

'You're fine – you'll warm up in bed.'

Downstairs again, she opened the press above the fridge and took out the remains of the brandy that someone, she couldn't remember who, had brought. She'd lost count of the visitors who'd come to the house over the last few weeks, who'd arrived in

31

their Sunday clothes and perched on the edges of armchairs, speaking in hushed voices as if noise would kill Cormac sooner than the cancer.

She eased the cork off the bottle and walked into the chilly sitting room, home to the Sacred Heart picture and his little red light that had hung on the wall since Cormac's grandmother's time, the only memento that he'd insisted on keeping. Helen looked at the face that gazed back at her serenely. 'Still here,' she told it, 'just like yourself.'

She crossed to the tiled mantelpiece and lifted down the envelope that sat there. *To my parents*, she'd written – had it only been last night? It seemed like a thousand years ago. She slit it open and unfolded the single sheet and read the brief message.

> I hope you can forgive what I am planning to do. I can't go on. Please look after Alice.

No salutation, no signature. She'd never been able to communicate on any meaningful level with them, never felt any real connection with them. On the face of it, her upbringing would have been the envy of a lot of others. Her parents had money, tons of it – they were rolling in it, thanks to the ludicrously high salary paid to her father– and as their only child, Helen had enjoyed the best of everything growing up.

But they had no conception at all that what their daughter had needed, more than any expensive outfit or gourmet meal, was a modicum of affection. Helen didn't remember a single goodnight kiss from either of them, or any declaration of love. There'd been no embraces on meeting or leaving them, no sign that they were ever genuinely moved by her. All her life she'd felt unwanted by them, as if she'd been an accident – or maybe a hasty decision, regretted the minute they'd conceived her.

She tore the sheet and envelope into pieces and tossed them into the fireplace on top of last evening's ashes. She raised the bottle to her lips and gulped down the remaining brandy, gasping as the burn hit her throat.

She looked at her face in the spotted mirror above the mantelpiece, saw the havoc wrought there. Cheekbones like blades: Alice had been the only one eating regularly for as long as Helen could remember. Shadows under her eyes so deep they might have been painted on, a testament to her broken nights. An eerie emptiness in the eyes, nothing left to shine out.

She pulled her hair back with both hands and gathered it into a bunch at the nape of her neck and stood silently in this position for several seconds. Eventually she dropped her hands and returned to the kitchen, where she took the scissors from the cutlery drawer.

She undressed slowly and completely, putting her clothes in a pile on the table. She spread overlapping sheets from the previous day's newspaper in a rough square on the worn lino and stood in the centre, feeling the cold worming its way up through the bare soles of her feet. She worked methodically, without a mirror, beginning above her left ear and feeling her way slowly around. The scissors made a sawing sound that reminded her of a purring cat. The hair dropped silently, sliding past her naked shoulders and falling onto the newspaper.

When she had finished, she went back into the sitting room and looked again at her reflection. The right side was shorter than the left, the ends blunt and higgledy-piggledy, the top too full without its counterbalancing length. With her gaunt, blank face she looked like a doll whose owner in a fit of spite had hacked off her toy's beautiful curls.

But Cormac had adored her hair, and without him it had become one more painful reminder: twining his fingers in it when they slow-danced, trailing it along his body when they were drowning in one another in bed, or wherever they got the chance. Washing it for her, both of them squeezed into the bath as he lathered and massaged and rinsed. Hadn't she some chance of surviving without him if it wasn't around to torture her with memories?

She didn't care how she looked, but she wasn't about to give strangers any excuse to stare at her. Tomorrow she'd take a tenner from the dwindling supply in Rick's envelope and find someone to take off the rest of the curls, give it a shape that nobody would look twice at. She hadn't been to a hairdresser in years. She'd go to some place that didn't look like they'd rob you.

She lowered herself to the floor and lay on her side on the awful orange and yellow carpet that Cormac had chosen six months before they'd met. She brought her knees up to her chest and wrapped her arms around them. The cold air raised goose pimples on her bare skin but she stayed there, wound up tight, eyes open and unseeing, until she heard the doleful notes of the national anthem playing on her neighbour's television.

She uncurled slowly and got to her feet, shivering now. She rubbed her arms and stamped her feet, feeling the lightness around her head. Back in the kitchen, as she was bundling up the newspaper sheets, a *help wanted* column caught her eye. She eased the page out from the rest, smoothed it flat and ran down through *dental technician, typist, lorry driver, seamstress, legal secretary, waitress, crane operator.*

She crumpled up the page and returned it to the bundle. Nothing she wanted, nothing she was qualified to do, apart from waitressing. Anyone could carry a plate from A to B, but she didn't want to. She didn't want to do anything.

She'd flatly refused to consider any kind of third-level education after secondary school, much to her parents' dismay. 'Have you any idea how many girls would give their eye teeth for the chance to go to university?' her father had demanded, and Helen had resisted the urge to tell him to send

35

one of them instead of her. She'd held her tongue and refused to budge.

His subsequent offer of a secretarial position within his brother's legal practice had left her equally cold – she had no intention of working in a place where she was known as the boss's niece. Instead she'd found a job without his help behind the counter of the glove department in Burke's Department Store.

It wasn't in the least demanding – in fact most of the time it bored her stupid – but it paid enough to allow her to move out of home and into a shared house, with a few pounds left over to have a couple of good nights out every weekend.

Twenty-seven and having the time of her life, marriage the last thing on her mind. Why would she tie herself down, give up her freedom in exchange for some man's ring? And then twenty-eight-year-old Cormac Fitzpatrick had come in one day looking for a pair of gloves for his mother's birthday, and while Helen was wrapping the sheepskin ones he eventually chose, he asked her if he could take her out to dinner.

And within six months they were living together in the house his grandmother had left him, arguing about the merits of The Beatles (him) over the Stones (her), and talking politics, which thankfully they agreed on – they both leant sharply to the left and despised the Church's stranglehold on Ireland – and all she wanted was to take his name and to wear his ring for the rest of her life.

She went along when he and the band were performing, followed them around the ballrooms and dancehalls of Dublin and beyond, although up to this she'd despised the middle-of-the-road music put out by the showbands, giving a nod to jazz and pop and country-and-western with none of the grit of Led Zeppelin or Procol Harum, none of the fierce excitement of Grateful Dead or The Doors.

It didn't matter: if he'd been playing organ music in cathedrals around Ireland she'd have sat in the front pew, mesmerised. He had bewitched her, he had swept into her life and taken it over. She watched him perform, the other band members invisible to her. She saw the way the women in the crowd eyed him up, all frosted lipstick and blue-lidded eyes, batting their false lashes at him and the other musicians, and she wanted to slap the smiles off their faces. She counted the minutes until the dancing ended and everyone went home, and he walked off the stage to her.

Needless to say, her parents had been horrified. Not so much at the idea of their only daughter living in sin – this was bad; but provided the neighbours, or their parish priest, didn't find out, they were willing to endure it. Far worse was the fact that he was a member of a struggling showband and not at all wealthy or famous. But Helen hadn't given a damn about her parents: all she cared about was the incredibly wonderful state in which she now existed.

She'd suspected, walking up the aisle a year later

to Cormac – her father stiff with disapproval beside her – that she was already carrying his child, and she'd been right. Alice had been born seven months after the wedding, much to her parents' fresh dismay. Bad enough that she'd married a musician from the wrong side of the tracks: far worse that he'd got her up the duff in advance.

She'd handed in her notice at Burke's when she was eight months pregnant, told her boss she wouldn't be back; much, she suspected, to his relief – they hadn't exactly seen eye to eye over the years, but she'd been careful never to give him enough ammunition to sack her. The prospect of becoming a full-time housewife and mother didn't exactly fill her with joy, but she'd bide her time until Alice started school, and then hopefully she'd find a more exciting workplace. In the meantime, they'd make do on Cormac's sporadic earnings.

But now Cormac was gone, and his earnings were no more, and she needed to find some other way to support Alice and herself, and she had no idea how she was going to do that.

She pushed the newspaper into the bin. She took her clothes from the table and went upstairs to bed.

SARAH

'She wasn't suicidal, it was a cry for help.' Christine took a biscuit from the plate and sniffed it. 'Is there ginger in these?'

'No. How can you be so sure she wasn't going to kill herself?'

'Because of the scarf.' They both looked at it, folded on the table by Christine's mug. 'She left it there deliberately, it's obvious. She knew someone would come along and find it, just like you did, and stop her.'

'But why didn't she take it back when I offered it?'

Christine shrugged. 'Maybe she was sick of it.'

Sarah wasn't convinced. The woman had seemed in real distress – she'd seemed so wretched and defeated. But in the five days since their encounter there'd been no mention in the paper of an abandoned car, or a body found in a river, so thankfully it looked like she hadn't gone through with it.

Christine stroked the soft silk. 'It's gorgeous. Are you sure you don't want to keep it?'

'I'm sure – I couldn't possibly wear it.'

'Well, I could.' She opened her bag and slipped

the scarf inside. 'Are you delighted about the new job?'

'I am – thrilled.'

The letter had come the day before, very formal, offering Sarah the position of head cook at St Sebastian's, and signed by the secretary of the board of management, who hadn't been at the interview. Sarah was to start, if she accepted the position, as soon as possible.

Uncle John had received the news of her departure from the hotel with rather less dismay than she'd been expecting; in fact, the prospect of losing her hadn't seemed to put him out much at all. 'It's time you spread your wings,' he told her. 'You'll make a terrific head cook, no bother to you. Give me a week or two to sort a replacement.' And that was that.

So she was moving on, with full responsibility in the nursing-home kitchen, and around twenty-seven mouths to feed each day. Her hours were half past eight to half past four, Monday to Friday – someone else, some man, covered the weekends. Breakfast was at nine, lunch at one and tea, which she could prepare in advance to be served by the nursing staff, at half past five. She would have an assistant cook and a kitchen junior – two people working under her, taking their orders from her.

Within a week Uncle John found a replacement, so she phoned the nursing home and told them she could start the following Monday. As the days passed, she found herself becoming increasingly anxious.

What if the assistant cook had been there for ages, and resented being told what to do by a newcomer? What if Sarah burnt something on her first day, or didn't make enough to go around? What if she poisoned them all with underdone chicken, or the first batch of queen cakes she made in the unfamiliar oven fell flat?

Maybe she'd been too ambitious, applying for the position of head cook at twenty-four. Maybe she should have bided her time at the hotel, or looked for a position in a restaurant kitchen with a little more responsibility. She wondered what the other candidates had been like – they surely couldn't have been younger – and how the board of management had decided on her. What if she let them down, what then?

Her parents had a lot more faith in her abilities.

'We're very proud of you, love,' her mother told her. 'Not many people your age would find themselves in charge of an entire kitchen. It's a big honour for you.'

'She'll be well able,' her father put in from behind his newspaper.

'Of *course* she will: I *know* that.'

They'd been astonished to hear of her encounter with the woman on her way home from the interview. Sarah hadn't been going to mention it, but she couldn't help blurting it out as soon as she'd arrived home. 'I hadn't a clue what to say. I was afraid I'd put my foot in it, and make things worse.'

'She was lucky you came along,' they'd assured her. 'You did what anyone would have done, you handled it very well. Now go and change out of those wet clothes,' her mother had added, 'before you get pneumonia. Why you didn't let your father drive you is beyond me' – and, just like that, they'd put the episode behind them.

But over the nights that followed Sarah found herself replaying the whole thing as she lay in bed. She didn't think Christine was right: it hadn't felt like a cry for help. She could still easily conjure up the woman's haunted expression – the empty, shadowed eyes, the starkly defined cheekbones. It was the face of a tormented woman, not someone looking for attention.

What had happened to cause her to be so miserable? A broken romance maybe, a betrayal by someone she loved. Or bad news of another sort, a terminal diagnosis; told she was going to die, and unable to face a slow, painful end. It could have been anything, and Sarah would never know.

Monday came and her new job started, and the woman on the bridge was forgotten as Sarah concentrated on settling into St Sebastian's – and to her delight, she discovered very quickly that her years of experience in the hotel had prepared her well, and she was more than capable of handling the demands of head cook.

She revelled in every aspect of the work, from planning the weekly menus and ordering supplies to preparing the dishes and plating them up. Right from the start she took to visiting the dining room towards the end of lunchtime to chat to the residents and get their opinions, and she also tapped on the bedroom doors of those unable to make it to the table.

By and large, she was positively received. Her elderly charges invariably expressed surprise at her young age, but most seemed perfectly satisfied with her efforts. They welcomed her attention, and were eager to offer their food preferences – and their life stories, if she had time. It wasn't hard to warm to them, to want to feed and nourish them.

Within a week, she knew she'd made the right choice in coming to St Sebastian's. It was the perfect fit for her; it was where she was supposed to be.

And, best of all, she had Bernadette, her cheerful sixty-plus assistant cook, who'd worked in St Sebastian's kitchen since it had opened in the fifties, and who had no ambitions at all to be the boss. 'I'm happiest carrying out orders,' she told Sarah. 'Tell me what you want done and I'll do it.'

Not surprisingly, she knew all there was to know about the workings of the nursing-home kitchen, and was invaluable in pointing out where things were kept – and she also had no problem in rearranging them to Sarah's satisfaction.

'You're the youngest boss I've had by a mile,' she told Sarah at the end of the first week, 'but you know what's important. The last cook never once set foot in the dining room. They love you here, even Martina.'

Sarah doubted that. Martina Clohessy would find something to complain about if the fanciest French chef was cooking her meals. She'd already informed Sarah that the beef in the stew was on the fatty side, and that pastry gave her hives.

But for every Martina there were half a dozen Stephen Flannerys.

'You're a better tonic than all the pills in the world,' he'd tell her, cradling her hand in both of his trembling ones. 'I'd swim the Atlantic for one of your fruit scones.'

Barely thirty-nine when Parkinson's had struck, turning him into a shaking old man by the time Sarah met him, shortly after his sixty-sixth birthday, she'd never heard a single cross or self-pitying word from him.

And there was Jimmy Doohan, who played 'The Mountains of Mourne' and 'Come Back to Ireland' on his battered accordion when anyone requested it, and often when they didn't. And poor Dorothy Phelan, who rarely spoke any more, who didn't recognise her daughter and son-in-law when they visited, but who smiled so sweetly whenever Sarah visited her room with a helping of trifle or a slice of still-warm ginger cake.

Sarah grew very quickly to love them all. She rose each weekday morning looking forward to getting back to them. The sad woman with the curly hair was called to mind just twice a day, when

Sarah cycled over the bridge on her three-mile journey to and from work. The ghost image of the Beetle was there, and the lonely figure standing behind it – but gradually even these faded, and the episode settled into a dim corner of her mind, to lie largely undisturbed over the months and years that followed.

HELEN

'Mama.'

'Just a minute.'

Her irritation increased as she read the article. Clumsy metaphors, clichéd rhetoric, nothing new, nothing to grab the attention, nothing controversial or thought-provoking. She checked the by-line: written by a man, like ninety per cent of the articles. She folded the newspaper and replaced it on the shelf. She could do better, miles better, given half a chance. She wouldn't write for that rag, though – she'd choose a better class of paper.

'Mama, jellies.'

'I'll get you some in a second, hang on.'

She'd always loved reading. She'd worked her way through an impressive number of novels during the hours in her bedroom when she was supposed to be doing homework. She'd been a reader all through her twenties and beyond, up to the time that Cormac had been diagnosed, and then she suddenly couldn't keep her mind on a newspaper column, let alone a book.

At school, English had been the only subject she'd felt any enthusiasm for. *Helen has a clever turn of phrase* had been one of the few positive comments on the report cards her parents had opened silently. Helen would watch her mother scanning them with pressed-together lips.

She *had* a clever turn of phrase: in fifth year she'd written a few pieces for the school magazine, before boys had begun to distract her from any kind of schoolwork. She remembered one in particular – her favourite – in which she'd scoffed at the ridiculous new Barbie doll. *I bet it was designed by a man,* she'd written. *No woman in the world could have a chest that big and a waist that small and still be alive, let alone capable of walking without toppling over. And this is what passes as an acceptable toy for little girls.*

Lying in her darkened room, she remembered the ripple of attention it had caused among her classmates, the kick she'd got from seeing her name in print, even if it was only in faint purple type on a sheet of paper that had been cranked out on the school's spirit duplicator.

Why hadn't she kept writing? Why hadn't she gone in that direction when she'd left school? Young as she'd been, her articles had been a damn sight better than the drivel she'd just read. Drivel that someone, presumably, had been paid to write.

Helen shows promise, another English teacher had written, somewhere along the line. And she'd got a B in English in the Leaving Cert, even though she'd never really studied for it. She'd shown promise, and she'd done nothing about it.

But maybe it was time to start again.

'*Mama.*'

'Coming.'

She scanned the newsagent's shelves and found the newspaper she used to read before she'd stopped reading anything. It was also her parents' newspaper of choice – one of the few things they had in common – and by far the most respected of the nationals. She turned the pages until she came to the editorial, saw *M. Breen* beneath it. He'd been editor for years; he was practically a household name. She had no idea what his first name was; maybe he felt using an initial gave him some sort of cachet – or maybe his parents had christened him Montgomery, or Mortimer.

What was to stop her writing something and submitting it to him? What was to stop him printing it, if it was any good? She wondered if you needed some kind of qualification to write for a newspaper. Only one way to find out.

But she needed an interesting subject, one she was familiar with, one she could write about confidently. She knew all there was to know about being widowed young, about the hell of watching your husband withering away and being helpless to stop it – six months on, the pain of his death was no less sharp – but that was probably not what people would choose to read about over their toast and marmalade.

She could write about the day she'd driven to the bridge, she could spell out the abject misery of not wanting to go on living, and the dawning horrible realisation that she didn't have the courage to stop the world and step off – but again, who wanted to begin their morning with someone else's nightmare?

She needed something light but also revealing, something that would inform as well as entertain. A topic that would give people something to think about, and send them off to work with a smile on their faces.

What about life as a female shop assistant? She'd witnessed enough in her ten years behind the counter at Burke's to fill a book. She could write about the long hours on her feet, the pitifully short breaks, the uniform that had to be kept spotless, even if it meant hand-washing it at midnight. She could write about the injustice of earning just over half the salary of a male assistant doing precisely the same job, only with less efficiency.

But she could also pull awkward customers from her memory, detail the odd requests she'd heard over the years, make it funny as well as revealing.

She'd have to make up a pseudonym, so nobody at her old workplace would know it was her. She couldn't be Fitzpatrick or D'Arcy: they'd recognise her married and maiden names. But she could use her grandmother's name. O'Dowd, she could be.

'Helen O'Dowd,' she said to Alice. 'Like that?'

Alice shook her head irritably. 'I'm *hungry*.'

'OK, we're going now.'

She'd write the piece and send it off, and if it was rejected she'd write another. She'd wear M. Breen down, she'd make a nuisance of herself until he gave in.

The more she thought about it, the more the idea appealed to her. She could write in the afternoons when Alice took her nap, and in the evenings after she'd been put to bed. She could work from home so no childminder would be needed, and she wouldn't have to call on her parents for help. If she had to interview anyone, she'd do it over the phone.

It would be even easier when Alice started school, just two months from now. And if – when – Helen began reading books again, she could try submitting a few reviews. A whole new career at the age of thirty-three.

Or maybe not. Maybe when she tried it, she'd discover that she wasn't half as good as she thought. And even if she did well, even if editors loved her, it wouldn't make her any happier. It wouldn't take her pain away, or even lessen it. But she had to earn money somehow, and this seemed like something she might manage, a thing she might have a flair for.

At the counter she paid for the newspaper and got jelly babies for Alice. She pushed the buggy out of the shop, and as she turned onto the street she caught sight of her reflection in the window.

Now that she'd got used to it, she quite liked her short hair. So much easier to manage – towel it dry after washing and that was it. Her mother's face when she'd seen it, though: not a word said, but the look had been enough.

'It was time for a change,' Helen had told her, as if the question had been asked, and thankfully her mother had left it at that. She'd been lucky with the man she'd got to fix her botched attempt, only two quid he'd charged, and no comment made on the state of it, which she'd appreciated. She'd given him a two-bob tip, and been back twice for a trim since.

She walked home with Alice, starting her shop-assistant piece in her head.

SARAH

They went to her uncle's hotel for dinner, her old workplace – hard to believe that she'd been gone for over nine months. They always went to Uncle John's when one of them had a birthday. They sat at the same table, set into the left bay window, a reserved sign on it until they arrived.

It was 1975, with America finally admitting defeat and pulling troops out of Vietnam, and three members of an Irish showband massacred by terrorists, and the British Conservative Party getting its first female leader. The world was full of change, every week bringing new upheaval, and the Kelly birthday celebrations carried on merrily. Sarah wondered if she'd be blowing out the candles on her sixtieth birthday cake here, accompanied maybe by Christine's children, who would turn up for their unmarried aunt's party out of pity.

The presents were good though. From her parents she got the black jacket she'd picked out the previous week. Not at all fashionable but handy for the bike, zipped and hooded and not too heavy. Christine's gift-wrapped box held a pair of chunky tortoiseshell bangles, and Brian gave her a book token.

'When you're married, you and Christine can give me a present between you,' she told him, 'and Christine will pick it out, so you'll be off the hook.'

He grinned. 'You mean my mother will be off the hook. I haven't a clue when it comes to presents.'

'You haven't done badly with me so far,' Christine told him.

'Only because you drop loads of hints – I'd have to be blind and deaf not to pick up on them.'

'That's true.'

Sarah watched them together, so comfortable, so at home in each other's company. She thought again how lucky her sister had been to find the man she wanted, and to discover that he wanted her too. Sounded so simple, but here she was at twenty-five still without a single prospect.

Unless you counted Neil Flannery, whose father Stephen Sarah had been cooking for since she'd got the job in St Sebastian's. Even though she hadn't even met the son, she supposed he was a faint possibility.

Stephen certainly thought so. 'You'd be ideal for each other,' he'd told her more than once. 'He's a good lad, just hasn't met the right lady. And he's about your age.'

His wife Nuala silenced him whenever he brought up the topic in her company. 'Stop that, you'll embarrass Sarah. I'm sure she's well able to find her own boyfriends.'

She came to see her husband often, nearly every second day – they were from a small market town less than twenty miles from St Sebastian's – and she sat by his bedside or armchair for much of the afternoon. Their only son, the mysterious Neil, worked during the week as a gardener and visited his father at weekends, when Sarah was off-duty.

'But he's starting a job soon just up the road,' Stephen had told her, 'and he says he'll be in more often while that's going on, so you'll get to meet him then.'

'Shush, stop that,' his wife had said automatically.

What must it be like, Sarah wondered, to have your life partner struck down so young, to watch him deteriorate, see the strength and vitality washing out of him, to be forced eventually to put him into care because you could no longer look after him yourself?

'Of course we would have loved to keep him at home,' Nuala had told her once, when they happened to be leaving together. 'This was the last thing Neil and I wanted, but it just became too much. And it wasn't fair on Neil either. He has his own life, and his work takes him all over the place.'

Awful to have husband and wife living apart from one another, never sharing a bed at night, never waking up together or sitting down to a family dinner. What kind of a marriage was that for anyone?

The loneliness Sarah had already witnessed in the nursing home and the poignant stories she'd heard from some of the residents had broken her heart several times over, had reduced her to private tears more than once. But she still felt convinced that the job was right for her – she could make a difference to them. She *was* making a difference.

She looked around the hotel table at the faces she'd grown up with. So lucky she was to be surrounded by a caring family, with so much heartbreak out there. She smiled at the chocolate cake that was being wheeled across the dining room on the dessert trolley – chocolate for her, coffee on Christine's birthday – with the half-dozen flickering candles stuck into the top.

She was aware that everyone in the room was looking at them now, waiting for the birthday girl to blow out her candles. If she were married she'd cook a birthday dinner herself, invite her family around. But without a husband or a home of her own, she was still the child who got taken out by her parents.

She blew out the candles and watched her mother sipping the single Babycham she ordered each birthday dinner, the only alcohol she ever took. She listened to her father making his usual jokey speech about how hard he'd had to work to afford the birthday dinner, and about how he and Martha looked forward to the day when they could retire and be supported by their children. Same speech every year, same everything every year.

'Won't be long,' he said to Sarah, 'with your new job, and Christine marrying into money, your mother and I will be heading off on the world cruise any day now.'

Brian grinned. 'I think you might have to wait until Sarah writes her bestseller.'

'Any day now,' Christine added, cutting the cake into slices.

'You can laugh,' Sarah told them, 'but I *am* going to write a book.'

She was. She just had to find the time. After work tomorrow she'd make a start for sure, or sometime very soon anyway. A period tale she thought, set in a big house with servants – that kind of story was always popular. All she needed was to sit down and make a start.

She joined in as they sang 'For She's A Jolly Good Fellow' and wondered, not very seriously, when she would finally get to meet Neil Flannery. Might be a big let-down, not her type at all, but it would be nice to find out, either way.

She didn't have long to wait. The following Friday, as she was helping Donna, the kitchen junior, to wipe down the stainless-steel worktops after the lunch clear-up, she glanced out of the window that overlooked the small car park. There was Nuala Flannery on her usual visit to Stephen – but the car was wrong: that wasn't her blue Mini. And Nuala wasn't getting out on the driver's side.

Sarah watched as the other door opened and a fair-haired man emerged. Long legs, tall, slim.

Grey tweedy jacket, blue jeans, too far away to make out facial features. She watched him take his mother's carrier bag from her – it must be him, it must be the son – as they walked together in the direction of the main door.

She waited twenty minutes, making out the following week's menu plan and writing up the shopping list for Dan, the nursing-home driver and general handyman, before making her way down the corridor towards Stephen's room. She would have been dropping in anyway, she told herself. They'd think it odd if she didn't appear: she always put her head in when Nuala was there to ask if they wanted tea.

She tapped on the door, her stomach fluttering slightly. *Stop, don't build it up.*

'Come in.'

Stephen's voice. She opened the door. 'I just wondered,' she began, not looking in the direction of the man who stood by the window, not looking at him at all, 'if anyone wanted a cuppa.'

'Sarah,' Stephen said, reaching a quavering hand towards her. 'Come in and meet my son. Neil, this is the best cook in Ireland – apart from your mother, of course.'

'Oh, shush.'

Grey eyes, magnified behind large, thick glasses that gave him a scholarly look. Regular features, longish nose, fairish hair. Outdoorsy complexion, a ruddiness to his cheeks, not surprising given the job he'd chosen. She was conscious of both his

57

parents observing them as they shook hands, could feel her own cheeks becoming hot. Hopefully he'd think it was from the kitchen.

'Hello,' she murmured, having to look up several inches to meet the grey eyes. His palm felt slightly rough – from wielding a spade, she presumed. She wondered if he wore the glasses when he worked. They'd look a bit incongruous with his gardening gear.

'I've heard a lot about you,' he said, their hands still clasped together. 'Apparently you make a terrific scone.'

She smiled, glad of the opportunity to turn towards Stephen. 'Well, your father seems to like them.'

'He must have gained half a stone since Sarah came along,' Nuala put in.

'And you should taste her lemon meringue pie,' Stephen added. 'I made Nuala get the recipe, didn't I?'

'You did – and mine didn't turn out half as nice.'

'Get away, it was lovely.'

It seemed to Sarah that along with the spoken conversation there was another, unarticulated exchange taking place between the older couple: *How's it going? Are they getting on? Were we right?* Something in the way they both looked from her to Neil, in the heartiness of their voices, in how Nuala's glance flickered to their hands as they separated at last. All that was needed was for Stephen to say something about how lucky the man would be who got Sarah, but thankfully he didn't.

'I'd love a cuppa,' Nuala was saying – Nuala who never took one normally. 'Can you sit with us and have one yourself?' Oh, clever Nuala.

Sarah made a show of looking at her watch, even though she knew the time practically to the second. 'I have a few minutes,' she said.

Nuala turned to her son. 'And maybe you'd fancy one?'

'I'd love one, thanks.' The grey eyes met Sarah's again. 'Can I give you a hand?'

'Oh, no, honestly—'

For goodness' sake, was she blushing again? You'd think she was fifteen, not twenty-five. It was Stephen and Nuala looking all pleased with themselves – it was the obvious matchmaking that was going on. Really, as if they didn't think either of them capable of finding a partner on their own.

She escaped from the room and hurried back to the kitchen, where she made tea and cut slices from one of the coffee cakes she'd baked that morning. 'Who's that for?' Donna wanted to know, and Sarah said Stephen Flannery had a few visitors, and were the salt cellars refilled yet?

First impressions had been favourable, she decided, taking a tray from the stack on the shelf by the window. Nothing objectionable about his appearance – the glasses made him look intelligent, they were a plus – and clearly he was on good terms with his parents, which reflected well on his character.

She scalded the teapot and spooned in tea. Had his own house too, which was good; and being a gardener meant he appreciated nature, also a lovely quality in anyone.

But there was no point in building it into anything at this stage: he might well have a girl-friend his parents knew nothing about, or he mightn't fancy Sarah in the least. A possibility, that was what he was. A slightly less faint one, maybe, than he'd been before they met, but still just a possibility.

Chances were nothing would happen – life didn't fall into place as easily as that – but for now she'd keep an open mind. No harm in doing that.

1976

HELEN

Dear Miss Fitzpatrick

Thank you for your piece on the death of Agatha Christie which you submitted recently. Please find attached our cheque payment.

Regards

Typed underneath was *M. Breen, Editor*, but the signature above the typed name was Catherine Fortune's. Word for word, apart from the subject of Helen's submission, it was identical to the half-dozen or so other letters – hardly letters, more like notes – that she'd received from the newspaper since the previous August. All signed by Catherine Fortune – M. Breen, Editor, being too busy, presumably.

And paper-clipped to the note was the identical cheque that had accompanied all the rest. More than she'd expected, enough to keep her and Alice in bread and jam for a month or two, with a few quid left over for a bottle of Powers Gold Label.

'Mama!'

She opened the kitchen door. 'What?'

'My sausage fell on the floor. There's stuff stuck on it.'

'Rub it off and it'll be fine. I'll be in in a minute.'

She slipped the cheque out from under the paper clip. She folded it in two and tucked it into the pocket of her jeans. She tore the note and its envelope in two and dropped the pieces into the ashtray that shared space on a kitchen chair with the phone.

She opened the front door and lit a cigarette and stood looking out at the garden. Gravelled rectangle roughly the size of a double grave, narrow cement path running alongside it to the gate. A waist-high privet hedge separating her from her neighbour, immaculately cut on his side and across the top, left alone to do whatever it wanted on hers.

The grey sky was striped with ribbons of pale blue. A teenage girl passed in the street, her cream cheesecloth top surely not warm enough for the chilly February day, her platform-soled clogs poking from beneath the wide, wide legs of her jeans. Helen leaned against the door jamb and marvelled all over again that she was being paid to do what came so easily to her, that this occupation which gave her so much satisfaction was proving to be her salvation.

It hadn't started the way she'd planned, with the shop-assistant piece. She'd begun writing it, she'd been more than halfway through, early on the morning of August the first, when a newsflash on the radio had announced the massacre in Northern Ireland of three members of the Miami showband, returning to Dublin in the early hours after performing for the evening in a County Down dancehall.

Her heart had stopped. The Miami. She'd never met them, but Cormac had. Their paths had crossed often, all the showbands knew one another. He'd known them, he'd spoken to them and now three of them were dead, ambushed on a country road in the middle of the night and shot.

She'd put her head in her hands and cried at the thought of their wives and children and parents, at the years of grief and anger and pain that had only begun for them. Christ, was there no end to the madness of Northern Ireland? Would the slaughter of innocents never stop?

When she could see straight, she'd wiped her face and set aside the article she'd been writing, and rolled a fresh sheet of paper into the second-hand typewriter she'd bought with her father's money. She'd written without stopping, more tears spilling out of her. She cried for the just-killed men and for Cormac, her fingers blindly finding the right keys until Alice had appeared, rumpled and pink-cheeked and demanding breakfast.

All that day she'd kept at it, any chance she got. She'd introduced herself as the wife of a former musician. She'd outlined the lifestyle of a typical showband, the camaraderie between the members, the rehearsals in draughty garages, the endless travelling to venues, the dingy B&Bs when getting home after a night's playing wasn't an option.

She'd written her imagined account of the atrocity, describing the chat in the van beforehand, the happy banter of the men after a successful evening's performance. Their acceptance of the checkpoint, their slight annoyance maybe, at their journey being delayed, their assumption that they'd be on the way again before long.

She hadn't lingered on the actual killings. She'd spoken of the horribly quiet aftermath, the lingering tang of smoke in the air, the pieces of the blown-up minibus strewn across the road and scattered over the surrounding fields, the ripped-apart guitar cases, the destroyed instruments. She'd mourned the senselessness of killing three young musicians.

She'd moved on to describe her own reaction on hearing the news; the shock and disbelief the newsreader's calm voice had caused. She'd imagined the families of the dead men hearing the same words from policemen, being woken up on a Friday morning to have their hearts smashed to pieces.

She'd skimmed over it when it was finished, but she'd changed nothing. She'd scribbled a note to M. Breen, asking if he'd like to print it, and she'd signed it *Helen O'Dowd*. She'd slipped it into an envelope and walked with Alice to the letterbox at the end of the next street.

Two days later she'd opened the paper and there

it had been: a half page of her words accompanied by a picture of the crime scene. The headline, which she hadn't written, read *The Day the Music Died*, and underneath, in smaller print, *An insider's view of the Miami Showband Massacre*. Her name – her pseudonym – was there too, in even smaller print.

The following morning a cheque had arrived, accompanied by the first of the letters. Helen had phoned the number at the top of the page and asked to speak to Catherine Fortune.

'Oh, I *loved* your piece,' she'd said warmly, as soon as Helen had introduced herself. 'So moving. Well done. Sorry it had to be cut a bit, to make it fit.'

'It's not my name, though,' Helen had replied. 'Fitzpatrick is my name: O'Dowd is just . . . one I'm using.'

Catherine Fortune had understood immediately. 'Oh – right, so you need a new cheque. That's no problem, just send me back the old one and I'll pop a replacement into the post.'

'Thanks a lot – and when can I send another piece?'

She'd heard the smile in the other woman's voice. 'Anytime you like – but of course it's up to Mr Breen what goes in.'

'Of course.'

'And you need to make it a definite length – either five hundred or a thousand words usually.'

Clearly, no special qualifications were needed to

have an article published; it just had to pass muster with the boss, which she'd accepted was fair enough. She'd better wait a while, though, didn't want to seem greedy, in case it put him off.

She'd finished the piece on the shopgirl – so light it seemed compared to the other, but maybe it was good to show him that she was versatile. She'd forced herself to wait three weeks before posting it off – and the following week there it was, accompanied by a shot of a model (Helen presumed) posing behind a department store counter, a look of utter boredom on her perfectly fresh face.

Since then she'd sent roughly one article a month. She'd written about the second marriage of Richard Burton and Elizabeth Taylor, eighteen months after their divorce, and the ordinary suburban house in Monasterevin where a Dutch businessman was imprisoned by terrorists for over a fortnight, and a new law that was passed in Britain which introduced equal pay rights for women – and every article she submitted to M. Breen had found favour, and had been printed, usually word for word.

In November Catherine had attached a hand-written note to the usual letter, asking for a photo. *Just a small head and shoulders will be fine*, she'd written. *Something we can put with your pieces, since you're becoming a regular with us!*

Helen had bought a new film for the camera she hadn't used since before Cormac's illness. She'd snapped herself as best she could half a dozen times – no front views, all three-quarter profiles, all taken slightly from above so her eyes weren't visible – and she'd used the rest of the reel to photograph the amazingly beautiful sunset that evening.

The head and shoulders photos, when she collected them from the chemist, were nicely out of focus. She picked the best of them and sent it off to Catherine. The sunsets were disastrous, the glorious sky reduced to smears of over-exposed, watery colours. As she was stuffing them into the bin, she realised that taking a snap of her only child hadn't even occurred to her.

Her phone had rung early on the morning of January the twelfth.

'Mark Breen here,' an unfamiliar, brusque male voice had said, and it had taken Helen a few seconds to realise who was on the other end.

'Nice to—'

'I'm assuming you're a reader.'

'Well, I—'

'Agatha Christie has just died. Are you familiar with her books?'

'Of course I—'

'Good. Can you do a thousand words by the end of tomorrow?'

And just like that, she'd got her first commission, along with an introduction to her employer, who clearly didn't believe in wasting words. What did she care, as long as he paid up?

She ground her cigarette under her shoe and

threw the butt into the privet hedge. Ten minutes later, as she was bundling Alice into her coat before letting her out to play in their scrap of back garden – same size as the front, straggly excuse of a lawn – the doorbell rang.

To her surprise, her mother, who hardly ever called unannounced, who hardly ever called full stop, stood outside, looking as perfectly groomed as ever.

Tailored grey coat, under which she most likely wore its matching dress; silk stockings, black patent handbag and shoes, hair backcombed into submission. Looking as out of place in the humble street with its shabby terrace of houses as it was possible to look. No car in sight, of course not: her parents had always come to Helen and Cormac's by taxi, afraid to chance leaving a car unattended.

'Happy birthday,' she said, offering Helen a cream envelope. Her birthday, completely forgotten about for the second year running. The one time in the year that Margaret D'Arcy felt entitled – or obliged – to cross her daughter's threshold uninvited.

'Come in.'

Helen stood back, picturing the mess of the kitchen, dishes piled in the sink, the remains of Alice's breakfast still on the table. What the hell: let her take them as she found them, her own fault for not ringing ahead.

Her mother made a pretty good show of not

appearing to notice the untidiness as she accepted Helen's offer of coffee. Supermarket brand, not the good stuff her parents were used to, but it wouldn't kill her.

'Where's Alice?'

'Out the back.' Helen put on the kettle and slit open the envelope, conscious of her mother's eyes on her. She pulled out the card it contained and opened it without reading the message on the front. Two twenty-pound notes lay inside, the same amount they'd given her each birthday since she'd turned eighteen.

The money had kept coming when Helen had committed the cardinal sin of moving in with a musician, but it had become a cheque that was posted to Cormac's address rather than personally delivered. This arrangement had continued after Helen and Cormac got married, and the only contact she had with her parents was one strained phone call from her to them each month.

The fact that Cormac hadn't lived long enough to cause them more than a few years of outrage had changed things, of course: once it became apparent that he was not, after all, going to outlive them, they'd reappeared, turning up at the house with bottles of wine and fruit cakes, offering to take Alice for a few hours, asking if there was anything they could do, anything they could pay for. Pretending a concern they couldn't possibly feel.

Each time they appeared, Helen had made them

tea and cut slices of whatever cake they'd brought. She had updated them on Cormac's condition and watched them trying to interact with the grand-daughter they barely knew. She'd taken the money her father had handed over – pouring money into the gulf between them, imagining he could fill it – and thanked him with as much grace as she could manage.

At the funeral she'd listened as people sympathised with her mother and shook hands with her father. She'd thought about how much of a disappointment Cormac had been to them, how they'd despised the fact that he didn't go to work in a white shirt, how they'd done little to hide their disdain in his company. She'd recalled her wedding day, the pinched, strained smile of her mother, the contempt for his new son-in-law plain in her father's face, and she'd known that she could never, ever forgive them for their snobbery and heartlessness.

Since Cormac's death they hadn't been invited to Helen's house. She couldn't care less if she never laid eyes on either of them again, but she was damned if she was going to deprive Alice of whatever wealth they left behind, so every Thursday afternoon she took Alice to visit them. They sat in the kitchen and made small-talk for as long as it took Helen to drink a cup of her mother's admit-tedly very good coffee.

While she waited for the kettle to boil she busied herself with jug and filter, searching in her head for something to talk about. When she turned around, her mother was gathering up Alice's crockery, trying to keep her sleeve out of the puddle of ketchup on the plate.

Helen went to the back door and opened it. 'Granny's here,' she told Alice. 'Come in and say hello.'

Alice was no conversationalist, but she'd do. Anyone would do.

SARAH

'You'll be glad to hear I've made a start on the book.'

'About time – you've talked about it for long enough. How far have you got?'

'Well, I haven't begun the actual writing yet. I'm still thinking up a plot and getting the characters together.'

'Oh.'

'Still, it's a start . . . Stop eating those cherries. I'll have none left for the cake.'

Christine pushed the tub across the table. 'So where's Lover Boy taking you tonight?'

'The cinema, *Barry Lyndon*. Why don't you make yourself useful and line those cake tins?'

'You're blushing.'

Sarah laughed. 'I am not.'

Still too soon to tell, only a few months since they'd laid eyes on one another; and even though this felt so right, she would hug it to herself and let nobody know how she was really feeling, not even Christine. Not yet.

It had begun slowly, with a handful of further encounters in his father's room, during which

Sarah noticed that he had a habit of placing a finger at the corner of his mouth and tilting his head to the side when he was listening. And his smile was delightfully crooked, sliding up more on the right. And his aftershave, or maybe it was whatever shampoo he was using, reminded her of the sea. And she liked the shoes he wore, and the fact that his fingernails were always clean, despite his job.

On the whole, she'd decided, she approved of Neil Flannery. As potential boyfriends went, he was definitely in with a chance. Once or twice their eyes had met, and he'd held her gaze for a scatter of seconds, and she'd thought, with a delicious flip in her stomach, that maybe there was something there.

But she was also acutely conscious, during each of these episodes, that they were being observed by his parents, who, no doubt, had had them marched down the aisle and happily married after their second meeting. Even if Neil was at all interested in her – and she had no real idea that he was – what chance did any kind of a relationship have of developing in Stephen and Nuala's well-meant but terribly inhibiting presence?

And then one afternoon towards the end of November, about two weeks after they'd first come face to face, there was a knock on the kitchen door as Sarah was putting cups onto trays in preparation for the tea.

'I'll go,' Bernadette said, wiping her hands on

her apron. Callers to the kitchen at this time were commonplace: someone looking for a mid-afternoon cuppa or glass of milk, or maybe a hot-water bottle refilled. Sarah continued to assemble the cups as she planned the next day's lunch in her head: stuffed pork steak with roast potatoes and turnip, followed by treacle pudding and—

'It's for you.' Bernadette winked at her. 'Stephen Flannery's son.'

Sarah added another two cups to the tray, feeling the blood rushing to her face. 'Probably wants another round of tea.'

'Yes, I'm sure that's what he wants,' Bernadette replied, plunging her mop once again into the bucket of steaming water. 'That'll be why he asked for you specially. He must have heard I can't make tea.'

'Sorry to bother you,' he said, his leather jacket slung over an arm. 'I know you're busy, but I just wanted to say thanks for looking after my father so well. I'm starting another job in Tullamore next week, so I'll be back to visiting here at the weekends.'

Sarah forced a smile. Not interested then, just being polite. Just saying thanks before he left. 'It's my pleasure. He's a lovely man.'

He began to shrug on his jacket. 'Well, he thinks the world of you, I know that, and it means a lot to my mother too, that he's being looked after so well.'

She remained silent, the smile stiff on her face.

'I don't suppose . . .' not meeting her eye as he fumbled with the zip '. . . you'd let me buy you dinner some time? I mean, only if you want to.'

He looked up then and she saw his crooked, charming smile.

'That would be lovely,' she said, delight fizzing inside her.

'Good.' The smile slid further up his face. 'I can't guarantee the standard of food would be up to yours, but we might be lucky.'

He took her to Bannigan's in Kildare town and bought her sirloin steak and strawberry cheesecake. He drove her home and kissed her cheek, and asked to see her again.

The following Saturday night they went to see *Shampoo* at the cinema. He bought her a box of Black Magic and didn't attempt to put his arm around her in the darkness, which was a bit of a disappointment. He drove her home and leant across to kiss her cheek, and she turned her head and met his mouth with hers. He tasted of chocolate.

For their third date he took her to a performance of *The Field* in a concert hall of a town about twenty miles away. During the interval they drank orange juice and he told her about a garden he was restoring in the grounds of a Tullamore hotel. As they resumed their seats after the interval, he slipped his hand into hers, and she moved closer and touched her thigh to his.

Their goodnight lasted twenty minutes. He cradled

her head and whispered that he was very, very happy to have found her, and she wanted more than anything to stay in the dark car, within the warmth of his arms.

They saw each other every Friday and Saturday night. He'd given her a silver bracelet for Christmas, she'd given him Queen's *A Night at the Opera* LP. All she could think about was him, and all that mattered were the weekends. It was 1976, and she was finally, finally in love.

'You're blushing again,' Christine said, and Sarah threw a cherry across the table at her.

HELEN

Twenty-three minutes into the evening she'd knocked back two large glasses of awful red wine, and eaten a single stuffed mushroom, and rejected everything else on offer – sausage rolls, chicken drumsticks, skewered something or other – from the long trestle tables that lined one side of the room.

She couldn't remember the last party she'd attended, except that it must have been with Cormac, probably before Alice had been born. She was deeply regretting her decision to come to this one – what had possessed her to let Catherine talk her into it?

She'd escaped the newspaper's last Christmas party by playing the widow card. 'It's the first Christmas without my husband,' she'd told Catherine. 'I really don't feel up to it' – and Catherine had been all sympathy and understanding, as Helen had known she would. Anyway, with just a handful of articles written by then, and no direct contact at that stage with Breen, she hadn't felt particularly affiliated with the newspaper.

This year she hadn't got off so lightly.

'Say hello to him,' Catherine had urged her on the phone. 'You needn't stay long, just enough to show your face and tell him you're happy to be on the payroll. It'll stand you in good stead, believe me. And I'd really like to meet you too.'

Catherine might like to meet her, but Helen wasn't convinced that Breen would. In fact, she considered it a safe bet that he wouldn't give a damn if they never came face to face. Over the eighteen months or so that she'd been working for him, from the few conversations they'd had over the phone – he called her with commissions, she called him with queries – she'd got the impression of someone who was always on the verge of losing his patience.

'Breen,' he'd snap as a greeting, managing to make her feel she was already in trouble. No 'Hello', no 'Hope I'm not interrupting anything', no small-talk at all. After the briefest possible conversation, his sign-off was usually an equally clipped 'Right' – because 'Goodbye', presumably, was out of the question.

Helen had never heard a word of praise from him, never got a hint that he'd actually liked any of her pieces, even though he had turned down not a single one of them. When she'd taken a chance and submitted her first unasked-for book review, a couple of weeks after the Agatha Christie piece, it had appeared in the following day's paper – and not long afterwards she'd taken delivery of two book proofs by authors whose names she didn't recognise.

500 words on each by Friday week latest he'd written – *latest* underlined twice – on the compliments slip that had accompanied them, *MB* at the bottom so she'd known it was him. Even his spiky handwriting looked annoyed.

God help Mrs Breen, in the unlikely event that such an unfortunate creature existed – would any woman in her right mind take him, for better or worse? Anyone who did would have to be as cantankerous as him. Maybe she'd turn up on his arm tonight, lording it over the plebs.

To make things worse, getting to the party had involved enlisting the help of her parents. There'd been little choice but to ask them, with Anna from across the road, Alice's regular babysitter, having taken the ferry the day before to spend Christmas and New Year with her married daughter in England.

Helen was well aware that her career as a journalist was a source of continuing bemusement to her parents. Writing for a newspaper wouldn't be much of a step up, in their eyes, from earning a living as a musician, and the fact that she was working in a male-dominated area – according to Catherine, Helen was one of just two female writers on the paper's list of freelancers – didn't help.

Then again, she was working for her parents' newspaper of choice, which she knew her father held in high regard, and she was supporting herself and Alice, so there wasn't much they could legitimately object to.

'A Christmas party,' her mother had said. 'How sociable. Of course we can take Alice. Have you got something to wear?'

Helen had resisted the impulse to tell her that actually she'd decided to go nude. 'My black trouser suit.' *The one I wore to Cormac's funeral,* she might have added, but didn't.

'That old thing? You've had it for years. Let us treat you to something new.'

Throwing money at her, like they'd always done. Still believing she'd mistake it for love.

The trouser suit *was* old – Helen had bought it before she met Cormac – but it would do fine for a party where she knew nobody, where she didn't give a damn what anyone thought of her, or her outfit. Far cry from the hours she'd spent getting ready to go out to the parties Cormac and the boys would be invited to.

She felt the alcohol begin to soften her up around the edges, despite its unappealing taste. The not-very-large room – presumably the main working area of the paper – was full of noisy, laughing people, the air heavy with their cigarette smoke. Helen had spoken to nobody apart from Catherine, who thankfully had been on the lookout for her, and who'd turned out to be both older and heavier than Helen had envisaged, and every bit as friendly as she had always sounded on the phone.

'I just love your writing,' she'd told Helen, dabbing at her large, rosy face with a red napkin. 'So original and witty, and you can write serious as well as funny. And your book reviews are always so direct.'

Breen, apparently, had yet to arrive. 'He's not really a party person,' Catherine had admitted, which didn't surprise Helen in the least. 'He'll definitely show up at some stage, though, and I'll introduce you.'

But Catherine had gone to the toilet a few minutes ago and hadn't reappeared – tired, no doubt, of having to babysit the freelancer. One more glass of bad wine and Helen would make her escape, Breen or no Breen. She edged her way through the crowd to the makeshift bar and refilled her glass, managing to splatter her jacket in the process when someone's elbow connected with her.

'Helen!'

In the act of reaching for a napkin, she turned. Catherine was making her way back through the crowd, followed by someone in a dark suit – presumably the famous M. Breen, dragged over to meet her so he could be duly thanked for his patronage. Helen gave a quick swipe at the damp stain with her sleeve and summoned as much of a smile as she could muster.

'There you are,' Catherine said. 'Mark, this is Helen O'Dowd – or should I say Fitzpatrick? Helen, meet Mark Breen.'

The navy suit looked expensive – having grown up with her father, she knew a well-cut suit when she saw it. Immaculate white shirt, dark grey tie.

Almost-black hair, cut so short it stood in bristles around his head. Startlingly blue eyes that met hers full on, the barest ghost of a smile on his face as he nodded once, crushing her fingers briefly in his.

Not handsome – the nose a shade too wide, the cheeks a little pocked, the skin about the eyes deeply creased and shadowed – but a face you wouldn't easily forget, with the intensity of that gaze. Hard to put an age on him: somewhere between forty and fifty, she thought.

She opened her mouth to say something suitably grateful, like Catherine had suggested – but the words refused to come. She was working for her cheques, for Christ's sake, he wasn't handing out charity. She was a decent writer: if she wasn't, he'd have told her to take a running jump.

She raised her glass. She'd say what she chose. 'Happy Christmas. Thanks for the invite. Good to put a face to the voice.' There, that would do him.

He inclined his head again, the smallest hint of a nod. She had the feeling he was taking her measure. She saw his glance flick to the darker patch on the front of her jacket. 'Someone bumped into me as I was pouring,' she said. 'I'm not blotto yet.'

'It wasn't an accusation,' he pointed out mildly. The voice was familiar, if less peremptory than she was used to.

'Just thought I'd explain.' She indicated the bottle. 'Can I get you one?' It was a party, for crying out loud. Did he have to look so damn serious?

'Not just now.' As he spoke, his gaze drifted from her face to wander off to her left. 'I'm afraid you'll have to excuse me,' he went on, extending his hand towards her again. 'Good of you to come, help yourself to the wine.' Another finger-crushing shake and he was gone, disappearing into the crowd.

Helen looked after him, prickling with annoyance. Clearly, the great M. Breen didn't consider her interesting enough to spend more than thirty seconds in her company. Help yourself to the wine indeed, as if she should be grateful for his atrocious plonk. As if all she'd come for was his free booze.

She turned back to Catherine. 'That went well.'

The PA didn't notice, or chose to ignore, the sarcasm. 'It went fine. I'm delighted you finally got to meet him. Let me introduce you to some more of the gang.'

But Helen decided she'd had more than enough. 'Thanks,' she said, setting down her untouched glass, 'but I really must be going – I promised the babysitter I'd be home by ten.'

The white lies she told, the fronts she put up, the hard shell she'd grown around her heart over the last two years. She stood on the path outside the newspaper offices, pulling the cold, crisp air into her lungs, ignoring the people who pushed past her. Everyone looking happy, three days before Christmas.

On the way to the bus stop she went into an

off-licence and bought a bottle of their second cheapest whiskey.

'Happy Christmas,' the youngish bearded man behind the counter said, and Helen took her change and wished him the same, because for all she knew he deserved one.

Back home she felt her way along the tiny darkened hallway until her foot touched the bottom stair. She climbed halfway up and sat, taking the bottle from its brown paper bag and unscrewing the cap. As she drank, she conjured up her first Christmas with Cormac, just a few weeks after they'd met. The marvel of what they'd found still new and fresh, their hunger for one another all-consuming.

This house had been their sanctuary, all they needed under its roof. The Christmas Day chicken drying and shrivelling in the oven, everything forgotten in the wonder of their entwined bodies, the miracle of the love that had swept away everything else.

People passed in the street outside, their cheerful shouts climbing the dark stairs to her. She pressed a black-jacketed sleeve to her wet face, remembering the length of tinsel that he'd threaded between her toes, trailed up her calves and thighs and across her abdomen and breasts. She remembered the tantalising tickle of it along the mounds and valleys of her body, the delicious tease of its feathery touch making her hot with desire, forcing her finally to pull it away from him and draw him closer—

She put the half-empty bottle down gently and bowed her head to rest it on her knees. Her sobs shuddered from her and merged with the sound of the group on the street outside who had gathered with their collection buckets to sing about angels they had heard on high.

1978

SARAH

'This is awful.'

Neil made no response.

'This book review, it's horrible, really cruel. Here, have a look.'

He glanced at the newspaper page but made no move to take it. 'What's the book?'

'It's a debut novel, a thriller, and Helen O'Dowd is tearing it to shreds. Imagine how he must feel.'

'How who must feel?' His eyes drifting back to the sports section.

'The *author*, of course. I hate when you only half listen to me. Read it and see – it's awful.'

'I'm already reading,' he pointed out mildly. 'Or trying to. I'll get to it later.'

'Sorry.' She dropped the newspaper onto the bed as Helen Reddy began to sing. 'Oh, I love this, it's so spooky.' She reached out and turned up the radio before leaning back to lift his arm and slide under it. 'I adore Sunday mornings, don't you?'

'Mmm.'

She turned to look up at his face. The rectangle of the window was reflected in both lenses of his glasses. 'You have a lot to put up with, don't you?'

He smiled, eyes still on the paper.

'I never let you read in peace, do I?'

'Nope.'

She grinned as she settled into his chest. 'But you married me, so you're stuck with me forever.'

'Or until divorce comes in.'

'In holy Catholic Ireland? Not a hope.' She eyed the newspaper section she'd just discarded, lying in a crumpled heap on the eiderdown. 'I've a good mind to write to her.'

'Hmm?'

'I feel like writing to Helen O'Dowd and saying I thought she was far too harsh.'

Neil lowered his paper. 'My dear soft-hearted wife, the woman is reviewing a book. It's her job to tell it like it is, even if it's not what you want to hear. If you had your way, nobody would ever say anything vaguely negative, in case someone's feelings were hurt.'

'But she's being so cruel,' Sarah insisted, reaching again for the page. 'Just listen to this bit – *If he wants to write so badly, let him keep a diary: that way, nobody else has to read it.* Now you have to agree that that's just downright nasty. It doesn't add anything to the review. Stop *smiling.*'

'It's funny, though. Helen O'Dowd has a sharp tongue, you know that, but she's also entertaining. She loves to court a bit of controversy – it's what makes her interesting. You don't have to read it if you don't want to.'

'Well, I've read it now, and I think it's too harsh.'

'And have you read the book she's talking about?'

'That's beside the point. Even if it isn't much good, the review is still cruel.' She folded the newspaper. 'I'm going to write and protest. I think it needs to be said, even if I'm the only one saying it. It might make her choose her words more carefully in future. She can still tell the truth, but in a kinder way.'

'Well, if you feel that strongly, go ahead.'

'I will.' She nestled into him again. 'Imagine if it was my book she was talking about.'

He laughed. 'You'd be inconsolable – probably want to top yourself.'

She slapped his arm lightly. 'Don't joke about that, it's not funny. But I *would* be devastated. I'll be terrified to even show it to a publisher, in case they turn me down.'

'I know you will,' he said, folding his page in two, 'but let's not worry about that until you finish it.'

'No.' She turned her head to see the clock. 'Damn, I'd better get up. I *hate* working on Sunday. Why did I ever agree to it?'

'Because they asked you to, and you're incapable of saying no.'

She sighed as she pushed back the eiderdown. 'They said it was temporary, just until they replaced Austin.'

'Of course they did, because they know you won't complain.'

She searched with her feet for slippers. 'Well,

they might be short of funds or something. I wouldn't like to put them under pressure.'

'Perish the thought that you'd ever upset them like that.'

Standing in the shower, she imagined the book's author opening his Sunday newspaper and discovering what Helen O'Dowd thought of his first book. Probably slaved over it for months, years even. His wife going out to work to support them maybe, both of them hoping he'd make it as a writer. The excitement when he'd got his publishing deal – they'd probably gone out to dinner to celebrate – and now this.

Oh, she knew there were plenty of bigger things to worry about: the Lebanon torn apart by war, the IRA still planting their bombs, horrible racial prejudice in South Africa – but this mattered too, it mattered a lot to the author.

She pictured herself in his shoes, her book out there for all the Helen O'Dowds of the world to say whatever hurtful things they felt like saying about it. She'd die – she'd be completely destroyed if a book she'd written was slated like that.

Then again, at the rate she was going, Helen O'Dowd would probably have retired long before Sarah's book got finished, let alone published. Over two years since she'd begun plotting it, and less than fifty thousand words written – about half as many as she needed, according to any writer's guide she looked at. So hard to get it right, her plot constantly changing as she ran out of steam with a storyline, but she was determined to keep at it.

She rinsed shampoo from her hair. She'd write to Helen O'Dowd when she got home from work, before she had a chance to forget. Her letter would probably be tossed into the nearest bin – book reviewers probably didn't take kindly to criticism, despite being well able to dish it out themselves – but the act of writing it would make Sarah feel better. She'd have spoken out against an injustice; she'd have taken a stand.

And starting tomorrow she'd get back to her own book, write for at least an hour a day, rather than hopping in and out of it at random. It didn't even have a title yet – or, rather, it had had a succession of titles, all of which she'd rejected one by one.

She towelled herself dry and reached for the talc, thinking of the five-hour shift that lay ahead of her in the nursing home's stuffy kitchen. Sunday lunch of roast chicken for twenty-seven, roast and boiled potatoes, peas, mashed carrot and parsnip. Apple tart and custard for dessert, a batch of raisin scones for their tea later on, after their Sunday visitors had gone home.

Poor Martina, the only resident with no visitors at all. She'd never married, never had children, but there had to be a niece or nephew, or a cousin maybe, who was aware of her existence. How sad to think that nobody in the world cared enough about her to come and see her. You could hardly blame her for being a bit cranky.

On Sunday afternoons Martina steered clear of the two common rooms, where the others congregated to show off the sons and daughters and in-laws who dropped in with boxes of Double Centre and plastic bags of dog-eared magazines. Unless the weather was unusually warm, Martina generally stayed in her room – and for the three Sundays she'd been filling in for Austin, Sarah had paid her a visit.

Martina would be sitting by the window where she always sat. 'Is that you heading home?' she'd ask, and Sarah would tell her no, not quite, she'd just taken the currant loaves from the oven and was letting them cool down before putting a bit of icing on them. And without waiting for an invitation she'd take the chair opposite Martina and stay for a quarter of an hour or so, and Martina wouldn't seem in the least bit pleased to see her. But she had nobody else, and Sarah couldn't bear the thought of her sitting alone there all afternoon.

Back in the bedroom she pulled on cream cotton trousers and a navy top. Didn't matter what she wore to work, with a big white apron to throw over it as soon as she got there.

Neil watched her from the bed. 'You'll be home about half five so.'

'Yes, should be.' She crossed the room and bent to kiss his mouth. 'Try to behave till then.'

His hand cupped the back of her head. 'Only if I can be very bad afterwards.'

'We'll see about that.'

She left the house and got her bike from the shed, smiling already at the thought of their evening ahead, just the two of them. Still wonderful to think of herself as someone's wife. Engaged on her twenty-sixth birthday, a year after they'd met. Married the following September, just five months ago. Despite Christine's predictions of the nursing home being a non-starter for meeting men, St Sebastian's – and, of course, Stephen Flannery – had brought Sarah and Neil together.

Poor Stephen had been so delighted with the engagement, so thrilled that he'd played his part. 'Just call me Cupid,' he'd said as Sarah had held his trembling hands in hers, the day they'd broken the news to him. Gone from them now, bless the man – a massive stroke three months before the wedding had denied him the chance to be her father-in-law.

She wheeled her bike down the front path and set off. Still cycling to work, even though Neil's house – their house – was five miles further from St Sebastian's than her parents'. A round trip of fifteen miles wasn't a problem for her: she had grown up on a bike, had cycled all over the county as a teenager. Rain and wind were challenges, that was all. And, of course, cycling that distance every day kept her figure trim – no mean feat when she had to cook and bake so much, and had so little willpower.

Brian had taught Christine to drive when she was eighteen. Sarah remembered her crawling down the road behind the wheel of his battered blue Anglia, traded in since for a Morris Minor. He'd offered to teach Sarah too – and so had Neil, when they were going out – but she had no desire to learn. A bike would always be her transport of choice, no matter what the weather did. And since she'd moved house her route to work was different, so she no longer crossed the bridge where she'd met the woman in the sheepskin coat, the day she'd had the interview for St Sebastian's.

Three years ago now – where had the time gone? So much had changed since then, her life so much better now: she was in a fulfilling job and married to a wonderful man. And considering that she and Neil had met at St Sebastian's, you could say that the day of her interview had been the beginning of a whole new future for her.

She wondered if the curly-haired woman was any happier now. Was she still alive? Had she found peace of mind? Sarah hoped so.

For the rest of the day, the letter she planned to write to Helen O'Dowd was on her mind. As she slit scones in two for the residents' tea, phrases hopped around in her head. *No need to have been so blunt . . . debut novelist, surely you could have given him a chance . . . very hurtful, after all his hard work—*

'I forget where the spare butter dishes are kept.'

Eve was seventeen and not blessed with any great initiative, but she was all that was to be had on

Sundays. Sarah indicated a press. 'In there. Give them a rinse before you use them. They might be dusty.'

Anyone else would have opened doors and found the butter dishes. But Eve was young, and no doubt resented that she was stuck in the kitchen of a nursing home when her friends were probably off enjoying themselves. Maybe there was a boyfriend on the scene: she'd be quite nice-looking if she smiled more often.

'You can slip away a bit early if you want,' Sarah told her, 'as soon as the tea prep is done. I'll manage the rest.'

The rest was washing down the worktops, putting tea towels and napkins to steep overnight, planning tomorrow's lunch menu and shopping list. Easier, almost, if Eve wasn't underfoot, asking questions she really should be able to answer herself.

And Neil wouldn't mind if Sarah was slightly late getting home; give him a chance to sort his records alphabetically, like he was always threatening to do, T. Rex after Queen after Dylan after Bowie.

'Cut the butter into narrower strips,' Sarah said, watching as Eve thumped a solid half-pound onto each dish. 'Some of the residents are a little shaky. They find it easier to manage the small bits.'

She was briefly tempted to point out that this was at least the third time she'd issued that particular instruction, but she held her tongue. Kinder simply to repeat it, and hope that it eventually sank in.

It was just as easy to be nice as to be nasty. Maybe Helen O'Dowd needed to learn that.

HELEN

'Don't play with your food.'

'I don't like it. It's sour.'

Helen took an orange segment from her daughter's plate and ate it. 'It's fine. Anyway, there's nothing else till I go shopping, so you'll have to put up with it.'

'There's biscuits.'

Helen sighed, stubbing out her cigarette. 'Alright, you can have one.'

'One is no good. Why can't I have two?'

'Because you shouldn't be having any. And brush your teeth after.'

Dramatic groan. 'I *hate* brushing my teeth – it's *boring*.'

'Well, you'd hate the dentist more, trust me.'

A battle every morning to get through breakfast, Alice fighting her every step of the way. Turned seven last week: what would she be like at seventeen?

School was a different kind of battleground. Alice had been a reluctant student from the start, her teachers each year complaining to Helen of untidy work and disruptive behaviour. Her copybooks, within a week of use, dog-eared and torn, every margin filled with doodles of cats and elephants and horses.

Since she'd gone into First Class in September, spelling and sums tests had become part of every Friday, the corrected tests being sent home for parental signature on Monday. Alice's results in both subjects were invariably disastrous.

'Why don't you make more of an effort?' Helen would demand. 'Didn't you get those for home-work?' and Alice's only response would be a shrug – and Helen would let it go, knowing she was partly to blame.

Other parents, no doubt, sat dutifully beside their children, making sure that the homework was presentable. Helen couldn't imagine anything more boring, so her supervision of Alice's home-work was sporadic at best. Serve her right if Alice got three out of ten for spellings, and not a single sum right.

Alice had Cormac's dimple, tucked into her left cheek. She had his long limbs and pale skin and grey eyes – and, so far, not an ounce of his musical ability. Cormac had held her, aged two, on his lap at the piano that his grandmother had owned, and she'd slapped the keys with her flattened-out palms. Nothing much had changed since then.

When Helen, eighteen months after his death, had found herself able to open the piano again and had plinked out 'Oh Can I Wash My Father's Shirt' and 'Chopsticks', Alice had looked up briefly and regarded her mother solemnly before returning to the doll's house Cormac's mother had got her for her fourth birthday. Not musical, whatever about her possible artistic leanings.

Becoming a mother a week after her twenty-ninth birthday hadn't been an easy transition for Helen. Once the horror of the birth had subsided, she found herself confronted with a creature whose tiny bowel spat out disgusting emissions with alarming regularity, who belched and shrieked and farted, and slept when she felt like it, and spewed milky gouts onto Helen's pyjama top; whose little red wrinkled face, just before tears, resembled a seriously annoyed Winston Churchill's.

The idea of breastfeeding repelled Helen: the sight of other babies clamped to their mothers' nipples reminded her of nothing more than giant gorging leeches. It was not for her, despite the coaxing of the younger nurses, who promised it would help her get her figure back more quickly, and also help her bond with the baby.

Helen hadn't given a damn about her figure – before the pregnancy she'd never weighed more than eight and a half stone, despite eating and drinking whatever she wanted. Alice hadn't caused her to gain much more than a stone, everyone exclaiming how neat she was, her jeans still fitting up to the sixth month. She'd presumed she'd be back to normal in no time, and she'd been right.

And as for bonding . . . she'd regarded the little downy head of her days-old daughter – for once, blessedly silent and emission-free. She'd run a finger along the ludicrously soft cheek, she'd cradled the tiny feet in one hand and conceded that, yes, there was some feeling within her for this small creature. Not the overwhelming, all-consuming love that Hollywood and magazines would have you believe came rushing in once the nightmare of childbirth had passed – not that flood of emotion, not yet anyway – but there was some positive connection that would in all likelihood grow along with the child.

And it had, to a degree. Helen and Cormac had muddled along, in the manner, she imagined, of all new parents. They'd had good days and bad days, and Alice passed all the usual milestones. In due course she figured out how to roll onto her stomach. Eventually she sat up on her own. Then she crawled, and then she walked.

As time passed, she learned to say *mama* and *dada*, she pointed to her nose when questioned as to its whereabouts, and she began to string words together, to form them into some semblance of a sentence.

Of course there were times when her actions didn't cause her parents to applaud. On one memorable occasion she emptied the contents of Helen's makeup purse into the toilet bowl, where they lay unnoticed for several hours. Another time she covered the bottom half of her white bedroom wall in pink crayon scribbles, and once she poured almost an entire jar of honey into Cormac's unattended, and much-loved, slippers.

He was always ready to forgive Alice – *She's still*

a baby, she doesn't know any better – or at the most issue a gentle scolding, but Helen would look at her little daughter and feel nothing but a strong desire to smack. She'd watch Cormac speaking quietly and lovingly to Alice, and wonder if whoever had put her together had forgotten to include a fully-formed maternal gene.

Then again, maybe her lack of warmth towards her daughter wasn't so surprising, given her own emotionally barren upbringing. With such little affection shown to her as a child, was it any wonder that she found it hard to be affectionate with her own child? Just as well Alice had a father who took care of all that.

But then Cormac had been diagnosed, shortly after Alice's third birthday, and when he'd died less than a year later, and Helen had missed being there because of Alice, she'd struggled to overcome deeper feelings of resentment towards her daughter. It wasn't Alice's fault, she'd told herself repeatedly. You couldn't hold a three-year-old responsible for anything. So she'd smothered her bitterness and battled on, and she'd somehow managed to keep their shaky relationship alive.

And now, three years on, things were better. Not hugely better, just not as abysmally sad as they'd been. Helen still ached for Cormac: the hole he'd left was still there, bloody and gaping inside her – till the day she died it would be there – but the sharp pain of his absence had dulled and softened, and she'd learnt to live with it. She and Alice were muddling along, because there was nothing else for them to do.

Her choice of profession was continuing to pay the bills. She was making enough as a journalist – a journalist! – to keep herself and Alice tolerably well fed and clothed. She wrote features on the events of the day, she reviewed books and films; she'd even profiled Tommy and Jimmy Swarbrigg last year, shortly before they'd made their second failed attempt to win the Eurovision for Ireland. While Breen remained her main employer, she also sent occasional reviews to other publications.

And on the home front, relations were cordial, if as reserved as ever, with her parents. Things could be worse, that was for sure.

A small shuffling sound came just then from the hall. Helen went out and saw the scatter of envelopes on the floor, only one of which looked like it might contain a cheque. When she returned to the kitchen, Alice's mouth was full, and an untouched Marietta biscuit sat on the plate before her.

'Did you take two?' Helen asked.

Alice shook her head, crunching rapidly.

'So what are you eating?'

'Orange,' Alice replied, spraying crumbs.

Helen slit open the first envelope. 'If you're going to lie, learn to do it properly.' She pulled out the final reminder from the phone company and wondered, not for the first time, if there was any point in calling it a working expense and passing it on to Breen.

Precious few perks in working for him – unless you counted the Christmas parties, which Helen had avoided since her first one. She'd never ended a phone conversation with him feeling anything less than irritated, and she regularly gave thanks that she didn't have to be in his company all day. How Catherine managed to keep going as his PA was one of life's little miracles. No, Helen would sort the phone bill on her own – no point in giving him another opportunity to make her want to throttle him.

The second envelope, thankfully, held a cheque from her least favourite editor. He wore sandals and picked at his toes while he talked to her breasts, but a cheque was a cheque. She folded it and tucked it into her bra. Wouldn't be there long, with nothing in the fridge apart from three more sour oranges, a can of grapefruit segments, half a jar of lemon curd and a third of a bottle of whiskey.

'What's for dinner?' Alice asked.

'Fish fingers.'

'Yuk.'

Yuk was right. Bits of fish's arse probably, covered with orange muck – but Helen was damned if she was going to waste time cooking for just two people, particularly when one was so unapprecia-tive, and the other couldn't care less what – or if – she ate. Helen was well aware of her strengths, and producing a home-cooked meal had never been one of them.

Cormac had cooked. Not very well, but better than Helen. Depending on their finances he'd fed her lamb chops and grilled fish and steak, among other things.

'You're a musician,' she'd told him, 'you shouldn't know how to stuff a chicken.'

'You can't beat a decent bit of homemade grub,' he'd replied. 'I need to keep my strength up for the gigs.' But all the homemade grub in the world couldn't give him enough strength to beat cancer when it had picked him out of the crowd.

'We've no milk,' Alice announced, standing at the open fridge door.

'I'll get some later. Have water.'

'Yuk.'

Thin Lizzy erupted on the radio. Helen nodded along, although Phil Lynott was no Rory Gallagher. The third envelope, addressed to *the resident*, was a printed invitation to a fundraiser for a local sports club. Spot prize's! it told her. *Music provided by Two's a Crowd! Finger Food! Dancing! A fun night guaranteed! Support you're local club!*

She screwed it up and threw it in the general direction of the bin. Even if she'd been gagging for a breaded chicken wing and a turn around the dance floor, she'd have had to pass on grounds of bad grammar and overuse of exclamation marks. Screamers, Breen called them, to be avoided at all costs. It was one of the few things they agreed on.

The fourth envelope had *Sarah Flannery* hand-written in purple ink in the top left-hand corner. There was an address underneath, a small town about forty or fifty miles away.

Sarah Flannery. The name meant nothing.

The envelope had been sent to the newspaper office, and was addressed to Helen O'Dowd, c/o M. Breen. Care of M. Breen, as if Breen cared a jot about her. The O'Dowd had been crossed out and changed to Fitzpatrick in Catherine's tidy, cramped writing – in safe blue ink – and Helen's address was written off to the side.

Someone else she'd offended, no doubt. Lots of sensitive souls out there, went running for their Basildon Bond at the smallest little thing. A woman had written to Helen once to complain about her use of the word 'laughable' in describing the chart success of a song called 'Money, Money, Money', when Ireland was in such deep recession. *There's nothing laughable about a recession,* her letter had read. *My husband lost his job eight months ago, and he's certainly not laughing. I wonder if Abba would laugh if I asked them to pay our ESB bill.*

Another time, when Helen had had the temerity to suggest that Ireland was being led by a man who was more at home in Croke Park than in Leinster House, an avalanche of outraged letters had arrived at the newspaper office, most of them with Cork postmarks, all of them insisting that Jack Lynch was the best Taoiseach the country had ever known, and more than a few of them demanding that Helen retract her statement.

Breen, when he'd told her, had sounded almost gleeful. Helen had assumed he was taking pleasure from her having landed in trouble.

'Do I need to issue an apology?' she'd asked.

He'd snorted. 'An apology? You'll do nothing of the sort. You stirred things up – that's what sells papers.'

'But what about all the—'

'I wasn't ringing about that. I want a thousand words on Steve Biko's autopsy findings by noon tomorrow. Give us your take on how white security police could be let off when a black anti-apartheid leader died of a brain haemorrhage brought on by repeated blows to the head while in their custody. Lay it on thick: I want righteous outrage here.'

He was fearless, like Helen. That much they had in common, that much she admired about him.

'What time is it?' Alice asked.

Helen glanced at the clock on the wall. '*Fuck*,' she breathed, dropping the envelope and pushing back her chair. 'Get your coat.'

'I don't need—'

'Just get it.' She threw the breakfast things into the sink and found the car keys on the worktop, under a red and pink striped sock.

'I forgot to brush my teeth,' Alice announced in the car. Waiting until she knew there wasn't time to go back inside, clever little madam.

'They'll fall out,' Helen told her, reversing out of

the driveway. 'You'll have to get false ones and *they'll* keep falling out into your dinner, and everyone will laugh at you.'

Alice turned her head to look out of the window, unconcerned. 'No, they won't. Patricia O'Neill brings Lemon Puffs for her lunch every single day and her teeth didn't fall out.'

Helen drove past the house next door, giving a cheery wave to Malone, pottering around in his tiny, immaculate garden. He scowled at her like he usually did. One day he'd smile and she'd keel over with the shock.

The principal was standing by the school door, scanning the road. Lying in wait. As soon as Helen pulled up she came over, plump arm raised, moving as fast as her long black habit would allow. 'Mrs Fitzpatrick, just a quick word, if I—'

'Sorry, Sister,' Helen told her, practically pushing Alice out. 'I'm rushing for an appointment, can't stop. Terribly sorry.'

Who cared if Alice was a couple of minutes late every now and again? What the hell was so important in First Class? Let Sister Aloysius write Helen a letter if it was so important.

Back home she rinsed the breakfast dishes and left them to drain. She made a fresh pot of coffee, forgetting that they were out of milk until she went to look for it. She swore loudly, slamming the fridge door.

Malone – he could hardly say no, even if it killed her to ask. And she needed coffee if she was to

111

write a thousand words on Joe Dolan, of all people, by the middle of the afternoon. 'He's planning a tour of Russia later in the year,' Breen had told her. 'First Western entertainer to go there. Give me a piece on that, from Mullingar to Moscow kind of thing.'

Helen had groaned. 'Joe Dolan? Please.'

'Just do it,' Breen had replied, in a voice you didn't argue with.

Joe Dolan sang the kind of songs Helen had always run a mile from. Some challenge, to make it sound like she had the slightest interest in a would-be Elvis from the back end of nowhere, strutting his stuff in the dancehalls of Russia. But she couldn't afford to turn down the cheque, so she'd ordered a couple of magazines from his fan club, and she had the bones of her piece put together. She'd squeeze out a thousand words on anything, if someone was willing to pay for it.

Thankfully, she had a few far more interesting ideas waiting to be worked up. She wanted to write a feature on the Yorkshire Ripper, his latest victim, just eighteen years old, discovered six weeks ago. She was also planning to interview mothers of Irish soldiers headed for the Lebanon: Breen would definitely go for that.

And if she could swing it, she was hoping for an interview with Eamonn Coghlan before he headed to the European Athletics Championships in August. Plenty in the pipeline, along with her usual stock of book and film reviews.

She left the house through the front door, where she found Malone clipping the dividing hedge. Small as it was, his lawn was an immaculate perfect green, not a dandelion or daisy to be seen. Two shrubs that she didn't recognise sat neatly inside his front wall. Probably loved the fact that he was showing up her gravel patch.

'Milk?' His scowl deepened, if that was possible. He lowered his shears slowly, probably dying to shove them between her ribs.

Helen resisted the impulse to say, *Yes, you know, the white stuff that comes from cows.* 'I've run out,' she told him, in as civil a tone as she could manage. 'Just need a drop for my coffee, if you can spare it.'

He continued to scrutinise her suspiciously. At least he kept his eyes on her face. Probably wouldn't know what to do with a pair of tits if they were handed to him on a plate.

'Don't know if I have any,' he said eventually. 'Don't use it much.'

'I just need a small drop,' she told him. *Quick as you like, you old fart.*

He turned and made his way up the short path to his front door. Last thing he wanted to do, help her out in any way. Banging on the wall between them anytime she turned her music up, even in the middle of the afternoon. Lately she'd taken to banging back, which must really get his blood pressure going. With any luck she'd finish him off one day, blast Black Sabbath out till she gave him a coronary.

She stood waiting on her side of the hedge. His house probably stank of that ratty old cat of his, no sign of a window open. Come to think of it, the milk might well smell of cat too. She should have gone to the shop, might still have to. What was keeping the old goat?

Eventually he reappeared and offered her a half-full blue and white striped cup. Broke his heart, barely enough for two refills.

'Thanks, appreciate it.'

'I'll need the cup back,' he said.

As if she'd want to hang on to anything that belonged to him. 'You'll get it,' she said tightly. 'I have plenty of my own.'

'And keep that music down,' he added, as she turned away.

She made no reply. Just her luck to end up living beside such a grump. *His bark's worse than his bite*, Cormac had said, *just give him a chance*, but the less Helen saw of him, with his threadbare jumpers that smelt of Zam-Buk and his baggy grey vests strung across his washing line, the better.

Back in the kitchen she turned on the news. A British soldier and a woman civilian shot dead in Belfast by gunmen posing as Rag Week students in fancy dress. Charlie Chaplin's body snatched by grave robbers in Switzerland. *The Spike*, RTÉ's big new drama, shot down in flames after just five episodes because it had dared to feature a nude actress playing the part of an art class model – now *there* was something to get her teeth into, once Joe Dolan was out of the way.

As she brought her mug to the table, the letter she hadn't got around to opening before the school run caught her eye. She slid her finger under the envelope flap and pulled out the notelet. The front image was a watercolour of a vase with masses of daisies stuck into it. Maybe not a letter of complaint after all, maybe one of the very few she got with something positive to say.

The handwriting inside was rounded, with giant loops under the *ys* and *gs*. The ink was the same purple as on the envelope.

Dear Miss O'Dowd

I am writing to protest in the strongest possible terms at your review of *To Kill with Kindness* in today's newspaper. I feel you dealt far too harshly with this book, which I admit I haven't read, but surely you could have been a little less blunt in your criticism, particularly as it's a debut novel. Imagine how hard the author must have worked on it. I especially thought your remark about him keeping a diary was unnecessarily cruel. Perhaps you could choose your words more carefully in future. I'm sure you won't object to a little constructive criticism.

Yours sincerely,

Sarah Flannery (Mrs)

She dribbled some of Malone's milk into her coffee, hovering between amusement and annoyance. Seemed like Pollyanna was alive and well, living forty miles down the road and worried that Helen might have upset the poor little author with her horrible review. Sarah Flannery (Mrs) must have time on her hands. Probably delighted with the chance to use one of her twee little notelets.

And naïve enough to admit that she hadn't even read the damn book. *Imagine how hard the author must have worked on it* – how the hell did she know he'd worked hard on it? If she'd bothered to scan even the first few pages she'd have seen that he'd put precious little work into it, but she'd been too busy writing to the nasty lady who'd offended him.

I'm sure you won't object to a little constructive criticism – what was so constructive about telling Helen she didn't like her review? Another cliché whose meaning had clearly escaped her. The woman was laughable.

She could just imagine Sarah Flannery in her country cottage with roses growing around the door. Married to Mr Flannery with a square jaw, who treated her like a queen and never got sick.

The perfect little housewife – no working outside the home, she bet, for Mrs Sarah Flannery – waving hubby goodbye in her frilly apron as he went off to work each morning. Cooking dinner for him and their two perfect children, one of each, who got top marks in everything at school.

Helen had a good mind to send her *To Kill with*

Kindness, let her see what rubbish she was standing up for. She pulled a cigarette from its pack. Why not? She'd send her the book, ask Catherine to let it go through the post at the paper, say it was work-related. That should shut her up, silly Mrs-in-brackets Flannery.

She stuck the cigarette between her lips and looked around for matches, eyeing the typewriter that sat waiting for her to tap out a thousand words about the wonderful Joe Dolan. Her deadline was five o'clock, so delivery could wait till ten to.

She enjoyed making Breen sweat a bit. Did him no harm at all.

SARAH

'She bought the land two years ago, and she plans to build a new house there. Imagine, a real princess coming on holidays to Mayo.'

'Bet Rainier couldn't believe his luck when he got her.' Christine gazed at the photo on the front of the magazine. 'She even looks good in a headscarf. Mind you, the open-topped sports car helps.'

'She's gorgeous, shame she had to give up acting . . . Oh, by the way, you'll never guess what I got in the post the other day.'

'What?'

'That book, the one Helen O'Dowd reviewed a few weeks ago. Remember I wrote to her because I thought she was too hard on it?'

'I'd completely forgotten that . . . So she sent you the book?'

'Well, there was no note or address or anything, but I presume it came from her.'

'Did you tell her you hadn't read it when you wrote?'

'Well, yes. I thought I should be honest.'

Christine laughed. 'Sarah, you're so innocent – I find it hard to believe we came out of the same womb. Obviously she felt you needed to see what you were talking about. Let's have a look then: where is it?'

Sarah took the book from the dresser and handed it to her. Christine's nose wrinkled as she took it. 'Stinks of cigarettes.' She opened it and turned the pages.

Sarah crossed to the window and looked out at the cherry tree that Neil had planted at the bottom of the garden six months earlier, the day after they'd got home from their honeymoon in England. She'd watched him placing the sapling in the hole, thinking, *I might be pregnant already*. Now March was almost over, and the little tree had its first scatter of blooms, and she was still being disappointed every month. Not to worry, she was only twenty-eight. They had plenty of time.

The silence in the kitchen was shattered suddenly by a loud squawk. Christine took no notice, continuing to read.

'Oh, let me.' Sarah crossed to the pram and lifted out the warm, wriggling bundle. She cradled it against her, rocking and shushing and pressing her lips to the soft, damp cheek.

'Needs a nappy,' Christine said, not looking up. 'I can smell him from here.'

'I'll do it.'

She couldn't get enough of him, wanted to smother him in kisses, tickle his fat little toes, press her face to the tight drum of his belly and inhale his sweet, powdery scent. Four months old and already well aware that his aunt adored him, she was sure of it.

'Aidan,' she whispered into his ear, and he hiccupped at her. Born nine months after Christine's wedding, the honeymoon baby that Sarah had wished for, but hadn't got. Some wives had all the luck.

After they'd left, Sarah cleaned the kitchen and put on a wash. So little time on a Saturday to carry out all the jobs she didn't get around to during the week. She remembered a time when all she'd wanted was to get married, have babies and give up working outside the home. But now that she had a job she loved, she was having second thoughts.

Raising a family and going out to work was undoubtedly a challenge, but it was 1978, and mothers in the workplace were becoming the rule rather than the exception – especially since women could now earn as much as men, in theory anyway. And it would be a bit demoralising, wouldn't it, if she had to go running to Neil anytime she needed money?

So much was changing, with the eighties just around the corner. The way things were going, it seemed only a matter of time before married couples would be able to get contraceptives from their doctors. Not that Sarah would ever be looking for those, of course: the more children they had, the better. But she'd try to keep her job too, for as long as she could.

Of course, she had to get pregnant first.

She returned the empty laundry basket to the bathroom and went outside to cut the back lawn. She was married to a gardener who kept everyone else's grounds looking lovely and never gave a minute's attention to his own. Some days she spent more time in the garden than in the house, but she enjoyed it as long as the weather held out.

Pushing the mower up and down in neat stripes, she thought about the woman who'd sent her the book. Impossible to know how she'd received Sarah's letter, when she hadn't sent a word in response. Mind you, the book was probably response enough. *Take that*, it said. *Read it and see what I'm talking about.*

And in fairness, Sarah probably *should* have read it before she'd protested at the review. She'd begin it this evening, now that she'd finished *The Girl with Green Eyes*. Really, she couldn't see what all the fuss had been about. Certainly Edna O'Brien's writing was a little risqué in parts, but to have banned it, and even burnt copies of it, seemed a bit harsh.

She raked up the cut grass and added it to the compost heap. But even if *To Kill with Kindness* wasn't very good, there had still been no call for Helen O'Dowd to be so mean about it. She could surely have found one single positive thing to say, even if it was only to compliment the characters' names, for goodness' sake.

She returned the mower to the shed and walked into the house, stepping out of her gardening shoes at the back door. Time for a quick shower before Neil got home. As she put a foot on the first stair, the phone rang.

'Sarah,' her father said, his voice thick with fear, 'it's your mother.'

HELEN

Dear Miss O'Dowd

Thank you for sending me *To Kill with Kindness* last week. No doubt you thought I shouldn't have criticised your review without reading it, and you were quite right. And now that I have read it, I have to be honest and say that it didn't really grab me. I found the plot a little thin, and none of the characters particularly appealed to me, especially the detective, whom I found slightly full of himself.

I still feel, though, that you could have been a bit kinder towards it, maybe held back a little in your review, even if you couldn't see any positives. I suppose I feel empathy for the author because I'm writing a book myself, and would hate to get a bad review like yours for it. Maybe when you're writing your next review, if you can't think of anything good to say, say nothing. Just a thought.

Thank you again for the book. I'm assuming you don't want it back, and unless I hear to the contrary from you in the next week I'll bring it to my local charity shop. They're always grateful for donations.

Yours sincerely,

Sarah Flannery (Mrs)

Helen read the letter with growing irritation. What a ninny she was. *If you can't think of anything good to say, say nothing.* How could Helen write a review if she said nothing? Such a load of bullshit – and what was with the ridiculous purple ink?

She could just imagine Mrs Goody-Two-Shoes Flannery throwing compliments around like snuff at a wake, spreading happiness wherever she went, never a bad word spoken about anything or anyone. If Helen had to button her lip every time she felt like saying something that might upset someone, she'd be struck dumb most of the time.

Mind you, there were plenty who'd probably prefer her that way. 'You have a mouth on you,' Breen had told her once, 'that would scour toilets.' As if he couldn't let fly himself with a few four-letter words, as if he hadn't turned the air blue on the rare occasions that Helen had dared to disagree with him.

'This is an effing newspaper I'm running here,' he'd bark. 'I'm in charge, not some Johnny-come-lately who thinks she's the next Hemingway. Don't think I won't give you your effing marching orders if you push me too far.' Only of course he hadn't said effing. And then he had the gall to point the

124

finger at her if she dropped the occasional exasperated four-letter word into their conversations.

But he wouldn't let her go: he knew as well as she did that they were too good a team. Much as she hated to admit it, Breen was the sharpest editor she worked for. He spotted a hanging participle or a lazy reference at a hundred paces, and for all his guff, Helen knew he respected her work. Not that she wouldn't drop *him* like a stone if she could afford to, ordering her around like he was God almighty. No wonder she felt compelled to push back against him now and again.

He wasn't all bad, though. The time Helen had had to turn down a commission because Alice had broken her wrist when she'd fallen from the monkey bars in the park, a courier had called to the house with a big blue elephant: most unexpected. And although Helen was reasonably certain that the idea had been Catherine's, she'd still have had to get the go-ahead from Breen. Somewhere beneath his well-cut suit there beat a heart that wasn't made totally of granite.

She scanned Sarah Flannery's letter again. *I'm writing a book myself:* Helen could imagine what sort of a happy-ever-after load of tripe that was going to be. Everybody being nice as pie to everybody else, nobody dying, nobody cursing, nobody so much as having a bad thought. She must remember Sarah Flannery's name, make sure to get her hands on an advance copy. Of course, that was assuming any publisher in his right mind would want it, which sounded a pretty unlikely prospect.

She tossed the letter and its envelope into the bin. Silly woman, nothing better to do than write preachy messages in poncy cards, in between embroidering a few cushions probably, and doing the church flowers.

As she reached for a cigarette, the phone rang. She walked out to the hall and lifted the receiver.

'Mrs Fitzpatrick?'

The female voice was familiar – breathy, polite – but Helen couldn't immediately place it. 'Yes.'

'Sister Aloysius here. It's about Alice.'

Damn, fuck, blast: another complaint. Helen decided to launch a pre-emptive strike.

'I know she was quite late yesterday morning,' she said, eyeing the cobweb that dangled from the far corner of the hall ceiling. 'It's totally my fault: I forgot to set—'

'Mrs Fitzpatrick,' the nun broke in, more brusquely, 'I'm not ringing you about Alice's lateness, although I do think it's important that she learn early on about the importance of punctuality.'

Helen's free hand balled into a fist: snooty frustrated bitch. She waited to hear what was coming, wondering what else Alice could have done to merit a call to her mother from the principal. Robbing someone's sweets at lunchtime? Breaking someone's crayons? Wasn't that as bad as seven-year-old crimes got?

'The reason I'm calling is to point out that Alice's

head is full of lice – in fact, she's had them for several days now. I'd appreciate if you could attend to it, if you wouldn't mind.'

Lice? Helen's mouth dropped open.

'I realise you're a busy woman, Mrs Fitzpatrick, but it really is essential that you keep an eye out – so easy for lice to spread within the confines of the classroom, as I'm sure you'll understand.'

Alice had *head lice*?

'Mrs Fitzpatrick? Hello? Are you there?'

Helen blinked. 'Yes.'

'You really need to keep an eye on Alice's schoolbag.'

Keep an eye on her schoolbag? Did it have lice too?

'Miss O'Keeffe sends notes home on a regular basis, Mrs Fitzpatrick, dealing with various topics, one of which is to remind parents to check for head lice. She puts these notes into the schoolbags personally. Maybe you're not aware of this.'

Notes? Alice had made no mention of notes. Helen couldn't remember when she'd gone through her schoolbag. Never, probably.

'Thank you,' she managed. 'I'll see to it.'

She hung up while Sister Aloysius was still bleating, the little voice becoming fainter and fainter as the receiver moved further from Helen's ear. She returned to the kitchen, her head buzzing with anger, although who it was directed at, she couldn't have said.

Alice, who didn't bother passing on notes. Or

Sister Holier-than-thou Aloysius, who no doubt took great pleasure in telling another woman that her child's head was full of lice. Or buck-toothed Miss O'Keeffe, who probably warned the other children in the class not to get too close to Alice Fitzpatrick, with her dirty hair and her careless mother who didn't bother cleaning it.

But of course she herself was the one at fault. She was the mother who'd never bought a fine-tooth comb, despite dim memories, now that she thought about it, of her own mother drawing one painfully across Helen's scalp on a regular basis. *Jesus*, she should have thought of a bloody fine-tooth comb: what kind of mother didn't even own one? Useless, she was useless.

She pulled a cigarette from the pack and lit it with trembling fingers. She paced the kitchen tiles, puffing angrily. *Christ*, to have that thrown at her at ten in the morning, for her not to have noticed that Alice had lice. Her insides heaved at the image of the tiny squirming things living on her daughter's head, maybe for weeks.

How had she missed Alice scratching? She must have scratched, with a head full of lice. How had she not seen them when she'd washed Alice's hair on Saturday nights, Alice whingeing that she had suds in her eyes, that Helen was scrubbing too hard? She *did* scrub hard, for Christ's sake. How had the little buggers survived?

And if Alice had them, wasn't there a chance

that she did too? Her scalp crawled at the prospect. She scratched furiously at it – *Jesus*, that was all she needed. A trip to the chemist as soon as she'd put her face on: deadlines could go to hell.

She stamped upstairs and wrenched sheets from beds, pulled pillows out of cases, yanked towels from rails. She brought her load back downstairs and dumped it in the twin tub. She attached the washing machine's length of rubber hose to the kitchen tap and began to fill the drum, blood still racing. Where the hell was Malone when you needed someone to yell at?

When the water was heating, she took the last of her toast to the bin and flung it in, on top of Sarah Flannery's sugary-sweet letter. No lice in that household, you could bet your last cent. Checked her little darlings' heads twice a week at least, had whatever necessary bottle or tube tucked away in the bathroom cabinet, just in case.

She reached abruptly into the bin and pulled out the notelet and its envelope. She brushed away crumbs and sped through the purple words again. She dropped the notelet back on top of the crusts and grabbed a sheet of paper from the bundle that sat by her typewriter.

She typed fast, without pausing. When she'd finished, she yanked out the page and read it rapidly, eyes darting along the handful of lines, before scribbling her signature at the bottom. She found an envelope among the scatter of magazines and newspapers on the table, and a stamp in the cracked cup on the windowsill.

She'd post it right away. She'd drop it into the pillar box around the corner from the chemist. That should shut the silly cow up.

SARAH

She sat alone in the blessedly quiet kitchen. The table was piled with haphazard stacks of plates holding half-eaten sandwiches, and little wobbly pillars of coffee-stained cups, lipstick crescents daubing several rims. Just about every glass in the house was out too, along with the remains of the various cakes and tarts that her neighbours had delivered the day before, when the news had filtered out. Showing their sympathy with a Victoria Sandwich, saying sorry with a fresh cream flan or pear crumble.

Neil was gone with her father, driving him back to the house where he would live alone now until his turn came to die, or until he became unable to live on his own any more, and moved in with one of his daughters.

Christine had wanted to stay and help, but Sarah had insisted she go: 'I'll be fine. Neil will be back in a little while.' This wasn't true – Neil had been instructed to stay with their father for the rest of the evening, make him tea, pour him a drink, watch the news on television, anything – but

Christine had Aidan to feed and put to bed, and Sarah had nothing else to do but clean up.

For now, though, she sat at the table in the silent kitchen, her mind replaying the last heartbreaking week. An aneurysm, the doctors had said, no way of predicting it, her mother's blood pressure normal at her last check-up just a few months before. It happened like that sometimes, they had been told.

The past few days had blurred into one another, with Mam lying unconscious in a hospital bed, tubes pumping air and food and medicine into her from various beeping machines, and the three of them taking it in turns to sit with her, overlapping their visits to talk in whispers across the bed, as if she might hear them if they spoke any louder.

Nothing much to do during Sarah's evening shifts at the hospital but work her way through *To Kill with Kindness*, which, even in her distraught state, she could recognise as not very accomplished at all. She wondered how on earth anyone had thought it worthy of publication – what could they have seen in it? Helen O'Dowd's assessment, she had to admit, had been pretty accurate, even if she'd worded it a little strongly.

When she'd finished, Sarah had felt obliged to respond to the woman who'd sent her the book, although in her present state she had little enthusiasm for the task. Still, manners dictated that she acknowledge the book's receipt and give her honest feedback.

She'd written for the second time to Helen O'Dowd as she'd sat late at night in the too-warm hospital room. The following morning she'd given it to Neil to post on his way to work – and just a day after that, her mother had died.

This evening sixty-three-year-old Martha Kelly lay in a wooden box at the top of the local church, and tomorrow they were lowering her into a hole in the ground, and Sarah couldn't think about that. She got to her feet and began gathering plates and cups and bringing them to the sink. She turned on the radio and ran water and squeezed in washing-up liquid.

Over the next forty minutes she emptied and refilled the sink several times, washing and drying and putting away, blocking out her thoughts with Fleetwood Mac and The Boomtown Rats and The Undertones.

When a handful of plates remained, she ran out of washing-up liquid. She dried her hands and went to the pantry for a new bottle – and saw the envelope, propped on a shelf.

This morning it had come, as she and Neil were leaving the house to go to her father's. Her name and address had been typewritten, with no return address, no indication of its sender's identity or whereabouts, apart from the Dublin postmark. She'd put it on the pantry shelf, out of the way of the busy day she knew was ahead, and she'd forgotten all about it.

She took it off the shelf and considered it.

Not a bill: she knew what they looked like. Not a letter of sympathy, nobody wrote those on a typewriter.

She sat at the almost-cleared table and slit open the envelope with a buttery knife and pulled out the single sheet.

Dear Mrs Flannery

Many thanks for your advice about writing a book review. I'll bear it in mind for the next time. In the meantime, I have some advice for you. Take your half-baked manuscript and tear it up – better still, burn it. If, as I suspect, you think it's possible to write an interesting, credible book without anything bad happening, you are sadly mistaken. Bad things happen, Mrs Flannery – disease happens, rape happens, infidelity, terrorism, vandalism all happen in this real, ugly world of ours – and like it or not, it's generally the bad stuff that makes for an interesting book. Therefore I suggest you take your little goody-goody clichéd characters with their happy little lives and stamp them out, Mrs Flannery, choke the life out of them before they send the readers of the world to sleep.

And in future, if you don't agree with one of my book reviews, despite not having bothered to read the goddamn book, I suggest you turn to the gardening page, or the cookery page, and try to forget all about it.

H. O'Dowd

When she had finished reading it, Sarah remained still, her gaze fixed on the scrawled signature. How could anyone be so cruel? Why would someone who'd never even seen Sarah's manuscript advise her to burn it? Had Sarah made Helen O'Dowd so angry with her criticism that she'd felt compelled to write such a horrible letter in response?

She sat on the hard kitchen chair and forbade herself to cry. They were strangers to one another. Helen O'Dowd meant nothing to her, and Sarah wasn't going to give her the power to upset her. She had enough to cry about right now without wasting tears on a spiteful, vindictive letter.

Easier said than done. A drop splatted onto the page. Sarah brushed another away before it had a chance to fall, and squeezed her eyes shut. If Helen O'Dowd had any idea of the work Sarah had put into the book, if she knew the hours that had been spent on it, the dream Sarah had of one day seeing it sitting on a bookshop shelf, surely she wouldn't have been so cruel about it.

She opened her eyes and folded the letter, left it on the table and went back to her washing-up. She worked until every plate and cup and glass was clean and back where it belonged, the fridge was filled with leftovers and a pile of dishes and platters that didn't belong to her was sitting on the table, ready to be returned.

She went out to the garden – still bright at almost nine o'clock – and placed the mound of half-eaten sandwiches on the bird table that Christine and Brian had given her on her last birthday. Back inside she wiped down the draining-board and swept the floor.

She undid her apron and draped it over the side of the sink. She sat at the table again and unfolded Helen O'Dowd's letter, and forced herself to read it through a second time.

I suggest you take your little goody-goody clichéd characters with their happy little lives and stamp them out.

The characters weren't goody-goody, far from it. Mrs Hastings the housekeeper had a really sharp tongue on her: look how she regularly reduced poor Betsy, the under-housemaid, to tears. And Lord William Delahunty was a proper philanderer – that was obvious from the way he'd seduced Betsy in the woods, having proposed to Lady Penelope Smith just the week before—

She stopped. It wasn't exactly bursting with originality, she knew that. She wasn't writing the next *War and Peace*. She didn't for a minute imagine she was going to set the literary world alight. She was writing a gentle story, a comfort read if you like. Something you'd reach for at the end of a trying day—

She came to another stop. Gentle story. Comfort

read. Even to her own ears, it sounded like she was writing the literary equivalent of a hot-water bottle.

She looked down at the letter again. *Clichéd characters . . . send the readers of the world to sleep . . .*

The characters *were* clichéd. She'd read countless novels with identical people in them, blunt-spoken housekeepers and timid, vulnerable housemaids and upper-class cads who took advantage when they got the chance. She was addicted to period dramas, and all she was doing, all she'd been doing for what seemed like forever, was regurgitating various scenes and characters and storylines from books she'd already read. There was nothing new in what she was producing; there wasn't an ounce of originality or creativity in it.

Helen O'Dowd was right. Without having read a word of Sarah's book, without meeting her or even speaking to her on the phone, she'd hit the nail on the head. *Trouble at Thornton Manor*, or whatever title she might finally have settled on, would do nothing but send readers to sleep. It was as lacking in originality and freshness as *To Kill with Kindness* had been.

Sarah sat for a while longer, as the fridge gave its every-now-and-again bubbly whirr, and a sudden dribble of water fell from one of the kitchen taps, and a dog barked sharply a few gardens away.

At length she got up and left the room. She climbed the stairs and opened the door of the smallest bedroom. She stared at the thick bundle of handwritten pages that lay on the desk she'd brought with her from home, and she thought of the hours she'd sat there, the countless words she'd written and scribbled out and rewritten. The pages she'd discarded, the scenes she'd replaced. All worthless, all for nothing.

She lifted the bundle and brought it downstairs to the kitchen. Someone was singing about match-stalk cats and dogs on the radio. She took the lid off the bin and began tearing the pages into quarters, a dozen or so at a time, and tossing them in.

It took just a few minutes. She didn't think about what she was doing. When she'd finished, she replaced the lid and left the kitchen without looking back.

HELEN

She reached out and checked the luminous face of her watch again: five eleven. This was ridiculous, her third sleepless night in a row. Not good, and not normal. Most of the time she slept like a stone, had to drag herself awake in the mornings, cotton-woolish until her first coffee. Even while Cormac had been sick she'd slept through most of the nights, despite the horror of their situation waiting to tumble afresh into her head each morning.

Fuck it. She threw back the blankets and swung her legs out of bed, rubbing the sting of tiredness from her eyes before making her way through the blackness to the door. She opened it quietly, meeting the muted light of the lamp that was plugged into the landing socket for Alice's benefit. She paused, listening for her daughter's breathing on the other side of the always-ajar bedroom door – and there it was, a rhythmic series of abrupt inhalations, as if Alice, in her dreams, was being repeatedly surprised.

Helen padded downstairs in the half-dark, yawning, fingers trailing along the wall, meeting the bump of the mounted family photo halfway down. A second-wedding-anniversary present from Cormac, a professional shot of the three of them. The only time he'd got it wrong.

The photo itself was inoffensive, Helen's curls still there, tumbling loose over the bodice of the blue and green gypsy dress she'd worn, her scarlet toenails poking from white cork-soled platform sandals, an ankle bracelet of tiny multicoloured love beads above.

Cormac's hair was long and thick too, his smiling face showing no sign of the ruin it was to become, his arm around her shoulders as they sat side by side on the photographer's white couch. And nineteen-month-old Alice, perched on her father's blue-jeaned knee in her best yellow dress and matching headband, had beamed obligingly at the puppet the photographer had waved at her. A perfectly fine family snap, nothing wrong with it.

But Helen had always hated having her photo taken and her smile, each time she looked at this one, appeared horribly false. 'Think sunny thoughts,' the photographer had urged, which of course had increased her desire to tell him exactly what he could do with his camera. The only reason the photo remained on the stairway was that Cormac looked happy in it, and Helen needed to keep seeing that.

She reached the bottom of the stairs and felt her way along the wall to the light switch. In the kitchen she tipped the contents of the bin onto the lino and rummaged through them until she located the crumpled envelope on which Sarah Flannery had written her address.

A little worse for wear now after its three days in the bin, stained with coffee grounds and ketchup, greasy with butter and damp with moisture, but the rounded purple letters were still legible, just about. The address was becoming familiar, Helen's third time to use it.

She copied it onto a fresh envelope, wording the accompanying note in her head. The fridge gave a shudder as she fed a sheet of paper into the typewriter – but as her fingers moved to their accustomed positions on the keys she changed her mind and pulled out the page again. Better do this one by hand.

For the past three days she'd been feeling increasingly uncomfortable. As she'd scraped the new fine-tooth comb across Alice's scalp, shushing the child's protests, as she'd deposited the tiny black grubs into a basin of water, as she'd applied the bottle of foul-smelling liquid afterwards to kill off any leftovers, she knew she'd been needlessly cruel to Sarah Flannery.

It was one thing to trash a badly written book – fair game, once it was out there on the shelves – and quite another to lash out at someone whose only offence had been to offer what had, after all, been a fairly mild criticism of Helen's review. She'd had a lot worse things written and said to her after nearly three years of making her honest opinions known to the general public.

Sarah Flannery was undoubtedly a bit of a softie, and possibly couldn't write a book to save her life, but she hadn't deserved the letter Helen had written. For all Helen's faults – and she recognised and acknowledged every one of them – she strove to be fair, and in this case she'd failed. She'd been angry, and she'd lashed out at Sarah Flannery, who'd chosen the wrong day to cross her path.

She had to put it right, or run the risk of never sleeping through the night again. She unscrewed the fountain pen she'd treated herself to with Breen's first cheque, and began to write.

Dear Mrs Flannery
A few days ago I wrote to you in anger, and I said some things which I now regret. As you know from my review of *To Kill with Kindness*, I'm not one to mince my words: I prefer to speak the truth as I see it, and hang the consequences. In your case, however, my anger was wrongly directed and my remarks, particularly in the area of your writing, wholly unwarranted. I'd been annoyed at something else entirely, and you simply provided an outlet for my anger.

I'm writing now to apologise unreservedly, and I hope you can forgive my thoughtlessness.

I wish you all the best with your book.
Sincerely,
Helen O'Dowd

There. It was prim and horribly stilted, but it would have to do. She folded the page and slid it into the envelope. She'd post it later, on the way home from dropping Alice to school, and that would be an end to it.

She turned off the light and left the kitchen. If she fell asleep in the next ten minutes she'd get a good two hours before the alarm went off. Less than ideal if she was to do justice to the thousand words Breen had demanded on the Wood Quay situation, but it would have to do.

SARAH

'That forsythia wants tidying up,' Martina said. 'It's a disgrace.'

'Cutbacks, I'm afraid. Apparently the nursing home has no money to pay a full-time gardener. But I'm sure Matron would be happy to let you do it, if you wanted.'

'*Me*? I'm a resident, not the hired help. I'm paying well to stay here.'

'Well, of course, but you'd enjoy it, wouldn't you? And it would look so much better. You could be happy that you'd improved it.'

Martina sniffed. 'I can tell you I have no intention of going near it.'

'Right . . .'

Silence. Sarah checked her watch: another ten minutes and she'd have to get going with the apple buns for tea. She cast about for a new topic of conversation, and found it.

'Imagine Elvis is dead a year already. Hard to believe, isn't it?'

Martina snorted. 'That fellow? No loss.' She pulled her grey cardigan more tightly around her. 'All that shaking himself around, and marrying that poor child when she didn't know any better: disgusting. He should have been arrested.'

Sarah hid a smile. 'It was his anniversary last week. Helen O'Dowd wrote a bit in the paper about him.'

'Who? Never heard of her.'

'She's a journalist. She does book reviews on Sunday too. I thought it was quite good, what she wrote about Elvis. Quite touching, even if you didn't like him.'

No response. Martina frowned out at the forsythia. Sarah tried again.

'Actually, I wrote a book,' she said. 'Well, half a book.' Maybe that would get a reaction.

Martina turned. 'What – a cookery book?'

'No, a novel, set in the past. About people who lived in a Big House, you know, kind of an *Upstairs, Downstairs* story.'

'Oh, that was good. The Bellamys . . . and the housekeeper, what's this her name was again?'

'Mrs Bridges.'

'That's right. She was priceless.'

'Yes, well, mine was about another—'

'And that strap who ran off with the footman. And the butler, Mr Hudson, he was great.'

'He was,' Sarah said. 'He was very good alright.'

Just as well, probably, that the conversation had veered away from the manuscript she'd destroyed. Four months on, the loss of it still caused a small pang.

When she'd told the others about tearing it up, the reactions had been pretty much as she'd expected. It had been a week or so after her mother's funeral. The family was gathered in Christine and Brian's conservatory, the sun slipping down behind the line of spruce trees at the bottom of their garden. They were letting mugs of coffee go cool, punctuating the silence with brief murmured exchanges, each of them still battered from the emotions of the previous week.

Sarah's admission, slipped into one of the pauses, had caused a stir.

'You tore up your book, just like that?' Christine had asked incredulously. 'The whole thing is gone in the bin, after a letter from someone you don't even know? What possessed you?'

'I can't believe you let her influence you like that,' Neil had said. 'You've never met her, she hadn't read a word you'd written. How on earth would she know what you're capable of?'

Her father's reaction had been more measured, but he was saying pretty much the same. 'If you felt yourself that the book wasn't going anywhere that's one thing, but to tear it up because of what someone else says seems a little . . . impulsive. I hope you won't regret it.'

Sarah had made no reply, reluctant to admit that she was already regretting it. Why had she been so rash? Why hadn't she at least slept on it before ripping up over two years of thinking and plotting and writing and correcting? All that effort, destroyed in a few minutes because some stranger had suggested it mightn't be any good.

She said nothing to them about the second letter, slipping through the door a few days after the first. Short, handwritten, astonishing. *I'm writing now to apologise unreservedly . . . I hope you can forgive my thoughtlessness.*

Helen O'Dowd, apologising unreservedly. Too bad the damage had already been done. Reading the few brief lines, Sarah hadn't been sure if this letter made the situation better or worse. She'd felt a twist of anger, directed towards both of them. What right had Helen O'Dowd to criticise something she'd never seen, and how could she herself have been so foolish as to be led by it?

I wish you all the best with your book – a fat lot of good all the wishes in the world would do, now that the book no longer existed. Too little, too late – and in the week that her mother had died too, just to make things worse.

For the rest of that day Sarah had felt crotchety, clattering dishes in the nursing-home kitchen on her first day back to work since the funeral, aware that the rest of the staff were keeping their distance. Let them – for once, she wasn't concerned with making sure everyone else was happy.

By the end of the day, though, she'd talked herself back into a more resigned state of mind. What was done was done: no point in crying over it now. And this second letter showed, didn't it, that Helen O'Dowd had a conscience, that she wasn't as ruthless as she seemed? That had to be a good thing.

So she'd put it behind her, and life had settled

back into its normal rhythms, except that everything was sadder without Mam around. Sarah went to work each day and phoned her father when she got home, inviting him to dinner at least twice a week. Hinting, every so often, that the offer to move in with her and Neil was there, if he was too lonely on his own.

And every now and again she would see Helen O'Dowd's name on a piece in the newspaper, and it would remind her of the book that had never been completed. Maybe she'd try another one some time, but for now all that was in the past.

'So what happened to it?'

Martina's voice broke into her thoughts. 'What happened to what?'

'Your *book* that you were writing.'

'Oh . . . I tore it up. It was no good, really.'

And there was the truth of it, no matter how much she might regret its absence or resent Helen O'Dowd's part in its destruction. But there were other things she was good at. She was a cook, and she loved it. And she was a wife, and she seemed to be good at that too.

And maybe, just maybe – a jab of excitement at the thought – she was on her way to being a mother for the first time. Too soon, much too soon to be sure, she was less than two weeks late, but every day that went by gave her more hope. Almost a year since the wedding – surely it was time. And if it happened, *when* it happened, she thought she'd make a pretty good mother.

'There's that boy of Mary's,' Martina said, watching a Sunday visitor walk from his car. 'You'd think he'd cut his hair. It's a disgrace.'

Poor Martina. Sarah got to her feet. 'Well, I'd better get the apple buns made, or you'll have no tea. Thanks for the chat.'

Tipping butter into sugar, she thought again about trying to write another book. Just because she'd failed the first time didn't mean she'd never succeed. She might take a more modern approach, set it in the present day. Make it a bit racy, even, like Edna O'Brien.

She imagined Helen O'Dowd doing a review, slicing it to ribbons, declaring that Sarah should keep a diary if she wanted to write. Then again, maybe Helen O'Dowd was no good at cooking. Each to her own.

And then the very next week she opened the paper and saw *Slave over a hot stove? Not me* – and below, Helen O'Dowd's name. She began to read.

Cooking is not an activity that turns me on in any way. I fail to understand the attraction of spending hours preparing a meal that takes ten minutes to eat – all that chopping and whatever else cooks do, for such little return – so I've never bothered to learn how to do it. Consequently, I've never managed to cook anything that anyone in his or her right mind would want to eat.

149

Recipes make me shudder; all those ingredients and instructions and oven temperatures, as if I'm in a science lab trying to put together a more efficient version of the atom bomb. On the few occasions that I've attempted to follow a recipe, I've ended up with a dish that's either burnt or undercooked. It doesn't help that I have a remarkably picky seven-year-old child (although I'm willing to acknowledge the possibility that my abominable cooking skills might be somewhat to blame for her pickiness).

These days I tend to slide a couple of fish fingers under the grill, or throw a few sausages onto the pan, and presto, dinner's done – and, yes, yes, I know it's not a balanced diet, and it's lacking in this vitamin or that mineral, and my daughter wouldn't recognise a vegetable if it hit her in the face (although ketchup is made from tomatoes, and she eats plenty of that), but, folks, it works fine for us. And guess what? I don't even own an apron.

Sarah read the article with growing disapproval. A child who was being brought up on fish fingers and sausages and not a single vegetable – Helen O'Dowd couldn't seriously think a blob of ketchup counted as one. Apart from the fact that tomatoes weren't technically vegetables, she must realise that what came out of a ketchup bottle couldn't possibly be compared in terms of nutritional goodness to a ripe, juicy tomato.

Of course she realised it. The woman was intelligent – she knew that she wasn't feeding her child properly. She was well aware of the deficiencies in her daughter's diet, and still she wasn't prepared to do anything about it. On the contrary, she seemed almost proud that she was raising her child on convenience food which had little or no nourishment in it: how irresponsible. And boasting that she didn't own an apron, for goodness' sake.

How could she say preparing a simple meal was complicated? What on earth was complicated about cutting a head of broccoli into florets and adding them to boiling water for a few minutes? Who couldn't top and tail a handful of green beans, or slice an onion and fry it up with a few chopped mushrooms and a sprinkle of black pepper?

It sounded like she had just one child – hardly a big family to feed. Presumably there was a husband too, if he hadn't left her in favour of a woman who could feed him properly. Had she never roasted a chicken? Could she not even grill a chop or poach a bit of salmon for her family?

Sarah had a good mind to send her a few easy recipes. Minimal ingredients and instructions, since she seemed to be allergic to them. Ones with vegetables in them, definitely. She thought suddenly of the vegetable croquettes she made regularly in the nursing home, an experiment one time to use up leftover vegetables. They'd gone down so well she produced them now at least once a week.

Surely Helen O'Dowd could manage those. Really, a child could put them together, and even Martina hadn't found fault with them. And they looked a bit like fish fingers, so they'd seem familiar to the poor malnourished little girl.

'You're daft,' Neil said, when Sarah told him what she was planning. 'Why would you want anything more to do with her? Didn't she rubbish your book without even seeing it? Have you forgotten that?'

'Of course I haven't forgotten, but that's all in the past. The point is, she needs help now, and I can give it to her.'

He shook his head. 'The point is, she can tell you to mind your own business – and anyway, I bet she can cook fine. She's just making this up to be controversial: they all do that.'

Sarah took a cookbook from the shelf and opened it. 'You could be right, but maybe you're not. We have no way of knowing, so I'm going to take the chance and send her a couple of simple recipes. She might be delighted.'

'Delighted that you're criticising the way she's raising her child?'

'That's not what I'm doing at all. She's already admitted that her daughter isn't being fed properly, and I'm just trying to help her to fix that. How could she take that as criticism?'

He shook his head. 'Have it your own way – but don't say I didn't warn you.'

He pulled off his work T-shirt and dropped it into the washing-machine. She'd take it out and transfer it to the laundry basket as soon as he went upstairs for a shower. A year of marriage had taught her, among other things, to pick her arguments carefully, and this one didn't make the cut.

At least she'd trained him to leave his boots outside: no more grass and earth scattered all over the kitchen floor every time he came home. She watched as he sat on a chair to pull off his socks before bundling them into the washing-machine on top of the T-shirt – like he'd done countless times, no doubt, before she'd come along. Pile clothes into the machine as they come off you, repeat till it's full, then switch it on. No wonder all his underwear had been the same shade of mottled grey before she'd replaced it.

'So,' he said, coming up behind her, bare-chested and barefoot, wrapping his arms around her waist, 'what's on Helen O'Dowd's dinner menu then?'

He smelt strongly of sweat, hardly surprising after a day of gardening in the late-August sunshine. She didn't mind male sweat: on the contrary, she quite liked the rough headiness of it.

She turned pages, trying to stay focused with his body pressed against hers. 'I'm thinking about vegetable croquettes, and maybe a chicken pie – they're both dead easy. And I'll tell her I have plenty more if she wants them.'

'Just don't get your hopes up,' he said, his mouth against her ear, his breath hot. 'Don't expect her to shower you with gratitude.'

Sarah smiled down at a picture of a casserole in a green dish sitting on a gingham tablecloth. 'No, I don't think that'll happen.' She was beginning to respond to his nearness, his smell, his body against hers. She was starting to feel the pleasant heat of arousal.

'Have we time,' he said, his lips against the side of her neck now, his hands pressing her pelvis into his, 'to make a baby before dinner?'

Make a baby: her heart flooded at the thought. Maybe we already have, she wanted to say. Maybe things have already started. But she remained silent, afraid to say it out loud, afraid to give him hope in case she was wrong. She'd wait. She'd hug it to herself until she was sure.

She turned in his embrace and pressed her open mouth to his. She was so glad she'd stayed a virgin until marriage, shying away from other boyfriends' straying hands, hating the idea of sex as a casual act between people who hardly knew, let alone loved, one another.

She hadn't been Neil's first lover, which had secretly dismayed her, but he'd been hers. Her first and her last, however corny that might sound these days, when sex before marriage had become the norm, and fidelity seemed to be a thing of the past.

'Have your shower – I'll be right up,' she murmured,

drawing out of his embrace. Alone in the kitchen she found Easy Chicken Pie and marked the page before closing the cookbook. She turned the oven down to gas three and lowered the heat under the saucepan of potatoes. She untied her apron strings and refreshed her lipstick at the little mirror she'd hung on the back of the door.

She left the kitchen and followed her husband upstairs. A baby already begun, maybe. A big happy family, waiting for them in the years ahead.

HELEN

'What are they?' Alice looked suspiciously at her plate.

'They're Golden Surprises. I made them.'

Alice poked at one with her fork. 'You always make dinner.'

'No, I mean I didn't buy them in the shop, I bought stuff and made them, all by myself.'

'What stuff?'

'Oh, just a few different things. Try them.'

Alice sniffed dubiously.

'You know Godmother in *Wanderly Wagon*?' Helen asked.

'Yeah.'

'She makes them for Rory and O'Brien.'

'How d'you know?'

'I read it in a magazine.' Helen put two croquettes onto her own plate. 'Go on, try them – they're yummy.'

They *were* yummy. She'd eaten one while she was setting the table, and she'd had to stop herself having another. They were crispy on the outside and soft on the inside, and they were the first thing

156

she'd ever cooked from scratch, and they tasted far better than she'd been expecting.

Alice still made no move to eat. She watched Helen dunking a croquette into a dish of ketchup. 'How did you know how to make them?'

'A woman called Mrs Flannery told me,' Helen said. 'She's a real cook. That's her job.'

'I don't know her.'

'No, you don't.'

Sarah Flannery's name on the envelope had taken a few minutes to register. When it had, Helen's heart had sunk. What did the silly creature want now? Had Helen said something nasty about another book? Had she been awfully mean to some poor theatre actor? Didn't the woman have anything better to do than write sanctimonious letters?

The envelope had been addressed, like the others, to the newspaper, care of Breen, and had been readdressed as usual by Catherine. Helen pulled out the notelet – yes, looked familiar, water-colour blobs of flowers in a prissy vase – and a separate sheet of paper slipped from it and fluttered to the floor. A novena prayer, maybe, to save Helen's immortal soul.

It wasn't a novena prayer: it was a recipe for some kind of a chicken dish. Helen turned it over and saw Vegetable Croquettes on the reverse. Sarah Flannery was sending her recipes?

She opened the card.

Dear Mrs O'Dowd

You'll probably be surprised to hear from me again. In case you've forgotten, I wrote a few months ago after you'd reviewed a book called *To Kill with Kindness* as I thought you'd been a bit harsh, and you subsequently sent me a copy of the book.

I hope you won't take this amiss, but I read your piece about cooking a few days ago in which you admitted your lack of experience in producing a balanced meal, and since I cook for a living I'm taking the liberty of sending you a couple of recipes that you might like to try for your family. They're both very easy and don't require a lot of ingredients. I chose the Vegetable Croquettes because they look a little like fish fingers (only they're much tastier and more nutritious) so they'll appear familiar to your daughter, who you mentioned is a picky eater.

The chicken pie is really simple to make too, and delicious. Strictly speaking, it's not a pie because it doesn't have pastry, just a top of mashed potatoes. It's one of my husband's favourite dishes. I do hope you don't mind my sending these along, and if you would like any more, I'll be happy to provide them.

Yours sincerely

Sarah

PS I took your advice and tore up my half-written manuscript. I think you were right, it wouldn't have made an interesting book at all. In future I'll stick to cooking – at least I know I'm good at that!

PPS I appreciated your letter of apology, and I accept it completely. It came after I'd got rid of the manuscript but, like I say, it was for the best. No hard feelings.

She'd destroyed her manuscript.

She accepted Helen's apology completely.

She'd sent Helen two recipes because Helen had written about not being able to cook.

She'd included a recipe for Vegetable Croquettes because they looked a little like fish fingers, which Helen had mentioned in the article.

She'd signed her letter 'Sarah', as if Helen was a friend.

Was she for real? Six months ago Helen had rubbished her manuscript, which she might well have spent years working on. She'd torn it up, she'd destroyed her embryo book because of Helen – and now she was sending recipes. She was a professional cook, and presumably scandalised by Alice's diet of sausages and fish fingers, but there wasn't a word of criticism directed at the mother who was responsible for it.

Helen reread the letter slowly. She turned to the recipes and scanned the croquette one.

Peel and chop three carrots and one parsnip into small chunks, about the size of sugar

159

cubes. Put them into a saucepan of cold water with a pinch of salt and pepper and bring to the boil. Reduce the heat, cover the saucepan and simmer until you can easily stick a fork in, about fifteen minutes. Drain off the water and mash the vegetables until smooth. If you don't have a potato masher use a fork.

No ingredients list, just instructions a child could follow. Sarah Flannery was making it all very easy for the woman who couldn't abide recipes. And she wasn't assuming that Helen had any kind of kitchen equipment, even something as basic as a potato masher.

When the mixture is cool enough to handle, break an egg into a cup, beat it lightly with a fork and pour it onto a dinner plate. Scatter about half a cupful of flour onto another dinner plate. Scoop out handfuls of the mixture and roll into fat sausage shapes: you should get about a dozen. Dip them one by one into the egg and then roll gently in the flour so they're lightly coated. (It might be a bit messy at the start but you'll get the knack as you go on!)

Heat a dessertspoon of sunflower oil on a pan and fry the croquettes over a medium heat for a few minutes, turning carefully so that all sides become golden brown. Don't have the pan too crowded, as you need room to turn them. Depending on the size of your pan, you might have to fry them in two batches.

Helen hadn't been sure whether to be amused or offended. Don't have the pan too crowded – did Sarah Flannery think she was dealing with a complete idiot? Cooked for a living: employed, no doubt, in the kitchen of some backwater hotel. Thought she knew it all, delighted with the opportunity to lord it over the nasty woman who'd made her tear up her little book.

No, it wasn't that. Sarah Flannery was simply being nice. She was a good person with no ulterior motive.

Helen turned the page over and read the chicken pie recipe. Chicken, carrots, onions, celery, potatoes, stock, a few herbs. Nothing unfamiliar, nothing that couldn't be easily got.

No harm in giving one of them a go. Might be a laugh, might even produce something halfway decent. Might manage not to burn the house down in the process.

She'd try the croquettes. She remembered liking the mashed carrots and parsnips her mother used to serve with roast beef. And she did have a potato masher – inherited, like all the kitchen tools, from Cormac's grandmother.

She'd added the ingredients to her shopping list, and half an hour ago she'd made her first batch of eleven fat vegetable croquettes, only two of which had fallen apart in the pan.

She pretended she wasn't watching as Alice took a cautious bite. She said nothing as her daughter chewed and swallowed. She waited until Alice was halfway through the croquette.

'You like it?'

Alice nodded, her mouth full. Helen had just served her daughter a home-cooked meal – well, not entirely home-cooked: the chips that accompanied the croquettes had come from the takeaway on the corner. But it was a start. And it was thanks to Sarah Flannery.

She wasn't a friend, far from it, but she'd done Helen a kindness, with nothing at all to gain in return. She'd simply seen an opportunity to help and taken it.

Helen couldn't remember the last time someone had done something nice for her, just for the hell of it. Since Cormac's death, she'd distanced herself from the people who'd known them both, not that any of them had tried too hard to keep in contact. Her school friends, such as they were, had long since drifted, and she'd forged no solid friendships during her time behind the counter at Burke's. She had plenty of acquaintances, but no real friends to speak of.

Then again, who'd want her as a friend? She tormented her elderly neighbour. She tore badly written books and mediocre plays to shreds. She spoke her mind, even when nobody wanted to hear it. She was mouthy and uncompromising. She drank more whiskey than was good for her

162

whenever she got the chance, and most of the time she probably smelt like an ashtray. She could hardly blame people for steering clear.

When she thought about it, her most significant adult relationship these days was probably with Breen, which was very sad indeed, seeing as most of their conversations were conducted through mutually gritted teeth.

'Can I have another one?' Alice asked.

'Course you can.'

Helen transferred a croquette from the serving dish to her daughter's plate. Tomorrow she might try the chicken thing. She liked a bit of chicken, and the mashed potato topping would make a nice change from chips.

She liked beef too. Sarah Flannery probably had a stack of beef recipes.

Dear Mrs Flannery

Many thanks for the recipes you sent last week: it was a generous gesture, and quite unexpected. Miraculously, I managed to cook both dishes without any major disasters occurring. Even more amazingly, my daughter ate both without complaint, and demanded a repeat performance of the croquettes.

Could you send one or two simple red-meat recipes when you get the chance? No rush. I've put my home address at the top, so you don't have to go through the newspaper.

Thanks again,

163

Helen Fitzpatrick (O'Dowd is a pseudonym)

PS Sorry to hear about your manuscript. Thank you for not being horrible about my part in its destruction: I had no right to write what I did, and your magnanimity is more than I deserve.

Dear Helen

I'm delighted the recipes were a success, and so glad I didn't offend you. My husband was sure you'd tell me to mind my own business, and I was also afraid you'd give me a bad review if they didn't turn out well, ha ha!

I'm sending two more recipes. The first is a beef casserole, which you can prepare really quickly – even the day before if you prefer – and the other is simple meatballs made from minced lamb. Do let me know how you get on, and also please ask if you'd like any more – I don't want to overwhelm you!

All the very best, and happy cooking!

Sarah

Sarah

You worry too much about giving offence: trust me, I have the hide of a rhinoceros. You've noticed I write the truth as I see it – this attracts all sorts of responses, ranging from the polite (yours) to the obscene (practically everyone else's). Doesn't cost me a thought.

Thanks for the new recipes. The beef

casserole worked, and will be a regular. The meatballs fell apart a bit, but tasted fine with the tomato sauce. I'm still pinching myself that I'm cooking stuff from scratch, and that it's edible – and now that I'm on a roll, any easy white-fish recipe? I'm guessing I could do a bit healthier than the battered cod the local chip shop cooks for us on Fridays.

Thanks again,

H

PS Still humbled that you forgave my rant about your book. Please don't let it stop you trying another one some time – what do I know?

1983

SARAH

The bedroom wallpaper was getting on her nerves. She couldn't understand how it had ever appealed to her. Rows of silly daisies in lavender and blue marching up the walls, trapped within pompous gold swirls and curlicues. All the go in 1977, bedroom walls covered with colour and loud patterns. She could update it now by adding a border, like Christine had done in her house, but she was heartily sick of it.

She tried to think back to the time she'd chosen it, coming on for six years ago. Revelling in her newly married status and eager to put her stamp on Neil's house, which had marvellously become their house. She remembered buying new curtains for the sitting room, rearranging the contents of his kitchen presses, replacing his shockingly dilapidated mop and ancient vacuum cleaner, throwing out the vast numbers of empty bottles and jars and paint cans that had been living under his stairs for what looked like years.

All the details were there, but the emotional memory of that time refused to return. She couldn't recall what pure happiness felt like. She couldn't imagine ever feeling happy again.

'You don't need to stay in bed,' the doctor had told her. 'In fact, it would do you good to be up and about' – but the thought of getting up held no appeal. What was there to get up for? What was the point of getting dressed? Easier to stay put and hate the wallpaper.

'We can try again,' Neil had murmured last night, both of them lying sleepless, side by side but not touching. 'You're only thirty-two, we've still got lots of time.'

Sarah had made no response, the tears sliding silently down her face. The thought of another failure was impossible to contemplate – not now, not yet, maybe never – but the prospect of admitting defeat brought fresh, sharp anguish.

'And they've told us there's no medical reason why we can't have a baby. I'm sure it'll happen for us.'

She'd turned onto her side, away from him, and pressed her wet face into the pillow, willing him to stop talking. No reason why they couldn't have a baby, apart from the fact that her womb kept rejecting the idea. It let her get started, it allowed her a few weeks of hope, it waited until the doctor had confirmed it – and then, a week or two later, it changed its mind and emptied itself out. It rid itself of her baby, and left her hollow and useless and destroyed.

Three times it had happened, in six years of

trying. Three lots of hoping and dreading and praying – real prayers, down on her knees by the bed, like she used to do as a child – that had all come to nothing, ending with cramps that folded her in two, and blood that came out of her in clotted waves, and tears. So many tears.

The third time was just five days ago, the same day that Karen Carpenter had died, a month before her thirty-third birthday. The world was mourning a tragic young singer who'd starved herself to death while another barely begun baby was draining out of Sarah.

She should have been a mother of three now. Two boys and a girl, maybe, or a clutch of daughters, too early to tell when she'd lost them. Neil taking boys to football matches, Sarah teaching all three how to cook – no reason why the boys shouldn't learn, with all the talk of equality now. The kitchen table strewn with eggshells and jars of spices and cake tins, the house full of laughter and delicious scents.

A dog chasing a ball around the garden, a cat sitting on the windowsill. Birthday parties, days out at the zoo, picnics, bedtime stories. A family making memories that she and Neil could pull out in old age and be warmed by. Torture . . . torture to conjure up the life that was being denied to her, and yet she couldn't seem to stop doing it.

She reached for a folded sheet that sat on the bedside locker. She opened it and reread the letter that had come earlier that morning, in response to the brief, heartbroken note she'd sent the day after it had happened. Helen must have written back by return of post.

Christ, I can't believe it. It shouldn't happen, not to someone like you who spends her time trying to make everyone else in the goddamn world happy. You of all people don't deserve this crap.

Helen, as direct as ever. Helen, whose honesty Sarah clung to.

I'm racking my brains here to find something to make you feel less horrible, but there isn't anything. All I can tell you, and I know it's cold comfort, is that this time will pass. You won't forget, and it will always be painful, but things will get better than they are now, and you'll be stronger. And you <u>will</u> laugh again. Trust me: I know what I'm talking about.

And Sarah did trust her, because Helen did know what she was talking about. Because Helen's husband had died.

He got cancer, she'd written, a few months after they'd begun to exchange letters. *He was thirty-three. I was a basket case for a while, but life went on. I had Alice, I had no choice.* And that was all, and Sarah had never asked any more, sensing that questions would not be welcome.

This morning's letter had been stuffed into a peculiar cardboard container that appeared to have been glued together using pieces of an Ajax box – *Stronger than dirt*, Sarah read on one side of the blue and green card – along with a small jar that was wrapped in newspaper.

'Eight Hour Cream', the jar's label read. 'Relieves chapped lips, soothes grazes and minor burns, moisturises and softens skin.' It had a slightly musty smell, but it was something to do as Sarah lay in bed. It passed a few minutes, every so often.

> Don't know if you already use this – I can't survive without it. Did you know Elizabeth Arden was the first woman to be featured on the cover of Time magazine? She was a suffragette; she marched with 15,000 other women past her salon in New York, and they all wore red lipstick as a sign of strength. Don't you love her?

In five years of letter writing, one or two each a month, they hadn't met, even though they lived about an hour's drive apart. Neither of them had suggested a meeting, nor had they exchanged photographs, although the same small head and shoulders shot accompanied most of Helen's articles.

Impossible to make her out clearly, with her face in three-quarter profile and her gaze tilted down so you couldn't see her eyes. Her dark hair was

173

cut close to her head, pixie-like, and the colour of her skin suggested dark eyes too. It was as if she was trying to be unrecognisable. Not necessarily a bad thing, given some of her views – surely deliberately controversial sometimes – and the awful things she still said about books or plays that didn't appeal to her.

You're heartless, Sarah would write after a typically unflinching review, but Helen remained unrepentant. *I'm a critic*, she'd reply, *I'm paid to be heartless. And besides, someone has to compensate for all the allowances you make, Mrs Benefit-of-the-Doubt.*

They were different. They were as different as it was possible for two women to be. They shouldn't have fitted together, but somehow they did. Something kept them writing to one another – maybe it was the very fact that they were such opposites; maybe they recognised in the other what was lacking in themselves. Whatever the reason, Sarah welcomed Helen's letters in all their bluntness, particularly at a time like this when she felt so bereft, so alone. Helen understood sadness.

The bedroom door opened and Neil appeared with a tray. Could it be lunchtime already? Sarah hoisted herself up to sitting, although the last thing she wanted to do was eat. But he was trying his best, and he was in mourning too, even if he was better at hiding it.

'Soft-boiled egg,' he announced, laying the tray across her lap. 'Toast and tea.' He sniffed. 'What's the smell?'

'Helen sent cream.' She looked without appetite at the food. He'd cut the buttered toast into strips, chopped the top off the egg. Making it as easy as possible for her, as if she were a small child learning to feed herself. She picked up a piece of toast – and let it fall back onto the plate.

'Sarah,' he said gently, 'you have to eat, love.'

She didn't have to eat. She didn't have to do anything except wake up each morning and wait for the night to come back. But she reached again for the toast and bit into it and forced herself to chew and swallow, conscious of his eyes on her. She took a spoonful of egg – he'd forgotten the salt – and a sip of tea.

'Your father phoned again,' he said, crossing to the window. 'I told him you were asleep.'

'Good.'

'And Christine wants to call around. She thought you might like to see Aidan and Tom.'

'No,' Sarah said quickly. 'I hope you put her off.'

'She said she'll phone again later.'

'Tell her I'm not up to it yet. Tell her I'll be in touch when I feel better.'

She couldn't face them, it was too hard. Aidan running to her like he always did, two-year-old Tom tottering after his big brother. And Christine, growing a third baby in her hospitable womb, five months to go until she held him in her arms.

It was too much. It was too unfair.

But Christine meant well. Everyone meant well. Matron at the nursing home, telling her to take what time she needed, they'd manage. Neil's mother, Nuala, bringing rock buns and Milk Tray. Nobody at all mentioning the miscarriage, everyone acting as if the pregnancy had never existed. Everyone except Helen.

'It's nice out,' Neil said, looking down on the garden. 'Not as cold as yesterday, and the rain has finally stopped.'

'Oh.'

She couldn't give a damn about the weather. Let it rain till kingdom come for all she cared.

'The cherry blossom will be budding soon.'

'That's good.'

He turned to face her. 'By the way, Shergar's been kidnapped. It was on the radio just now.'

'Who?'

'Shergar, a racehorse. He won the Epsom Derby two years ago, by ten lengths. You must remember, it was big news.'

A horse, kidnapped. She smiled weakly at her boiled egg. 'Oh dear.'

'He's worth a fortune. They think it might be the IRA.'

'Really.'

But she'd lost interest in Shergar and his problems. She laid down her spoon, unable to face more food.

'Would I run you a bath?' Neil asked.

'No.' Her fingers tightened around the edge of the blanket. She pushed the tray aside. 'Just . . . give me more time, OK?'

He crossed the room and sat on the bed. 'Darling,

176

it's been nearly a week.' He reached for her hand and held it between both of his. 'It's not doing you any good, lying here moping.'

She resisted the impulse to snatch her hand away, to tell him to shut up, leave her alone. She'd never told him to shut up, never. They rarely rowed.

'Tomorrow,' she said, watching his fingers curled over hers. 'I'll get up tomorrow, OK?'

'And you'll think about going back to work? Maybe next week?'

'Yes.'

But the prospect of going back to work seemed marginally more challenging than climbing Mount Everest on her knees. She eased her hand from his and slid back down, pulling the blankets around her.

'I'd like to sleep now,' she said, closing her eyes. She felt the mattress lifting as he stood, heard the soft clink of cutlery on crockery as he took away the tray. She listened to the sound of his footsteps, muffled by the carpet. The gentle click of the door closing, the low thud of his feet on the stairs.

She would get up tomorrow because he wanted her to. She would have a bath and wash her hair and put on clean clothes. And some time in the afternoon she would phone the nursing home and tell Matron she'd be back on Monday. Life would go on. That was what it did.

Life went on, no matter what happened. Princess Grace dead, all that beauty wiped out in seconds when her car had smashed into a mountain last year. No holiday home in Mayo after all.

John Lennon gunned down outside his home, the IRA blowing up bandsmen and horses, wars and floods and famines all over the world, and still the sun came up each day and people carried on.

But not everyone carried on, did they? She remembered the woman she'd met on the bridge the day she'd done the interview for St Sebastian's, eight years ago now. She remembered the horror she'd felt when she'd realised what the woman wanted to do, what so many people did, year after year. Throwing themselves into rivers or over cliffs, climbing onto chairs to hang themselves from rafters, swallowing bottles of pills.

The bridge was still there. Sarah cycled over it anytime she went to visit her father. In eight years the only change had been a fresh coat of paint to the railings every now and again. There was vague talk of a reconstruction, but so far nothing had been done.

The bridge wasn't far from their house, about twenty minutes on a bike. She could wait until Neil had gone back to work, she could be there by mid-afternoon. She could prop the bike against the railing and climb—

She shook her head sharply, cutting off the thought. No, never, no matter how sad and bleak everything became. There was always hope – wasn't there always hope? There was always the possibility that tomorrow things would be better.

But right now it was so hard to go on remembering that, so hard to keep the darkness from taking over.

She propped herself up on an elbow and reached again for Helen's letter. She read it for the umpteenth time, her lips forming the words silently. She clung to them; she wrapped them around her like a much-loved, tatty old dressing-gown.

HELEN

On the morning of her forty-first birthday Helen O'Dowd observed herself without joy in the bathroom mirror. A web of lines splaying from the outer corners of her eyes: permanent residents now, whether she laughed or not. More lines, an accordion of them, scored into the skin above and below her lips. Nearly a quarter of a century's worth of smoking to thank for those, begun behind the bicycle sheds in school with Maura Curran and Frances Lynch when they were all seventeen, and not stopped since.

Long before she met Cormac she'd been on twenty a day, blackening her insides with the poison from thousands of cigarettes. And yet it had been Cormac, smoker of just the occasional joint, whose lungs had been withered away by cancer, years before his forty-first birthday.

She tamped down the flare of pain his memory still caused and patted the loose skin beneath her chin – when had that happened? And look how crêpey the skin of her neck had become, and the ugly criss-cross of creases meandering down her chest. Some sight, at ten past eight in the morning.

Her appearance wasn't helped in any way, of course, by the night she'd just had. Too much alcohol, too many cigarettes, not nearly enough food: repeated often enough – and she was still repeating it as often as she got the chance – it was bound to put years on anyone.

Forty-one admitting to thirty-six, the only thing she didn't tell the truth about. Forty-one, on the verge of sliding disgracefully into middle age.

Sarah was one of the few people who knew her real age. Sarah, in fact, probably knew more about Helen than anyone, including Helen's parents. Especially Helen's parents. She wasn't sure exactly how it had happened, but over the course of the last few years she and Sarah had become friends.

Never meeting up, maybe that was how they'd managed it. If Sarah spent ten minutes with Helen she'd probably want to run for the hills – and Helen might well feel the same. Chalk and cheese, that's what they were.

But however opposing their personalities, the truth was that on some level they clicked. Sarah was impossibly romantic, always believing the best of people, always ready to trust the stranger. But maybe that wasn't such a bad thing. Maybe people like her balanced out cynics like Helen.

So they'd continued to write after the last of the recipes had been sent, they'd fallen into a correspondence that seemed agreeable to both, and with each letter that passed between them they connected a little more. And while Helen often shook her head at what she regarded as Sarah's hopeless naïveté, she found herself looking forward to the letters with the Kildare postmark.

Scanning the paragraphs of the first few letters, the overriding feeling they conveyed to her was happiness. Here was a happy person, in love with her husband, fulfilled in her job. The kind of person you'd love to hate – but hating Sarah, with her enormous capacity to see goodness everywhere, was impossible.

When she'd lost the first baby, only a few weeks after she and Helen had been corresponding, she'd been upset, of course, but also philosophical. *These things happen to so many*, she'd written. *Please God next time I'll be luckier.* But two years later it had happened again, and it was heartbreaking to witness her struggle to stay positive then.

Reading about the miscarriages, sensing the raw grief within the lines, Helen had felt real sympathy. You didn't need to meet Sarah to know that she was a mother waiting to happen. What rotten Fate had decreed that she should be denied the chance, over and over, while the likes of Helen, who would never win a parenting prize, could have got pregnant so easily?

She'd conceived without trying, coming off the Pill just a few months before Cormac's sperm had done the business – and there was Sarah, desperate for a baby, but only able, it appeared, to miscarry them.

Helen felt helpless in the face of her friend's anguish. What could she offer, other than useless jars of cream and equally useless words? But maybe Sarah was glad to have someone to write to; maybe that helped in some tiny way. And surely, eventually, she'd manage to hang on to a foetus for nine months. Time enough, she was still only thirty-two.

Helen left the bathroom and crossed the landing to Alice's room. She opened the door and stepped over the trail of crumpled garments to pull the curtains apart and push the window open.

'Time for school.'

A muffled groan from the humped shape in the single bed.

'Five minutes, and bring those clothes down.'

A week away from twelve years old: on the cusp of her teens but already fully qualified. Sulky, monosyllabic, doing as little to help around the house as she could get away with. Helen ignored as much as she could, insisting only that Alice kept her room moderately tidy and did the washing-up after dinner. It wasn't as if housework came top of her own agenda, so she could hardly blame her daughter's lack of interest.

But school was another story. *Alice isn't trying* was the continuing mantra at the parent-teacher meetings, *Alice can be disruptive* was the variation. Alice's dog-eared copies were littered with doodles and deletions and the red biro marks of her teachers, and comments like *disappointing* and *could do better*. Alice's test marks hovered in the bottom quarter of the class.

'What the hell is wrong with you?' Helen would demand, after another teacher had taken her through the catalogue of Alice's failings. 'You could be top of the class – you have brains to burn. Why don't you use them, for Christ's sake?'

And Alice would shrug and twirl her hair around a finger and wait for her mother to finish ranting, and Helen would use all the self-control she could muster not to grab her daughter's skinny arms and shake some sense into her. Eleven going on teenage nightmare, eyelashes catching in the muddy blonde fringe she refused to cut, frayed ends of her jeans trailing the ground, soaking water up to her knees when it rained. Nails bitten to the quick, just like her mother's.

Helen walked downstairs and lifted the newspaper from the floor in the hall. One of her few luxuries since becoming a journalist, having it delivered five days a week. She pushed open the door that led into the poky kitchen; unchanged, like the rest of the house, since Cormac's time. Helen couldn't care less about the brown Formica worktop, the gas cooker in the corner, the rickety steel-legged table pushed up against the geometric-patterned yellow and cream wallpaper, the narrow cheap presses whose doors had hung crookedly for as long as she'd known them, the cracked brown lino that Cormac's grandmother had chosen. Décor had never interested Helen – what difference did the colour of a wall make?

The toaster popped as Alice slouched in. Without

a word she took the slice and brought it to the table and began to butter it.

'Plate,' Helen said, not lifting her eyes from the newspaper. Alice sighed loudly and took one from the stack that sat on the worktop.

'Did you bring down those clothes?'

'Forgot.'

She crunched the toast, drinking nothing. Helen had long since given up trying to coax juice or milk or any liquid into her.

Duran Duran sang on the radio. Upstairs a toilet flushed. Alice looked accusingly at her mother. 'He's here again.'

Helen went on reading.

'Isn't he?'

'If you mean Oliver, yes, he is.'

Alice bit into her toast. 'Fuck,' she said, mouth full.

Helen looked up sharply. 'Watch your tongue.'

'You say it all the time.'

'And if I stepped off a cliff you'd do it too?'

Alice mumbled something that Helen didn't catch: probably wishing her mother would do just that: disappear out of her life, tumble over the edge of a cliff, never to be seen again. Helen wondered what reaction she'd get if she lowered her newspaper and said *I nearly jumped off a bridge into a river once. You were three, your father had just died and I was a mess.* That might wipe the sulk off Madam's face for a few minutes.

Helen thought of it, on the rare occasions that

185

it crossed her mind, as the turning point: the day she'd gone out to kill herself and come home alive. She remembered taking the kitchen scissors and cutting off her hair that evening – her first step forward, she'd realised later. Her first attempt to claw herself out of Hell, to leave the nightmare behind.

Of course, it had been several more months before she'd found the strength and inspiration to begin writing about the experiences of a shopgirl, but she believed her recovery had begun that night, after the blackest day of her life.

And it had been writing that ultimately saved her. Discovering something she was good at, and that paid the bills, had been her redemption. With each subsequent article she'd begun to inch her way further out of the darkness. It had taken her till her mid-thirties to find her vocation, and now, nearly eight years on, she couldn't imagine making her living in any other way.

Where did the years go? Cormac, dead eight years last month, his daughter growing up so fast. Time galloping on, stopping for nothing, and today Helen was forty-one, like it or not. No doubt her mother would be around later with the usual little birthday remembrance, and they'd drink coffee and pretend that even one of them wanted to be there.

Her father had retired from the bench four years earlier, working right up to his seventy-second birthday, and since then her parents had been on a Caribbean cruise and two extended holidays to the south of France. Making the most of their free time, plenty of money to spend on whatever they chose. In fairness, they'd offered to finance a holiday for Helen and Alice, and Helen had thanked them for the offer and said sometime, maybe.

She and Alice still called once a week, still made conversation for an hour in her mother's immaculate kitchen, still exchanged gifts at Christmas and birthdays. And still Helen felt a gulf between them, a distance that she could never imagine closing.

The kitchen door opened again and Oliver walked in. He wore jeans and a black T-shirt, and his feet were bare. 'Morning,' he said to Alice, who pushed back her chair and walked past him out of the room, leaving her half-eaten toast behind.

'I'm still flavour of the month then,' he said, taking up the toast and biting into it, cocking his head at Alice's angry stomps up the stairs. 'Good to know.'

Helen sipped her coffee, watching him fill a mug from the percolator. 'I thought you were going to stay in bed until we left.'

'Oh, come on, she's eleven years old.' He put his coffee on the table beside hers and dropped onto his haunches beside her chair. 'You can't let her dictate what you do,' he said, opening the top buttons of her shirt to slide his hands inside and cup her breasts. 'You're the adult, she's the kid,' he said, squeezing gently.

Helen ignored the desire that flared into life at his touch. He only had to look at her, damn it. 'I'd rather keep my private life private, that's all,' she said lightly, drawing out of his reach and gathering plates and cups. 'Help yourself to breakfast. There might be eggs.'

'Coffee's fine.' He leant against the table and crossed his arms. 'You are one sexy lady, you know that?'

Helen put the crockery into the sink and did up her buttons. 'So they keep telling me.'

She hadn't mentioned her birthday. They'd met three months earlier, at the welcome reception of a press convention to which Helen, out of curiosity, had wangled an invite.

'Oliver Joyce,' he'd said, in a voice as dark as cocoa, looking her over with lazy cat-green eyes. 'I like your writing.' He wore an open-necked black shirt under a grey suit, and shoes with no socks, which she'd never seen before. Dark hairs poked out from the open V of the shirt. He had a dangerous feel to him.

'Any connection to James?' Helen had asked, swimming pleasantly after a generously poured free whiskey on an empty stomach.

He'd lifted one shoulder. 'I've read *Ulysses*. Does that count?'

It did with her. They'd sneaked off to his hotel room an hour later, gone out afterwards and eaten oysters, and washed them down with Guinness before making their way back to his room for the rest of the night. Picking Alice up from her parents' house the following evening, Helen had felt bruised and exhausted and wonderfully satisfied.

He was thirty, recently escaped from a six-year marriage, and living on the far side of Dublin with one of his brothers. He wrote for a variety of publications, reporting mainly on Ireland's music scene: the phenomenon that was U2, the new Celtic punk sound of the Pogues, the family from a Donegal Gaeltacht who were bridging the gap between Irish traditional music and pop rock.

He didn't own a tie. His hands were always warm. He claimed to be a quarter Spanish on his mother's side. Helen didn't give a damn about his ancestry, or his fashion sense. He was insatiable, and he knew his way around a woman's body – not that he limited himself to women, if you could believe him. He was the first man she'd brought to her bed since Cormac.

Her parents would have hit the roof if they'd known – bringing a man home with Alice in the house – but Helen had little choice if she wanted his company at night.

Not surprisingly, Alice objected.

'I don't like him.'

'Why not?'

'He smells. And he calls me Allie.'

'It's aftershave, and tell him you prefer Alice.'

But Helen kept them apart as much as she could. He wasn't permanent, she knew that. And he certainly wasn't husband material, which was fine by her: she wasn't looking for another of those, too afraid of the possibility of pain that love and marriage second time around would expose her to. Oliver was a diversion, no more than that. He'd leave her when somebody younger caught his attention, and she'd let him go with no regrets, or not many.

Her life had settled into a comfortable routine, very different from the wild early years with Cormac. Mornings were generally spent researching in the library or meeting up with interviewees while Alice was at school, afternoons and evenings were for writing up articles and reading.

Once a week there was usually a visit to the theatre to check out a play she'd been asked to review, Alice left in the capable hands of Anna, her long-term babysitter who thankfully still lived across the road. Oliver occasionally accompanied her to the plays, but more often than not she went alone.

Maybe she'd mention him to Sarah in her next letter. She hadn't said anything yet, sensing that the happily married Mrs Flannery wouldn't approve. If Helen was sure of anything, it was that Sarah had saved herself for her wedding night. She could imagine her getting undressed in the bathroom, pulling on a long white nightie before presenting herself, blushing, to her new husband.

Talk of promiscuity of any kind would probably scandalise her – but maybe it would also serve as a diversion, give her something else to think about, however briefly. And she must be used to Helen's outspokenness by now.

She found her car keys and opened the kitchen door. 'Alice,' she called, and The Smiths stopped singing upstairs. The Smiths were one of the very few things mother and daughter had in common, much to Alice's disgust.

'Have a good day,' Oliver said, topping up his coffee. 'I'll give a shout, yeah?'

No arrangement, no plan. He never made a plan. For all she knew, he was going straight from her bed to another.

'It's my birthday,' she said to Alice, as they drove to school.

Alice turned to her. 'Is it? You never said.'

'I'm saying now.' Helen took her place behind a line of cars waiting to turn right. 'Anyway, you know it's a week before yours.'

'Is that why he stayed over?'

Helen inched forward. 'He has a name.'

No response.

'I'm twenty-one again,' Helen said. 'Isn't that great?'

'Whoop-de-doo,' Alice replied, waggling her fingers at a boy who was pedalling past them on a bicycle. 'Look,' she said, 'he's eating ice-cream in the rain, the dope.'

'Ice-cream for breakfast,' Helen said, not looking.

SARAH

'T hanks for replacing the tyre,' she said to Neil.

'No problem.'

'The bike is much steadier now.'

'I'm glad to hear it,' he said, and that was all. They'd stopped talking like they used to, and it was her fault. She'd pushed him away when he tried to get close, kept pushing until he'd stopped trying. In the six weeks since the miscarriage they hadn't once made love. Her fault, completely hers.

'Neil and I are drifting apart,' she told Christine, over the phone. 'We never talk now.'

'I wouldn't worry about it – Aidan, leave him *alone*. Sarah, hang on a sec.'

She heard wailing in the background, and more sharp words she couldn't make out from Christine. She waited, watching a woodlouse making its careful way across the floorboards.

'Sorry,' Christine said, returning. 'I wonder if Rolf Harris would like his two little boys back.'

'You're busy.'

'Not at all – they're just acting the cod, as usual.

192

What were we saying? Oh yes, Neil. Listen, you've been through a rough patch, it'll pass.'

'I hope you're right.'

'Of course I am . . . Sarah, you know that woman in Kildare I was talking about?'

'Yes.' The woman in Kildare had been brought into their conversations at least once a week since the miscarriage.

'I told you, did I, that Dorothy Furlong went to her last year after her husband died, and she said she helped her a lot?'

'Yes.'

'Would I just give you her number? I can easily get it from Dorothy. I'll be meeting her on—'

'No, don't do that,' Sarah said quickly. 'If I decide I want to talk to someone I'll let you know.'

'Promise you'll think seriously about it?'

'I will.'

But she didn't want a counsellor. She couldn't bear the thought of some stranger, however highly recommended, picking apart her grief, feeding her tissues as she cried for her lost babies. Stirring it all up once a week, sixty minutes of regurgitated sadness in some drab little room with framed certificates on the walls, and maybe a photo on the woman's desk of the children she'd had without any bother at all.

Better to get on with things. Better to go to work each day and fill her mind with recipes and menu plans. Better to chat as usual to the nursing-home residents, who looked at her so pityingly each time she went back to work after a miscarriage – all except Martina, who treated her exactly the same as she'd always done, for which Sarah was profoundly grateful.

'You're back' – her only comment when Sarah had returned the last time, and that had been it, apart from asking, somewhat accusingly, if Sarah had lost weight. Bless Martina, who didn't force her to keep saying she was fine, honestly.

She checked the time on the kitchen clock. Five minutes before she needed to leave for work, enough to refill her cup and read Helen's latest letter, which had just arrived.

> Lashing rain here. I'm looking out at my neighbour clipping his hedge with a plastic bag stuck on top of his head, silly man. Thinks more of his precious garden than he does of anything else, apart from his scruffy old cat. He's the one who bangs on the wall when I play my music – I think I've told you about him. Bet you're thanking your lucky stars you don't live next door to me: I'm not what you'd call ideal-neighbour material.

Sarah smiled. Helen's letters were such a tonic. She wouldn't put it past her to have invented this next-door character just to have something entertaining to report. Plastic bag on his head, indeed.

She turned the page.

Now, brace yourself: I have a confession to make. I've taken a lover – isn't that what they say? And get this – he's thirty. Yes, I said thirty, which makes him even younger than you, and all of eleven years my junior. (Forty-one yesterday, hurrah.) I met him a few months ago at a press thing, and we've been an item ever since. It won't last, of course, but I have to say I'm having a whole lot of fun. He knows what's what in the bedroom. Let's leave it at that, and spare your blushes. We're both free agents, Missy, so stop judging.

Alice isn't impressed, needless to say, but these days nothing I do would find favour with her. She's turning twelve next week, one step closer to her teens, God help us all.

Hope you're not too shocked: I know you're a much better-behaved person than I am. What can I say? I have needs, and he's fulfilling every one of them.

Helen had a lover, a man eleven years younger than herself. She was having sex – lots of sex, by the sound of it – with a man she barely knew. He wasn't her husband; he hadn't committed to her in any way. On the contrary, it sounded like their relationship, or whatever you'd call it, could come to an end at any minute.

Sarah wasn't shocked, not really. Everyone seemed to be at it: every problem page she read had letters on the subject of sex, both inside and outside marriage. Sometimes she wondered if she was the only adult female on earth who wasn't planning to have more than one sexual partner in her lifetime.

But Helen had lost her husband when she was still a young woman, and this was the first mention of any kind of romantic attachment in all the time they'd been writing to one another. Maybe no man had shown an interest in her since she'd become a widow, maybe this thirty-year-old was the only one. Who could grudge her the chance to be physically intimate again, even for a little while?

And if they were both free agents, like Helen said, they were presumably hurting nobody – except poor Alice, who seemed to be affected by this new development. Hopefully, she didn't realise he was sleeping in the same bed as her mother; surely Helen was being discreet in that respect. But even so, to be introducing a man into their home, when the chances were he'd be gone in a matter of weeks, or months, didn't seem right to Sarah.

She laid the letter aside and got to her feet. Helen would live her life as she saw fit, and raise her daughter in her own way, and Sarah would mind her own business. What right had she anyway to criticise someone else's mothering skills when she wasn't a mother herself, when she hadn't gone through the undoubted challenges associated with bringing up children?

She felt the familiar pinch of sorrow as she pulled on her coat. When she wrote back to Helen, she wouldn't mention her qualms about Alice. She'd be glad her friend was happy, and leave it at that.

And tonight she'd cook Neil his favourite rib-eye steak; she'd attempt to make amends for being so distant with him. He was a good man, a good husband. None of this was his fault.

I've taken a lover. She smiled faintly as she left the house, pulling the door closed behind her. Honestly, so dramatic.

HELEN

She opened the sitting-room door and was met by the blare of the television. Alice lay sprawled across the couch, her hair wrapped in a towel. Helen picked up the remote control and reduced the volume considerably. No reaction.

She stood for a minute, arms folded, watching the characters on the screen. *Coronation Street* still going strong, older than Alice, more than twenty years on the go. A man appeared whose face Helen dimly recognised – in it from the very start, wasn't he, from the first ever episode? He looked older but no happier, a lifetime of on-screen struggles. She wondered if he ever confused his two lives, if he ever addressed his real wife by his pretend wife's name, ever woke up in the night and listened for the sound of glasses clinking in the pub next door.

She'd watched *Coronation Street* – she'd watched all the soaps – in the months after Alice was born, when all she and Cormac had had the energy for, between the never-ending rounds of feeding and burping and nappy-changing and singing to sleep, and fevers that came and went with frightening speed, was sitting on the couch in a half-trance with the cause of all the upheaval on one of their laps, ignoring the little glass bottles and rubber teats and Liga-encrusted bowls piled in the kitchen sink, the bucket of steeping nappies outside the back door.

Cormac had mostly dozed his way through the programmes, but Helen had watched as people had fallen in love and married and cheated and divorced on the screen in front of her; as delirious with exhaustion as she'd been, she'd recognised the improbability of the storylines and cringed at the uninspired dialogue and the two-dimensional characters.

When the bewilderment of having to cope with a new and completely helpless human had abated, and life had more or less returned to normality, they'd left the soaps behind and never gone back. But here Coronation Street still was, visiting sitting rooms twice a week, impervious to Helen's lack of interest.

'What's for dinner?'

'Quiche, ten minutes.'

The recipes she'd got years earlier from Sarah had become their staple diet. *Twelve will be plenty*, Helen had written. *That'll be enough for a fortnight's worth of dinners, with one night off a week for beans or scrambled egg on toast, or fish fingers for old times' sake.*

You can make your own fish fingers, Sarah had pointed out in her next letter. *They're really easy, and much more nutritious.*

Or I can buy them in Quinnsworth and have a night

off from cooking, Helen had replied, and that had been that. Now she had a dozen dishes that included pork ribs, mushroom stroganoff, salmon puffs (*wrap the fillets in ready-made puff pastry – I won't tell!*) and ham and leek quiche.

Alice ate what was put in front of her, more or less. Helen had offered to teach her how to cook any or all of the dishes, but so far her offer hadn't been taken up. *Make the dinner or wash up*, Helen had ordered, and Alice had chosen the latter.

Oliver, on the odd occasion when he joined them for dinner, seemed satisfied with the food too – although the atmosphere, with a silent, glowering Alice across the table, didn't make for a happy meal. Oliver's initial efforts at conversation had been met with muttered monosyllabic responses. These days he and Alice acted as if the other wasn't there, and Helen did her best to ignore the tension.

Alice's twelfth birthday party had come and gone. Five pre-pubescent girls dressed like mini prostitutes watching *Grease 2* on video, hair stiff with mousse, all giggles and high-pitched squeals, enough makeup between them to keep Helen supplied for a month, bowls of crisps and popcorn and sausage rolls (ready-made) scattered around the sitting-room floor.

Helen's offer of a cake had been turned down. 'Cake is for *kids*,' Alice had told her, rolling her eyes at her mother's ignorance.

'Didn't you bring home some cake from Patsy McMenamin's party last month?'

200

'Her dad works in a bakery, that's why.'

Her dad. When Cormac had died, three-year-old Alice had looked for him, naturally. 'Where is he?' she'd asked, coming home from her 'holiday' at Anna's house, the day after he'd been buried. Looking over Helen's shoulder, as if he might materialise there at any time.

'He had to go away.' Every word like a knife slicing Helen in two. 'He was very sorry that he couldn't say goodbye.'

'But when is he coming back?' Alice had demanded – Daddy's girl, from the second he'd seen her – and the best Helen could manage had been a whispered 'Soon.'

Every day for over a week she'd asked, searching for him every morning, pattering into Helen's bedroom, pulling back the bedclothes on his side, still playing the Hide and Seek game they'd often played, her face falling each time that he didn't pop up with a 'Boo!' like he'd always done.

And then one morning she'd come into the room and stood by the bed. She'd looked at the empty space next to Helen, and she'd made no attempt to touch the blankets. Over the days that followed, her questions about him had become fewer and fewer, until they'd finally petered out – and even though it spared Helen the agony of having to talk about him, she'd mourned this new disconnect with fresh tears.

When Alice had started school, eight months after his death, she'd come home one day asking why she had no dad. Helen looked at her and realised with a shock that she'd forgotten him. She'd brought her to the stairs and pointed to the family portrait that still hung there.

'That's your dad,' she said. 'He got sick and went to Heaven. That's why we can't see him any more.'

Alice had gazed at the photo for a few seconds. Helen had waited for questions, wondering how much detail about death and mortality a four-year-old would need.

'Your hair is funny,' Alice had said finally, and just like that, the subject had been closed. Since then, Cormac's name was rarely mentioned between them. Alice had been too young; he'd died before she could properly remember or mourn him, and maybe that was no bad thing.

'Have you finished your homework?' Helen asked now.

'Most of it,' Alice replied, her eyes never leaving the screen.

Helen picked up the remote control again and switched off the television. 'You know the rule. Go.'

Alice slithered wordlessly off the couch. The sitting-room door banged after her, and Helen listened to the angry thump of shoes on the stairs. If she got a pound every time her daughter stormed off she could give up writing.

By mutual consent, Alice worked alone on her homework. They fought enough over other things: this, at least, was one battleground they could avoid. Helen carried out cursory spot checks about once a week, and signed the homework diary when it was presented wordlessly to her before dinner each evening.

The phone rang as she was taking the quiche from the oven.

'You free tonight?' Oliver's dark drawl. 'I could come over around eleven.'

Eleven. Too late for them to go for a drink, even if she could get Anna to babysit at this short notice. No mention of where he'd be before eleven, no clue as to what he'd be doing, or who he'd be doing it with. He was asking, in essence, if she was free for sex.

Helen took a cigarette from the pack that sat by the phone. She could tell him she wasn't just someone he could phone anytime he didn't feel like going to bed alone – but of course she wouldn't, because she wanted it as much as he did. Even the thought of his hands on her made her hot inside.

Sarah wouldn't approve of making a date with nothing more than sex in mind. Easy to be right-eous with a husband in your bed every night.

'Make it half ten,' she said, striking a match against the wall. 'I feel like an early night.' She lit the cigarette and drew smoke into her lungs, wondering if she had any massage oil left. Whatever else you could say about him, Oliver Joyce gave a mind-blowing massage.

SARAH

She looked at him, aghast. *'Adoption?'*

'Look, I'm only saying maybe we could think about it. It's just an option.'

An option: someone else's unwanted baby. She could feel the blood racing, outraged, to her face. 'How could you even bring it up? How could you possibly imagine I'd want to do that? When have I *ever*—'

'Hang on, why are you getting so upset? Can we not at least discuss it?'

'There's nothing to discuss.'

'I think there is. I don't see why you're dismissing this out of hand. You want a baby—'

She glared at him, her eyes filling with hot, angry tears. '*I* want? There are two of us here. Don't you care whether we have a child or not? Am I the only one who gives a damn that I've miscarried three times?'

He reached for her hand, but she snatched it away. 'Sarah,' he said patiently, 'of course I care. That's why I'm bringing this up. You know I want children as much as you do. But if this is going to keep happening, it'll destroy you.'

She rose, pushing her chair from the table with such force that it almost tottered. She crossed the room to the window, thumbing the tears from her eyes. Was it going to keep happening? Were all their babies doomed to die before they were born? The thought was simply unbearable.

'We're not going to stop trying,' she said, looking out at the branches of the cherry tree. So beautiful when it was in bloom, so different now at the end of June after the blossoms had all fallen, leaving it ordinary and dull. 'I'm not going to give up. I can't.'

'I'm not asking you to give up – of course we'll keep trying, if that's what you want. But I'm concerned about you, and how unhappy this is making you. If we could give a home to some unwanted child . . . I know you'd make a wonderful mother. Just think about it, that's all.'

She leant forward until her forehead pressed against the window. The glass was ice cold. She *would* make a wonderful mother. She made a wonderful aunt. She closed her eyes and thought about Christine, younger than her by a year and soon to give birth for the third time, due in just three weeks. She pictured her two little boys, rushing up the driveway anytime Christine brought them over, delighted to be visiting.

She remembered Angela Ryan in school, adopted along with her two brothers. She remembered the unspoken pity that had hung like a fog around the three of them. She could see Mrs Ryan, older than the other mothers, dropping them outside the school on wet days in a green station-wagon, waving behind the swishing wipers as they crossed the yard, even though they never looked back.

But why pity them? Hadn't they been taken in by someone who'd wanted them? Mr and Mrs Ryan who ran the corner shop, Mr Ryan who'd slip you a barley-sugar stick when you came in with your mother for slices of corned beef or a block of ice-cream, who'd ruffle your hair and exclaim at how tall you were getting, and ask what class were you in now.

And, for all Sarah knew, maybe their real mothers had wanted Angela and the boys too, but hadn't been in a position to keep them. What did she know about their situation, what right had anyone to condemn or pity them?

She opened her eyes and turned from the window. 'Don't forget you said you'd fix the shed door for my father after work.'

Neil looked at her for a moment, an index finger tapping out a slow rhythm on the edge of his plate. 'I know,' he said, getting up, sweeping the crumbled shell of his boiled egg into the bin.

Sarah watched him leaving the room. That was the end of it: they wouldn't talk about adoption again. If he brought it up she'd ignore him, or walk away. He'd get tired of it eventually, and stop.

But for the rest of the day, as she chopped and stirred and whisked in the nursing-home kitchen, the topic insisted on turning itself slowly around in her head. Would it be so terrible after all to take possession of someone else's baby? Couldn't she learn to care for it? Wouldn't any woman's mothering instinct take over in the face of such helplessness? Care for it – and surely, in time, love it.

But the idea of never feeling a child growing inside her, never giving birth herself, never experiencing that miracle, still felt unutterably sad. However deserving of a happy home the babies were, however good an adoptive mother she might make, she didn't think she could face the awful implications of defeat that adoption held for her.

She'd ask Helen what she thought, next time she wrote. Helen's opinion was always worth hearing: she'd say exactly what was in her head. Funny how her forthrightness had brought them together in the beginning, how her savaging of that awful book had provoked Sarah into a response, and how her honesty was precisely what Sarah appreciated now.

She'd get her a present, she decided suddenly. Helen had sent that jar of cream when Sarah had been so desolate, and she'd been touched by it. She'd find some little gift next time she went shopping – not for any specific occasion, because Helen mightn't want that precedent set. It would just be a present, out of the blue.

And while she was at it, she'd get something for Alice too – why not? Poor Alice, having to cope without a father and get on with her mother's boyfriend. Sarah would hunt down something suitable, parcel it in nice wrapping paper and tie it with a pink ribbon. Alice was just twelve, still a little girl, whatever Helen said about her, and what girl didn't like pretty packages?

Work is busy, she wrote later that week, with my right-hand woman Bernadette out with flu. A few of the residents are quite sick with it too – one of them is gone to hospital, poor thing. I went to see him last evening and brought him a bit of lemon meringue pie, but he didn't look as if he had much of an appetite.

The weather isn't exactly helping – isn't it chilly? We're nearly going through a bag of coal a week at home. Neil comes in frozen every evening, takes him half an hour in a hot bath to feel human again. The joys of working out of doors, but he loves it, thank goodness.

I'm having my father and Neil's mother to dinner on Sunday. Nuala is just back from a week with friends in Jersey. Seventy-one and not a sign of slowing down. What a shame Neil's father got sick so young – they could have done so much together. I'm secretly hoping she and my dad will hit it off, but so far I've seen no evidence!

I'm enclosing a small token, for no particular reason other than I saw it and thought you might like it. I hope I got it right – difficult to know what to get for someone you've never met, even though I feel that I know you quite well in some ways! And I hope you won't mind if I send a little present to Alice too, under separate cover. I didn't want her to feel left out.

Helen, <u>please</u> don't feel you have to reciprocate – this was just something I wanted to do. It's as much for me as for you! Anyway, you got me that lovely cream (and no, I didn't feel like I had to reciprocate, honestly!).

How's your romance? I hope it's going well. Hope Alice is getting used to him.

She chewed the end of her pen. Chit-chat, small-talk, instead of what she really wanted to write about. Come on, out with it.

I want to ask your advice about something. Neil asked me a few days ago, out of the blue, if I'd consider adoption. I must admit I flew off the handle a bit. I know he means well – he says he's worried about the effect more miscarriages might have on me – and I know there are lots of babies who need loving homes, but I so desperately want one of my own, and I feel that considering adoption is like accepting defeat. Am I being terribly selfish and short-sighted?

She read it over. It would have to do. She began a new paragraph.

Neil got a window box for outside our sitting room – after much nagging from me! – and I filled it at the weekend with begonias I'd started in pots. They're such colourful little flowers, aren't they? Wonderful how they last all summer long.

Her letters weren't remotely exciting, or entertaining in the way that Helen's were. But maybe Helen appreciated the normality of Sarah's life, her steady job in the nursing home, her gardener husband, the routine of her days. Maybe Helen, living with the uncertainty of freelance work and lacking the stability of marriage, even envied elements of Sarah's safe, settled existence.

But Helen had a child. For that privilege, Sarah would happily have traded everything.

HELEN

'He's a little off today,' Catherine said. 'Between you and me, things are a bit troubled at home. Just so you know.'

'You're joking.'

Wife had a headache in bed last night, or loaded too much on his credit card, and along comes Helen the following morning to ask him for a rise: wonderful timing. Then again, was there ever a good time for broaching a pay hike to the likes of Breen?

Catherine pressed the intercom button on her desk. 'Mr Breen?'

A moment's silence. Helen eyed his office door, just down the corridor. *M. Breen, Editor* in black peel-off letters on the frosted glass. No expense spared.

'Yes.' The machine flattening out his voice, lending it a robotic quality.

'Helen Fitzpatrick is here,' Catherine told him. 'She'd like a word.'

He responded with a grunt that could have meant anything.

'I'll send her in.' Catherine took her finger off the button. 'Good luck.'

'Thanks.' Helen strode to his door and tapped. No response. Bugger him. She opened the door and stuck in her head. 'Good morning,' she said.

Breen stood by the open window, arms folded, shirt sleeves rolled to his elbows as usual. 'Well?'

Hello to you too. Helen closed the door behind her and took the chair facing his desk. No point in waiting to be asked.

Her third visit to his office in eight years, the last two times at his instigation, to brief her on commissions that needed more than just a phone conversation. This time, she was showing up of her own accord.

'I've brought the piece you wanted on the abortion referendum.'

'You could have left it with Catherine. Or posted it.'

He sounded weary more than cranky. Maybe he'd just had a bad night.

'I could,' she said, 'but I thought I'd come in and give it to you in person. I'm nice like that.' She reached into her bag and drew out the envelope.

'You're after something,' he said, as she laid it on his desk.

She gave him her most innocent look. On some level, and given the right mood, she almost enjoyed their exchanges. 'You're such a cynic. Can't your favourite freelancer come and say hello without being suspected of having ulterior motives?'

He came and sat at his desk then, interlaced his

fingers as he studied her, ignoring the envelope. 'O'Dowd, you were born with ulterior motives.'

She resisted telling him, again, that her name was Fitzpatrick. There were dark shadows under his eyes, a droop to his shoulders. Something had taken the fire out of him. Not her problem. 'Actually,' she said, mentally crossing her fingers, 'there is something I thought I'd run by you.'

His expression didn't change. He regarded her stonily. Mightn't be bad-looking if he bothered to smile. He was no Al Pacino, but there was nothing you'd run screaming from either. Eyes shockingly blue, still less grey in the dark hair than you'd expect from a man who must by now be on the wrong side of fifty. Teeth OK, on the rare occasions she was allowed a glimpse.

'I've been writing for you for almost eight years,' she began. 'I presume you like my work, you've never turned anything down—'

'You want more money.'

The same resigned tone as before. Something banged to the floor outside, clattered a few times before it went silent. Someone laughed, a long, rich peal.

'It's the first time I've asked,' Helen said. She couldn't read him: nothing in his face gave her any clue. 'I've never looked for parity with your male freelancers, although I'm assuming you're paying them more.'

He got to his feet abruptly. She was going to be thrown out, told never to come near him again.

He walked to the door and opened it. The end of a beautiful friendship. Just as well she had a few more irons in the fire, although his cheques would be sorely missed.

'I'll talk to Accounts,' he said. Just like that.

Helen, ready for a fight, was thrown. She reached to the floor for her bag, got slowly to her feet. Probably best not to pin him down to actual figures.

At the door she stopped. 'You OK?' she asked, the question out before she'd had time to consider the wisdom of it.

For the first time she saw a change in his face, a slight narrowing of the eyes. 'Why wouldn't I be?'

'Just asking,' she said, holding his gaze. 'Well, thank you for that.'

He inclined his head a fraction as she walked past him and left the room. She heard the door clicking shut as she approached Catherine's desk.

The PA smiled brightly at her. 'Everything all right?'

'Everything's fine,' Helen told her. 'Everything is just dandy.'

Walking back to the car, she wondered what, or who, had knocked the stuffing out of him. She'd never met his wife, had no idea if he had children. He knew she had Alice; he'd sent her a blue elephant when she'd broken her wrist once, years ago. It still sat at the bottom of Alice's bed, dressed these days in one of her old Talking Heads T-shirts.

She was getting a rise: she'd splash out on the strength of it. She stopped at the shopping centre and bought a bra and knickers in black lace. It amused her to think that Breen was paying, but Oliver would get the benefit.

When she got home, she washed the breakfast dishes and cleared the table. As she was feeding paper into her typewriter, the doorbell rang.

'Morning.' The parcel postman gave her his usual cheery wink. 'Two for the price of one.'

She'd never seen him without a smile on his face. Maybe it was easy to be happy when you spent your day driving around delivering parcels to people. Maybe Breen should think about a change of career, drive a florist's van or something.

In the kitchen she regarded the two packets. One a light-as-a-feather A4 padded envelope addressed to herself, the other a smaller, more solid rectangle, wrapped in lavender paper stamped with cavorting kittens and tied with a pink bow, and addressed to Alice.

They were both from Sarah, her return address printed neatly in the top corner of each package. A padded envelope for Helen, a parcel for Alice. What was going on?

She put Alice's delivery aside and turned her attention to her own. She slit the top and reached inside and pulled out a wispy scarf in swirls of gold and burnt orange and burgundy.

She turned the envelope upside down and Sarah's letter slid out. She scanned it till she got to *I'm enclosing a small token, for no particular reason other than I saw it and thought you might like it.*

A small token. A present. Helen's first present in years, if you didn't count the money she got from her parents every birthday and Christmas.

But this wasn't her birthday, it was nowhere near it, and Christmas was months away. And they never exchanged birthday or Christmas presents anyway. She ran a hand along the scarf, pressed it to her face. Not silk, like Cormac's scarf, the one she'd given to the woman on the bridge, but similar in design, with its swirls of colour.

She closed her eyes and was back there, alone and terrified until the stranger on her bicycle had come along. She tried to summon up an image of the other woman. She could remember a trouser suit – green, was it, or blue? – and fairish hair, but the face was gone.

Helen recalled how upset the woman had become, once she'd realised what was going on. Did she ever think about that day now? Did she shudder at the memory of it, or had she forgotten all about it as soon as she'd got to wherever she'd been going?

She had Helen's scarf, though, as a reminder. Or maybe she'd never worn it. Maybe she'd dropped it into the river as soon as she could, or left it tied around the railings in case the owner came back for it.

Helen opened her eyes, unsettled by the memory of that day. The sheepskin coat she'd worn, Cormac's coat, much too big for her but the only one she'd used since his death. Stuffed a few weeks later into a bag in the attic, the sight of it suddenly too sad for her to cope with. The maroon Beetle – his car – traded in a few months after that, another reminder that had become too painful.

She returned to Sarah's letter.

How's your romance? I hope it's going well.

Her romance, as if Oliver was arriving with flowers and chocolates, as if he was taking her out every week to dinner and the theatre, or whisking her to Paris for the weekend. Of course Sarah would find a quaint name for it, even though Helen had made it clear that romance played little part in what she and Oliver had been doing together for the past several months.

Hope Alice is getting used to him.

Her smile faded. Alice was decidedly not getting used to him. Last time he'd shown up for dinner she'd stayed in her room, coming out only after he and Helen had moved to the bedroom. Helen had heard her pattering down the stairs, the sharp click of the kitchen light switch.

She'd pictured her wolfing down the remains of the chicken pie, and had felt little sympathy. Alice was twelve, not a toddler, and her mother was far from past it. Let her sulk in her room when Oliver came around, if it kept her happy: Helen was going to enjoy having a younger man in her bed for however long it lasted.

Neil asked me a few days ago, out of the blue, if I'd consider adoption.

So they'd finally arrived at adoption. Helen had

217

wondered how long it would take them. Three miscarriages would be enough, surely, to set anyone thinking about alternative means of coming into possession of a child.

I must admit I flew off the handle a bit.

She tried to imagine equable, reasonable, soft-hearted Sarah flying off any handle, and found it difficult.

Am I being terribly selfish and short-sighted?

Selfish, from someone who probably couldn't bring herself to swat a fly in case it had a family that cared about it.

She finished Sarah's letter and laid it aside, and returned her attention to Breen's latest demand: a piece on the buying frenzy that had descended on American toyshops as parents fought one another, literally, for a doll that had supposedly been 'born' in a cabbage patch, and came complete with its own birth certificate.

'You want me to write about dolls?' she'd asked him incredulously.

'It's the madness of consumerism you're writing about. A thousand words by the end of Tuesday.'

So she'd done her homework, with the help of her local library's collection of US magazines and newspapers, and she'd visited the American Embassy and eventually found someone willing to tell her what they knew about the Cabbage Patch dolls phenomenon.

When she got home from school, Alice regarded the lavender-wrapped package silently.

'Aren't you going to open it?' Helen asked. 'Don't you want to see what she sent?'

Alice began to untie the ribbon. 'Why did she send me a present? She doesn't even know me, and it's not my birthday. And it looks sissy anyway.'

Helen counted to ten in her head, a little too rapidly. 'She knows me,' she said evenly, 'and she probably thought it would be a kind thing to do. And I'm sure she spent a long time making it look pretty.' Poor, innocent Sarah, thinking her present would be appreciated.

Alice undid the wrapping paper and lifted out a book. 'It's got my name on it,' she said.

It was a beautiful hardback edition. 'It's very famous,' Helen told her. 'I read it when I was your age.'

Alice picked up a slip of paper that had fallen from the book. Over her shoulder Helen read *Happy Unbirthday, Alice – when you read the book you'll know what it means! Love, Sarah Flannery (your mum's friend) xxx*

Alice dropped the slip and began to turn the pages. 'What's it about?'

'It's about a girl who discovers a secret place called Wonderland. There's a talking cat in it, and a baby who turns into something else, and a weird guy called the Mad Hatter. It's very cool, actually.'

She'd forgotten *Alice in Wonderland*. She'd forgotten the marvellous escape of it, curled on her bed while the rain lashed outside. She wondered if Alice, who rarely picked up a book, would get beyond the first chapter.

'Was that why you called me Alice, after her?'

'Yup.'

Little white lie, did nobody any harm. She'd been named after Alice Cooper, whose music Helen had loved – Cormac had been going to name the next baby – but for the purposes of interesting her in Sarah's present, let her think Lewis Carroll's Alice had been the inspiration. 'You must write and say thank you,' Helen said.

'Why can't you just tell her I said thanks? She's *your* friend.'

'Because she sent it to you, not to me. And because you won't get any pocket money till you do.'

Never five minutes away from a battle, the two of them.

SARAH

Both letters arrived on the same day, less than a week after she'd sent the presents. Both envelopes had been addressed in Helen's forward-tilting handwriting. Sarah brought them back into the kitchen.

Neil looked up. 'Anything for me?'

'No.' She stood by the sink and opened the envelope with Helen's return address in the top corner.

Sarah

Presents for both of us, and nowhere near our birthdays – what a lovely surprise. Thanks so much, the scarf is beautiful. Reminds me of one I had years ago and lost, so this will be a fitting substitute.

Alice was charmed with her book, loved the girly wrapping too. When I saw what you'd sent I wondered if you'd wasted your money, as she's not a big reader, but she actually started it that evening, and she's had her nose stuck in it ever since, so well done.

She's written you a letter; I'll post it off with

221

this. Apologies for the misspellings that I'm sure it's littered with – she refused to let me see it. Spelling is definitely not her forte. The only school subject she shows any interest in is art, and her drawing is quite good, but how many people make a living out of drawing pictures? I have visions of supporting her till I'm ninety. Hope she finds her vocation in secondary school, hard to believe she's starting in just over a month.

Bit of good news – I asked Breen for a rise, and I got it. Wasn't sure how much it was going to be till today, when I got a pretty decent cheque, more than I thought he'd give. Must be getting soft in his old age. Not that he's old – fifties-ish – just a cranky bastard most of the time. But what do I care, as long as he goes on paying me?

And speaking of cranky bastards, my neighbour gave me a particularly filthy look over the hedge this morning. I'm guessing he'd spotted my younger man leaving earlier, and I've decided he's either scandalised that I'm enjoying a healthy sex life or hopping mad that he isn't getting any himself.

Right, on to the serious stuff: Neil's talking about adoption and you don't want to hear. The way I see it, you were born to be a mum. Naturally you want to produce your own baby, and so far it hasn't happened, which is not to say it never will.

You say adopting would feel like accepting defeat, which I don't get. What's defeatist about giving a home to a child? How would it change your chances of conceiving? You and Neil could still keep trying – only difference is you'd have a real live baby to keep you company while you do. Just don't dismiss it out of hand.

Think about having a baby in the house. How long would you say it would take you to fall in love with it? I'd put a tenner on less than five minutes. And once it was rocking your world, would it really matter that you hadn't given birth to it? Same feeding, changing, burping, same sleepless nights . . . all the gain (if you consider that gain) and none of the pain – and believe me, giving birth is like discovering a whole new city of pain.

You'd soon get used to never, and I mean never, sleeping as long as you wanted – not to mention the tantrums and the spills and the falls and the fevers and your grandmother's antique vase in pieces and your lipstick in the toilet bowl and the trips to A&E with a broken something or other. The many joys of having a little person in the house.

I rest my case. I'm not trying to influence you, just telling you how I see it. Feel free to ignore me if none of this is making sense to you.

Must fly, a piece on the Divorce Action Group to deliver to Breen in three hours, and only halfway through it. He'll be demanding his rise back. No prizes for guessing which way you'd vote in a divorce referendum, Mrs Happily-Married-Forever.

Be good. Look after yourself. Thanks again for our surprises.

H

She folded the letter and slid it back into its envelope, and ripped open the second.

'More tea?' Neil asked. She shook her head and read the short, ink-stained message on the lined sheet.

Dear Mrs Flanery
My mother said I had to write to you or I wouldent get any poket money. Thank you for the book. I was called after the Alice in it. I think its a good storey but I didn't like wen the baby turned into a pig, that bit was yuk. I liked the cat, he was cool. OK I hav to go and do my homework.

from Alice Fitzpatrick

'Good news?'

Sarah looked up.

'You're smiling,' he said.

She handed him the sheet. 'I sent Helen's daughter a copy of *Alice in Wonderland*.'

He read it, a grin spreading across his own face. 'Was it her birthday?'

'No . . . I just felt like it.'

He held out the note, and as Sarah took it he grabbed her hand. 'I love you,' he said, 'and I don't deserve you.'

It was unexpected. He wasn't good at romantic pronouncements. Sarah squeezed his hand, met his grey gaze behind the glasses. 'Of course you deserve me,' she said, pulling him to his feet. She rested her head against his chest, raised the fingers still entwined in hers and put them to her lips, felt his heart beating under the checked flannel shirt she'd bought for him the week before. They stood unspeaking for a minute or so, his free hand cradling her head.

They'd make good parents: they'd give a baby a settled, loving home. She'd think about adoption. It couldn't hurt to think about it.

1987

HELEN

She squinted through the landing window. Was that a *dandelion* on Malone's lawn? She stared at the small bright yellow splotch in the middle of the otherwise immaculate rectangle of perfectly striped grass, and tried to remember when she'd seen him last.

Not anytime during the past week she was sure, up to her eyes with three books waiting to be reviewed, and Breen yelling for her take on AIDS in Ireland, and the drama with Alice last Thursday. Yes, at least a week – more, maybe two – since Malone had been spotted.

She frowned at the weed. Was he sick? Did she care? She had no idea if he had family – she'd never seen a visitor calling. Not that she was keeping track, but with the houses so huddled together, and her working from home, it was hard to avoid being aware of the general comings and goings in the neighbourhood.

The only people who passed Malone's gate were ones who had to, like the postman and the meter reader – and if there was an election coming up, a canvasser or two might ring his bell, but that was it. From what she could see, her neighbour was as friendless as herself.

And she was fairly sure he hadn't gone away. In all the years they'd lived beside one another he'd never travelled further than the supermarket. Probably afraid someone would break in and steal his ratty old furniture, or find his fortune under the mattress.

She should probably call to make sure he was still alive. Wasn't that what neighbours were expected to do, even if she didn't give a damn whether he'd kicked the bucket or not? And she'd look a right idiot if he simply hadn't noticed the dandelion, unlikely as that seemed.

She could imagine Sarah heading up his path with a homemade apple pie and a face full of neighbourly concern. Pity he didn't live next door to her. Shame Helen couldn't put him in a box and ship him off to Kildare.

Maybe he was starting to go gaga. Maybe that was why he hadn't been out with his little trowel at the first sign of the dandelion. If that was the case, he'd probably tell her to mind her own business and slam the door in her face before going in to leave the cooker on all night, or wander around the neighbourhood in the nip.

She'd leave well enough alone for the time being: if there was no sign of him over the next few days, maybe someone else would investigate. Hardly his other next-door neighbours – for as long as Helen had lived on the road, the house had been rented to various combinations of young women who, she was sure, hardly knew his name. But the meter reader might turn up and raise the alarm if he couldn't get in, or the postman might spot letters still lying in the hall.

She walked downstairs. He wasn't Helen's responsibility, and she had enough to do without worrying about him. She'd wait to see if any more dandelions appeared, or smoke started to pour out of a window. She could try cranking up the music for a few days, see if he reacted.

In the kitchen, Alice flicked the pages of a magazine. A huddle of crockery sat in the sink from breakfast: perish the thought that she'd wash them up. Johnny Logan sang 'Hold Me Now' on the radio, practising for his second Eurovision in a week's time. The man was addicted.

Helen lifted out the plates and ran water into the sink.

'I'm bored,' Alice said, without looking up.

'I'm not listening,' Helen replied, reaching for the washing-up liquid.

'Can I phone Karen?'

'You can not.'

Alice sighed loudly. Helen turned up Johnny Logan, and sang along.

SARAH

Sarah
Hope this finds you as wonderfully happy as in your last several letters. Life here continues to be the barrel of laughs that it always was. I'm still man-less, not a sign of a fling since Toyboy decided to give his marriage another go. Imagine it's nearly two years since he and I were making the earth move. Wonder if he's still enjoying wedded bliss, or if she kicked him out again.

You'll be sorry to hear that my cranky neighbour has gone missing – no sign of him for about two weeks, and there's a dandelion in his garden. In case you don't get the significance of this, I should remind you how fanatical he is about that lawn – if he could roll it up and bring it in at night he would. I suppose I should check and see if he's still in the land of the living, but the thought gives me hives. I'll wait another while, hope someone else gets there first. (Don't judge me: I'm kind in other ways. Well, I'm not, but if you knew him you'd understand.)

On a cheerier note, I got a call last week from the manager of a chemist in our local shopping centre. Alice was caught with a couple of unpaid-for lipsticks in her pocket. I squeezed out a few tears and played the poor widow card, and she was let off with a warning never to darken their door for the rest of her life.

She's grounded for two weeks, not allowed to step outside the house after school, and no phone calls either. I can't decide who's being punished more, her or me. She swears she never did it before: I told her I'm more concerned that she never does it again. But she will, watch this space.

I don't think I mentioned that I found cigarettes in her coat pocket last month. What could I say, except that I didn't start until I was older than her? I didn't add that I was just a year older at seventeen (sorry, shocked you again). I'll just have to hope she doesn't move on to anything more sinister than ciggies.

Wonder what I did to deserve this kid. I thought puberty was bad – remember the meltdown when I wouldn't let her get her ears pierced at thirteen, and the time she put that bleach in her hair and it went bright yellow, and that whole business with the history teacher, to mention just a few highlights?

The only chink of light is her art. She's definitely got talent – and that's not maternal blindness, believe me – and she's mentioned art college a few times, but I've told her without a few more subject passes she hasn't a hope of getting in. Inter Cert in three weeks and she's finally doing a bit of study, but I'm not holding my breath. The scary thing is, she reminds me a bit – a lot – of me when I was that age, except that I was nicer. (I think.)

You wouldn't like to swap, would you? No, didn't think so – and I'm not sure I'd want to go back to the start anyway. Be happy with your little bundle of joy while you can – as far as I recall, Alice was fairly manageable up to about two and a half. That gives you another six months of baby-honeymoon.

Sarah laid down the letter, smiling. She smiled a lot these days. Everything made her smile. Even the thought of Alice slipping a couple of lipsticks into her pocket didn't unduly upset her. Silly girl: but there were worse things she could be doing, and she was still only sixteen, she'd surely grow out of it. Maybe Sarah should write to her again; maybe she just needed someone to show an interest in her.

She stretched her arms over her head, relishing the unaccustomed peace, the precious solitary cup of tea. The others would be back soon and she'd have to think about what to cook for lunch – something without cheese, which she seemed to have gone off lately – but for another few minutes she was happy to sit and marvel at the way every-thing had turned around for them over the past few years.

Who would have thought that one small child could change their lives so very much? The house hadn't been clean, not properly clean, for well over a year. The sitting room had become a jumble of toys, jigsaws, books, playpen, miniature jackets, hats and shoes, teething rings, doll's pram, buggy, tricycle – you had to pick your way through them to get to the sofa. The carpet, what you could see of it, was stained in several places, the tiles around the fireplace constantly smeared with small fingerprints.

Most of the kitchen worktops had been comman-deered by bundles of dribblers, stacks of nappies and jars of powders, creams and lotions devoted to the business of warding off nappy rash, eczema, flaky scalp and a myriad other baby-related condi-tions. In the freezer, miniature tubs of homemade ice-cream and stewed fruit nestled among the salmon cutlets, minced beef and chicken fillets.

Upstairs was no better. The bath was piled with cloth books, rubber ducks, star-shaped sponges, plastic boats and a little yellow watering can. In Sarah and Neil's room the bed had been joined by a cot, a changing mat, a rocking chair and yet more toys.

After much deliberation, Sarah had decided to keep her job but reduce her hours – now she worked mornings only, finishing straight after she'd plated up lunch, and getting home by half past two. Shorter hours, smaller pay packet – and less time with the residents, which was the hardest part.

But home life was wonderful, better than it had ever been. And today was Saturday, and for once Neil didn't have to work, and it wasn't raining. This afternoon they were going to Christine and Brian's house for Tom's seventh birthday, and later she and Neil would watch the Eurovision, Johnny Logan the Irish entry for the second time. Not that he'd win again – nobody could win the Eurovision twice – but she couldn't care less if Ireland came last.

She heard the front door being opened and she rose immediately and went out to the hall, where her husband was manoeuvring a buggy across the threshold. 'You're back,' she said, bending to kiss the wonderfully soft, beautifully warm and rosy cheek of her little daughter.

Dear Alice
Remember me? I'm your mum's penfriend, the one who sent you Alice in Wonderland a few years ago. You wrote me a very nice letter in return. In fact, I still have it. I just thought I'd drop you another line, see how you were doing.

236

I can't believe you're sixteen already. I don't remember very much about being sixteen, it's so long ago! But one thing I do remember is watching a singer called Butch Moore singing for Ireland in our very first Eurovision, around the time I was fifteen or sixteen – gosh, that makes me sound really ancient, doesn't it? Were you watching the Eurovision last week? Imagine Johnny Logan won it again, I was sure he wouldn't.

I don't know if your mum ever talks about me, but if she does you'll know that my husband and I adopted a little baby girl two years ago, and I can honestly say that my life has been utterly changed by her. Even though I'm not her natural mother I don't think I could possibly feel any more love for her if I was. Before I even considered adopting, your mum said something in a letter that I'll never forget. She said if I adopted a baby, it wouldn't take more than five minutes for me to fall in love with it – I'm guessing it was the length of time it took her to fall for you – and she was right!

I'm sending a photo of her, so you can see how adorable she is. We called her Martha after my mother, who died nine years ago. My sister is really jealous – she has three boys, and would love a daughter! Your mum is so lucky to have you. She often mentions you in her letters.

Well, I'd better stop – sorry for going on about Martha so much, I can't help it!

All the very best,

love Sarah xx

PS You don't have to write back, honestly!

HELEN

'So how's school? You're getting on all right?'
Alice lifted a shoulder. 'Yeah, fine.'
    'You won't feel it now till the Inter Cert – three weeks, is it?'

'Two.'

'Two? You'll be glad when it's over, I'd say.'

'Mmm.'

'What's your favourite subject?'

'Art.'

Her grandfather's smile dimmed somewhat. 'Art. I see.'

Helen sat in her parents' kitchen, happy to let her father struggle through a conversation with his only grandchild while she sipped coffee and thought about Malone.

The dandelions plentiful now, almost a month since she'd spotted the first. Still no sound from next door, no reaction to Meatloaf at full volume for two hours yesterday afternoon. His cat mewing outside Helen's back door last evening until she'd thrown the dustpan at it. Something was up, and she might be the only person who'd realised it.

'Some more?'

Her mother stood beside her, holding the coffee pot. Still elegant at seventy-six, still capable of keeping the four-bedroom Dalkey home running smoothly for herself and the retired judge.

'No thanks,' Helen said. Every time she and Alice visited, a coffee refill was offered and declined.

Was he dead? Was he lying in a heap with a broken neck at the bottom of the stairs, or slumped across the kitchen table with a fishbone in his throat? She should have investigated before now, even if he was a gnarly old goat. If he'd died before the first dandelion had shown up, he'd be mouldy by now.

Nearly a month, *Jesus*, and she'd done bugger all about it.

'Helen.'

She looked up.

'I asked,' her father said, 'if you'd read any good books lately.'

Books, the last resort of the desperate conversationalist. Maybe she should tell him about his granddaughter's recent brush with criminality: that would kick-start a lively exchange.

'Only a few I had to review, nothing worth mentioning,' she said, pushing back her chair. 'Well, we'd better get going, Alice has revising to do. Thanks for the coffee.'

They stood side by side at the front door as Helen drove off, waving at the little Fiat until it was out of sight. As relieved, no doubt, to be rid of them as Helen and Alice were to be making their escape. The tyranny of family ties, condemning them to maintain some form of contact as long as they all should live.

Helen turned onto the main road. 'Do you want to be dropped in town? Are you meeting Karen?'

The grounding period had ended the day before: peace of sorts had been restored to the household.

'She's gone to Kilkenny to stay with her dad.'

'So you're coming home, then?'

'Yeah.'

Helen approached a roundabout and signalled right. 'Have you seen Mr Malone lately?'

'No. Why?'

'No reason. He doesn't seem to be around.'

Silence. Helen entered the roundabout, wondering again what had prompted Sarah to send a second letter to Alice.

It had arrived the day before. Helen, seeing the familiar writing, the purple ink, had almost opened it before she'd realised it wasn't addressed to her. Not another package, just an envelope this time. Nothing in it but a page or two, by the feel of it. She'd held it up to the light and hadn't been made any wiser. She'd have to wait until Alice got home.

But Alice had taken it without comment and brought it upstairs, and no mention of it had been made for the rest of the evening. Helen vowed not to ask: Alice was sixteen, and entitled to her privacy. Still, she wondered what Sarah had had to say. She turned onto the road that ran along by the canal.

'Have you any photos of me?' Alice asked suddenly.

It was unexpected. 'Photos? You mean your school ones?'

'No, when I was a baby. Did you take any?'

A scatter of raindrops hit the windscreen. Helen flicked a switch and the wipers scraped against the glass. 'Yes,' she said eventually. 'We took lots of photos – well, your father took them mostly, he was much better than me. He took piles of them.'

The camera had never been far from Cormac's hands, those first few hectic months. Alice asleep, nestled against Helen's chest. Alice yawning, her whole face getting involved. Alice crying, Alice feeding, Alice lying on her back, looking solemnly at the line of plastic animals that dangled on a line of elastic above her.

And later, Alice sitting on the kitchen floor, propped up by cushions. Alice crawling, Alice pulling herself up to standing, Alice dragging a doll around the garden by the hair, Alice in a high chair, clapping podgy hands at a cake with two lighted candles that sat on the tray in front of her.

There must be dozens, more than a hundred maybe. Helen had forgotten all about them, hadn't looked at them in years. Hadn't laid eyes on the camera in years either, hadn't a clue where it was. She wondered why Alice was asking about photos out of the blue.

'Can I see them?'

'Of course you can. They're in my room. I'll bring them down when we get home.'

After Cormac's death the photos had stopped. No,

242

they'd stopped before that, when he became too weak to hold the camera, and by then the last thing on Helen's mind had been taking photographs. In fact, she was pretty sure she hadn't taken a single photo of Alice since then – which was probably, now that she thought about it, a bit shameful. One more reminder of her pathetic parenting skills.

There were half a dozen albums, covered with fake white leather and pushed to the back of the wardrobe shelf, behind a tumble of tights and scarves, and a scatter of discarded paperbacks. Helen brought them downstairs and laid them on the kitchen table.

'Here you go.'

She lit a cigarette and leant against the window-sill, studying her daughter's profile. Alice turned the pages slowly, head bent, looking intently at the snaps. Her pale hair was cut high on her forehead – she'd butchered her long fringe without warning one day – and short as a small boy's at the back. As she examined the photos, she scratched absently at a scab on her left wrist.

Her nails were bitten, a Fitzpatrick family trait. Alice had a small dark freckle, or a mole, at the point where the side of her neck met her right shoulder. Shoved up on her arm, almost to the elbow, was the thin, gold-plated bangle Cormac's mother had sent her for her last birthday.

'I remember that doll,' she said, 'but I forget what I called her.'

'Juju.' The name came to Helen without thinking.

'She was Julie, but you couldn't manage it. You wouldn't go to bed without her. We left her on Sandycove Beach once. You screamed the place down till we drove all the way back. She was sitting on the sea wall: someone had wrapped her in a plastic bag.'

'I don't remember that.'

Juju had been a present for her first birthday from Rick, the lead guitarist in the band, and his wife Jenni. After Cormac's death they'd drifted away, like everyone else. Better things to do than keep in contact with the piano player's widow and little girl. Bookings to fulfil, parties to go to.

Alice turned another page. 'Oh my *God.*'

'What?'

'My face is *covered* in ice-cream, or yogurt, or something.'

Helen smiled. 'You were a baby. That's what they do.'

Look at them, having a normal conversation. Nobody scowling, nobody giving out. When had that ever happened? Helen felt the top of the sill against the back of her thighs as she watched her daughter turning the pages slowly. She remembered Cormac coming home from town with each wallet of photos, spreading them out on the table. The look on his face as he'd gazed at them.

'He's not in any of them,' Alice said suddenly, on the last album. 'My dad.'

The brushing-up against Helen's thoughts was

disconcerting. 'That's because he took most of them,' she said. 'But he's in some, isn't he?'

Alice turned pages. 'Oh,' she said, stopping and staring down at a photo. Helen resisted the impulse to cross the floor. Alice turned another page, slowly, and studied it with the same intensity. For several minutes she was silent, looking at pictures of the man she didn't remember.

Finally she closed the album. 'Can I keep this one in my room?'

Helen stubbed out her cigarette. 'If you want.'

The phone rang in the hall. Alice got to her feet. 'I'll go.'

Karen probably, or one of the other girls who asked for her when Helen answered – nine times out of ten the voice at the other end looked for Alice. No male callers, not yet.

At sixteen, Helen had French-kissed three boys and let one of them under her top. Brazen behaviour in 1958, when nice girls didn't allow boys much more than a chaste goodnight peck on the cheek after a red lemonade and a swing around the local dancehall. Helen had always pushed further, curious to see what was waiting behind the next taboo.

She took eggs from the fridge, broke them into a bowl and beat them with a fork. As she grated cheese, Alice reappeared.

'I'm making omelettes,' Helen told her.

'Karen's dad has a new girlfriend,' Alice replied.

'Does he?'

Jonathan Nugent had made a pass at Helen once. She'd called to the house to collect Alice from a birthday party, and he'd answered the door. Must have been around three years ago, when he and Karen's mother were still together, and supposedly happy, and Oliver was an intermittent visitor to Helen's bed.

Jonathan had stood back to let her in. His blond hair needed a cut and his belly pushed at his shirt buttons, but he wasn't bad-looking, in a sort of Robert-Redford-gone-to-seed kind of way.

'Helen,' he'd said, 'good to see you. Drinks in the kitchen, away from the birthday madness.'

Presumably his wife was holding the fort inside, poor woman, while he got sloshed with the other parents in the kitchen. Helen, only too pleased to avoid the clutch of over-excited girls she could hear on the other side of the sitting-room door, had followed him down the hall. To her surprise, the kitchen was empty.

'You're the first,' he'd told her, lifting an open wine bottle from the table and waving it at her. 'A little Piat D'Or for the lady?'

From his too-loose grin she'd realised that he'd already had a few. 'Any whiskey?' As long as it was free, might as well go for it.

He'd bashed ice from a tray into a glass – a few cubes skittering away from him across the worktop – and added a decent amount of Paddy. 'Bottoms up,' he'd said, handing her the glass.

'Cheers.' She'd raised it to her lips, aware of his

246

gaze sliding down to her cleavage as she drank. Let him look, didn't bother her.

He topped up an almost-empty wine glass that sat beside the sink. 'So,' he said, moving back to stand close to her, 'here we are.'

His eyes were watery blue. She could have reached out and pulled his head down, she could have shoved her tongue into his mouth, and he wouldn't have complained; he'd have loved it. She took another sip, enjoying the burn of the whiskey. Enjoying, to be perfectly honest, his eyes on her.

'You wouldn't have a cigarette, would you?' she'd asked, and he'd drawn a packet of Major from his pocket. For the laugh she'd held eye contact with him as she'd leant towards the lighter he'd offered.

'You don't look old enough,' he'd said then, 'to have a daughter Alice's age. You must have been a child yourself when you had her.'

She'd laughed: he was ridiculous. She'd been twenty-nine when Alice was born – any fool would know, looking at her, that she was well over that now. But it was harmless, a bit of flirtation in a suburban kitchen – and the knowledge that his wife could walk in at any minute had only added to the fun.

'God,' he'd said then, his eyes openly on her breasts, his smile still in place. 'I'm so attracted to you. I want to fuck you right now on that table.'

She'd kept her eyes on his face, waited until he'd looked up. 'What's stopping you?' she asked. Call his bluff, dirty old man.

And before he could react, the kitchen door had burst open and there was Karen in her blue party dress, cheeks aflame, holding an empty jug and demanding more MiWadi. And as her father was refilling the jug the doorbell sounded, and Helen had grabbed Alice and slipped away in the ensuing flurry of more parental arrivals.

Lying in bed alone later that night – no sign of Oliver – she'd imagined starting an affair with the married father of her daughter's best friend. Arranging for him to collect Karen when she was visiting Alice so they could snatch a quickie while the girls were still upstairs, or sneaking him into the house at night after Alice was asleep. Meeting his wife at the school gates in the afternoons, meeting both of them at the end-of-term concert in a couple of months' time.

She'd waited to see if he made contact – let him come to her, she wasn't that desperate – but he never did; and before the term ended he'd walked out on his wife, and Helen hadn't laid eyes on him since. No loss.

'By the way,' Alice said, taking cutlery from the drawer, 'there's an ambulance outside Mr Malone's house.'

Dear Helen
I hope you didn't mind that I wrote to Alice last week. I just felt a bit sorry for her being grounded, even though of course you had good reason – and you needn't worry, I didn't

mention the lipstick business. I probably bored her to tears going on about how wonderful Martha is! I sent her a photo of the second birthday party – she probably showed it to you, not that you need to see any more!

You must have loads of baby photos, and older ones as well, of course. It's fascinating to watch the changes as Martha grows – although I must confess I feel a little sad when I look at our first few photos of her, when she was so tiny and helpless. Just over a week old, not a hair on her head – remember how bald she was when we got her? – but the biggest, bluest eyes, and I remember how frightened I was at the thought of her being dependent on us for every single thing. It seems now that she's becoming more her own person every day, learning to do so many things for herself, which of course is wonderful, but it makes me lonely for that little helpless creature.

So – brace yourself – I've decided I want another one! And in fact I can reveal that we've already applied to the adoption agency!! The good news is that they've said we shouldn't have as long to wait this time round. Fingers crossed, and I'll let you know as soon as there's any development. I have constant butterflies these days. I can hardly eat, I'm so keyed up at the thought that I might be a mother of two in just a few months!

Other than that, there's not a lot of news. Work is the same as ever, can't believe I've been at the nursing home for over twelve years! Neil is well, and still managing to work his hours around my schedule so we can look after Martha ourselves, which is wonderful. We don't see a lot of each other at weekends – he works most of them to make up for missed time during the week – but it's a price we're willing to pay, for the moment anyway.

There's a possibility of a big commission coming up for him though – a new golf course in the offing just a few miles away, and he's put in a tender to maintain it. If he gets that he'll be a lot busier, which of course would be great in one way, but it would mean we'd have to think about a childminder, especially if we get a second baby. I suppose it doesn't help that I can't drive – I really should learn, but I love the bike.

Don't be too hard on Alice. I know it's easy for me to say, and I should probably mind my own business, but I'm sure she's sorry for what happened. Maybe it was just a bit of bravado in front of the pals. And I know you're raising your eyes to Heaven now at me being so soft, but one of us has to be!

All the best,
Sarah x

Dear Mrs Flanery

Thank you for your letter. I like your little girl, she's cute in her red dress. I asked my mum if she had photos of me and she brought out a stack of them. There were some of my dad, who died when I was three, so I don't remember him, but it was wierd seeing him with me.

I'm sending you one of me, just to give you a laugh. Look how messy I am.

Yours sincerly

Alice Fitzpatrick

SARAH

It was happening again, and she was terrified. She lay in the bath, door ajar, listening to the up and down swing of Neil's voice as he read Martha's bedtime story in the next room. This week she was demanding 'Winnie the Poor' every night. Sarah could picture her curled up in bed, Baba tucked firmly under her chin. Baba was a soft black sheep with creamy-coloured ears, a present from Helen that had arrived in the post two days after they'd brought Martha home.

The miracle of her daughter, their daughter, had overwhelmed Sarah. The months of waiting, once they'd started down the adoption route, had seemed endless. No, not months, years. Almost two years after she'd agreed to put in an application for someone else's baby, still not at all certain that it was what she wanted.

But Martha, with her shiny little head and enormous blue eyes, Martha, with her miniature fingernails and tiny, perfect ears – Martha, whose gaze had fastened on Sarah's face as she'd sucked determinedly at her very first bottle in her new home – Martha had won her over without even

252

trying, had found the empty place inside her and settled right in.

And now, just when everything was going so brilliantly, when they were planning to do it all over again, this.

'Congratulations,' her doctor had said that afternoon – because he was programmed to look on a pregnancy as a good thing, even if you'd tried and failed three times, even if the thought of another failure was unbearably frightening.

'We'll take very good care of you,' he'd assured Sarah, no doubt guessing exactly what she thought of the news. 'There's no reason why you won't carry this one to term.' Sarah didn't remind him that he'd told her that three times before. He meant well.

She lay in the bath and wondered when to tell Neil that she didn't have a tummy bug after all, that her nausea and indigestion of the past few weeks had a very different cause. She'd suspected the truth, naturally, and refused to consider it, doomed to failure as it most likely was. But now it had been confirmed, and there was nothing to do but let nature take its cruel course for the fourth time.

Maybe she'd say nothing to Neil. Maybe it was best to keep it to herself this time. What was the point in setting him up for more heartbreak?

They had Martha, and they were in line for another baby: let that be enough for them. Let this seedling inside her go the way of all the others.

She'd tell nobody – although it would be hard, with Christine and the boys due tomorrow for lunch, and her father coming on Sunday to spend the day with them, which he did most Sundays now.

Presently she heard Neil sneaking from Martha's room. Seconds later his head poked around the bathroom door. 'Will I put on the kettle?' he whispered.

'Do. I'll be down in a minute.'

And maybe after it was over she would talk to the doctor about going on the Pill, although the thought of that brought hot tears that ran down her face and dripped almost silently into the cooling water.

HELEN

The house was definitely empty. No lights, no sound for more than a week, not since Alice had reported seeing the ambulance. Helen had gone straight out, but there had been no sign of it. She'd looked about for anyone to ask, anyone who might have witnessed the scene, but nobody was around.

She should have called to his door. She should have enquired, even if he'd told her to get lost, even if he'd run her off the premises. At least her conscience would be clear now: she wouldn't feel like the worst kind of person. It was perfectly clear that he had nobody: it wouldn't have killed her to ring his doorbell.

The dandelions had taken over his front lawn. Every one a reproach, a reminder of how Helen had ignored his absence until he'd been carted away in an ambulance. Jesus, it wouldn't have killed her to show some neighbourliness.

She checked the death notices each day and saw no sign of his name, which didn't mean he wasn't dead. But with nobody to ask, she had no way of knowing. The postman still walked up his garden path every few days – junk mail probably, building up on the mat inside – but no other person appeared; no one came to cut the grass or open the curtains or feed the cat.

The cat: she'd forgotten the cat. Was it still in the house, slowly starving to death with its owner gone? And then she remembered flinging the dustpan at it one night when it had sat mewing outside her back door. Not trapped inside then, which was something. But that had been ages ago.

She opened the fridge and saw eggs, butter, a block of Cheddar cheese, two carrots, a parsnip and a bowl of jelly. The only food that seemed remotely suitable was the cheese. Cats did dairy, didn't they? She cut a wedge into small cubes and left them on a saucer outside the door. If it was still around, and hungry enough, it would eat it.

The next time she looked out, an hour or so later, the saucer was empty. The cheese could, of course, have been eaten by any number of creatures – not all of them cats – but she decided to assume it was Malone's pet that had found it.

She wrote *cat food* on her shopping list. It wouldn't make up for her shameful neglect of its owner, but it might go some small way towards making her feel less despicable.

SARAH

He broke her heart.

A scarecrow, skin and bone, grey trousers bunched with a belt at the waist, shirt collar badly frayed, stubble on his scrawny chin as pure white as the wisps of hair that trailed across his head. Shuffling in slippers from his bedroom each day to pick at the dinner that was put in front of him. Not making any effort to talk to the people around him, leaving the dining room as soon as he'd finished.

'He lived alone,' one of the nurses had told Sarah when she'd enquired. 'He'd been ill, pneumonia I think they said. He couldn't get out and about, he ran out of food – not that I'd say he ate much in the first place. Practically starving by the time anyone realised he was there. He was a month in hospital.'

'Who found him?'

'No idea. Some neighbour, I suppose.'

Charlie had lived in Dublin all his life, but a shortage of beds in the capital's nursing homes had resulted in his being sent to St Sebastian's, forty miles away, to convalesce. In the two weeks

257

he'd been there Sarah had seen no visitor, and as far as she knew, nobody had phoned the home to enquire after him. Nobody at all seemed to care what happened to him.

On mild afternoons he'd make his way to the garden and sit on one of the wooden benches, wrapped in the tartan rug that was folded at the bottom of his bed. Sarah would see him from the kitchen window, his balding head poking from the rug that dwarfed him as he sat there alone, and her heart would contract with sympathy.

And because she was trying not to spend all her spare time keeping count of how long it had been since her last period – seventy-four days – she'd taken to wandering into the garden when she had a few spare minutes to sit on the bench beside him.

At first there wasn't much talk. She'd remark on the weather, or wonder if he was warm enough, and he'd respond with as few words as he could get away with. He wasn't unfriendly, just detached, as if he'd had nobody to talk to for a long time, and had got out of the habit of conversation. She asked him once what his favourite food was.

He considered the question, his head to one side, his gaze fixed on a twiggy furze bush. 'I don't know,' he said finally. 'I've never been that bothered about food.'

Sarah imagined him lying in bed, too weak to leave the house, barely able to make his way downstairs and find whatever meagre offerings his fridge had yielded. Wouldn't have taken him long to run out, by the sound of it. Hard to imagine a man living in the middle of the city, surrounded by others, almost dying of malnutrition.

He had the appetite of a small bird, ate practically nothing, but he needed food now to build him up. She'd try chicken soup with a soft bread roll, that might tempt him, and a finger of apple tart with custard afterwards. Surely he'd manage that.

Towards the end of his third week at St Sebastian's (eighty-three days since her period), while they sat in silence on the garden bench, he turned to Sarah, out of the blue, and said, 'I had a cat' – and to her dismay she saw his eyes were brimming with tears.

'Oh,' she said, putting a tentative hand on his arm, her own eyes filling at the sight of his distress, 'oh, please don't cry.' She couldn't bear it if he cried.

His face collapsed. 'I don't know where he is,' he said, pulling a crumpled grey handkerchief from his trouser pocket. 'He went missing while I was sick. I couldn't feed him. I didn't have anything to give him—' Oh, the heartbreak of having to watch the tears spilling from his eyes, stuttering past the crevices in his face. 'I don't know how to find him. I asked in the hospital, I asked them to send someone to look for him, but they said they couldn't do that, but I don't know where he is.'

'I'll help,' Sarah cried impulsively, swiping her

own tears away. 'What can I do? Is there anyone I could phone? You must have a neighbour who'd go and have a look.'

She wanted to ask who'd found him in the house – surely that person would oblige by hunting around a bit – but the question sounded insensitive. Besides, it had been . . . how long now? Almost two months since he'd left the house? The cat could be anywhere – did cats hang around houses, waiting for their owners to return? Did they die of loneliness if no one came back, or did they simply find someone else to feed them?

Charlie blew his nose noisily, dabbed at his eyes again. 'Well, there's George,' he said doubtfully, 'but he doesn't live near. I went on the bus . . .'

'Let me ring him anyway. Let me ask him. He's a friend of yours, is he?'

'Well . . . he has a garden centre. I used to go there a bit. He'd have my address – he delivered plants to me. He knows where I live.'

A garden centre. The only person he could come up with was someone with a garden centre a bus ride away.

'I'll ring him,' Sarah promised. If the man had a heart she'd get around him: he'd surely oblige an old customer in need. She'd give him the number of St Sebastian's, ask him to call if he saw any sign of the cat. What would happen after that, she had no idea. Let them find the cat first, if it was to be found. Maybe this George would take it in, look after it until Charlie was ready to go home. If all came to all she'd send Neil to get it and bring it back, and she'd look after it herself. There was always a way, if you wanted something badly enough.

She got a description of the cat from Charlie and found the garden centre in the *Golden Pages*. She rang it first thing in the morning from Matron's office. She asked for George, and was told he was out doing a delivery. 'I'm his partner,' the man on the other end told her. 'Maybe I can help you.'

It was a long shot – he might never even have met Charlie. But she'd made the call, she might as well try, and he sounded nice. 'It's a bit of a long story,' she said. 'Allow me to explain.'

HELEN

"You got a cat?"

From the look on her mother's face, Helen might as well have told her she had the plague. They sat in her parents' spacious drawing room, the September sun a red ball slipping behind the roofs of the houses across the road, red and purple sky reflected in the giant gilt-framed mirror that hung above the fireplace.

Her father's eightieth birthday, Black Forest Gateau and sherry all around, except for Alice who was drinking Fanta. Helen had given him a copy of Frank Delaney's *Silver Apples, Golden Apples: Best Loved Irish Verse*. Alice had sketched Malone's cat and put it into a frame that she'd found selling for thirty pence in a charity shop. No doubt her grandparents would find a suitable spot for it; the downstairs toilet maybe.

'It's not our cat,' Helen told her mother. 'It belongs to our neighbour. Alice looks after it mostly, don't you?'

'Mm.'

'So what are you doing with it?'

'The neighbour's in hospital. We're just looking after it until he gets home.'

Three months, maybe more, since Malone had been last sighted, she'd lost track. The chances of him ever returning to his house becoming slimmer, surely, with each day that passed. His cat making himself at home next door, Alice sneaking him into the kitchen whenever Helen wasn't around, feeding it leftover meat from the fridge last week that Helen had been planning to turn into a curry, a suggestion from Sarah some time ago.

She'd seen a man from her bedroom window a couple of days earlier getting out of a van that had *F&G Garden Centre* on the side. She'd watched him pushing open next door's gate and decided she'd better ask him about Malone, but by the time she'd finished dressing and gone downstairs, both man and van had disappeared.

She ate cake and listened to Alice telling them about her Inter Cert results. A relief that she'd scraped through: on to the next two years. Still talking about art college, but Helen wondered if an accomplished portfolio, which she'd already begun assembling, would be enough to secure her a place.

'She'll have to work hard across all subjects,' her art teacher had told Helen. 'She has the artistic talent, and definitely the drive, but there's stiff competition for art college, and she should pull up in the other areas too, to give her a fighting chance.'

She studied her father, still an air of authority about him at eighty, well honed from years of putting criminals in their places. Her mother in a duck-egg blue twinset and grey tweed skirt, cutting more cake, pressing another slice on Alice, who would eat Black Forest Gateau for breakfast, lunch and dinner if she was allowed. Shame Helen had never baked a cake in her life.

Sarah probably made her own Black Forest. Helen could imagine her piping on the cream, dotting the swirls with plump black cherries. More on her mind these days than cakes, according to her last letter.

> I'm still terribly anxious, even though I'm past the three-month danger period. The doctor keeps reassuring me, and Neil is over the moon, and convinced that this time everything will be all right. We've told the adoption agency to take us off the waiting list – it didn't seem right to stay on it, just in case things didn't work out.
>
> We've said nothing to Martha yet – anyway, she's too young for it to mean much. Christine is convinced I'm having a girl. She just has a feeling! I couldn't care less what I have . . . Please keep your fingers tightly crossed for us. A first baby at thirty-seven, with my history – I'm trying to relax and enjoy being pregnant, and I am happy, of course, I'm so terribly happy that it might be happening at

last, but I'm also very frightened. I'm due mid-December, and I know I won't relax till I hold him or her in my arms.

Helen, after some thought, had sent her a tapestry kit.

Take it out after Martha has been put to bed. It might stop you worrying for a while – and if you stick with it, you'll have a thing that says 'Home Sweet Home' that you can hang in the hall, or wherever. It seemed like the sort of thing that would suit the kind of home I imagine you to have (which is not in the least, as you've probably gathered, like the kind of home I have).

My fingers are tightly crossed. Let's hope for the best here. I've told Alice – presume that was OK – and she sends her good-luck wishes.

'She's having a *baby*?' Alice's face had been full of disbelief. 'Isn't she as old as you?' Ah, the tact of a teenage daughter.

'Actually, she's eight years younger than me. Not quite an old hag yet.'

Helen wondered sometimes, lying alone in bed, if she would ever meet another man, ever have another relationship. Forty-five wasn't old, far from it. She had years ahead of her, thirty or forty if she lived a natural life. Was she to spend it all alone once Alice had moved out, as she inevitably would? Was Helen destined to live out her days with just a second-hand cat for company?

No, not even the cat: they didn't live that long. On her own, then, unless someone came along who liked the look of her – and how likely was that, with no social outlets, no friends to go hunting with, no opportunities at all to meet people, apart from the various Christmas parties thrown by the publications she wrote for, which she still avoided?

'You'll have another drop,' her mother said.

'Better not, thanks.'

The other dire possibility, of course, was that her parents would become dependent on her. She might be forced to have one or both of them living with her – and since she couldn't see either of them moving willingly into her neighbourhood, she would probably be expected to return to their house: unthinkable prospect.

Maybe Sarah would take them into her nursing home. Or maybe her parents would totter on together without her help, dying conveniently in their sleep, preferably simultaneously, one fine night.

'I hope that cat doesn't have fleas,' her mother said. 'Especially if Alice is handling it.'

Helen was tempted then to tell the story of Alice's head lice, and the phone call from the school principal. So long ago that was now – Alice had been, what, five or six?

266

'Remember the fine-tooth comb?' she asked.

Her mother frowned. 'What?'

'You used it to make sure I had no head lice. I remember how it dug into my scalp.'

'*You* did it to *me*,' Alice put in. 'I hated it.'

'Why on earth would you bring that up now?' Helen's mother asked.

'No reason. I just remembered it. Must have been the talk of fleas.'

She'd say nothing. Whatever Gorbachev might believe, openness wasn't always the best policy.

SARAH

From the sitting room there came a sudden shriek. Christine carried on tossing clothes from the top shelf of the hotpress onto the little heap that was growing on the landing.

'Should we investigate?' Sarah asked, looking anxiously downstairs.

'Why? Oh, look,' pulling out a little orange jumper, 'Mam knitted this, remember? I must admit I always thought the colour was a bit sissy on Aidan, but everyone admired it.'

'Well, I love it,' Sarah said. 'I'd put that colour on girls or boys. I'd have put it on Martha if I'd known you still had it.'

'Would you? Sorry . . . Oh, here, these are sweet.'

Sarah took a miniature pair of blue and white checked trousers from her. Doll's clothes they looked like, all the tiny garments Christine was pulling out. Had Martha ever been that small?

'Oh God, look what I just found.' Christine held up a little mustard and green striped cardigan. 'I thought I'd thrown it out. Isn't it vile? Gráinne made it for Paddy. The only times I put it on him was when we were visiting them. I'll drop it into the next charity shop I pass.'

The relationship between Christine and her mother-in-law had been strained for years, largely because Christine had refused to name any of her sons after their paternal grandfather. 'I can't stand the name Victor,' she'd declared – and even though the remark had not, of course, been addressed directly to Gráinne, the message had been received.

No further sounds came from the sitting room. Presumably nobody was dead or badly injured. Sarah bent with difficulty and began gathering the clothes into her arms.

'Stop, I'll do that.' Christine closed the hotpress doors and scooped up the pile. 'I think that's everything – if I find any more I'll drop them over to you. You can go through them in the kitchen: it's warmer.'

Sarah followed her downstairs, holding tightly to the banisters. Feeling her way past each stair edge, unable to see her feet when she walked. An elephant, that's what she'd become. A big fat happy elephant, or maybe a deliriously joyful hippopotamus. Giant breasts, huge bottom, enormous balloon of a stomach. A mother-in-waiting, twenty-seven days to go till her son or daughter was born.

Blooming, she felt.

As Christine passed the sitting-room door, she called: 'Everything all right in there?'

'Yeah.' A ragged chorus.

In the kitchen she tumbled her armload onto the table. 'Right, have a look while I put the kettle on.'

'No tea for me,' Sarah told her, beginning to pick her way through the clothes. 'I'll be going to the loo all night as it is.'

'I remember that – it was awful. I was up every five minutes.'

'I don't mind.'

'I know you don't – you're the most uncomplaining pregnant woman I've ever met.' Christine rummaged under the sink and pulled out a couple of plastic bags. 'Here, you can put the ones you want into those. By the way, ye must be thrilled that Neil was taken on at the golf course.'

'We are. It's great news. They're opening in the New Year.' Sarah smiled at a little lilac T-shirt with a cartoon penguin on the front. 'This is so cute. The only thing is, he won't be able to take mornings off any more, so we'll have to find someone to look after Martha and the baby when I go back to work.'

'Have you anyone in mind?'

'Not yet, but we're saying it to everyone we know, so hopefully we'll get a recommendation.'

Christine took a blue cardigan from her and added it to the basket. 'Brian has a cousin, Noreen. She's a widow. Her husband died in a boating accident a few years back. You might remember.'

'Can't say I do.'

'Well, anyway, the reason I mentioned her was that Brian was telling me lately that the crèche where she worked closed down, so she might be interested if she hasn't found another job.'

In the act of folding a pair of pyjama bottoms, Sarah stopped. 'She worked in a crèche? Has she children of her own?'

'No, no children. She's a bit older than us, mid-forties, I think. I haven't met her all that much but she seems nice.'

'Where does she live?'

'Well, that's the only thing. She's on the other side of Naas, about twenty miles away, but I'm pretty sure she drives, so that mightn't be a problem.'

'Sounds promising. I'll mention her to Neil, see what he thinks . . . Right, that's it, thanks so much. And sorry that you have to run me home. I really must learn how to drive sometime.'

'No problem. I'll get the car keys.'

She disappeared as Sarah manoeuvred herself into her coat. One more week at the nursing home, then her maternity leave started. Five more lunches to cook, five more mornings of lumbering around the kitchen, her apron needing a pin for the past two months to keep it fastened at the back.

She regarded the basket of tiny clothes and imagined the little creature she'd be pulling them onto in just a few weeks. Never mind that it was a fortnight after her thirty-seventh birthday: she was fit and strong, and everything would be fine this time.

Her baby, her own flesh and blood, at long last. Was anyone as blessed as her?

HELEN

Sarah
The countdown is on, won't feel it now to your big day. Any urge yet to clean the house from top to bottom? Not that that happened to me with Alice, surprise surprise, but I believe it's a common enough phenomenon. Nesting, they call it. Maybe that's why my little fledgling and I are always at loggerheads – I didn't spring-clean the nest before she hatched.

You must be high as a kite. I wish you all the blessings in the world – if anyone deserves them you do, lady. Just don't forget to wait till they tell you to push, and squeeze Neil's hand to death – that's what it's there for. Good for him getting involved in the whole business: not many men have the guts. When Alice was born in '71 my husband wasn't allowed in, although he wanted to. I kicked up the king of all fusses, but got nowhere. At least that's changing now.

I'm sending my favourite bath oil. Put Neil on bedtime-story duty, fill the bath, add a generous slosh and wallow in all your enormous glory. It will make you feel sexy and sleepy and deliciously scented, a glorious combination. (And yes, in case you're wondering, Mrs Ripe-as-a-Peach, gentle sex is not only allowed but <u>recommended</u> at this stage, to encourage Baby to think about putting in an appearance. As regards positions, I'm sure you'll figure it out. Oh, stop blushing: you're a married woman.)

On to more mundane matters. The house next door is for sale. A sign went up the other day, which I presume means cranky neighbour must have died. I feel a bit guilty now for all the times I wished him a million miles away. Wonder who'll move in. Wouldn't say no to a rich widower, or maybe another toyboy. At this stage I'm not fussy.

Brace yourself – Breen is retiring. I know, I was devastated too. Actually he's not the worst of them. I may even find myself missing the withering sarcasm now and again. I can gather from his PA that the home front isn't the happiest – you'd wonder why they don't just split up if they're not getting on. Maybe she's loaded, and he can't bring himself to leave all that cash. Anyway, he's clearing his desk next week, end of an era. He's taking early retirement, can't be more than sixty. Must have made a pile.

There's a big farewell do at the newspaper

office, so I'm leaving Alice with my parents for the night – much to her disgust – and putting on my glad rags. I figure at forty-five my days of catching anyone's eye are numbered, and I fancy a last fling before hanging up my lacy bra.

Alice continues to cause me sleepless nights. She's sulking at the moment – what's new? – because I wouldn't let her go to an all-night party last Saturday at someone's friend's house. An all-night party at sixteen. And I'm sure I caught booze on her breath the other evening, when she was supposed to have been in the library with Karen. Plus ça change. Maybe you can send her a photo of the new baby when it comes – might keep her on an even keel for a while.

Right, time for my lonesome double-bed-for-one. I'll be thinking of you over the next while. Let me know the minute there's news – get Neil to send me a postcard or a telegram or something.

H xx

SARAH

'You're doing it all wrong,' Martina said crossly from her garden seat. 'You're cutting it back far too much. There'll be nothing left.'

Charlie snipped off another twiggy stalk. 'You don't know what you're talking about. It's been neglected for years, it needs a hard pruning.'

'Well, the way you're going at it, it hasn't a hope of flowering next spring.'

'Maybe not, but in the long term it'll be healthier.' He continued working his slow, shaky way around the bush, Martina glaring at him.

'What's the matter?' he asked, after several seconds of silence. 'Cat got your tongue?'

'I still say you're taking off far too much,' she snapped.

'You've made that perfectly clear, thank you. Now, unless you have anything more constructive to say, I suggest you keep your mouth shut.'

From the other side of the open kitchen window, as she chopped carrots for the lamb casserole, Sarah could hear their conversation quite clearly. If someone didn't intervene soon they'd kill each

275

other. Martina would stab him with the pruning shears, or Charlie would goad her to death.

Or maybe they secretly enjoyed the encounters. Martina had certainly never spent as much time outdoors as she did since she'd appointed herself guardian of the shrubs – and if nothing else, she was company for Charlie as he set about putting a shape on the much-neglected nursing-home grounds. He seemed well able for her.

Sarah tipped the carrots into the casserole dishes, marvelling at the difference a few months had made. Charlie would never be robust – the pneumonia he'd been suffering from when they'd found him had weakened his heart – but as the weeks had passed he'd recovered enough strength to approach Matron, about a month after his arrival at St Sebastian's, and offer to do a little light gardening.

'I couldn't turn him down,' she'd told Sarah, 'even though I had no idea whether he'd make it better or worse. But I figured he wouldn't have the stamina to do much damage, and if it gave him a reason to get up in the mornings . . .'

As far as Sarah could see, Charlie was doing no damage at all. He couldn't manage more than an hour or so in the garden on the fine days, but even with such slow progress there was sureness about the way he worked, confidence in his movements that spoke of some expertise as he clipped and pruned and weeded. Six months on, everyone was remarking on the difference he was making.

Everyone apart from Martina, of course, who seemed outraged at his presence in the shrubbery. Maybe she resented the newest arrival having the gall to get involved, however peripherally, in the running of St Sebastian's. Since Dorothy Phelan's death last year, Martina had become the nursing home's longest-serving resident; probably felt Charlie should have asked her permission.

Poor Charlie, not physically capable of living on his own again – which meant, inevitably, that his house had gone on the market, needing to be sold to fund his nursing-home fees. Sarah had always thought it must be a terrible wrench, knowing that you'd seen the last of your old home. All the apple tarts or chicken soup in the world wouldn't make up for that loss.

Her efforts to locate his cat in the spring had come to nothing, despite a hopeful start. The affable-sounding man from the garden centre had taken the nursing-home number and the cat's description.

'We'll drop by anytime either of us is in the area and have a scout around,' he'd promised Sarah. 'We'll let you know if we see any sign of it.'

And to give him his due, he'd rung back the following week, and the week after that, but he had no good news.

'We've both dropped by a few times, went around the back and had a good look, but there's no sign.'

Sarah had thanked him and told him not to worry about phoning again unless the cat was spotted.

Her hopes weren't high: what were the chances of the cat still hanging around a deserted house, months after anyone had fed it there? All she could hope was that it had been taken in by someone who'd seen it wandering about.

'George and his colleague are still looking,' she'd told Charlie – but she'd known by the resigned expression on his face that he had as little hope as she did, and her heart had gone out to him.

She added chopped onions to the casserole dishes, checking the time on the kitchen clock and wondering what was keeping the new junior. How long did it take to set a few tables for dinner? Bernadette would have had it done long before this. Two years since her retirement, replaced with a succession of lesser-paid juniors due to cutbacks, and Sarah still missed her cheerful efficiency around the kitchen. Another few minutes and she'd have to go looking for help to lift the casseroles into the oven.

She took jugs of stock from the fridge and spooned off the thin layer of fat that had formed on them. No matter, Una would reappear soon – and today Sarah wasn't letting anything bother her. Today her maternity leave was beginning, with just three weeks to go until her baby arrived.

At the thought she felt another butterfly of nervous energy – all morning she'd been having queer little flutters. She poured the stock onto the meat and vegetable mixtures. They weren't unpleasant as much as uncomfortable, more of a twinge than a flutter. She'd have a cup of pepper-mint tea when she got home. That would settle her.

Neil was coming with Martha to collect her. She hadn't cycled to work since the fourth month, doctor's orders. 'We're taking no chances with this one,' he'd said, and Sarah had obeyed. If he'd told her to sleep with an ice block under her feet and live on raw onions for the duration of the preg-nancy she'd have done it, so anxious was she to look after her precious growing baby.

But the only change to her routine he'd suggested was to stop cycling, so Neil, her father and Christine had been taking it in turns to ferry her to and from work. Such a nuisance she'd become: just as well she was finishing up today.

Another twinge as she added seasoning to the casserole dishes. Stronger than before, strong enough to stop her in her tracks and put a hand to her bump. Had she eaten anything funny? Was it a touch of indigestion? She walked slowly to the back door: maybe she just needed some fresh air.

And maybe she should phone the doctor when they got home, just to see what he said. She opened the door and stepped outside – and as she did, she felt a strong gush of warmth between her legs. She looked down and saw dark spatters on the pale grey gravel, below the mountain of her white apron.

Her heart stopped. She gripped the door jamb and held on tightly. Sweat popped on her forehead.

'Martina,' she called, in a voice that was far from steady.

Helen
I'm under strict instructions to send this postcard as soon as I can. As of yesterday, Tuesday, we have a son, Stephen, seven pounds two ounces. He arrived three weeks early but all is well. Sarah will write as soon as she can with details.
  All the best
  Neil Flannery

Dear Helen
Thanks so much for the beautiful little bootees and hat that arrived this morning – and I'm afraid you're right: I didn't for a minute think you'd knit them! And you're so good not to forget Martha – she loves her pink umbrella, takes it everywhere, and I mean everywhere: it was floating in the bath last night!
  Sorry it's taken me over a week to write. Things as you can imagine have been hectic since they let us go home. I'm snatching the chance now, with both children asleep at the same time – minor miracle! Let's hope I can get this done before all hell breaks loose again, or before I fall asleep myself!
  Helen, it was terrifying. My waters broke while I was still at work, three weeks before my due date – in fact, it was the day my

280

maternity leave was due to start! I was on my own when it happened – my junior was setting tables in the dining room – and I'd stepped outside for some air, and of course when it happened all I could think of was the other times, and I couldn't bear the thought of things going wrong again. Thank goodness two of the residents were in the garden so I called them – and Helen, would you believe one of them was Martina, the one I'm always quoting who finds fault with everything! Well, I have to say she was simply wonderful. She sat me down and told me I was going to be fine, and she sent Charlie, the other resident, off to get help (you should have heard her ordering him around – I suspect she was in her element!). While we were waiting she actually patted my shoulder and said all the right things – it was just a baby, and women had been having them for thousands of years, and they came when they were ready, not when we were, and why should mine be any different – and you know, it was just what I needed to hear to stop me going hysterical!

Thank goodness our driver Dan was around. He drove me straight to the hospital with one of the staff nurses, who waited with me until Neil arrived, in a complete flap. He'd tried to call Christine and his mother so he could drop Martha off to one of them, but both of them were out, and then he couldn't find my address book to get Dad's number, so in the end he left Martha with a new neighbour we hardly know. Such a fuss I caused everyone!

Helen, what an experience – well, you know what giving birth is like. And I know it was terribly painful, and it seemed to go on forever, and poor Neil's hand was black and blue from my squeezing it during the contractions – I'm surprised I didn't break something – but when they laid Stephen on my chest and I looked at his squashed little face, I forgot completely about the pain and flooded over with emotion – well, you can imagine, you know how soft I am! My very own darling child, at long last – I could hardly see him for tears! (And yes, even writing this is setting me off again – I'm hopeless!)

The other great news – not that it can compete – is that Neil has got the maintenance job at the golf course, which he's thrilled about, and Christine was telling me about a cousin of Brian's who might be interested in looking after the children when I go back to work in January. We're going to meet her as soon as we can and see what she's like. She's been working in a crèche so it sounds as if she would be suitable. I hope she is – the fact that she's Brian's cousin makes her family, practically.

I can hear Stephen – he's just woken up – just as well I'd pretty much finished this!

Thanks again, you're a love,
Sarah xxx

Dear Alice

I've sure you've heard our wonderful news from your mum, but I wanted to send you your very own photo of our darling Stephen. He's just adorable, with my husband's eyes and my nose (so I'm told) – and just look at all that black hair! When we got Martha she was completely bald, so this baby is very different!

Everyone is mad about him: his three cousins (all boys) are delighted he's a boy, and Nuala, my husband's mum, is thrilled that we called him Stephen after her husband, who died ten years ago, just before I married Neil. Martha is very happy to have a new brother, but disappointed that she's not allowed to wheel him around in her doll's pram!

I hope you're well, and that school is going OK. (Congratulations on the Inter Cert, by the way – you've probably forgotten all about it by now, but I was delighted to hear the news.) Your mum tells me you're hoping to go to art college; really hope that works out.

I'm sending a picture that Martha drew for you. It's an elephant, in case you don't recognise it! She loves drawing too.

Well, it's time to feed my little man – I can't believe how hungry he is! – so I'd better stop.

Take care, Alice.

Love from an exhausted, but terribly happy, Sarah! xx

HELEN

'It won't be the same without you.'

Breen eyed the glass in her hand. 'How many of those have you had?'

'Not as many as I'd need,' Helen told him cheerfully, 'to tell you what I really think of you.'

She was on her third generous whiskey, at the safe stage of inebriation. Happy enough to be pretty much at peace with the rest of the world, Breen included, and lucid enough not to mess it up by talking rubbish.

'You must admit,' she went on, 'that we've had our moments.'

'We certainly have. I've lost count of the times I wanted to strangle you.'

She laughed. 'Not half as many times as I've wanted to push you off the nearest cliff.'

He gave a small smile as he raised his coffee mug to his lips.

'You're not drinking?' Helen enquired. 'Afraid you'll lose the run of yourself and say something nice to me?'

The left corner of his mouth twitched. 'Something like that.'

There were about fifty of them milling around the hotel function room that had been booked for the event. Pretty much the same crowd here tonight, she imagined, who had attended the long-ago Christmas party, but the surroundings were slightly more impressive than the newspaper office building.

The refreshments were better too: the departure of the newspaper's longest-serving editor – twenty-six years of telling everyone what to do – clearly warranted something more exciting than a chicken drumstick and glass of cut-price wine. *Goodbye and Good Luck*, a banner proclaimed, hanging on the wall above the small but beautifully stocked bar.

Breen had noticed her dress – or, rather, he'd noticed the length of it. Helen had seen him taking it in as she'd approached. She had good legs, and the dress, hanging in her wardrobe since minis had been fashionable, made the most of them: an inch higher and her underwear would show. Let the fashion magazines with their longer hemlines get stuffed – she'd wear what she liked.

Breen, no doubt, disapproved. Look at him, with his snow-white shirt and dark grey suit: the essence of respectability. Not that he didn't look well, even if it pained her to admit it. Still could do with taking the scowl off his face, though. She wondered where his wife was, why she hadn't bothered to come to her husband's retirement party.

'You never once told me that you were happy

with my work,' she said. 'In all the years I've been writing for you, I never heard a single positive comment.'

'Fishing for compliments, O'Dowd? You disappoint me.'

O'Dowd again. He did it to annoy her, she was sure.

'I never rejected anything you submitted,' he went on, 'even the ones I didn't ask for. You were paid on time, and paid well. Isn't that enough for you?'

'*Jesus*,' she said in exasperation, 'you just can't do it. You wouldn't recognise an encouraging word if it hit you in the face, you cranky old bastard.'

And before he could respond to that, they were approached by one of Breen's assistant editors, who slapped him on the back and asked loudly what he wanted to drink. Hoping, no doubt, to step into the soon-to-be-vacated slot, no replacement announced yet.

Helen moved away and wove through the crowd back towards the bar, to where the interesting-looking blond barman who'd caught her eye earlier was pouring drinks and opening mixers. Foreign accent – Scandinavian, maybe.

She didn't talk to Breen again. She pulled up a barstool and introduced herself to Torvald from Norway, and discovered that he was tending bar in the evenings while he studied Celtic literature in Trinity.

She was still sitting there when Breen was presented

with a set of golf clubs. She listened as he made a brief acceptance speech and joined in the clapping when he'd finished.

And by the time, an hour later, Torvald was helping her into her coat and whispering what he was planning to do to her, Breen had long since left the building.

Dear Mrs Flannery

Congratulations on your new baby, he's lovely. Martha's elephant picture is so cute. I drew our neighbour's cat for her in return, I hope she likes it. We started looking after the cat when our neighbour got sick, but now he's dead so it looks like we get to keep it.

My mother just shouted up that dinner is ready. She's in a bad mood today. She was out at a party last night and I bet she got really drunk.

love Alice x

1990

SARAH

'Martha, leave your brother's plate alone. You know he doesn't like you touching his food . . . Stephen, eat your yogurt, please, lovey – no, no honey in your hair, darling. Martha, you put that cracker down *right* now, or I'll tell Noreen there's no park allowed. I mean it.'

Breakfasts were hectic, with Neil usually gone to work and Sarah coping on her own till the cavalry arrived. Two-year-old Stephen at the stage where he was insisting on feeding himself, and not quite capable of carrying it off without mishap; Martha, almost five, starting school in September, and equally determined to inject her unique brand of mischievousness into the proceedings.

Sarah slapped toast onto a plate and cast around for the butter. 'One of these days I'll wake up and my hair will be completely grey.'

Martha regarded her mother's light brown head with interest. 'Who'll make it grey?'

'You will, you monkey,' Sarah replied, dropping a hasty kiss onto her strawberry blonde curls, 'you and your brother. But I still love you.'

She never tired of telling them; she drenched them

with love from morning to night. Neil said she smothered them, but she didn't care. She was their mother: she had every right to tell them how much they meant to her, every opportunity she got.

It frightened her sometimes, this overwhelming love. Its power terrified her. She would study other parents, in the supermarket or the doctor's waiting room, or in a queue for the cinema, and she would wonder if they felt the same crushing weight of love for their children that she did whenever she looked at Martha or Stephen.

She wondered if Helen felt it for Alice. It didn't come across in her letters: Helen rarely said anything positive about her daughter. In fact, her comments about Alice, who admittedly sounded like a handful, were mainly disparaging, but Sarah assumed that was just Helen's way. Of course she loved Alice – what mother didn't love her own child?

As she was taking the marmalade from the fridge, a sudden smash made her wheel around. Martha's cup lay in fragments on the floor, in a puddle of milk.

'Oh, what happened here?' Sarah cried, dropping the marmalade on the worktop and reaching for the dustpan and brush. 'What did you *do*?'

'My jumper just knocked it by an accident,' Martha said, her voice wobbling. 'I didn't do it on purpose, Mummy.'

Sarah shovelled the shards into the pan. 'I know you didn't, pet, but you need to be a bit more—'

'Morning, everyone!'

All three turned. Stephen's chubby face lit up. 'Nory!'

He reached his arms towards her – and Sarah tamped down the stab of jealousy as Noreen slipped out of her coat and crossed the room, laughing, to gather him up and hug him.

'Haven't you finished your breakfast yet, you scallywag?' Without waiting for his reply she sat on his chair, set him on her lap and began spooning up the remaining yogurt – and he, the traitor who refused to let Sarah feed him, took it from her uncomplainingly.

'My cup falled down,' Martha told her. 'It got all broke. Mummy putted it in the bin.'

'Oh dear . . . Sarah, leave that, I can do it when you're gone.'

'All done.' Sarah took the dishcloth to the sink and squeezed it out. 'Neil might be back early, he's not sure.'

'No problem.' Noreen regarded the two children. 'So what'll we do today? How about a picnic in the park?'

'Yaaay!'

Cycling to work a few minutes later, her nose pink in the February chill, Sarah tried to recall what life had been like before Noreen's arrival. Hard to imagine how they'd coped, given how invaluable she'd become to them.

She turned up without fail each morning and stayed until either Sarah or Neil got home, and timing was never an issue. In between keeping the children fed and entertained she somehow managed to deal with whatever household tasks were outstanding. She emptied the laundry basket and pegged out the washing, she cleaned windows, made beds and ironed shirts. She'd even mown the lawn once, laughing when Sarah had protested the following morning.

'What else would we be doing? Martha was a great help, emptying the grass box for me, weren't you, dote?'

The children adored her, and Neil approved of her too. Sarah had come home from work on one memorable occasion to find the four of them sitting cross-legged on the sitting-room carpet, each holding a tiny plastic cup. A tea towel spread on the floor between them held a miniature milk jug and sugar bowl, a normal-sized plate of real biscuits and the small, battered metal teapot that Sarah used for her single breakfast cup if Neil had left the house before her.

Martha wore one of Sarah's aprons, doubled over several times at the waist. Stephen scattered biscuit crumbs on the carpet as he munched.

'Tea party,' Noreen had said, straight-faced. 'You're just in time. Martha, anything left in that pot?'

And Martha had poured her mother a cup of 'tea', and Sarah had sat and eaten biscuits, and given thanks, for the umpteenth time, for Noreen.

Shame that she didn't make more of an effort

to smarten herself up, though. No makeup, no attempt to disguise the white strands scattered through her reddish hair. Out-of-date clothing in pastel shades that didn't suit her pale colouring, shoes that never seemed to match what she was wearing. And that awful brown canvas bag, winter and summer.

Clearly, she needed help – which was why Sarah had come up with her plan. Their birthdays were days apart at the end of October, with Noreen almost exactly ten years older. Sarah hadn't given this year's birthday too much thought – who wanted to be reminded that a milestone birthday was on the way? – until Christine had suggested a party.

'You really should – when do you get a chance to dress up? I've already warned Brian I'm going to have a big bash for my fortieth. And you'll get lots of gorgeous presents.'

And the more Sarah had thought about it, the more the idea began to appeal. Why not celebrate the fact that at forty she was happier than she'd ever been, with two beautiful children and a wonderful husband? Why not mark this milestone by dressing up and eating cake with friends and family? It was only a number.

And then she thought of Noreen, hitting fifty a few days earlier. Why not make it a joint party? Why shouldn't both of them mark their birthdays? And to make it more of an occasion, why not invite Noreen's friends in secret and surprise her on the night? Even though it was still months away, where was the harm in planning ahead?

'She has a sister,' Christine said, when Sarah put the idea to her. 'I could get her number from Brian' – and, just like that, the plan was hatched. The sister, whose name was Joanna, had been briefed and had agreed to help. Everything was set.

And the best part, the part that Sarah had told nobody about, was that she'd also come up with a man for Noreen. Single, of course – never married, as far as she knew. Not handsome in the strict sense but terribly nice, and only a few years older than Noreen, ten at the very most. Sarah would invite him to the party and make the introductions, and Noreen would be looking her best, and hopefully they'd hit it off.

As she approached the gates of St Sebastian's, the man in question appeared behind the wheel of the familiar yellow minibus. Sarah raised a hand in greeting and Dan, the nursing home's driver and general handyman, waved back before turning onto the road and moving off.

HELEN

She sat in front of the television and watched as Nelson Mandela walked to freedom after being locked up for twenty-seven years. She looked at the beaming face of his wife Winnie, walking hand in hand with him. She listened to the loud cheers from the crowds of South Africans, black and white, who had gathered to witness history, and she could feel the hope that here, at last, was the beginning of the end of their struggle.

When the newsreader moved on to another item she got up, leaving the television on. She left the room and climbed the stairs. She opened the door to Alice's empty bedroom and stood on the threshold.

The single bed was unmade, the covers carelessly thrown back: in all her eighteen years, had Alice once made her bed? The art books, always piled higgledy-piggledy on the floor by the radiator, were gone. The top of the dressing-table was bare, except for a single lidless lipstick wand and the tiny curl of a silver earring back.

Alice's records were gone too, her Smiths and her Bruce Springsteens and her Pet Shop Boys, all vanished from the wooden crate under the window that she'd stacked them in.

Helen crossed the floor to the narrow wardrobe, on whose top sat Nelly, the blue elephant that Breen had sent to heal a long-ago broken wrist. She opened the door and saw a clutch of wire hangers. Was there anything as dismal as the clatter of empty hangers? Nothing, not even a shoe, not even a goddamn insole.

She opened drawers in the dressing-table and found a used postage stamp, still attached to a raggedy piece of envelope, a paperclip and one green ankle sock, balled in on itself.

She slipped off her shoes and got into the bed and pulled the rumpled blankets up around her. She closed her eyes and pressed them to her face. She breathed them in.

Alice.

Her torment, her scourge. The battles that had been fought between them, the doors that had been slammed. Alice, the cause of countless sleepless nights, grounded for half her life. Stubborn, sulky Alice, her precious rebel child.

'Don't forget to feed the cat,' she'd said to Helen the day before, looking unbearably young in her red plastic raincoat, the last bag slung over her shoulder as she'd stood waiting to pack it into the back of Jackie's battered van. 'His bowl is under the hedge.'

'I know where it is.' Helen, with her arms wrapped tightly around herself, biting the inside of her cheek to stop her mouth trembling. 'Ring

298

when you get there, OK? Doesn't matter what time. Find a phone. Reverse the charges if you can't get change.'

Off with two other art-college dropouts, the three of them having decided, after a single term, that working for nothing in an eco-something-or-other outfit in the middle of Wales was preferable to getting a proper qualification. Nineteen in a few weeks: what could Helen do except give her enough money to ensure she didn't starve and wave her off?

'So . . .' Alice had stood uncertainly in front of her, and Helen had reached across and given her a quick kiss on the cheek. No hug: a hug would have undone her. No declaration of anything: they'd never learnt how.

'Mind yourself. Take care. Don't do anything stupid.' Helen rubbing her hands together just to have something to do with them, all her effort concentrated on not falling apart. 'Get in, you'll freeze. Ring me.'

Alice had clambered into the van's single front seat beside Dermot, whose girlfriend had dumped him at Christmas and who was probably planning to console himself with his two travelling companions once they'd got to Wales. Jackie had ground the gears, and the van, which surely wouldn't take them as far as the end of the street, let alone Wales, had spluttered off. Helen had turned abruptly, before it was out of sight, and gone back into the empty house.

She pushed back the blankets and got out of Alice's bed and left the room. She closed the door softly – no more slamming now – and walked slowly down the stairs and back into the sitting room, where she stared unseeing at the television screen.

Alice's phone call had come several hours later. Well past midnight, long after Helen, sitting halfway up the stairs with an empty whiskey glass, had decided that the van had burst a tyre on a Welsh motorway and smashed into the central barrier, killing the three of them instantly.

She'd stumbled down and picked up the phone, sure it was the police, expecting an unfamiliar, concerned male voice asking in a singsong accent if he had the right address for Alice Fitzpatrick.

'Yes?'

'Mum?' Alice had sounded wide awake, and far away, and very much alive. 'I'm on a pay phone. It's gobbling money so I can't stay long.'

Relief had flooded through Helen. She'd closed her eyes. 'Where are you?'

'We're here – we're at the centre. We've just arrived. We ran out of petrol about twenty miles away. We left Dermot minding the car and Jackie and I hitched a lift to the nearest petrol station, and then we asked a lorry driver we met there to bring us back. His accent was gas.'

She'd sounded happy. Helen had decided not to dwell on the image of her climbing into a stranger's car, not to mention a strange lorry driver's cab. She'd leant against the banister, suddenly bone weary.

300

'Go to bed now,' she'd said. 'It's late. Drop me a line when you get a chance. Ring if you need money.'

After hanging up – keep warm, she'd forgotten to say keep warm – she'd refilled her glass and brought it upstairs to bed. This morning she'd woken with an impressive headache and a mouth as dry as straw. Forty-eight in a fortnight, and still giving herself hangovers.

She turned off the television. Nothing but bad news, apart from Mandela; nothing but wars and famines and terrorism, Ceauşescu and his wife shot to death in Romania on Christmas Day, two pensioners put up against a wall and riddled with bullets. More bombs in the North, no sign of peace after more than twenty years of bloodshed. People crushed to death at a football match, the ground splitting open in San Francisco. Who needed to have all that thrown at them night after night?

She lit a cigarette and sat alone in the sitting room. She listened to the ticking of the mantel clock and thought again about her daughter. Left home, the Irish Sea between the two of them now. No qualifications, nothing to show for thirteen years of education.

Artistic talent certainly, but what use was talent without something to harness it and structure it and make it work for you? What good was being able to draw if you'd thrown away your chance to channel it into some kind of career?

Listen to her: she sounded like her parents so

many years ago, scandalised when Helen had refused to go to college, horrified all over again when she'd thrown up her job to marry a musician and raise a child. And yes, she could see their point now, damn it. If she'd done a course in journalism after school she'd have been well established by the time she'd met Cormac, could have made a proper career out of it instead of living from cheque to cheque like she did now. No savings to speak of, nothing put aside for the future, when younger writers would push her aside.

Maybe Alice would go back to college. Maybe she'd see the attraction of a qualification and a decent job when the novelty of living on brown rice and lentils had worn off.

Helen stubbed out her cigarette wearily. This was it then. This was her life now. Watching for the postman every morning, waiting for the phone to ring. Drinking a little more each evening, telling herself it did no harm, until she woke up one morning on the kitchen floor.

Oh, for Christ's sake. 'Get a grip,' she said aloud. She left the room and went out to the back garden. She called the cat and he came padding slowly towards her from under the hedge.

'Come in,' she said. 'You're better than nothing.'

Back in the sitting room she pulled a writing pad from the drawer under the television. The cat jumped lightly onto an armchair and sat regarding her solemnly as she began to write.

Sarah

Sorry it's been a while, things have been a bit weird here lately. First thing that happened, just after Christmas, was that Alice announced she'd quit art college. Big shock, never saw it coming. I did a rant, of course, but it fell, as usual, on deaf ears. Long story short, she moved out yesterday, went to Wales of all places, with two others she met in college – seems they cooked up this big plan between them.

They're working for some environmental crowd based in the middle of nowhere – don't ask me what they'll be doing, keeping an eye on the world, it sounds like – and of course, all they're getting in return is meals and accommodation. Can you imagine the set-up? I'd like to think she'll have her own room, or at least share with other females (she went off with one of each) but who knows? I warned her to write, so she'd better.

In other news, my father, who's eighty-two, had a pretty major stroke last month, and has been in hospital since then. He can't talk or move his left side. I call to see him a couple of times a week, but all I can do is sit there. You may have gathered that I've never been close to either of my folks – I'm not entirely sure that having a child was ever on their to-do list – but I can feel sympathy for the way he is now. It's weird to see him so helpless; he was always a big shot with plenty to say. My mother has pretty much taken up residence there, spends practically all her time in his room. According to his doctor, he could last for years like this or go in the morning, which isn't much help.

Nothing else, really. Work is work. Two books to review and a piece (again) on Valentine's Day in the pipeline. Yawn. Bring back Breen: at least rowing with him kept things interesting.

My new neighbours are having work done on the house; I dread to think what condition it was in when they got it, empty for nearly three years. Probably paid nothing for it. The front is like a builder's yard right now, stacks of timber, towers of roof slates. Old owner would be spinning in his grave if he could see it. His lawn is ruined, and the hedge he was always clipping is a mess – they're replacing it with a wall, apparently. At least they haven't asked me to go halves, which I couldn't afford, now that I have a daughter earning nothing in Wales who'll probably look for cheques with frightening regularity.

She stopped and laid down her pen. She sat back and looked into the cold fireplace, the ashes from their last fire two nights ago still lying in a little heap there. The room was chilly, but it seemed wasteful to light the fire, or switch on the central heating, for just one person. Tomorrow she'd find a cheap fan heater. She picked up her pen again.

I've just realised something. I've never lived alone, never in my life till now.

She stopped again, rubbed at an itchy spot on her cheek, realised it was wet, tickled by a tear that had come out of nowhere.

I have to admit that I'm missing her.

Another tear splatted onto the page, just below the last line. She blotted it carefully with her sleeve.

'What are you looking at?' she asked the cat. 'Haven't you ever seen anyone cry before?'

He didn't blink, his yellow eyes fixed calmly on hers.

She laid the pad aside and sank her face into her hands.

SARAH

Sarah stood at the kitchen window and watched as the old woman with the bent back snipped excruciatingly slowly at the forsythia, as she'd been doing every dry day for the past two weeks.

No one had passed any remarks. No one had wondered aloud why she was doing the very same thing she'd objected to when Charlie was alive, clipping and pruning and weeding, maintaining the garden he'd restored. Taking up, literally, where he'd left off, working determinedly with set shoulders and pursed mouth, as if she was on a mission and would not be deflected.

Which, of course, Sarah thought, was exactly the case. Martina was atoning for her contrariness. She was attempting, by carrying on the work Charlie had begun, to make amends for her harassment of him. How sad that they hadn't been able to work together in the few years he'd been with them.

Martina was eighty-nine now and slower on her feet; arthritis had curved her back and swollen her knuckles. But each day that the rain stayed away she did what little she could in the garden, talking to no one as she worked. Alone with her thoughts, whatever they might be.

Had she ever confided in anyone in the whole of her life? Had she ever spoken of what was in her heart? Sarah still tapped on her door occasionally, but Martina seemed to have little interest now in conversation, barely responding to Sarah's comments, her gaze drifting more and more to the garden and the shrubs she tended.

And Helen, who as far as Sarah could make out had never been close to her parents, had lost her father in March, two months earlier. So sad to think they'd never connected in any meaningful way while he was alive. Did Helen regret it now, did she wish she'd tried to have some kind of relationship with him when they were both adults?

'I'm so glad I married you,' Sarah told Neil that evening, as they bathed the children.

He looked at her. 'What brought that on?'

She soaped Martha's arms. 'Nothing. I just wanted to say it. I'm glad you asked me, and I'm glad I said yes. I think it's terribly sad when people are afraid to communicate what's in their hearts.'

He lifted Stephen from the bath and wrapped him in a towel. 'I think your mum's been drinking.'

Sarah frowned. 'Don't say that.'

'Sorry,' he said, reaching for the talc bottle at the end of the bath. 'Just kidding.'

Sarah turned to Martha. 'Men don't know how

to talk about their feelings but ladies do. That's the big difference between us.'

Neil pulled a pyjama top over Stephen's head. 'I'll be late tomorrow, got a call from a potential new customer outside Naas. I promised I'd drop over after work and have a look.'

The golf course hadn't lasted; just two years before they'd admitted defeat and closed the gates. But Neil had survived, pursuing job leads doggedly, poring over landscaping books in his spare time, broadening his skills whenever he had the opportunity.

'Out you come, lovey.' Sarah helped Martha from the water. 'How late is late?'

'Could be eight or nine, could take a while. They've half an acre out the back they want to talk to me about: sounds like they want me to design a garden for them.'

'You'll be well able.' She dusted Martha with talc, stroked it onto the soft, warm skin. 'By the way, I invited you-know-who to the party and he's coming.'

'Who?'

'You know, the person I told you about, for N-o-r-e-e-n.'

'What does that spell?' Martha asked.

'It spells "only for grown-ups",' Neil replied, getting to his feet, lifting Stephen into his arms. 'Right, Mister, let's get you to bed.'

'What do you think?' Sarah called after him.

His voice drifted back. 'Fine, if you want.'

She turned back to Martha, who was pushing her feet into her rabbit slippers. 'OK? All set?'

He could show a bit more enthusiasm for her idea – and it would have been nice if he'd said he was glad he'd married her too. That was men for you, hopeless.

HELEN

She pulled the sheet from her typewriter and set it on top of the others: five thousand words on Ireland beginning to drag itself out of recession for a new magazine she'd approached last month. Unemployment at its lowest in years, emigration and inflation down, exports up, all the signs there for the long-awaited recovery. She'd pitched the idea to them and they'd gone for it, and now it was done.

She glanced at her watch. Send it off this afternoon, catch the half-four collection if she didn't delay. They'd have it a couple of days before the deadline, a mark in her favour.

She'd never delivered anything early to Breen – it was more fun to let him wait, let him sweat a bit. She remembered their testy exchanges, neither of them giving an inch. 'Don't push me, O'Dowd,' he'd warn, and she'd push a bit more, see how far she could go.

There were no heated exchanges with his successor at the newspaper, a younger man named Ryan. There weren't very many exchanges at all – these days she was contacted by various sub-editors, all of whom were terribly official, none of whom she could distinguish from any other. Breen, it would seem, had been unique.

'I miss him,' Catherine had confessed to Helen, a few weeks after his retirement. 'He wasn't always the easiest to work for, but at least he was interesting. Now everything's so samey and organised and . . . ordinary.'

Yes: whatever else you could accuse him of, Breen had never been ordinary.

Helen slipped the pages into an envelope. She'd drop in on her mother after the post office: she was due a visit. Twice a week she called these days, sometimes more often.

Different now, without her father and Alice around, just her and her mother. Easier, in a way – or maybe Helen was mellowing. Maybe she was finally learning to loosen her hold on the resentments of the past. For whatever reason, she didn't dread the visits to her family home like she used to.

Helen had heard the news of her father's death – less than two months after his stroke, and only a few weeks after Alice had left for Wales – with a detached sadness, the kind of one-degree-removed sympathy you might feel on hearing of a distant relative's death, or a fatal car accident on the news involving some perfect stranger.

Her mother, on the other hand, mourned him with a deep and genuine grief, often opening the door to Helen in those first few weeks with reddened eyes, or breaking off in the middle of a sentence to press a hand to her mouth. Her grief made her gentler, rubbed her corners soft. It also caused her, after the fierce rawness of it had passed, to draw her only daughter closer, to welcome her with what seemed like genuine warmth when she called.

'How's Alice?' she would ask. 'How's the job going in Wales? What are you working on now? Why don't you stay for dinner? Where did you get that lovely sweater?'

Showing an interest, listening to Helen's answers as if she cared. For Helen, lonesome after Alice, gone four months now, it was oddly comforting. She and her mother had no one around them now but one another, and they must make do with that, and be satisfied with it.

She slipped the envelope into her bag and took her umbrella from its stand – rain off and on for the past week – and walked to the front door. As she reached to open it the bell rang, startling her.

'Oh – hello there. That was quick.'

The man standing on her doorstep smiled, showing large, even teeth. He was a big, white-haired, white-bearded bear of a man, with the reddish-brown complexion of someone who spent more time out of doors than in. His grey corduroy trousers were bald in several places, his faded blue T-shirt strained over his wide chest.

'Can I help you?' Helen asked. A van was parked on the road outside that struck a faint chord. *F&G Garden Centre*: maybe they touted for business around the neighbourhood. Maybe he was hoping to flog her a few shrubs today. If that was the case he'd be in for a big disappointment.

'This will probably sound a little odd,' he said, his smile staying put, 'but I was driving by just now and I spotted a cat in your front garden. It's disappeared now – hopped over the wall when I opened the gate – but I'm just wondering if by any remote chance it's Charlie's.'

What was he on about? 'I don't know anyone called Charlie,' Helen told him, stepping out and pulling the door closed behind her, 'and actually I'm in a bit of a—'

'I beg your pardon, I should have made myself clearer. I meant Charlie Malone, who used to live next door.'

Helen, about to step past him, stopped. Charlie Malone. Malone.

'The thing is, this is going to sound a little strange, but we got a phone call at the garden centre – well, I did actually, a long time ago, two or three years it must be – asking about his cat . . .'

Charlie Malone. She'd never known his first name – or maybe she had, years ago. Maybe Cormac had mentioned it way back. But for as long as she could remember he'd been Malone. But he was dead, wasn't he? Why was this man, this stranger, looking for his cat now?

'. . . and it's a bit of a long story really, but he was trying to locate it, and he'd given the lady at the nursing home our number as a contact—'

'Nursing home?'

'Yes, he'd been sent there, apparently, when he came out of hospital, and the one thing that was bothering him was his cat. So of course I promised to keep an eye out for it, and I called around here a few times, we both did, my colleague and I . . .'

A nursing home. He'd managed not to die in hospital then.

'. . . but eventually we gave up, it just seemed pointless really, so much time had gone by. But then, like I say, I happened to be passing today, and I saw a cat in your garden, and of course it mightn't be his at all – I never actually saw it myself, but the description . . .'

Still alive in a nursing home, not dead like she'd assumed. Tough old Malone, not ready yet to shuffle off his mortal coil. She should have known.

'. . . and I was just wondering if maybe you took him in when Charlie got sick. I know it's a long shot, but I thought it was worth a try, you know?'

He stopped talking, finally, and stood towering over her. His story was ludicrous – trying to track down a cat he'd never seen, years after its owner had moved away – and yet his expression was so open, his face so completely without guile, that she was inclined to believe him.

'It *is* his cat,' she told him. 'I'm looking after it. I thought Malo— I thought Charlie was dead, so I put out food.'

His grin widened, nearly split his face in two. 'Well, that's very good news,' he said delightedly.

'I'm sure Charlie will be thrilled to hear that you have it. I'll give a call to the nursing home and—'

'Let me,' she said. 'Would you? Let me have the number, and I'll ring.'

She'd get a kick out of telling Malone that his precious cat was alive and well, and that she was the one he had to thank. Let him put that in his smelly old pipe.

The big man raised his eyebrows, which were growing as enthusiastically as his beard – such a very hairy face he had. 'Well, if you like, I could do that, but the number is back at the garden centre. I have it stuck on a notice board there—'

'Here,' she said, pulling a receipt from her bag and scribbling her number on it, 'you could ring me with it. There's an answering machine if I'm not at home.' She wrote *Helen* under the number. 'Thanks awfully.'

'No problem at all,' he said, the smile bouncing back onto his face as he pocketed the receipt. 'You want to break the good news to him yourself.'

'That's it,' Helen said, struggling to keep a straight face. He could get a job as Santa, no problem. Put him in a red suit, give him a sack and a queue of kids. No false beard required.

'Charlie was a nice old soul,' he told her. 'And knew his stuff when it came to plants, a real expert.' He gestured across the newly built brick wall to the paving stones that lay now in place of Malone's precious lawn. 'Look what they've done to his garden – wouldn't do him good to see it.'

'Don't suppose it would.' Helen felt the conversation had gone on long enough. She began to move down the path. 'I'm afraid I have to go. I'm trying to make the post.'

'Oh, I'm sorry,' he said immediately, following her to the gate, nipping ahead of her to open it. 'Would you like a lift?'

Helen looked at him, amused. The proverbial good Samaritan. 'Thanks, but I think I'll make it on foot. Goodbye now.'

'Much obliged to you.' He put out his hand. 'I'm delighted that the mystery is solved at last – thanks again for your help.'

He seemed genuinely happy. Imagine looking for a cat that wasn't yours, imagine keeping an eye out for more than two years, just because someone had asked you to. The male equivalent of Sarah, spreading goodness and light wherever he went.

His handshake was as firm and warm as she'd expected. She put him in his mid-fifties, a few years older than her, and at least a foot taller. Not to mention several stone heavier.

As she walked away she heard the van door slamming, the engine starting up. He drove past her, tooting the horn and waving cheerily.

She made the half-four collection by a couple of minutes. She called to her mother afterwards and they drank coffee and talked about Brian Keenan, still in captivity after more than four years, and Cardinal Ó Fiaich dropping dead in

France, and Alice's description of the basic living conditions at the eco centre.

When she got home, having declined her mother's offer of a salmon steak, she grilled a couple of fish fingers – no motivation to cook a proper meal without someone to share it – and tossed a green salad to go with them. She watched a film and fed the cat—

The cat. Malone.

She checked her answering machine and saw the message light blinking. She pressed *play* and the bearded man's big genial voice burst into the silence: 'Hello Helen, Frank Murphy here, we met earlier when I was looking for Charlie's cat. I have that nursing-home number for you.'

The area code was Kildare: what had brought Malone all the way out there? Wasn't there any nursing home good enough for him in Dublin?

Sarah was in Kildare – maybe he'd ended up in her nursing home: some coincidence if he had. She'd ask him tomorrow if there was a cook called Sarah Flannery working there, tell him to say Helen said hi.

She returned to the kitchen. 'Remember Malone?' she asked the cat. 'Old man you used to live with. He's still alive – can you believe it?' But the cat continued snuffling into his bowl and ignored her. She made tea and wrote a letter to Alice as she drank it, and told her about Malone not being dead after all.

Wait till he heard who had his cat.

SARAH

The door to Matron's office was open, which meant she was on her morning rounds. As Sarah passed, the phone on the desk began to ring. She could leave it, and the answering machine would pick it up, but she hated to ignore it. She entered the office and lifted the receiver.

'St Sebastian's Nursing Home, may I help?'

'Good morning.' The voice was husky, hard to tell if it was male or female. 'I'm looking for Charlie Malone. I believe he's staying there.'

Sarah's heart sank. Why hadn't she minded her own business and kept going to the kitchen? 'Er, may I ask if you're family?'

'No, I'm not family.' Marginally sharper. 'I'm a neighbour – I was a neighbour of his. Are you telling me only relatives are allowed to speak to him?'

'No, no, it's not that, of course you could talk to him—' Lord, a neighbour after all this time: maybe this was the person who'd found him. But why wait till now to look for him, years later?

'Hello? Are you still there?'

Say it, get it over with. 'It's just, I'm really sorry

to have to tell you this' – the words stuttering out – 'but I'm afraid Charlie, er, he'd been ill, you see, a few years back, with pneumonia – well, maybe you know that already – and it had weakened his heart, and he . . . suffered a heart attack, I'm afraid, and he, well, he died, quite suddenly, just a few months ago. One of the other residents found him, in fact, in the garden here. He had made such a—'

Stop, shut up, you're blabbering. She stopped. There was silence at the other end.

'Hello? . . . Hello? Can you hear me?'

The silence stretched, and she realised that the line was dead. The caller, whoever she was, had hung up. She replaced the receiver and left the room.

HELEN

Hi, Mum
Thanks for the cheque. Big news – Jackie and I have left the centre. We both had enough of it, and it was too full of weirdos anyway. I didn't tell you about them because I thought you'd freak out, but there was a guy who had a swastika tattoo and who wore a bulletproof vest all the time, even in bed, and a Dutch woman who thought someone was cutting her hair while she was asleep – and they were pretty normal compared to some of the others. Dermot is staying on there, but he's a bit weird himself so he fits right in.

We hitched a lift to Cardiff and we're living there now. We're sharing a house that belongs to Cait, who we met when she visited the centre a few weeks ago. When we told her we were thinking of leaving, she said we could stay with her till we got sorted. I've found a job in a pub, three nights a week to start, and Jackie is delivering groceries on a bicycle for a supermarket.

And the other good news is that we've signed up for Saturday-morning art classes. They're free, given by some student, and they're held in the university, which is just ten minutes from the house, and we're going to try and sell the stuff that we paint in a craft market that takes place every Sunday. Cait is a potter and has a stall there, and she says we can share it.

Cardiff is cool, lots of free stuff to do. It's freezing though – I bought a coat in a vintage charity shop for a fiver yesterday. It's one of those sheepskin ones, weighs a ton but very warm. Jackie says I look like a hippie in it. And I'm letting my hair grow, it's past my shoulders now and it goes a bit curly if I don't blow dry it. I like it. You'll see it when we come home at Christmas.

I've put the address of Cait's house at the top. You can write to me there for now, but as soon as we can afford it we'll try and find a place of our own, because it's a bit crowded here. Hope everything is OK at home. Tell Gran I said hi, and give the cat a hug.

love Alice

PS Stop asking me if I've met any nice boys. I keep telling you I'm not interested in boys. Seriously.

Helen lowered the letter. All it had taken for them to stop fighting was for Alice to move away: put a sea and a few hundred miles between them and they got on fine.

She found an envelope and copied the Cardiff address onto it. She'd get a postal order for two hundred pounds sterling next time she was in the post office. She had no idea how much apartment rental was in Cardiff, but it was all she could spare, and it would help.

She wondered who else lived in Cait's house, and if Alice had a bed to sleep in, or even a couch. Maybe she slept on the floor, and hadn't mentioned it in case her mother freaked out. She wondered what else wasn't being mentioned.

Saturday art classes, free because the tutor was a student, maybe with fewer hours of learning under his belt than Alice herself. A far cry from the fine-arts course Alice had turned her back on, but at least she was doing something arty. And if she sold a painting or two it might encourage her to go back and study properly again.

Working in a pub, three nights a week. Helen wondered what class of Welshman it attracted, and how Alice got home after closing time, and if working there was better or worse than cycling a bicycle around Cardiff with someone else's weekly shopping in the basket.

But she sounded happy, and she had Jackie with her, and they were coming home at Christmas, only nine weeks away. As Helen was slipping the letter back into its envelope, the phone rang. She walked out to the hall.

'Hello.'

'It's me.'

Sounding as happy as if he'd just won a million on the National Lottery, as usual. In four months she'd never known the man to be in a bad mood.

'How're you doing?' he asked.

'Fine, just reading a letter from Alice.'

'All well in Wales?' He had yet to meet her daughter but you'd never know it, the way he always asked after her, always showed an interest when Helen mentioned her.

'She's left the centre, her and one of the pals. They're living in Cardiff now, sharing someone's house. Alice is working in a pub, and her friend is delivering groceries on a bike.'

'Good for them, having an adventure. That's what you need at nineteen.'

He turned everything into a positive. She could picture the beam plastered across his face, and the image made her smile too. He could do that to her, even over the phone.

'You free later?' he asked. 'I got tickets for that play at the Olympia.'

Another thing he did, book tickets and then tell her. She should be annoyed that he didn't check to see if she was busy first, but getting annoyed with him was pointless – he never reciprocated, he was useless at arguments. If she told him she had something else planned, he'd simply laugh it off and pass on the tickets. Nothing bothered him.

'I'd love to,' she said.

'Wonderful – pick you up at half seven.'

They'd been dating, or whatever you wanted to call it, since he'd rung, a few days after giving her the nursing-home number, to ask if she'd be at all interested in going out to dinner with him.

He took her to restaurants and the theatre and the cinema. He drove her out of the city on Sundays, his only day off, and they walked along riverbanks and drank tea in little village cafés with lace table-cloths. He was the most generous person she'd ever known, presenting her regularly with chocolate and books and flowers. He paid for everything when they went out, wouldn't hear of her contributing.

He was pleasingly, but not overly, tactile. He would stroke her hand absently as they watched a play, and reach out to cradle her elbow when they crossed a street. Occasionally he draped a hand lightly across her shoulders as they walked. At the end of an evening he would bend his head and kiss her goodnight, his lips warm, his beard tickling her face, his huge arms enveloping her. And on most Saturday nights he stayed over.

There'd been no big seduction scene – they were both well beyond coyness. One evening, a few weeks after they'd got together, Helen had suggested he stay the night, and he'd smiled and accepted the invitation. He was gentle in bed, and as consid-erate as she'd thought he would be – and if their sex life wasn't as earth-moving as she would have liked, she'd felt cherished for the first time since Cormac.

He was good company. He laughed often, was never short of conversation. He could make a story out of anything. He loved his work: he got enormous pleasure from advising people on what to plant and where to plant it. His business, by the sound of it, was thriving.

He was fifty-two, four years older than her. He'd never been married, and he never referred to previous relationships, but it was obvious that there had been at least one or two: she certainly wasn't his first lover. His parents and sister, his only sibling, were dead, but he had various relatives scattered around Dublin – cousins, aunts, nieces, nephews – whom he saw regularly. One of the cousins, George, had started the garden centre with him more than twenty years earlier, and the two still ran it together.

His goodnight kisses were comforting; she enjoyed the feel of his arms about her. His bulk soothed her, made her feel safe. His default setting was happy, his good humour the perfect counterpart to her occasional black moods. Simply by being himself, he made her feel less prickly.

On paper he was perfect. In person he was perfect too, if you were looking for someone dependable and kind. And what was wrong with dependable and kind? She was forty-eight; she'd moved beyond fireworks. He was good for her, she'd been lucky to meet him. To think it had been Malone's cat that had brought them together.

Malone, who had been dead after all, who'd

never got to find out that Helen had taken in his cat. The woman on the phone stuttering out the news, assuming that Helen cared. Pity all the same he hadn't known that the cat was OK: sounded like the poor bugger had been attached to it.

I have a new boyfriend, she'd written to Sarah, after she and Frank had been seeing one another for about a month. *You'd approve. He's a real gentleman, treats me like a queen – and you'll be pleased to hear that this time I've gone for my own generation. He's fifty-two and looks like Santa, big fluffy beard, twinkly eyes, the lot. He actually dresses up as Santa in his garden centre on Christmas Eve – I didn't know whether to laugh or cry when he told me that.*

She made no mention of him in her letters to Alice: time enough to introduce them when Alice came home at Christmas. Frank would still be around, she was quite sure of that. She remembered Alice's rejection of Oliver, her silent treatment of him whenever they'd been in the same room, the tension at their shared meals. But Alice was older now and had moved out – and Frank was no Oliver Joyce.

She opened the front door and walked out to the garden, gathering her wrap more tightly around her. The days were getting chillier, now that winter was approaching. Where were the years going? She regarded the brick wall her neighbours had erected and saw Malone's ghost, clipping the hedge that had preceded it.

She remembered Cormac scooping her up to carry her into the house the first time he'd brought her around to see it. 'You only do that when you're married,' she'd protested, laughing, and he'd winked and said, 'Just getting in some practice.'

She pictured Alice as a toddler, insisting on wheeling her own buggy from the gate to the house, stumbling when the wheels bumped up against the path's raised brick border.

And now Malone and Cormac were dead, and Alice was grown-up and living in a different country, and in two years Helen would be fifty.

And it was Sarah's fortieth in little over a week, a big party was being planned in a local hotel – and typically of Sarah, she was incorporating a surprise party for their childminder, whose fiftieth was around the same time.

She has no idea! It's great that I'm planning a party anyway, so I don't have to do all the arranging in secret. We've invited every relative and friend her sister could round up, and I've even found a man for her – he's Dan, the driver at the nursing home for as long as I've been there, and longer. He's a really sweet man, and I think he and Noreen would be perfect together. I'll introduce them anyway, and you never know.

She'd invited Helen to the party.

Don't you think, after all these years, it might be time for us to finally meet up?? You could bring Santa with you (!!) and you could stay the night in the hotel. I'm sorry I can't offer a bed – our house will be bursting at the seams with various family members – but I'd love to meet you. Do come!

But Helen had turned down the invitation, saying Frank had already booked tickets to a play that evening. It wasn't true – and even if it had been, cancelling wouldn't have bothered him in the slightest: on the contrary, he'd have been delighted at the thought of a trip to Kildare to meet Helen's mysterious penfriend – but for some reason Helen resisted the idea of coming face to face with Sarah. They got on fine on paper: best to leave it at that.

The cat appeared suddenly, padding unhurriedly through the bars of the front gate and down the path towards Helen, tail in the air.

'Where have you been?' she asked. 'Account for your movements.'

It slinked around her, pressing its body against her calves. They'd grown used to one another, both abandoned by the ones closest to them.

'Come on.' She turned, and it followed her into the house.

SARAH

She rolled Stephen's buggy to and fro as she stood outside the junior infants classroom window, searching the sea of small bodies scrambling to get ready for home until she found Martha. There she was, by the opposite wall, reaching on tiptoe to yank her pink raincoat from its hook, looking both heartbreakingly grown-up and frighteningly young in her grey cardigan and too-long navy skirt.

As soon as the teacher slid across the door that opened onto the yard, the waiting parents moved forward to claim children, some already dropping to their knees to button coats and pull up zips. Sarah stood where she was, a smile in place for when her daughter found them.

Martha emerged and looked about, skimming over the adults until she picked out Sarah. Her face brightened as she skipped towards her mother, schoolbag bouncing against her legs. Sarah crouched and gathered her into her arms, pressing her lips against the soft, warm cheek. 'Hello, my precious. Did you have a good day?'

'Mmm. How come Stephen got jellies?'

Sarah released her and tucked her schoolbag underneath the buggy. 'I've got some for you too. Did you have a nice day in school?'

'Yeah. Cathal was bold again. Where's my jellies?'

Life was hectic. Working part-time helped, of course, but there were still busy afternoons and weekends with two small children who claimed all her attention, and a father, seventy-nine last birthday, who, despite his continuing independence, she felt obliged to visit at least twice a week.

Neil did his bit when he was around, but these days he was busier than ever, more involved now with the design side of gardening, Most weeks he spent one or two nights away from home, with customers from miles around looking for him to plan their gardens – and willing to pay him surprisingly well in return – and on the nights he did appear he was often too tired to do much more than eat dinner and go to bed. Sarah supposed it was a good complaint – worse if he had nobody looking for him – but still.

Thank goodness for Noreen, who continued to provide such wonderful help. 'I don't know what we'd do without you,' Sarah would tell her regularly, and Noreen would laugh and say anyone could do what she did: all it took was a bit of patience.

After much thought about a birthday present for her, Sarah had bought a very sweet wicker picnic basket, lined in blue and white gingham and stocked with crockery, cutlery and glasses for two.

'This wouldn't have anything to do with the blind date you're lining up for her, would it?' Christine had asked when Sarah had shown it to her.

'Not at all – she can use this with a friend, it doesn't have to be for a couple. And it's not a blind date, it's just Dan, and he would have been coming to my party anyway. I'll introduce them, that's all.'

'And you're hoping they'll take one look at each other and fall helplessly in love.'

'Of course not – well, not straight away. But you never know what might develop.'

Christine had shaken her head, smiling. 'It takes more than availability for people to fancy one another.'

'I *know* that. I'm not totally innocent.'

But it could happen, and maybe it would, and Noreen would be glad of the picnic basket then. Nothing like slices of chicken terrine and a glass or two of wine by a sunny riverbank to move a relationship on a little.

Look at Helen, almost fifty and with someone new, who sounded lovely. Shame about her not being free for the party: Sarah had been looking forward to them finally coming face to face. When you thought about it, the fact that they hadn't met up yet was pretty remarkable – they were only forty miles apart, for Heaven's sake.

But of course it was only a matter of time. You couldn't write to someone for so long, share so many confidences with them, feel that they were as much a part of your life as the others in it, and never meet. Sooner or later it would happen.

In the meantime, something else was preoccupying her. Maybe she was expecting too much: she was well aware that with Stephen's birth her most fervent wish had already been granted. Maybe it was the prospect of turning forty in just over a week. For whatever reason, the desire to conceive again, for her and Neil to give life to another baby, was becoming overwhelming.

She needed to talk it over with him. They needed to find time to reconnect. It seemed like forever since they'd made love – more often than not, on the nights he was home he was asleep before she got to bed – but if they were going to try again they needed to do it soon.

'Do you think we could go away, just the two of us, even for one night?' she asked. 'We could get Noreen to stay over, or bring the children to Christine's.'

With a night to themselves, with a chance for him to tune out of work and without Stephen and Martha to distract them, she could bring up the subject.

But he shook his head. 'Sorry, love, I'm just too busy right now. Maybe if work eases up a bit. We'll see.'

We'll see: what you'd say to a child to stop them demanding something you couldn't, or wouldn't, supply. Oh, she knew she shouldn't resent the fact that he was working steadily, but he didn't have to say yes to every job offer that came along, did he? It wasn't as if they needed the money, with him able to command such high fees, and her working too.

But she wasn't about to give up. She'd wait till the party was over and then she'd sort something out. She'd ask Christine to take the kids for a night, no need to involve Noreen. They'd stay at home, she'd fill a bath for him and cook his favourite dinner. She'd remind him why he'd fallen in love with her, and then she'd talk about what was uppermost in her thoughts.

They just needed to find the time, that was all.

HELEN

Was it him? Hard to be sure, with the evening sun lighting up the plate-glass window that separated them. Helen shielded her eyes and watched the man walking past the restaurant. Yes, definitely Breen – and look at the grey in his hair now. How long since they'd last met? Two or three years at least since he'd retired.

She remembered talking to him briefly at the party the newspaper had thrown to wave him off, but she couldn't remember what they'd discussed. That had been the night she'd brought home the Swedish barman – or was he Norwegian? The details were vague, her head fuzzy with the whiskey she'd drunk. She remembered trying to make coffee in the kitchen when she'd brought him home, spilling granules all over the floor.

Not that he'd been worth it. No thought except for his own pleasure, no idea where to go to keep her happy. Gone before she'd woken the following morning – taken one look at her, probably, in the cold light of day and headed for the hills.

'Someone you know?'

'My old boss, and . . . his wife, I presume.'

Must be the wife: scarlet lipstick in a washed-out face, enormous gold hoop earrings, pale hair pulled tightly into a knotted green scarf. Heavy brown coat, thin legs beneath, shiny black shoes whose high, high heels lifted her a couple of inches above him.

Didn't exactly look like the sunny antidote to Breen, same grim expression as his own. Not touching, both looking straight ahead as they walked. Hardly a barrel of laughs around that dinner table.

But still together, if she was the wife, despite Catherine's hints that all hadn't been well. Maybe they'd worked through it. She tried to imagine Breen agreeing to counselling; she conjured up the image of him sitting across a desk, taking advice from someone on how to conduct his marriage. Never happen, not in a million years.

'I think I'll go for the steak,' Frank said. 'I'm in a red-meat mood today.'

Helen wasn't hungry, not in the slightest. All day she'd felt off-colour, stabbing listlessly at the type-writer keys, her back aching, her head light. She should have rung him to cancel the date, gone to bed with a hot lemon drink. But the time had run away with her until it was too late to call it off, and here she was.

'Actually,' she said, 'I don't feel so good.'

He was instantly concerned. He drove her home, sent her upstairs while he boiled the kettle and filled a hot-water bottle. He fussed so much, drawing the bedroom curtains, hunting through the bathroom cabinet for a thermometer, taking the blankets from Alice's bed to pile onto Helen's, riffling the pages of the phone book to find a late-night chemist, that in the end, weary, she sent him home, pretending to feel much better now that she was tucked up.

He left reluctantly, threatening to return first thing in the morning until she insisted that a phone call would be fine, the phone next to her bed so she could answer it easily. She listened to the sound of the front door closing softly, his steps down the path, the creak of the gate, his van door opening and closing, and finally the engine, moving him away from her.

She was never sick, apart from the odd head cold or bout of indigestion. Her hangovers didn't count, being self-inflicted – and since she and Frank had got together they'd pretty much disappeared anyway, with him not being much of a drinker. No fun getting pie-eyed on your own.

She lay unmoving and assessed her current situation. A throbbing, small but insistent, around her temples. A stiffness across her shoulder blades and down her spine, as if she'd had a fairly challenging workout. A heat in her cheeks – her temperature was up a bit – a shiver in her limbs, an ache in her chest when she breathed deeply. Some bug that would have to work its way through her system.

After a while she pulled herself up, wincing, and sipped the lemon drink he'd left on the locker. He would have made a good nurse. She dressed him in white scrubs, put a thermometer around his neck, rubber-soled shoes on his feet. Nurse Murphy at your service, full of tender, loving, smiling care. He'd probably have to lose the beard.

She didn't love him, not in a romantic way. She wasn't in love with him, not at all. But she'd had a great love once, which was more than a lot of others got. And Frank had taken her home when she was sick, he'd put her to bed and flapped around her like a mother hen, and there wasn't exactly a queue waiting to do that. He was worth hanging on to.

She lay back and closed her eyes, waiting for sleep.

SARAH

Dear Mrs Flannery
You'll probably be surprised to hear from me, but my mum said your 40th birthday was coming up so I made you this card at my painting class. I hope you like it.

I'm living in Cardiff now, you probably know that from Mum. I'm working in a pub and sharing a woman's house, but my friend and I are hoping to find our own flat soon. Our budget is small but we don't need much room.

I hope your children are well.
Happy birthday,
love Alice x

It was lovely, a hand-painted card that had arrived the day before her birthday. A little red plane flying through a clear blue sky and trailing an orange banner that read *Happy Birthday*. So sweet of Alice, all the way from Cardiff.

The party hadn't been a disaster, nothing like that. Most of the people Sarah had invited had turned up, and they'd seemed to enjoy themselves.

Christine had ordered a gorgeous three-tier lemon sponge cake, decorated with yellow fondant roses. Sarah had felt good: quite a few had admired her new blue skirt and grey lacy top.

The music had been her choice, lots of Madonna and Eurythmics and Billy Joel, all her favourites. The party hadn't ended till well after midnight, past one by the time she and Neil had got home.

She'd received beautiful presents too, perfume and ornaments and photo frames and spa vouchers. Earlier in the week Helen had sent the new Ballymaloe cookbook that everyone was talking about – 'hope it's not coals to Newcastle'.

The children had stayed the night with their cousins, Christine's in-laws on babysitting duty. They'd been dropped back home at lunchtime the following day, along with colouring books, crayons and a box of chocolates for Sarah. All fine, all perfectly according to plan. On the whole, everything had gone splendidly.

It was just Noreen.

It wasn't that she'd done anything wrong; there'd been nothing to suggest that she hadn't enjoyed the evening. She'd seemed genuinely surprised to see her family and friends there when she'd walked in – maybe a little taken aback initially – but she'd thanked Sarah very cordially for having included her, and accepted the gifts people had brought with what looked like real enthusiasm.

She'd looked well too, or as well as she could, given the turquoise dress that didn't really flatter her complexion, the hair that still needed a decent cut, the face completely bare of makeup, apart from lipstick. Still, she'd looked perfectly pleasant.

And it wasn't as if Sarah had expected her to be bowled over by Dan, who you could see had made a real effort, even got his hair cut for the occasion – but Noreen hadn't seemed in the least bit interested in getting to know him. Sarah had introduced them, and the three of them had chatted for a few minutes – and really Sarah had said lovely things about both of them, how invaluable Noreen was to them at home, how Dan had sped her off to the hospital when she'd gone into early labour with Stephen – and then she'd made some excuse and left them to it, and the next time she'd checked, barely five minutes later, Dan was back with the nursing-home crowd he'd come with and Noreen had vanished.

Sarah had spotted her eventually, dancing with Neil to Whitney Houston, and thought, *Not much point in taking to the dance floor with someone else's husband.* But maybe she wasn't looking for a new romance, maybe she was afraid to fall in love again, after the heartbreak of her husband's death. Still, it had been a disappointment.

No matter – Noreen was old enough to know what she wanted, and Sarah should probably have minded her own business. Thank goodness she'd said it to nobody, apart from Christine and Neil. She was going to put it from her mind now and move ahead with the far more important matter.

'Can you take my two for the night on Friday?' she asked Christine. 'I need some quality time with Neil.'

'No problem. Everything OK?'

'Fine. We just never seem to get time to ourselves, that's all. Would you mind coming to collect them, maybe around five?'

She said nothing about what she was planning: that was between her and Neil for now. Time enough to share when she, all going well, found herself pregnant again.

A little girl this time, maybe. Neil, she was sure, would love another little girl.

HELEN

S he wasn't getting better. It wasn't going away. Two days in bed – or was it three? – sticking to the sweaty sheets that she didn't have the energy to change. Head pounding, throat burning, face flaming, back aching. Making her way every so often on stupidly shaking legs to the bathroom to slurp water from her cupped hands, the kitchen with its glasses much too far away.

Putting Frank off when he phoned, unable to summon up the energy for him. She'd wait until she started feeling better, let him come over at that stage and look after her.

And then, when she was hovering between waking and sleeping, the doorbell rang. She ignored it. It rang again. She swore weakly and turned over. A few minutes later the phone by her bed jangled into life, making her start painfully. She reached out a shaky hand and lifted the receiver.

'Hello?' Her voice sounded strange, more croaky than it should be.

'It's me,' someone said. 'I'm next door. Can you come down and let me in?'

Next door? It made no sense. Malone lived next door, but he was in a nursing home.

'Can you get downstairs? You can take your time, I'll wait.'

She dropped the receiver back into its cradle. This was part of a dream, she was asleep. A minute later, just as she was sinking gratefully into oblivion the doorbell rang again, and someone shouted something that sounded like 'Help!' She pulled the blankets over her head to drown them out, breathing in her own cloying musky scent.

When the phone rang a second time, she let it ring until it became apparent that it wasn't going to stop. She levered herself out from under the blankets and reached for it wearily.

'Ssh,' she told it. 'Go away.'

'It's me again.' The same calm voice. 'Can you get downstairs, or will I call for an ambulance?'

Suddenly it all became clear. Malone was sick: he needed an ambulance – that was why he kept calling.

'I saw the dandelions,' she said. 'Are you OK?'

'What?'

'The cat,' she said. Something about the cat she should say, but it kept sliding away from her. She closed her eyes and let the receiver fall onto the blankets, dimly aware that it was still making little squawking noises. She lay back, trying to swallow the rock that had lodged in her throat. She wanted water, but it was too far away.

Time passed. Alice wandered in, wearing a

bulletproof vest over her clothes. 'They're cutting my hair when I'm asleep,' she told Helen. And here was Breen, hands dug into his pockets, glaring at her from the top of the wardrobe. 'You have a mouth on you like a toilet,' he growled. 'You were born with an ulterior motive.'

'I got a blue elephant from you,' Alice said to him. 'I fell off the monkey bars in the park.'

'I saw you,' Helen told him, 'outside the restaurant,' but he mustn't have heard because he made no reply, just shimmered away. Helen closed her eyes again and dreamed of her father in his judge's wig shovelling coal into a huge furnace that roared flames at her.

And now there were different noises. There were people around her – Frank was there, his big face frowning as he looked down at her, his bushy eyebrows drawn together, and someone, some man she didn't know, was sliding something cold into her mouth and lifting her wrist, his hand cool against her burning skin, calling her Helen, and he was pushing up her eyelid to shine a light that hurt her eyes, and hands were underneath her, she was being lifted onto something that smelt like tyres, and she was moaning because she wanted to stay where she was and sleep, and because it hurt, all her bones hurt and her throat ached, and they were covering her with a blanket and wrapping it like a cocoon around her, and she was so thirsty, and they were telling her she'd be fine, Helen, and not to worry now, and stay with us,

Helen, and they were bringing her down a mountain, everything tilting as they wobbled her down, and the blessedly cold air on her hot face now, and still everything hurting, hurting, as they brought her into a small beeping room and laid her down gently in her cocoon and closed the door, slammed the door too loudly, like Alice, and then the room was moving and she was lying down in the moving room, and somewhere behind the beeping she could hear an ambulance siren, and someone was holding her hand, someone was stroking her hand and it hurt to be stroked, and she wanted water more than anything in the world.

And after that, a jumble of doors and lights and moving and voices, and then a sting in her arm.

And after that, nothing.

SARAH

'I'm desperately sorry. It just happened. It wasn't something we planned.'

Sarah watched his mouth opening and closing, his top teeth flashing into view every so often. He never showed his bottom teeth when he talked. She knew this about him, as she knew so many things. They'd been married for more than thirteen years, plenty of time to learn pretty much all there was to know about someone.

'We didn't set out to hurt anyone, that was the last thing we wanted. I'm really sorry.'

Her chicken and bacon lasagne in its pretty blue and white pottery dish sat untouched on the table between them, the cheese topping congealed. The tongs lay beside the bowl of green salad, the little white jug of dressing – oil, vinegar, mustard, garlic, honey – still waiting to be added.

'I had to tell you,' he said. 'I can't live a lie any more.'

Phil Collins was singing something about paradise on the radio. Hailstones tapped against the window, showers of them off and on all day. Sarah abruptly remembered her bicycle still leaning against the

346

back wall of the house, abandoned when Stephen had come running out to her as soon as she'd got home from work, waving a still-wet painting he'd done with Noreen.

'Say something,' Neil said.

She hadn't had a clue. She'd been blind and deaf. He'd fallen in love with someone else, he'd been in love with her for months, and for all that time Sarah had lived with him and argued with him and slept with him and sensed nothing at all.

Hadn't even taken much notice of the fact that they hardly made love any more, had put it down to hectic lives and nothing else. Blind and deaf she'd been.

'Please,' he said. 'Just say something.'

She found her voice. 'Who is she?'

Some customer, it must be. Some woman who'd invited him into her garden, who'd come out to him with cups of tea and slices of cake. Younger than Sarah, with no stretch marks, with breasts that didn't sag.

He made no reply, his gaze sliding down to the lasagne.

'Who is she?' Louder. A drumming in her ears, her hands pressing into the table to stop them from shaking.

'It doesn't matter who she is.'

She rose abruptly and reached across to snap off the radio. 'Who is she? Tell me. *Tell* me.'

'Sarah, you don't want to know. It won't make any—'

'Tell me,' she cried. 'I have a *right* to know.'

The silence stretched between them. She felt her pulse banging somewhere in her chest as she watched the man he'd become, this stranger sitting at her table, unable to look at her.

Finally, when she was on the point of shouting at him again, he lifted his head.

'It's Noreen,' he said quietly.

Sarah's mouth dropped open. The hail shower died away as quickly as it had come, the silence in the kitchen absolute as she tried to process the nonsense of what he'd said.

'Sarah, I'm really—'

'That's not *remotely* funny. You really scared me – and it's cruel, making fun of Noreen like that.'

'I'm not—'

'How could you do it?' she demanded. 'She lost her husband – and she's so great with our kids. I thought you liked her. And how could you *pretend* you'd fallen in love with another woman? That's really horrible.'

He got to his feet, stood in front of her. 'Sarah, please stop. Please listen to me. I'm not pretending.'

'Of course you are,' she said angrily. 'You don't expect me to believe you're in love with *Noreen*, for God's—'

'I am,' he insisted loudly. 'Whether you believe it or not, it's happened. I love her, I'm sorry. I love Noreen, and she loves me.'

Sarah glared at him. 'I want you to *stop* it,' she said. 'Why are you *insisting*—'

'Sarah, I am. We're in love. It's true, I swear it. Look,' he said, 'I hate having to tell you this – neither of us meant it to happen, honest to God. But I'm not pretending. It's the truth.'

And as he spoke, as the look on his face finally forced her to realise that it wasn't some kind of sick joke on his part, she felt the blood draining so quickly from her face that she swayed, dizzy from it. Noreen? *Noreen*?

He moved towards her but she backed out of his reach. 'Get *away* from me,' she told him in a voice she didn't recognise, grabbing the edge of the sink for support.

'Sarah, I'm so sorry, we never—'

She breathed deeply, trying to recover her balance. Without warning, her hand balled into a tight fist. With all her strength she lunged forward and punched his face as hard as she could. As her fist made contact, a sound, a throaty grunt, came from deep within her.

His head snapped back, the impact of the blow sending him toppling down into the chair he'd just left. Sarah's hand exploded with pain, causing her to cry out sharply.

'*Jesus*—' His hands flew to his face. He drew them away and looked at the blood on them.

'Get out,' Sarah said, her voice still alien to her. 'Get out. Get *out*.' Her hand throbbing, her heart going mad inside her. 'Get out. Get out.'

He met her eyes for an instant, hands cradling his nose, blood trickling between his fingers, before getting to his feet and staggering from the room. She heard the front door opening and closing. She waited, her breath unspeakably loud and ragged, until his car started up, until the noise of it was utterly gone.

She turned to the sink and ran the cold tap on the back of her hand until it went numb. She ducked her head and sloshed water onto her face and neck, drenching her top and the kitchen floor. She blotted her face with the towel and slumped onto a chair.

Noreen. He'd fallen in love with Noreen, who was fifty and plain and badly dressed. An image came unbidden into her head of the two of them sitting cross-legged on the sitting-room floor, holding tiny plastic cups.

Noreen. How could he? How could they?

She regarded her knuckles, which were bright red. Thoughts jumped into her head, collided together.

She'd shared her birthday party with Noreen just under a week ago; she'd bought her a picnic basket.

She'd told Neil she was trying to find a man for Noreen. She thought they'd been driving to the supermarket at the time, Stephen and Martha preoccupied in the back of the car. She strained to remember what his response had been, but couldn't.

She'd also told him lately that she was glad she'd married him, that she was glad he'd asked her, glad she'd said yes.

She'd introduced Noreen to Dan at the party,

and Noreen had walked away from him as soon as she could – and the next time Sarah had seen her, she was dancing with Neil.

Sarah had seen them dancing, seen their arms around one another, and thought nothing of it, nothing.

Noreen had sat at this table and drunk countless cups of tea with Sarah, she'd cuddled Sarah's children and put plasters on their cuts, and she'd fallen in love with Sarah's husband.

Noreen had been here this very day; she'd left the house at three, half an hour after Sarah had got home. Sarah had stood outside with the children like she always did, and the three of them had waved Noreen off. 'See you on Monday,' they'd chorused, and Noreen had smiled and waved back.

Had she known that Neil was planning to tell Sarah about them this evening? Of course she had. She'd stood at the table earlier; she'd chopped tomatoes and grated cheese while Sarah had stirred the meat sauce for the lasagne. Was she thinking that this was the last time she'd be in the house? Was she pitying Sarah as she imagined what lay ahead?

And even more horrible – was Neil going to her now? Was she getting ready to receive him, would they talk about what had just happened? Would she bathe his face, tend the injury that Sarah had caused?

She gritted her teeth hard and pressed the heels

351

of her hands into her eye sockets, trying to shut out the pictures of the two of them that pushed their way into her head, that made her insides clench with rage.

Time passed. She sat, unable to move. Eventually she became aware of a gnawing hunger. Her hands trembled as she cut a wedge of cold lasagne and ate it with her fingers, chewing and swallowing rapidly, taking no pleasure from it. The knuckles on her right hand were swelling slightly, turning from red to purple.

Her wet top clung to her, making her shiver. As she ate, another shower of hail began abruptly, flinging itself against the window in angry bursts. When she had finished, she stowed the lasagne dish and untouched salad in the fridge.

She tidied the kitchen, mopping the floor with the towel, and walked upstairs. In the bathroom the bath was still full, the water she'd run for him earlier completely cold. She pulled up her sleeve and yanked out the plug.

Still shivering, teeth chattering, she opened the bathroom cabinet and gathered up his shaving foam, his razors, his hair gel, his hay-fever drops, his nasal spray and his toothbrush, and dumped everything into the pedal bin.

In the bedroom she swept his clothes off hangers and pulled them from drawers and tossed them out of the window into the garden below. She threw out his shoes and his books and his spare glasses. She went downstairs and gathered everything up, rain pelting down on her as she stuffed it all into the big green refuse bin that sat outside the back door.

Back upstairs she ran a fresh bath and sloshed oil into it, the same oil she'd been buying since Helen had sent her a jar of it just before Stephen was born. She peeled off her damp clothes and left them lying in a crumpled pyramid on the bathroom floor and lowered herself into the steaming, fragrant water.

And through it all, she didn't shed a single tear.

HELEN

'O' Dowd?'

She turned slowly towards the sound of his voice, planting a hand against the wall to keep her steady.

'You look terrible,' he said.

She smiled faintly. 'Nice to see you too.'

He extended a raincoated arm. 'Here, grab on to that – I'm going your way.'

'I'm OK.'

'*Jesus*,' he said, 'you're hanging on to that wall like it was your best friend. If you collapse I have no intention of carrying you. Grab on.'

She reached out and curled her fingers around his arm. It was solid as a stone. 'I'm just two doors down,' she said. 'I'm supposed to exercise.'

'You can still do that – I told you I'm not carrying you.'

They moved off slowly. She was acutely conscious of the stains on Alice's old tartan dressing-gown. Her face was damp with sweat from dragging herself up and down the corridor. She must smell ripe, no proper shower or bath since they'd brought her in five days earlier, her hair probably cocked up all over the place.

Breen looked straight ahead as they walked, tapping the point of his big black umbrella on the vinyl floor. His hair was cut very short, as always, and more grey than dark brown now, which did it no harm. He smelt of the outdoors, the bottom half of his raincoat spotted with drops.

It occurred to Helen that apart from the handshake they must have exchanged on first meeting – at that Christmas party, aeons ago – this was the only time she'd made physical contact with him. He was an inch or so taller than her, no more.

A nurse swung out of a ward and walked briskly down the corridor towards them. She darted a look at Breen before scurrying past, her shoes squeaking.

'So what's wrong with you?' he asked.

Typical: in like a bull. She should tell him she'd been given six months, watch him deal with that. 'Meningitis,' she said. 'I'm on the mend, going home in a few days.' No response. Same old master of small-talk. 'How're things with you?' she asked.

'Fine. Still here.' His shoes were brown suede, and scuffed, which surprised her.

'I saw you,' she said, 'last week, just before I got sick.'

He threw her a pained look. 'I suppose I'm to blame then.'

'Don't flatter yourself. You walked by a restaurant

I was sitting inside.' She didn't mention the woman he'd been with, and he made no further comment.

They crawled past the first door, which was open. Helen glanced in and saw a bald man sitting on a bedside chair in dark green pyjamas, magazine splayed on his lap as he gazed instead at the wall in front of him. The absence of privacy, and dignity, that hospitals afforded.

They walked on, Helen conscious that she was leaning heavily on Breen's arm, glad of its stability. A man in blue scrubs wheeled an empty trolley past them, whistling a tune she knew but couldn't place.

'I come across your pieces now and again,' Breen said. 'You're still well able to stick the knife in.'

'I'll take that as a compliment,' she told him. 'How's retirement?'

He turned his head then to look directly at her, the way she remembered he'd always done. She'd forgotten how blue his eyes were. 'It's Hell,' he said mildly. 'Thanks for asking.'

She was thrown. Was he trying to be funny? Did he expect her to laugh? He hadn't sounded like he was making a joke – there wasn't a trace of a smile on his face. The silence sat between them until they reached her door.

'This is fine,' she said, releasing his arm. 'Thanks.'

'Want me to walk you in?'

'No . . . thank you.'

'So,' he said, 'home soon.'

'Two or three days, they tell me.'

356

He nodded. She felt awkward, standing there with him. They weren't meant to be polite with one another; they worked better when they were getting under one another's skin. He had no call to tell her his retirement was Hell. What was she supposed to do with that?

He pushed the door open, stood back. 'Take care,' he said. 'Look after yourself, O'Dowd.'

'You too.'

She shuffled inside. The door closed with a gentle swish. She heard his umbrella tapping its way down the corridor. She wondered who he'd been visiting.

Two days later her mother drove her home. Half an hour after she'd left, as Helen, showered and powdered and in a clean T-shirt, was about to climb into the freshly made bed, the doorbell rang. She looked out of her bedroom window and saw a florist's van parked by the path. Frank, any excuse for a bouquet.

But the blue bowl of three forced white hyacinths wasn't from Frank. She opened the little envelope and read, *Don't let me catch you in there again* in Breen's impossible scratchy writing.

He must have rung the hospital to see if she'd been sent home. And he must have looked her up in the phone book to get her address – she doubted he'd have remembered it from his days as editor, if he'd ever known it.

She brought the bowl upstairs and set it on her bedroom windowsill. She climbed into bed, her feet finding the hot-water bottle her mother had filled while Helen was in the shower. She closed her eyes and inhaled the tumbling, glorious scent of the flowers, and drifted off to sleep.

1991

SARAH

'Hold it higher, like this.' Sarah took the hand that held the sieve and raised it six inches. 'That way, the flour will get mixed with air while it's falling into the bowl.'

'Why does it have to get mixed with air?'

'Because air will make the buns lovely and light.'

'Why is it not coming out?'

'You have to tap the sieve gently, like this.'

Martha pushed Sarah's hand away. '*I'll* do it.'

Sarah watched the flour falling in little clouds, most of it landing in the bowl beneath. There was flour in Martha's hair, a smear of margarine on her cheek. The table was gritty with caster sugar. There were eggshells on the floor, and a scatter of flaked almonds.

The radio was on, Madonna singing about moving to the music on the dance floor. A few minutes earlier, a newsreader had announced the release after sixteen years in prison of the Birmingham Six. On the far side of the room Stephen was sprawled on his stomach, watching a little wooden train as it clacked around on its circular track.

It was half past four on a March afternoon, the rain beating against the window, the wind whipping the branches of the cherry tree – which only, Sarah thought, made it feel cosier inside the Aga-warmed, fragrant kitchen.

'Mum, what does a-e-r-a-t-e spell?' Martha had finished sieving and was now bent over the open recipe book.

'Aerate. It means to fill something with air, or let it breathe. That's what we've just done with the flour – and look, see how I'm stirring the mixture very gently with my spoon? That's called folding, so the air doesn't get pushed out again.'

She's so interested in cooking and baking, she'd written in her last letter to Helen. *I'd love to get her a few child-friendly cookbooks, but I can't find any. The language in all of my books is too advanced and I have to keep simplifying everything for her.*

As they were spooning the mixture into bun cases, the phone rang. 'I'll get it,' Martha said, dropping her spoon and scrambling to the floor. Less than a minute later she was back, deflated. 'It's Grandpa.'

Not the man she'd been hoping for. Sarah slid the baking trays into the Aga and closed the door. 'Leave everything. I won't be a minute.' She wiped her hands on her apron and went out to the hall.

'I'm heading into town,' her father said. 'I could pick up a takeaway and drop it in to you on the way home, if you wanted a night off cooking.'

'I have a chicken in the oven,' she told him, 'and we're making buns for dessert. Come and eat with us.'

He'd defied all their expectations, as healthy now at eighty-one as he'd been when his wife had died thirteen years earlier. Showing no sign of being unable to cope alone – on the contrary, he'd been her rock when Neil had left, when she'd woken the following day and the horror of what had happened had sunk in. Her father had been the first person she'd turned to.

He'd taken her tearful phone call, then hung up and packed a suitcase. Far from coming to live with them as someone who needed looking after, he'd moved into the spare room and taken over. Shooing her out to work each morning, looking after the children as best he could, steering her through the first terrible days and weeks.

He'd been there at the end of every day, when the hurt and the rage and the loneliness had become too much for her to bear alone, when she'd wept on his shoulder and tried to make sense of it. He'd made her hot chocolate and told her bad things sometimes happened to the ones who least deserved it.

He'd stayed with them until she found a neighbour to look after Stephen, and then he'd driven the five miles back to his own house, promising to return each morning to take Martha to school until a more permanent arrangement could be put in place.

Life had moved on, four months had passed since that terrible evening, and Sarah had adapted to her changed circumstances as best she could. The nights, of course, were the worst, full of memories and regrets and silent longings. However much she despised Neil's betrayal, and despite their lack of intimacy in the months leading up to his departure, she found herself mourning the physical absence of him, the smell of him, the sound of his breathing in the dark.

And her desire for another child hadn't dissipated, far from it. There were times in her loneliness when she wished he'd left her pregnant. Would it have distracted her from her melancholy, or would the idea that she was carrying a child whose father had abandoned them have made it worse? But torturing herself with what-ifs did no good: it hadn't happened, and now it was never going to happen, and this added its own layer to her sadness as she pushed herself through the days and endured the loneliness of the nights.

Christine, naturally, had been appalled.

'Oh, Sarah, the *bastard*! How could he have done that to you? And Noreen – I can't believe it. Brian will be mortified, just *mortified*, when I tell him. And to think I got that woman a present for her birthday – and you shared your party with her, and all the time . . . God, I could *hang* for her, for the *two* of them.'

I'm so very sorry, Helen had written. *He must be nuts, not that that's any comfort. I'm glad your dad is staying with you. Be strong, like I know you can be. Be good to yourself. Hug those children.*

She'd sent a box of notelets with watercolour birds on them in blues and greens and greys, and a thin slab of chocolate so dark it was almost black, and a pair of soft leather gloves the colour of blueberries. Sarah had pulled on the gloves and tried to feel something other than wretched and angry, but it seemed unlikely that she would ever be happy after this, ever want to smile again.

There had been no word from Neil for at least a fortnight. With Stephen's third birthday approaching Sarah had felt torn – knowing, despite what had happened, that he would want to be at the party, and willing him to show up for the children's sake, but dreading having to face him again.

She'd told Martha and Stephen that he'd got a new job far away. It was the best she could come up with, and they'd seemed to accept it readily enough. Inevitably, though, they also looked for Noreen.

'Where is she?' Martha had demanded. Five years old and not yet aware that her father had broken her mother's heart. 'Why isn't she coming?'

'She had to go away,' Sarah told them. 'She won't be looking after you any more.' Seeing their faces crumple, she'd felt a dart of pure hatred for Noreen. Had she cared so little about them? Had it all been an act to snare their father? How could she destroy their trust in her, how could she wound them like this?

A few days before Stephen's party, when Sarah had all but given up on him, Neil had finally phoned.

'It's me,' he'd said – and even though it wasn't wholly unexpected, the sound of his voice had brought all the hurt rushing back. 'I'd like to see the children. I'd like to come to the party, if that's alright. I'm assuming it's on Saturday.'

Sarah had clenched the receiver, tried to keep her voice from shaking. 'You have to come alone.'

'I will. And, Sarah . . . we need to talk, to sort things out.'

'No,' she said quickly. 'I'm not ready for that. I don't want to talk to you. You're coming for the children, that's all.'

A brief pause. 'OK.'

It had been horrible. She hadn't been able to look at him, had barely been able to acknowledge his presence. He'd given Stephen a far-too-expensive wooden train set, and Martha a pink coat that Sarah had seen immediately would be outgrown in a month. He'd hovered on the edges of the party, ignored by Sarah's father and Christine, for the best part of an hour.

Sarah had felt his eyes on her as she'd poured lemonade and distributed ice-cream, as she'd stood beside Stephen when he was blowing out the three candles on his gingerbread house. When Neil eventually made his excuses and left, the composure she'd managed to keep up all day had crumbled.

'Won't be long,' she'd said brightly, throwing Christine a look as she'd made her way from the room, weeping upstairs in her sister's arms, her father holding the fort until she'd felt able to patch herself together again.

The following week a letter had arrived. He'd asked to see the children one day a week, more if Sarah agreed. He'd told her he would meet them alone if that was what she wanted. Noreen's name hadn't been mentioned, but the address at the top of the page was hers.

Sarah had waited several days before writing back: *You can have them on Saturday afternoons from two till six. I would prefer if you met them alone, and I would also appreciate if you didn't bring them to that house. I haven't told them why you left, just that you had to move for a new job and you don't know when it will finish. Please don't contradict this.*

How horribly impersonal the words sounded, addressed to the man she'd been married to for so many years. Her first letter to him, she realised with a shock. In all the time they'd been together, they'd never been separated for long enough to warrant a letter.

The following Saturday he'd arrived promptly at two. At the sound of his car pulling up the children had screamed with delight and rushed outside. Sarah could hardly look in his direction as they'd scrambled in, as she'd buckled them into the two child seats.

'Have them home by six,' she'd managed to say,

before turning back into the house, a list of jobs lined up for her so she wouldn't fall to pieces, Christine and the boys due at five to further distract her.

The afternoon had dragged, as long as a century. Halfway through her first job – cleaning the windows – she'd dropped her cloth into its bucket and gone inside to pull the photo albums from the sitting-room bookshelves. She'd sat on the couch flicking through the pages, reliving the years of memories they contained.

Their wedding reception in Uncle John's hotel, her empire-line dress, so demure and pretty with its high lace neck and long sleeves, her hair coaxed into unfamiliar curls with rollers that had dug into her head the night before.

Neil wearing a grey suit – look how long his hair had been then, and the ridiculous sideburns – his arm around her waist as they stood under a beech tree, her impossibly happy smile, head tilting towards his shoulder.

Her mother in a lemon dress and matching coat, Christine in a loose blue frock that didn't hide her seven-month pregnancy bump.

Their honeymoon in England, non-stop rain for three of the seven days. York Minster in the rain, Manchester in the rain. In a Blackpool restaurant with an entire lobster on a plate in front of her. Neil holding a bingo card up to the camera, laughing. She couldn't remember how much he'd won.

Their first Christmas as man and wife, Sarah's parents – her mother's last Christmas – and Neil's mother gathered around the dinner table, coloured tissue-paper hats pulled onto their heads, plates of plum pudding in front of them.

The weekend in Paris they'd treated themselves to for their first anniversary, Sarah standing in a lime green beret on the steps of Notre Dame, and sitting on a stool in Montmartre, giggling as someone drew the caricature they'd left behind them in the hotel.

Her thirtieth birthday party, her father and Christine beside the cake with glasses in their hands, Christine pregnant for the second time, two-year-old Aidan perched on his grandfather's lap.

Neil in shorts and T-shirt on a beach somewhere – Wexford? Cork? – the blue jumper she'd knitted him slung over his shoulders, his hair cocking up in wet points.

Martha, almost two albums full of her first few months. In Sarah's arms, in Neil's arms, in everyone's arms. Happy, happy days, a child for them at last.

More happy days, her abdomen swelling with Stephen, Neil with a protective arm around her as they'd posed on the main street of Naas a month or so before she was due – shopping for a bag, as far as she could remember, that she could bring to the hospital, and probably some decent underwear too.

And then Stephen's arrival, a few moments after his birth, her exhausted, ecstatic, tear-blurred face as she'd cradled him, Neil looking on, shell-shocked.

There were no photos of her fortieth party: they'd all been burnt before they'd made it into an album, along with any others of Noreen. Sarah and Christine had done it one evening, about a fortnight after Neil's departure, when Sarah had still been a wreck.

When Christine and the boys arrived, it was an effort to pull herself out of the past, to put on the kettle and produce the biscuits she'd made with the children for their cousins that morning.

'You OK?' Christine had asked, her voice slipping under her sons' chatter.

'Just a bit melancholy, that's all, looking at old snaps.'

Christine had squeezed her hand. 'You still have plenty of happy memories with the kids, and plenty more to make. Don't forget that.'

At six o'clock, as she and Christine had sat on the garden seat wrapped in blankets and watching the boys kicking a ball around, the doorbell had rung.

Christine had got to her feet. 'I'll go.'

Sarah had let her, grateful that she didn't have to face him. She'd listened but couldn't hear how her sister greeted her brother-in-law – or maybe there'd been no greeting, just a stiff nod or a glare as she'd ushered in the children.

Inevitably, they'd wanted to see more of Neil, so

Sarah had reluctantly agreed to an overnight visit every second weekend, although the thought of them spending any time under Noreen's roof, the idea of their old childminder having any role in the family unit, turned her stomach.

'How do you propose explaining the fact that you're living with her?' she'd asked Neil, still unable to mention the other woman's name.

'I'll just tell them I'm staying for a while,' he'd replied. 'It'll help that they already know her.'

The words had sliced into Sarah as deeply as a blade. The youth and innocence of Martha and Stephen would allow them to accept the situation now, but when would they need the truth spelt out, and what would the discovery of it do to them?

She'd face that when she had to. For now, there was a more immediate problem, and the thought of solving it brought little pleasure.

Without Neil or Noreen she had no regular access to a car, and since the house wasn't on a bus route it meant that for the past several months her father had been setting his alarm in the mornings so he could bring Martha to school, a journey of just two miles from Sarah's house, but a round trip of almost fifteen for him.

'I really don't mind,' he told her, whenever she brought it up. 'It's something for me to do.' But she couldn't expect him to keep doing it indefinitely, and with the children getting older, it was inevitable that there would be more demands on a driver. They couldn't be dependent on him all the time: it wasn't fair.

She would have to learn to drive, even if the thought brought her out in goose pimples. She suspected she'd be useless at it, far too nervous to be safe, but she had no choice. When the weather improved and the days got longer, she'd find a driving school, take some lessons and hope that she didn't kill anyone.

She left the hall and returned to the kitchen. The aroma of baking buns wafted to meet her when she opened the door. She stood on the threshold, taking in her daughter as she flicked through the pages in the cookery book, her son as he played with his train set.

She thought back to the years when she'd imagined just such a scene, when it had seemed as if it would be denied to her forever. Now it was here, and she was looking at it through such different eyes.

But she had a lot to be thankful for. She had two healthy children, family support and a job she loved. She would appreciate it all, and not look back. And if she felt desperately lonely sometimes, that was only to be expected, and would have to be endured.

HELEN

'Well,' Helen said, looking around, 'this is nice.'

It was horrendous. Exposed silver pipework – was that supposed to be trendy? – running along the orange walls that clashed with the drab mustard units in the tiny kitchenette. A dark green Venetian blind on the little window above the sink, a brown Formica-topped counter that separated the area from the rest of the room. Plenty of colours, none of which looked remotely comfortable together.

She glanced down at the navy carpet, eyed its suspicious dark splotches – how long since it had been put down? Probably just as well it was navy. And no dining table or chairs: they must eat all their meals standing at the counter, or sitting on the couch. A bright purple blanket thrown over it, hideous against the orange walls, and hiding God alone knew what.

And everything was open plan, an entire living space for two people in one not particularly big room, with no effort made to hide the ancient-looking double bed pushed against the opposite wall. She tried not to think about how many had slept in it, or not slept, before Alice and Jackie had got to use it.

There was a smell too, an underlying thick odour that brought to mind boiling cabbage and wet socks. She longed to fling open the long, narrow window, despite the ice-cold biting wind that had met her at the airport. Wales in April was even colder than Ireland, which was saying something – and this horrible little space felt no warmer than the street outside.

But none of that mattered. None of it made her regret her decision to come. As soon as she'd read Alice's invitation, which had arrived out of the blue a fortnight earlier, she'd realised she'd been waiting for it. Hoping for it.

We thought you might like to come and see the flat, Alice had written, *if you feel well enough to travel. You could check out Cardiff, stay a couple of nights. We'd have to book you in to a B&B, we've no spare room, but there are plenty of cheap ones nearby.*

And Helen, who was becoming mightily fed up with convalescence, had thought, Why not? And here she was, fresh off the airport bus – which had dropped them, thankfully, less than five minutes' walk away.

'Have a seat,' Alice said, pushing buttons on a gas heater that looked at least as old as herself. 'I'll put the kettle on for coffee.'

'Actually –' Helen unzipped her case and lifted out a bottle of whiskey '– I might have a drop of this instead, but do boil the kettle because I think I'd like it hot.' Maybe one or two toddies would thaw her out, stop her gut clenching with the cold, take the numbness from her toes.

Alice looked at her. 'Are you OK? You're very pale.'

'Just a bit chilly, I'll be fine once I warm up.'

'Go and stand by the fire – it's actually quite good once it gets going.' Alice filled the kettle and plugged it in. 'I hope this trip wasn't too soon – after you being sick, I mean.'

'It was months ago. I'm well over it.'

It was five months ago, and she wasn't completely over it. Her chest still hurt slightly when she breathed. 'It'll take a while,' the doctor had told her, 'before you feel back to full strength. Just take it easy, let others do the running around for you.' So she'd scaled back on the writing, doing just enough to remind people that she was still out there.

To her slight alarm, her mother had taken to visiting every few days, bringing fruit and wedges of quiche and slivers of smoked salmon, and insisting that Helen not call to see her until the weather softened. And of course Frank had been in his element, keeping her supplied with chicken soup and oranges, fussing over her as much as he was allowed to.

Christmas had been interesting, for two reasons. It was their first without her father, and it was Frank's introduction to her family. Amazing that he and her mother hadn't already met, particularly during Helen's week in hospital, with both of them visiting daily – they'd missed each other by minutes once – and in the immediate aftermath, when Frank had been a frequent caller, watching Helen like a hawk to see if she showed signs of getting sick again.

But they'd never come face to face, until finally it was unavoidable.

'I'd like to bring a friend to dinner,' she'd said to her mother, the week before Christmas. 'He's a man I've been seeing for a while.' Her mother had agreed so readily that Helen had been thrown – had the prospect of just Helen and Alice at dinner been so distasteful that anyone else would have been welcomed? – until the thought had struck her that a male presence, whoever the male, might make it a little easier for a woman's first Christmas without her husband.

For whatever reason, Frank had been duly invited – and he'd been a godsend. He'd turned up in a suit, which of course had impressed her mother right away. He'd presented her with a jar of hand cream that smelt wonderfully of lavender – 'Organically made by one of my suppliers,' he'd told her – and he'd praised every course of her immaculately presented dinner.

Afterwards he'd pulled crackers with Alice – the two of them having hit it off, thankfully, when they'd met the night before – before treating them to a rendition of 'White Christmas' in an unexpectedly tuneful baritone that Helen hadn't previously encountered.

He'd charmed her mother on a day that would have been far more poignant without him; he'd prevented them dwelling on the fact that one of their number was missing. He'd delighted Alice, he'd made them all laugh. He was still perfect on paper, and Helen was still waiting to fall in love.

'You wouldn't have a lemon, I suppose,' she said now. Hot whiskey without a slice of lemon was like a boiled egg without salt.

Alice opened the fridge. 'Actually, we do. I sneak them home from the pub. Can't have a G-and-T without lemon.'

Helen raised an eyebrow. 'You drink gin, at your age?'

Alice laughed, pulling a knife from a drawer. 'For one thing, you probably had your first drink at ten, and for another, I'm twenty, as you well know, which means I've been perfectly legal for two years. I'm even going to join you in a hot toddy, so there.'

Helen stood in front of the hissing fire and watched her cutting the lemon into slices, taking two glasses down from a press. An adult, no longer the child who'd defied her mother at every turn. Helen's mothering, such as it had been, was done.

'For your information I was sixteen before I tasted alcohol. And it was cider, not whiskey. I didn't graduate to spirits until I met your father in my late twenties.'

'And I probably drove you to more drink,' Alice

said cheerfully, unscrewing the cap of the whiskey bottle. 'I didn't make it easy, did I? With you having to cope on your own, I mean.'

Helen felt the echo of a long-ago sorrow, remembering the wretch she'd been after Cormac's death, the resentment of Alice she'd struggled to overcome as they'd muddled their way through her childhood.

'You don't remember him,' she said. 'Your dad.'

Alice shook her head, spooning sugar into the glasses. 'Not really. I mean I know what he looked like from photos, but I can't . . . picture him, or hear his voice, or anything.'

The kettle boiled. She made the toddies and handed one across the counter to Helen. 'So what'll we drink to?'

'You,' Helen replied, cradling the glass in her frozen hands, inhaling the blessed warmth of the steam that rose to her face. 'All grown-up.'

'And you,' Alice replied, 'for getting me there.'

The conversation was bittersweet. Helen swallowed a lump in her throat: a legacy of her illness, tears threatening more easily these days, not that she gave in to them much. They clinked glasses and drank, standing in front of the fire. The sinking wintry sun hit the exposed pipes and made them glint, which didn't improve them much but brightened the room a little. The gas fire popped softly as it struggled to banish the chill.

'So where's Jackie?'

'Out with friends.'

Jackie had long since left the grocery-delivery business behind. These days she worked behind the counter in a little wholefood self-service restaurant whose proprietors didn't mind her taking home the leftovers at the end of the day. *We never have to buy dinner*, Alice had written. *It's great, all very healthy stuff. But once a week we get a takeaway, when we're both craving a bit of junk food.*

'Actually,' Alice said, looking into her glass, 'I kind of asked Jackie to make herself scarce this evening.'

Helen heard the new note in her voice, and some tiny alarm sounded in her head. She sipped her drink and waited.

'Well . . .' Alice looked up, and the expression on her face sent Helen's mind flying through possibilities. Alice was pregnant. It was always that, wasn't it, when a daughter had something difficult to say to a parent? Or she was emigrating to Australia. Or she was sick, with something bad.

The gas fire gave a sudden loud splutter, making both of them turn towards it.

'The thing is,' Alice went on, still watching it, 'I have a new job. I started last week.'

Relief washed through Helen. 'What kind of a job?'

Alice turned back, smiling. 'I'm working for a design agency as a graphic artist. I saw an ad and applied, and I did a test for them and they took me on straight away. They're paying me peanuts but I love it, and I don't care.'

Not sick, not pregnant, not emigrating. Working

in design, using her talent. All good. Helen began to speak, but Alice hadn't finished.

'I'm keeping on the pub work. It's just three nights a week and I enjoy it. But the agency job is permanent, Monday to Friday, and they'll review my position after six months, and I might get a rise.'

A new job, one that paid her so little she had to keep pulling pints three nights a week. But she loved it, and she was waiting for her mother's approval.

'That's great,' Helen said. 'Well done. I'm happy you're doing something artistic. You should be. You never said you were applying for jobs.'

'I wanted to keep it a surprise, in case nothing came of it. Then when you said you were coming over, I thought I'd save it and tell you face to face.' Alice's smile brought out her dimple. 'Mum, it's really brilliant. I'm working with a copywriter, and we're in a studio with three other teams. There's a great atmosphere, and everyone's been so nice and welcoming.'

She looked younger than twenty, with her father's grey eyes and pale skin, and limbs that had gone from gangly to graceful somewhere along the way. Her hair was the longest it had ever been, beyond her shoulders now, falling in gentle waves rather than Helen's wild curls before she'd taken the kitchen scissors to them.

Alice was beautiful. The realisation came to Helen like a key slotting quietly into its lock. Her daughter was a beautiful young woman.

'There's something else,' Alice said then, fishing the lemon slice from her drink to press it against the side of her glass. 'I have another thing to tell you.'

Helen's fears came tumbling back. Alice had given her the good news first. She'd saved the bombshell for after.

Alice raised her head and looked directly at Helen. 'Mum, I'm . . . gay.'

Helen stared at her, dumbfounded. The words sat in the space between them, the last thing she'd been expecting. For what seemed like an awfully long time, neither of them spoke. A toilet flushed somewhere. A woman, or maybe a child, shouted something. A siren sounded distantly, three floors below them.

Finally, Helen found her voice. 'Oh . . .' she began, the word scratching in her throat, making her cough. She was aware of Alice's eyes glued to her face as she caught her breath, trying to gather her thoughts.

Her daughter was gay; she liked women. The news wasn't going to cause the earth to topple off its axis. *Get a grip*, Helen told herself fiercely. *Whatever you say, don't fuck this up.*

'Well, that's a relief,' she said. 'I thought you were going to tell me you were pregnant.'

Alice blinked. Her anxious expression didn't change.

'That was a joke,' Helen said. 'It's OK, I'm fine with it.'

'Seriously? You don't mind?'

'Of course I don't mind. You think I give a damn about that, as long as you're happy?'

Alice's eyes brimmed suddenly. 'Wow,' she said softly. 'That might just be the nicest thing you've ever said to me.'

Helen watched her thumbing away the tears, listened to her blaming them on the whiskey. She refused Alice's offer of a second drink, still trying to feel her way around the revelation.

Alice was gay. Her daughter was gay. Why had the possibility never occurred to Helen? How could she not have guessed? No boyfriend all through her teens, not even a hint of one. Plenty of female friends, the odd male now and again, who never seemed interested in Alice that way. Had they all known? Was Helen the only one who hadn't?

The news brought her little joy. How could it, when she knew the prejudices Alice would inevitably face, the ignorance she was bound to come across over the years? In a heterosexual-oriented world it was harder to be gay than straight, a lot harder.

And another realisation struck her, taking her by surprise: she'd expected, one day, to become a grandmother. Not for years, of course, not for at least another decade, but she'd assumed it would happen sometime. And she'd wanted it to happen, to see echoes of Cormac and herself in brand new little faces, to feel that they were being carried on into the next generation. Who would have imagined that she, of all people, would feel that way?

But whether she wanted them or not, grandchildren didn't seem very likely now. A feeling of heaviness settled in her chest.

'Why didn't you tell me when you were home at Christmas?'

'I wanted to, but Frank was around, or Granny . . . and, anyway, you were still getting over being sick. It just didn't seem like the right time.'

'Well, I'm glad you've told me now.'

'Thanks, Mum.' Alice found Helen's hand and squeezed it briefly. 'For taking it so well, I mean.'

The two of them would probably never share a home again, but in due course Alice and Jackie, or whoever she ended up with, might move back to Dublin – or Helen and Frank, in the fullness of time, might buy a little holiday cottage in Wales. There were always ways of keeping your important people close to you.

'Come on,' Helen said, setting her empty glass on the counter. 'We'd better find my B&B or they'll give away my bed. And then you can take me to a nice restaurant and let me buy you dinner.'

And it wasn't until much later – after they'd eaten bowls of pasta, after they'd taken a taxi back to the B&B, Helen's tiredness making a walk impossible, after she'd waved Alice goodnight and watched her being driven off, after she'd climbed the stairs to her small single room – it wasn't until then that she allowed herself to give vent to the tears that had been waiting to fall ever since she'd seen Alice standing in the arrivals hall at Cardiff airport, waiting for her mother.

And after they'd been shed for Alice and herself, for all the useless, angry years between them, the heaviness in her chest lifted and she fell into an exhausted, dreamless sleep.

SARAH

'I'm writing a cookbook for children,' Sarah said. She couldn't think why it hadn't occurred to her. The minute she'd read Helen's letter, it had seemed so obvious a solution.

You're a trained cook. You cook for a living, for God's sake. And you have two young children, so you know your target market, and exactly what level to pitch a cookbook at. What are you waiting for? If nothing else, it'll keep you busy, take your mind off the crap that happened.

So obvious – and the more Sarah thought about it, the more ideas came rushing into her head.

'I'm going to have two children as the characters in it,' she said, 'a boy and a girl, so hopefully it'll appeal to both. They'll be making the dishes, and it'll be like a story, with lots of pictures. I'll have some recipes for no-cook dishes that the children can do all by themselves, but there'll be clear symbols wherever parents need to get involved.

It'll all be very easy to read, with no hard words or cookery jargon.'

She'd trawled through her selection of cookery books at home before finding more in the library. She was picking out recipes that could be adapted for children, and copying them carefully into the big hard-covered notebook Helen had sent with her letter.

I know you'll feel duty bound to use it, because you have a lovely active conscience that always makes sure you do what's expected of you. Gather your recipes together, then sort them into groups, maybe party food, picnic food, holiday food – oh, I don't know, you're the expert here. And by the way, I'm giving you a deadline of Christmas to have the first draft ready, because again you'll feel compelled to meet it. No pressure.

'I'm not really going to be making up my own dishes,' Sarah said. 'This is more about simplifying and adapting what's already out there and making it more accessible to any children who think they might like to cook. But I may throw in a few of my own creations. We'll see.'

She had confided in Martha and Stephen. 'I'm going to write a proper cookery book for children just like you,' she'd told them. Stephen was still a little young to grasp the significance, but Martha had been impressed.

'A real book? Like you can buy in a shop?'

'Well, I'm hoping someone will want to turn it into a real book.'

'And can me and Stephen be in it?'

'Absolutely – but I might have to change your names, just so nobody gets mixed up.'

She had no idea if anyone would go for her idea, but Helen was going to help with contacts she had.

I feel obliged to smooth your way if I can, after trashing the novel that I never even read all those years ago. I'll have a think about who I can get to read it.

And as the cookbook started to take shape in Sarah's head, as she added to her collection of recipes and began to sort them, her excitement grew. There was nothing comparable already published, she was sure – she would be breaking new ground. Surely some publisher would be interested in filling a gap in the market.

'So what do you think?' she asked.

Martina, confined to her bed for most of the day now since the fall that had broken her hip and arm in January, threw her a scornful look. 'A cookery book for children? I never heard such nonsense. Children don't want to be stuck in a kitchen with an apron on, they want to play outside with their friends, especially boys. No, I can't see anyone being interested in that at all.'

'Oh dear,' Sarah said, digging her nails into her palms to keep the smile off her face. 'Maybe I should forget all about it so.'

Thankfully, Martina's opinion wasn't shared among Sarah's family. Christine was all for it. 'Paddy would love it – he always wants to help me when I'm cooking.' Paddy was eight, and secretly Sarah's favourite nephew. Quieter than his two older brothers, and so patient with Stephen when his small cousin followed him around.

Her father approved too. 'Great idea, just up your street. Surprised no one thought of it before.'

Neil hadn't been informed. The first person she would have told in the past, now excluded from any events in her life that didn't concern the children. They met only when he came to collect Martha and Stephen, and again when he dropped them back. Sarah dreaded the encounters, her hurt still raw, and kept conversation to a minimum.

'He's living in Noreen's house,' Martha had said after their first overnight visit. 'She made us hot chocolate with marshmallows.'

'She's got a pond with goldfishes in it,' Stephen had said, and Sarah had had to grit her teeth and pretend to be impressed, and silently wish Noreen and her goldfish at the bottom of a much larger body of water.

In the same letter, Helen told Sarah that Frank was moving in with her, eleven months since their first date.

I'm a disgrace, living in sin at forty-nine. He wanted me to move to his house, which is the one where he grew up, but you should see it. It's about three times the size of mine, with mountains of giant mahogany furniture that was probably there since his great-great-grandfather's time. I'd feel like I was living in a museum – and I'm betting it's impossible to heat. There's a big yard out the back full of pots of things that he's bringing on for the garden centre, and that I'd probably kill in a week just by being near them. The only things that grow for me are weeds. Anyway, I want to stay put for when Alice and Jackie come home for holidays.

The news of Alice had taken Sarah by surprise. The only gay person she knew was Lawrence, who delivered vegetables from his farm to the nursing home, and who had them in stitches with his commentaries on the latest episodes of *Fair City*, which he loved, and *Glenroe*, which he claimed to despise, but which he still watched avidly.

Lawrence, of course, had never made reference to his sexual orientation but his gait, his voice, his whole demeanour said it louder than any words. He lived in a converted stable at the back of his married brother's house, and they farmed the land between them. Sarah had wondered, from time to time, how he coped in a small rural community, and where he went to find like-minded folk, and whether he'd ever been targeted because of his difference.

There was never talk of a partner, never a hint of a romantic interest. It must be hard for him, existing as he did within his locality in a minority of one. She tried to imagine Martha or Stephen in years to come telling her they were gay, and she wondered if she would be as accepting as Helen seemed to be.

Jackie is a decent girl and they seem happy together, which is all you want for your child, right? I'm just stunned that it never occurred to me. Maybe I didn't want it to. It's a tough road, but hopefully she'll be able for whatever's flung at her.

In the meantime there was a cookery book to be written – or maybe a series: maybe half a dozen slim little books were called for. In pastel colours – no, primary colours, bold reds and blues and yellows. With cartoon illustrations, or maybe photos of real children in action in the kitchen. And then there was a title to be decided on. So much to think about before her Christmas deadline.

But all good, all very good indeed. Just the tonic she needed.

HELEN

'Where should I hang my jackets?'

Sixteen years since she'd lived with a man, since anyone other than Alice had been given a key: even Helen's mother didn't own one. Helen had moved in when the house was Cormac's, and it had become theirs. Now Cormac was gone, and Frank was moving in. It was . . . She searched for a word and settled on 'strange'.

'Is it OK to put my golf clubs under the stairs?'

He wasn't selling his own house: that had never been up for consideration. For one thing, there were all the potted plants in his big back yard, destined for the garden centre when they grew strong enough – no room for them in Helen's poky space. And for another, the house had been in his family for five generations and wasn't easily parted with.

'I can leave those books in boxes, if you'd prefer.'

From the start, Alice had approved of him. 'He's a dote,' she'd said to Helen, 'and it's obvious he's mad about you.' When Helen had told her he was moving in, an envelope had arrived from Cardiff addressed to both of them. The hand-painted illustration on the card inside had been of a car disappearing into the distance, tin cans rattling on strings from the bumper and a *just shacked-up* sign stuck in the back window.

Delighted with your news, Alice had written. *Just make sure you don't turn my room into a nursery.*

A nursery. Pregnant at forty-nine: it didn't bear thinking about. Helen had barely survived motherhood at twenty-nine. Although Frank would probably be in his element – she could just see him with a toddler on his knee.

'My van will have to stay on the road. Hope the neighbours don't mind.'

She hadn't broken the news to her mother yet, but she didn't see any complaints being made. As far as Margaret D'Arcy was concerned, Frank was the knight in shining armour Helen had missed first time around. She'd get over no ring eventually.

'Are you completely sure about this?' he asked, standing in the middle of her living room, surrounded by boxes and bags. 'You can change your mind – I can stay in my own place. I won't be upset.'

Because he knew, after nearly a year of being a couple, after all their nights together, after countless days out, after meeting her mother and her daughter, that he was the one in love here. He was sensitive and kind and courteous, and a far better man than she had any right to, and she desperately wanted to return his feelings – because if anyone deserved to be loved, Frank Murphy did.

392

She put her arms around his waist and stood on tiptoe to press her lips to his. 'Of course I'm sure,' she told him. 'You're very welcome here. Mind you, I'm a bitch to live with. You'll probably have run out screaming within a week.'

He laughed his rich, happy laugh, enfolding her in his strong arms. 'Never.'

In time, he'd love his way into her heart. She was sure of it.

SARAH

'**M**rs Flannery, you need to relax a little. You're not making it any easier for yourself by being so tense.'

'I'm *trying*,' Sarah said crossly. 'I might manage it if you didn't keep going on about it.'

Easy for him to be relaxed: all he had to do was sit beside her and criticise. She was the one supposed to steer this monster down the road without careering into a gatepost, or sending a pedestrian flying. Her fingers ached from being clamped so tightly on the steering wheel.

'Now, Mrs Flannery, we're approaching a bend,' the instructor said. 'Time to change down in gear. Do you remember what to do?'

'Of *course* I don't,' she snapped. 'I can't possibly remember everything you've said.' Why did he insist on calling her Mrs Flannery? She'd told him a dozen times her name was Sarah. Stupid man.

His calm voice didn't change. 'No problem . . . Ease up on the accelerator, and at the same time depress the clutch gently.'

Sarah's left foot slammed down on the clutch.

'Now lift your foot slowly off the accelerator,'

the instructor repeated, 'and take hold of the gear stick.'

Sarah's hands didn't move from the steering wheel.

'The gear stick, Mrs Flannery, the bend is coming up now. Move it from third to second the way you practised. Nice and quick.'

Sarah grabbed the gear stick and jiggled it around.

'No, you're going into fourth now – back to second. Bring it into the centre and over to me, and then down again . . . Watch the road, keep your eyes on the road. Keep your foot on the clutch – no, no, that's the accelerator—'

She revved the engine loudly as the car jerked violently forward before cutting out, right on the bend. She thumped the wheel with her palms.

'Oh, this is *too* hard. I *can't* do it.' She looked pleadingly at the instructor. 'Will you drive it home? I don't think I'm cut out to be a driver.'

'You're doing fine,' he told her in his infuriatingly calm voice. 'This is just your second lesson. You can't expect to learn it all at once. Now, make sure you're in neutral gear before starting the engine again.'

She gritted her teeth and grabbed the gear stick. It wasn't working, she'd never manage it. She'd been a nervous wreck after her first lesson, and it was looking like she'd need to be hospitalised after this one.

And the worst thing, the most *horrible* thing was,

even if she did learn to drive, even if she became the world's most careful driver, she could still run into black ice, or a slick of oil on the road, or a drunk driver careening at full tilt towards her. She could die, or be horrendously maimed, without doing one single thing wrong.

She managed to get the car started and they jerked down the road. The hedges and trees flew past alarmingly fast – surely he should pull her up on that. She must be well over the speed limit, but she was afraid to try to slow down in case they cut out again.

'You could go a little faster,' he murmured. 'Get out of second gear, move up into third.'

Faster? She wanted to look at him to see if he was joking, but she didn't dare take her eyes off the windscreen. Oh, why had she started this? Her father was perfectly happy running the children around – and it gave him something to do; he'd said it himself. And he was a very steady driver – she need never worry when the children were in his car.

'Left foot on the clutch, down all the way, that's it. Now slide the gear stick over to you and then up . . . very good. Now ease off on the clutch again, and away you go.'

She'd wait until they were home, and then she'd tell him she didn't know when she'd be free for another lesson. She'd say she'd be in touch, she was under no obligation to keep going, and she didn't care about having paid for six lessons in advance: that was the least of her worries. She'd given it a go and it hadn't worked. Anyway, she had the children's cookbook to finish. She hadn't time for driving lessons.

'Watch the cyclist here. Check your mirror before moving out. Don't forget your indicator. Keep well out . . . not quite that far.'

So much to remember, pedals and gears and mirrors and indicators to keep account of – and that was before it got dark, and you had to think of lights too. She couldn't understand how people ever got the hang of it, and yet you'd see really young drivers, much younger than her, flying around in their cars.

Maybe she'd left it too late, maybe forty was too old to learn a skill as complicated as driving. Christine had learnt before she was twenty. But Sarah had never wanted to learn, and she didn't now.

'Approaching the bridge,' the instructor murmured. 'Slow down, check your mirror, use your indicator.'

The bridge, upgraded last year, its wooden surface replaced with concrete, much to the disgust of the inhabitants of the surrounding area, a few of whom had protested for weeks while the renovations were going on. The old railings were gone, a much higher structure in place on either side now, metal struts punctuating a mesh fence. Not attractive in the least but perfectly functional, and the river still clearly visible below. Safer too, no risk of anyone scaling that fence to jump in, with its crown of metal spikes.

Somehow she survived the hour without further mishaps, and turned finally onto her own road with relief. As she approached the house, she saw Neil's car parked outside. Had the driving lesson run late? She checked the dashboard clock and read a quarter to six, the time they were supposed to finish. But maybe the clock was slow.

'What time does your watch say?' she asked the instructor.

'Almost ten to six.'

Neil never brought them back early. Something had happened. There'd been an accident, or one of the children was sick. Sarah jammed on the brakes and the car lurched to a halt in the middle of the road.

'You need to pull in to the side,' the instructor told her. 'Put your gear stick into neutral, switch on the engine again.'

She ignored him, grabbing her bag from the back seat and yanking open the door.

'Hang on, d'you want to make another—'

'I'll ring you,' she called, as she half ran up the path. The front door was ajar. She pushed it open with trembling hands, her heart pounding. Martha had fallen off a tree – Stephen had run out onto the road. She stumbled down the hall and into the kitchen.

Neil sat at the table, Stephen on his lap. Beside him, Martha looked up from her open colouring book. All was calm.

Sarah scanned her children's bodies for bandages

or other evidence of calamities, and found none. No sign of tears recently shed, nothing at all amiss as far as she could see.

'Your face is funny,' Martha said.

Sarah forced a smile, aware of Neil's eyes on her. 'Is it?' She must be as white as a ghost. 'You're back early. It just gave me a surprise.'

It was disconcerting to have him in the house when there wasn't a birthday party going on. It was uncomfortable to see him sitting at the very kitchen table where he'd told her, just eight months before, that it was all over between them, that he'd fallen in love with Noreen. She waited for him to explain.

'We just arrived,' he said. 'I was hoping for a word. I thought you'd be here.'

He wanted to see the children more than once a week; he wanted more than one overnight visit a fortnight. She'd been dreading it but she'd assumed it would come. He was their father. He had every right, even if he'd smashed their mother's heart in pieces.

'You could have said whatever it was on the phone,' she told him, hearing how brittle her voice sounded. 'You didn't have to come in person.'

'Five minutes,' he said, getting to his feet and depositing Stephen on his vacated chair. 'That's all, honestly.'

She couldn't very well refuse, with the children in the room, with Martha, no doubt, taking it all in. She got Stephen's tub of Lego from a press and placed it on the table in front of him. She filled two plastic beakers with juice, then peeled and sliced an apple and divided it between two plates.

'I'm just going to talk to Daddy for a minute,' she told them, crossing to the back door. 'I'll be out here.'

'I'll', not 'we'll'. There was no 'we' any more.

In the garden she sat on the wooden bench and waited to hear what was coming, her eyes fixed steadily on the cherry tree.

'D'you mind if I sit?' he asked, and she slid over without replying. He stayed at the opposite end, leaving a good two feet between them. For a minute there was silence, which Sarah determined not to break. He was the one who wanted to talk.

Finally, he cleared his throat. 'Sarah,' he said, and she realised that he was nervous. She kept looking straight ahead, although she was aware that he had turned sideways to face her.

'I just wanted you to know,' he went on, 'that I've moved out of Noreen's house.'

This was so utterly unexpected that she swung her head to look at him.

'We made a mistake – I made a mistake. It should never have happened.'

She couldn't believe it. Moved out of Noreen's house. A mistake. She dropped her gaze, turned away to stare at the bottom of the garden again, trying to take it in.

'I'm so sorry. I know I hurt you badly. I behaved

abominably and I will never forgive myself for that.'

The grass around the tree trunk had grown to almost a foot high. She'd get the clippers to it after dinner. She didn't trust herself to speak.

'I'm living with my mother. I just thought you should know.'

Living with Nuala, less than ten minutes down the road.

He got to his feet. 'Well, that's it. That's all I wanted to say.'

Sarah looked up at him. 'You can see yourself out. Leave the children in the kitchen.'

After he'd gone she sat on, digesting this new turn of events. He'd left Noreen and moved in with his mother. He'd made a mistake – did that mean he'd never actually been in love with Noreen? And if that were the case, where did that leave Neil and Sarah now?

She stood, smoothing her dress over her thighs. It left them exactly where he'd put them last November: it left them separated. This new development didn't change a thing. He hadn't said he still loved Sarah, he hadn't pleaded with her to take him back. He'd given no sign that he wanted a reconciliation, which was just as well, since she had no intention of allowing him back into her life.

She'd keep up the driving lessons. She'd show him that she and the children could manage fine without him. She'd say nothing to Christine or her father about this latest development: for now she wanted to keep it to herself, and get used to it.

Noreen was gone. She was out of their lives, hopefully forever. Neil was alone. That would take some getting used to.

HELEN

Sarah

Commiserations on the driving test. If it's any consolation it took me two attempts – an ex taught me, which didn't help – but I'm a whiz behind the wheel now. Sending a Blondie CD to cheer you up, in the hope that you've got yourself a CD player by now. I love Blondie, which must mean I'm mellowing in my old age. When I was in my twenties I was such a rock chick you wouldn't believe: Suzi Quatro was the only woman for me.

Sounds like your kiddie cookbook is taking shape. You might be right about it suiting a series, but I wouldn't worry about that at this stage – time enough to sort a format when you've bagged a publisher. Yes, I said when. I've got this feeling that you're on to a winner here, girl – and I even have someone in mind who might be interested. He's a publisher – he works for a UK company but he's based here, sort of their man in Ireland – who often sends me books to review. Let me know when you're happy to have him look at it and I'll give him a shout.

Frank is surviving the cohabitation, which has shot him up in my estimation. Any man who can cope with living with yours truly deserves a medal. He's talking about us going to Scotland for Christmas, taking a house and inviting Alice and Jackie to join us. Trouble is, he wants my mother to come too, says we can't leave her on her own. I know, I know, I'm a rotten daughter, but I can't see us having a merry old time with her there. He's right though, damn it.

Brace yourself: the cat died. No idea how old it was, but I'm guessing it had a few years on Rip Van Winkle. Frank, old softie, buried it out the back, planted a rose bush on top of it. Probably bloom like crazy, just to spite me.

You haven't mentioned Neil and his hussy in a while. Presume things are unchanged on that front, although it would be nice if one of them had a non-life-threatening accident that laid them up for weeks to get on the other's nerves. Good on you for moving on, and do stick with the driving – you'll get there, and you'll wonder what took you so long.

H x

Hey there

I know it's still months away, but I wanted to mention it in case you two were booking tickets to Ireland for Christmas. Frank has had this corny idea of spending it in Scotland, and was wondering if you and Jackie would join us. He wants to rent a house, so we need to know if you're interested. He's threatening to write to you himself. You have been warned.

Hope all's well. How's work? Did you get the new heater? If you spent that cheque on gin I'll cut you out of the will. I mean it.

Let us know about Scotland. Could be fun.

Mum x

PS Granny will be invited too, so if she says yes, you and J would have to be just pals in her company. At eighty-four, I'm pretty sure the truth would be a bridge too far.

Dear Alice

Hope all is well in Cardiff. Frank here, just dropping a line to invite you and Jackie to spend Christmas with your mother and me – and hopefully your grandmother – in Scotland. I thought it might be nice to take a house there for a week or so. I've never been to Scotland, and would enjoy seeing it.

Of course, you may have your own plans, and if that's the case, no problem, but I know your mother would love to see you both, and so would I. We could pull a few more crackers, and I could make my special eggnog, which nobody can resist.

Looking forward to your response,
All the best,
Frank

Dear Mum and Frank
We'd love to come to Scotland, thanks for the invite. Jackie's been a few times, she says it's great. Let us know the plans as soon as they're in place. Presume we'll make our way to whatever airport you're flying to, and travel on from there.

Mum, we bought a heater, and we had enough left over for a bottle of gin! (Joke, just the heater.) Thanks again for the cheque – and the good news is that I've got another rise at work, just a fiver extra a week but it all helps.

Jackie says hi, and asked me to tell Frank that she LOVES eggnog. I foresee some sore heads this Christmas.

Alice xxx
PS You make such a lovely couple, har har.

SARAH

'An older brother of one of Aidan's pals got one of those Morrison visas for America. He's moving over in the summer. It's a great opportunity for him.'

'Mmm.'

'He has an uncle there, or maybe it's a cousin. They'll put him up anyway till he finds a job. He did engineering in college, so he'll probably get something easily enough. I'd hate to see any of mine going to live abroad though – I'm praying they all stay in Ireland. Does that make me really selfish?'

'What? No, of course not.'

'Did I tell you Aidan is saying he'd like to do medicine? I know he's only thirteen, he'll probably change his mind a dozen times, but wouldn't it be great to have a doctor in the family?'

'It would.'

'He was always a good student. I never had any problem getting him to do his homework. Not like the other two: it's a battle with Tom every night, and Paddy would spend his life daydreaming if I let him.'

'I know.'

Christine took another custard cream from the plate. 'So the cookery book is nearly done then.'

'Yes, nearly there.'

'You must be excited.'

'I am.'

'And Helen is going to talk to a publisher.'

'So she says.'

Christine lowered the biscuit into her tea. 'You don't sound too excited. Are you all right?'

Sarah shook her head. 'Sorry, just tired, that's all.'

'Are you upset about failing the driving test again?'

'I am a bit – but I didn't deserve to pass, I was hopeless. I went totally to pieces and forgot everything I'd learnt, just like the first time.'

'Have you applied again?'

'Not yet, but I will. I have to.'

'Good for you. Third time lucky. You know I'll sit in with you, anytime you want to go for a spin. Or Brian would – he'd probably be better.'

'Thanks.'

'And there's nothing else?'

'No . . . I just didn't sleep very well.'

Getting a good night's sleep, which Sarah had always taken for granted, was becoming more and more of a challenge. She fell asleep like she'd always done, but lately she'd begun waking around two or three, and it seemed to take an eternity before she dropped off again.

Maybe it was getting older, although forty was hardly old. Maybe it had to do with the cookery book, whose title she couldn't settle on, whose format she still wasn't sure about. Maybe she was mourning Martina, who had finally left them a few weeks ago.

Acerbic, contrary Martina, who'd squeezed her hand when she'd gone into early labour with Stephen, who'd told her fiercely that she was going to be fine as they'd waited for Dan to come with the van. Martina, who'd gone on clipping the hedges Charlie had begun to tame, who'd scoffed at the notion of a cookery book for children. Martina, who'd died as she'd lived, all alone, in the middle of the night.

'Look,' Sarah said, 'there's something I want to tell you.'

Because of course she knew what was keeping her awake, and maybe sharing it would help, after all.

Christine frowned. 'I hate when someone says that. It's usually something bad.'

'No, this isn't bad – at least . . . it's not bad, and it's not good. It's just something that happened, that's all.'

'Go on.'

A beat passed. A bird flew with a soft thump into the window before swerving away again.

'It's Neil,' Sarah said.

Christine's eyes narrowed immediately. 'What's he done now?'

'It didn't work out between him and . . . her. He's back living with his mother.'

'You're joking.'

'I'm not.'

'When?'

'A couple of months ago.'

Christine looked at her in disbelief. 'A couple of months ago? When did you find out?'

'He told me when it happened,' Sarah said, 'but I didn't—'

'Hang on – you've known about this ages, and you said nothing?'

'Christine,' Sarah said sharply, 'it was our business, mine and Neil's. I didn't have to tell anyone. I didn't have to tell you now, but I chose to.'

Christine clamped her mouth closed. For a handful of seconds there was a tense silence. From the garden Sarah heard Martha calling, 'My turn.'

'Sorry,' Christine said then, 'you're right. It's none of my business. It's just that I don't want to see you getting hurt again.'

'I won't get hurt,' Sarah replied. 'He hasn't – we're not getting back together, that's not the issue. It makes things easier, that's all, for the children, I mean. He's closer, and they get to see Nuala when he takes them at the weekend. And she's out of the picture, hopefully for good.'

Christine picked biscuit crumbs from the plate. 'Did he tell you what happened?'

'He just said he'd made a mistake.'

'Have you told Dad?'

'No. I will.'

Another short silence.

'More tea?' Christine asked.

'No thanks.' Sarah stood and unhooked her bag from the back of the chair. 'We should be going, we'll be late.' They were meeting her father in town to do the weekly shop.

'Sarah, don't take him back,' Christine said quickly. 'If he asks, I mean. Say no, OK?'

Sarah slung her bag over her shoulder. 'Of course I'll say no. I told you, it hasn't come up. There's no question of us getting back together.'

'Good . . . You sure I can't drive you into town? It's no bother.'

'No need, we're fine. Thanks.'

They walked the ten minutes to the bus stop and waited with a stout elderly woman in a cream coat, who nodded at Sarah and smiled at the children, and a teenage girl, whose headphones beat out a tinny rhythm that her left foot copied. Sarah sat on the narrow wooden seat, Martha on her lap, and rolled the buggy to and fro as she replayed her conversation with Christine.

So adamant her sister had been: *Don't take him back*, she'd said. As if Sarah had a choice, as if Neil had asked to come back.

Why hadn't he asked? If he and Noreen had been a mistake, why didn't that mean that he still loved Sarah? Why wasn't he begging her to forgive him? Why didn't he want to try again?

Because that was the crux, wasn't it? That was what had her tossing and turning at night. He'd left the woman who had broken up his marriage, but he hadn't even hinted at reconciliation with his wife. No wonder she was having trouble sleeping.

'Here comes the bus,' Martha said, and Sarah got to her feet with relief.

HELEN

'Six days and five nights,' Helen said. 'We're leaving the day before Christmas Eve and coming home on the twenty-eighth. We're flying to Glasgow and picking up a car there.'

'And the house is – where did you say?'

'Troon, a small town just a few miles away.'

'And Alice will be there, with her friend.'

Her friend. 'Yes, they're getting the train up from Cardiff and meeting us at the airport. So what do you think? Will you join us?'

Their second Christmas without Helen's father, and Frank adamant that her mother had to accompany them to Scotland, and Helen knowing he was right. But far from being grateful for having been included in their plans, her mother seemed dubious about joining them.

'You wouldn't want me along, cramping your style.'

Helen tamped down a flick of irritation. 'What style?' she asked. 'It's just a few days away, and it happens to be over Christmas, that's all. You'd be cramping nothing – and you'd be miserable here on your own.'

Her mother ran a finger along a fold line in the immaculate linen tablecloth that was sent to the dry cleaners once a week, whether it needed it or not. Helen felt like shaking her. If she was waiting to be told they really would love if she came, she was in for a long wait.

'Is there central heating?'

Helen had no idea. 'Of course there is. Frank would have checked all that out.'

'Because I'm sure it would be colder than here.'

'Don't worry about that.' *Jesus*, you'd think they were going to Outer Mongolia instead of a few days in bloody Scotland, an hour away on a plane. 'Frank is booking the flights tomorrow, so you need to make up your mind.'

'Well . . . if you're sure I wouldn't be in the way.'

Helen got to her feet: duty done. 'I'm sure,' she said, pulling on her coat. 'We'll book you in so.'

'Let me know what it costs. I'll pay my own way.'

'I know you will.' She fished her car keys from her bag.

'And I'd like to take you all out to dinner on Christmas Day. My treat.'

'Fine. That'd be nice.' Let her foot the bill for dinner for six if it kept her happy. 'Well, I'll be off then.'

Her mother didn't move. 'Helen,' she said, 'wait for a minute. Can you?'

Helen, surprised, looked back.

Her mother's face gave nothing away. 'Are you in a rush?'

'Not really.' What now? Helen lowered herself into the seat she'd just vacated. 'Was there something else?'

Her mother didn't respond right away. Her hands were clasped loosely on the tablecloth, the nails painted the same shell pink as ever, defying the swollen finger joints, the puckered skin criss-crossed with dark purple veins on the backs of her hands. Eighty-four since May.

'Can I tell you something?' she asked finally, her eyes meeting Helen's across the table. 'Something I think . . . needs to be explained.'

She seemed nervous. Nothing overt; a pinching around the mouth, a brittleness to the words. Helen lowered her bag to the floor. 'What is it?'

Her mother moistened her lips, the fingers of her topmost hand tapping softly onto the back of the other. 'Your father and I were married for nine years before you came along,' she began.

'I know that.'

She raised a hand slightly, let it drop again. 'Just let me . . . we'd given up expecting babies, and then you came along . . . and when you were born there were complications . . . I was very sick, I nearly died.' Tap, tap, tap, went her fingers. 'The priest anointed me.'

Helen hadn't known that. She remained silent, waiting for whatever was to come.

Her mother pressed her lips together, her tapping fingers finding and twirling the thin gold bands of her wedding and engagement rings, round and round they went; joints too swollen, surely, for them to come off easily now.

'And then they told us . . . that there would be no more children. They . . . they removed my womb, they said they had to—'

She broke off, mouth squeezed shut again. Helen sat unmoving.

'And . . . your father was so disappointed, he always wanted a son, and I'd hoped so much—' She broke off, drew in a steadying breath, gaze dropping to study her hands.

Helen watched dispassionately. She'd disappointed them by being a girl. Her only crime, something beyond her control.

'You see,' her mother went on, raising her eyes again to find Helen's, 'there was another baby.'

The words didn't register right away. Helen looked at her blankly for several seconds.

'You were a twin. You had a brother, but . . .' She trailed off, shook her head slowly, lips trembling. She fished a handkerchief from her sleeve and blew her nose.

Helen tried to make sense of what she was hearing. Two babies. There had been two babies, and the wrong one had survived – that was what she was being told, wasn't it? They'd wanted the boy and they'd got the girl.

As if she was reading her mind, her mother shook her head. 'It wasn't that we weren't grateful to have you – you mustn't think that. It was just . . . difficult to bear the other loss . . . and the thought that our chance was gone to have any more.'

Helen had had a brother who hadn't lived. Her mother had lost a baby and her womb all at once. No more children, Helen had been their lot. And her father had wanted a boy.

'I know we were never . . . demonstrative,' her mother said, eyes rimmed with red, nose pink-tipped. 'We were . . . distant. I know that. It wasn't deliberate, it was just . . . we were . . . you were . . . a reminder.'

And there it was. Every time her parents had looked at her they'd seen the ghost of her dead twin. There it was, the explanation she'd needed all her life.

And curiously, despite the terrible unfairness of her having been denied their affection, there was a measure of satisfaction in knowing why. There was even, she realised, some sympathy for their plight.

'Helen, I'm sorry,' her mother said brokenly. 'I know it wasn't easy for you. I wouldn't blame you if you were angry.'

She wasn't angry. She could have been: she had every right. But they hadn't done it deliberately, she recognised the truth of that. They weren't to blame. Nobody was to blame. She felt no anger.

'Why did you never tell me this?'

Her mother shook her head. 'I couldn't. I just couldn't. It wasn't . . . the done thing.'

No, not the done thing in the forties, or even

the fifties or the sixties. It wasn't until the nineties, not until she was an old woman, that she'd found a way to talk to her forty-nine-year-old daughter.

It didn't fix things between them; it was too late for happy-ever-afters in that respect. They'd still been snobs who'd turned their noses up at Helen's choice of husband. But an explanation had been offered. Knowledge had been shared, and that was something.

She got to her feet for a second time. She looked down at her mother.

'Thank you for telling me,' she said. 'Don't get up, I'll see myself out. I'll let you know when the flights are booked.'

Her mother nodded. 'Thank you . . . for inviting me.'

She looked small, her face pinched and reddened, her foundation blotchy beneath her eyes. The woman who'd given birth to Helen, who'd made sure, despite her torn feelings, that she was fed and warm and healthy. Who'd pulled a fine-tooth comb through her hair.

'You're welcome.' Helen pulled her car keys from her bag and left the room.

A twin brother, she thought, striding down the path, pulling open the wrought-iron gate. Imagine if he'd lived. Imagine how completely different her life might have been.

She walked through the gate, swinging it closed behind her. She turned left and collided with a man walking past. 'Sorry,' she muttered, stepping sideways out of his path and moving towards her car.

'Might have known,' he said.

She stopped, looked back. 'Bloody hell.'

He looked much the same as the last time they'd met, nine or ten months ago now. She remembered their shaky walk along the hospital corridor, the hyacinths that had been delivered after she'd got home.

'Thank you for the flowers,' she said, 'when I was sick. They were a surprise.'

The blue bowl they'd come in sat now on the kitchen worktop, filled with a clutter of biros, Sellotape, unmarked postage stamps teased from envelopes, rubber bands, paper clips. 'Keep the bulbs,' Frank had told her, 'they'll come again,' but she hadn't had the patience.

'Keeping well?' Breen asked. A heavy navy coat, a grey scarf wound around his neck. A couple of books tucked under his arm. 'No more hospital visits?'

'No, I'm fine . . . You? How are things?'

He moved his head in a gesture that could have meant anything.

'You live around here?' She'd never seen him in this neighbourhood.

'Not really, just walking.'

She nodded, turned her car key in her hand. 'Well . . .'

'You have time for a coffee?'

The invitation was totally unexpected. Her and

419

Breen having coffee. Her and Breen doing anything together that wasn't work-related.

He fixed her with a look she remembered. 'O'Dowd,' he said, 'it was a cup of coffee I was offering, not a marriage proposal. Don't worry about it.' He turned to go.

'I'd prefer a brandy,' she said, 'if it's all the same.'

Where was the harm? Let him buy her a drink, after all the pieces she'd written for him over the years. She could manage half an hour in his company – and after the conversation she'd just had, she could use a stiff drink.

She opened the car. 'Hop in, there's a place around the corner. I'm going that way.'

As long as he was paying, they'd check out the new boutique hotel on the sea front, opened recently enough for Helen never to have been inside. About two minutes' drive away, which was better than the ten minutes it would have taken them to walk there.

As he sat in beside her, Helen smelt his aftershave, or cologne, or whatever it was. A marine tang about it, not unpleasant. The wife, she supposed, every Christmas.

'So,' she said, pulling away, 'you miss the newspaper?'

'I do. I enjoyed it.'

She glanced at him, but his expression told her nothing.

'You were good,' she told him, 'much as I hate

to admit it. And so was I – so *am* I – much as you never admitted it.'

He smiled then, but made no response. She wondered why he'd asked her to join him; maybe he was already regretting it.

The silence lasted until she parked outside the hotel. 'This OK?'

'Fine. You've been here before?'

'No, it's not been open long . . . My mother had lunch with a friend. You?'

He shook his head. She wondered if he ever met a friend for lunch. She knew so little about him. They walked towards the entrance, her heels clacking over the paving stones. What was she doing, having brandy in the middle of the afternoon with Breen, of all people? He held open the door and she walked through, taking in the thick dark green carpets, the cream walls, the pleasant warmth after the outdoor chill.

In the bar she saw a scatter of armchairs and couches in various configurations of burgundy and cream, and heard jazz playing softly through discreet speakers. A fireplace opposite the counter held a little heap of coals that glowed red.

There were just three other occupants. Two foreign-looking men in suits sat side by side on a couch that was set into the wide bay window, both tapping at laptops, teapot and assembled crockery on the low table before them. At the far end of the room a younger man read a newspaper.

'Have a seat.' Breen turned towards the counter and Helen chose a pair of armchairs close to the fireplace, slipping out of her coat before sinking down, deciding to enjoy the decadence of brandy and jazz by a fire in the middle of a chilly October afternoon. Not Frank's scene at all; perfectly willing as he was to spend money on her, this padded luxury would make him uncomfortable.

Breen returned with two balloon glasses. 'Cheers,' he said, handing her one. No mixer: he'd taken her, rightly, for someone who drank it neat.

'*Sláinte.*'

She sipped the brandy, welcoming the golden warmth of it, watching as he set his books on the floor between them before taking off his scarf and coat and laying them over the arm of his chair. He wore a charcoal grey suit with a white shirt beneath. She couldn't picture him in anything other than a suit. He wore them well.

He sat, cradling the bowl of his glass. When he made no effort to speak, she cast about for a topic, and found it. 'I'm off to Scotland for Christmas,' she told him. 'Family gathering.'

He tipped his hands, swirling the brandy. 'You have people over there?'

'Alice, my daughter. She lives in Cardiff now. We're meeting up in Scotland.'

'Alice, yes.'

Silence. She tried again. 'That was my mother's house,' she said, 'where I met you.'

'You grew up there?'

'Yes.'

'And your father?'

She wondered if he'd recognise the name if she told him. 'Died last year.'

'I'm sorry.'

More silence. Helen leant back and looked at the fire, out of inspiration.

'Nice here,' he said. 'The hotel, I mean.'

'Lovely.'

She drank again, feeling the alcohol burning its way down. He still hadn't touched his, just held the glass in his cupped hands. At this rate she'd be finished before he started.

'O'Dowd,' he said then, 'can I tell you something?'

For the second time since she'd met him she was thrown. It didn't sound like he was going to share his plans for Christmas. 'What kind of something?'

He gave a short puff of laughter, gone as quickly as it had come. 'My wife—' He stopped, and raised the glass finally to his lips.

Helen stiffened. His *wife*? Was Breen about to get personal? Was that what they were doing here? Was she about to get the 'my wife doesn't understand me' line? She'd had more than enough revelations for one day. She waited in dread for him to continue, the brandy he'd bought her forcing her to stay and listen.

He lowered his glass – half-empty suddenly. 'My wife is bi-polar,' he said, fixing Helen with a stare so intense she had no choice but to meet it. 'She

423

was diagnosed nearly thirty years ago, at the age of thirty-three.'

His voice was so low and calm he might as well have been giving her the weather forecast. 'Unfortunately, she's never accepted the diagnosis, and tries periodically to do without her medication: not a good idea. She's also an alcoholic who won't admit it, which, as you can imagine, doesn't improve the situation.'

He stopped, still watching her face. Helen looked back at him, aghast. Why was he telling her all this? Did he imagine one brandy gave him the right to throw his problems into her lap? What did he expect, that she'd pat his shoulder and say, 'There there'?

'Tell me to fuck off,' he said then, in the same toneless voice. 'You look like you want to.'

Helen let out the breath she hadn't realised she was holding. 'Why are you telling me this? I mean, why are you telling *me*?'

He turned his head, looked towards the fire. 'Maybe you were handy, and I felt like sharing. Maybe because I knew you wouldn't feed me crap, like "Things will get better."'

And to her dismay, Helen realised that she felt some sympathy for him. If his story were true – and why would she doubt it? – he'd remained with a wife who, by the sound of it, needed round-the-clock care. He'd lived for years in a situation that a lot of people would have walked away from. Whatever else you could say about him, he hadn't walked away.

Thirty years ago she'd been diagnosed, presumably after they were married. He'd lived with it for thirty years.

That was why he'd given up his job, it must be. He'd loved being an editor – any fool could have seen how perfectly the job had fitted him. He'd been good at it, he'd been quick and sharp and fair, and whatever about their clashes, Helen had respected him for it.

She remembered suddenly asking him, the time they'd met in hospital, how he was enjoying retirement. 'It's Hell,' he'd said, or words to that effect. She remembered the thin woman walking beside him in the street. Bi-polar, and an alcoholic who refused to acknowledge it.

Little wonder he was cranky.

And desperate, if she was the only one he could find to talk to. As she hunted for something to say – what the hell could she say? – he drained his glass and got to his feet.

'You'll run a mile next time you spot me,' he said, folding his coat over his arm. 'Sorry about that – you just happened to be in the wrong place, nothing personal. I'll leave you in peace now. Have a good Christmas, O'Dowd. Tell Alice I said hello.'

'Do you want a lift somewhere?' she asked – but he shook his head and lifted a hand and strode from the room, depositing his glass on the counter as he passed, nodding farewell to the barman.

Helen sat on, cradling what was left of her brandy, imagining the Christmas they would have.

No mention of children, probably just the two of them sitting across the table from one another. Trying to make conversation, or maybe not bothering.

What could Helen have done? What help could she possibly be to him? He wasn't looking for help: he was like her, determined to solve his own problems. He'd needed an ear and she'd been there, that was all. But of all the people he might have chosen to confide in, it had to have been her. And of all days, with her mother's earlier news still sitting uneasily in her head.

She looked around the quiet, warm room. Tempting to stay there for a few hours, downing the brandies and getting quietly sozzled; she couldn't remember the last time she'd had too much to drink. She could phone Frank from Reception: he'd come and pour her into his van and bring her home. He wouldn't approve, sensible Frank, but he'd know better than to say it.

Breen could do with having a few too many drinks, forgetting his troubles for a night. He looked like he hadn't a clue how to be happy.

She finished her drink and got to her feet – no fun in getting drunk alone. As she put on her coat, she saw Breen's books on the floor. She stooped and picked them up: Gore Vidal and Kingsley Amis, which didn't surprise her in the least. She opened the Vidal and saw that it belonged to a library a couple of miles away, and was due back in a few days. Must have been on his way to return them when he'd met her, taking the scenic route to the library maybe, spinning out time until he had to go home.

She could drop them back; she could do that at least. She left a note for him at the reception desk, in case he came looking for them.

Outside a breeze was whipping up, the daylight almost completely gone. She scanned the dusky street in both directions but there was no sign of him. She got into her car and turned the heater on full blast, the taste of his brandy still in her mouth, and headed for home.

SARAH

'You could come here for dinner,' she said. 'You and Nuala, I mean.'

She saw the surprise bloom in his face. 'Are you sure about that? I know my mother would love it.'

'We missed her last year.'

She didn't say anything about missing him. She didn't tell him how miserable she'd been, how she'd sobbed her way through the cooking of Christmas lunch for the handful of nursing-home residents who hadn't had anyone to take them in, how she'd cycled home afterwards, still in tears, to cook another turkey for her father and the children. They'd been invited to Christine's for dinner but Sarah had refused, unable to face putting on an act all evening.

She made no mention of the effort it had taken to seem happy in front of the children as she'd opened her presents and pulled crackers, the terrible absence of Neil shouting out at her, how she'd tried not to think about him being with Noreen instead of with his family, but how it had been all she could think of.

She wondered if he remembered that she hadn't gone to the phone when he'd rung later that evening to wish the children a happy Christmas. She'd been terrified that his voice would cause more tears after the river she'd cried earlier.

'I've offered to do lunch at the nursing home again,' she told him, 'but I'll be home by three at the latest. You could come around half past. You could be there when the children are opening their presents.'

'We'd love that,' Neil said. 'Thank you, Sarah.'

She walked away from the car, conscious of his eyes on her. Nothing had changed: he was still taking the children on Saturday afternoons, and every other weekend they stayed the night with him and Nuala, and he phoned them just after dinner each weekday evening. Sarah wasn't offering any more; he wasn't asking for it. They spoke for a few minutes when he returned the children, that was all.

But where was the harm in inviting him and his mother to Christmas dinner? He was still the father of two children: he had a right and an obligation to be involved in their lives. And Nuala, who was innocent of any wrongdoing, certainly deserved to see her grandchildren on Christmas Day.

'You're mad,' Christine said. 'You let him back in and he'll turn around and do the same in three or four years' time.'

'I'm not letting him back in, I'm just having him to dinner. His mother is Martha and Stephen's granny. She deserves to be there, and I couldn't very well ask her without asking him.'

'Dad won't like it. He mightn't even go.'

'Well then,' Sarah replied lightly, 'he can go to you.'

Christine's sigh travelled down the phone line. 'Look, I'm sorry – it's just that I'm afraid you'll get hurt again.'

'I know, you keep telling me that . . . By the way, I've got a date for the driving test, Thursday week. Third time lucky, hopefully.'

And the subject of Neil and Christmas dinner was dropped, and not raised again during the conversation.

Her father, not surprisingly, was circumspect when he heard. 'Are you sure it's a good idea?' he asked. 'Are you certain you want to do this?'

'I'm certain. The children would love it, and I know Nuala would want to come.'

He made no response.

'You're OK with it, aren't you?'

The only time her family had been in the same room with Neil since his departure had been at the children's birthday parties, during which they'd studiously avoided any contact with him for the hour or so that he'd stayed. But this would be different, with her father and Neil thrown together for several hours, sitting around the same dinner table, opening presents with the children, making conversation before dinner.

'If you'd prefer to go to Christine's I'll understand,'

Sarah said, 'but I'd love you to be here – and so would the children.'

'I'll come, of course I will,' her father replied. 'And I'll do my best not to challenge him to a duel.'

She smiled at the idea of her eighty-two-year-old father standing back to back with Neil, six foot two and fifteen stone. 'Thanks, Dad – you're a pet.'

It was for the children. Christmas was all about families; they deserved to have both parents there. But lying in bed at night, safe in the darkness and silence of her room, she allowed herself to acknowledge that she wanted it too.

Dear Helen

Great news! I finally passed the driving test, third time lucky! I'm still petrified behind the wheel – I think I probably always will be – but I'll take it easy and hope for the best. At last I can let poor Dad off the hook and bring Martha and Stephen to school in the morning – and I've even got myself a car! Someone who works with Brian has a brother with a garage, and he found it for me. It's a Ford Fiesta and it's bright yellow, which I'm not mad about, but only four years old and apparently in good condition. I'm planning to put my bike in the boot every morning and drive as far as the school, then cycle on to the nursing home from there. I'll only drive when I have to.

And more news: I've invited Neil and his mother to Christmas dinner. I don't know what you'll have to say about that, but it just felt like the right thing to do. I'm still so confused about him. He hasn't said he wants to come back, hasn't even hinted at it, but maybe he's waiting for me to give some indication that I'd let him. Oh, I don't know, I'm so mixed up. I'll let you know how the day goes anyway.

Enjoy Scotland – only another week until you head off. Maybe Frank will propose over there! And I'm so glad your mother is going too. She'd have been so lonely without you and Alice, now that your father is gone. I'm sure you'll get on fine, and I'll look forward to hearing how it goes.

Right – deep breath: I think I've finished the cookbook! I'm terrified to show it to anyone, but I'm also very excited about it! I've tried it out on Martha, and on Paddy, my eight-year-old nephew, and they both said it was really easy to use. Martha did sausage rolls and Paddy made a batch of coconut castles. So if you're still happy to help, feel free to contact your publisher friend after Christmas – God, I'm full of butterflies after just writing that! Imagine if he actually wants to meet me – I'll be a nervous wreck!

I'm sending a tiny little gift, and one for Alice, which I hope you don't mind delivering,

since I haven't got her address in Cardiff.
Please give her a hug from me.

Happy Christmas, my friend, all the very
best to you and Frank for 1992, let's hope it's
a good one, as poor John Lennon would say.

Sarah xx

HELEN

Sarah Flannery

You little minx, inviting your ex to Christmas dinner. And his mother too, so it looks totally respectable, when you're probably planning to bat your eyelashes at him all evening. Just be careful, lady: I'm all for following your heart – and I suspect that he still has a hold on it – but look after yourself too, OK? Don't let him back into your life too easily. Make him deserve you.

Frank proposing marriage? He'd better not, unless he wants me to have a minor coronary. I've walked down the aisle once in my life, and I've no intention of doing it again, thank you.

You passed the driving test – fabulous. You'll be whizzing around the countryside in no time. Sending a dual Christmas/congratulations present of a road map and a compass, to keep you going in a straight line.

Cookbook is done, wonderful. I've gone ahead and contacted Paul the publisher, who is intrigued, and happy to have a look – he

434

says he'll bring it home and test it out on his kids. I've put his phone number at the top of this letter, and I've told him you'll call him first week in January to arrange delivery. See how I anticipated you chickening out, and made it impossible? Let me know what he says.

My photo frame is delightful, thank you. I'll put one of Frank and me in it and make his day, and Alice will be very happy to get hers – you're sweet to think of her. Frank asked why you and I have never met. I told him one day, when the time is right.

Oh, God, Cliff Richard has just started singing 'Mistletoe and Wine' again: must go and shoot the radio. Happy Christmas, hope it goes well. 1992 here we come.

H x

PS Met Breen a while ago – literally bumped into him. He bought me a brandy and gave me far too much information about his manic-depressive alcoholic wife. Poor sod, explains a lot.

Dear Mrs Flannery

Belated Happy Christmas – are you even allowed to wish someone Happy Christmas afterwards? Jackie and I have just got back from Scotland, which was great. We walked the legs off ourselves, and even swam briefly on Christmas morning! FREEZING, but great fun. Frank had a flask of coffee waiting for us on the beach, well laced with Scotch, which hit the spot and had us staggering back to the house. I think he may have got into a spot of bother with my mum about that. He's great. We went to a hotel for Christmas dinner, it was hilarious, like something out of the ark, but the grub was fine.

Thank you for the lovely photo frame, I've put the photo of Martha into it that you sent me when you got her. It was a bit small for the frame so I made a border for it. When I told Jackie the story of how you and Mum have written to each other for years and never met she thought it was incredible. I'm sending you a key holder, made by a friend of ours called Jake. He sells them in the market here in Cardiff, and they're very popular. Hope you like it.

Mum was telling us about your children's cookbook idea, sounds brilliant. Mum says a publisher is going to look at it, best of luck. I've told her to pass on any news. If you ever need an illustrator, I'm available.

Happy New Year to you and your family, love Alice xx

1992

SARAH

He was balding, although his face didn't look more than mid-thirties. His forehead was shiny, his nose long, his teeth crooked but startlingly white. He wore a blue denim shirt and beige corduroy jeans, and when he stepped around the low table to greet her she saw his cowboy boots underneath. He gripped her hand in both of his.

'Sarah,' he said, his voice as rich and warm as it had sounded on the phone. 'Paul Donnelly. Good to meet you.'

He'd come all the way from Dublin, even though she'd offered to travel to him. 'Not at all,' he'd said. 'I like any excuse to get out of the office. Give me the name of a hotel near you, and I'll see you in the lobby,' and here he was in Uncle John's old hotel, with a coffee pot already on the table in front of him, and a briefcase on the floor by his chair.

He indicated the pot. 'This is still fresh – or would you rather something else?'

'Coffee's fine, thanks.' She rarely drank it, and certainly not an hour before dinner – but it didn't

439

matter in the least what he poured, since she was far too nervous to touch a drop.

He'd given nothing away on the phone, simply said he thought they should meet and have a chat.

'Of course he's interested,' Christine had said. 'He'd hardly come all the way here if he wasn't.'

'Maybe he's just letting me down lightly.'

'Don't be daft.'

She hadn't stopped thinking about the cookery book since she'd finally plucked up the courage to lift the phone and ring him in January, like Helen had ordered, six weeks ago now, and he'd given her his address and asked her to send him the manuscript.

Five weeks and six days since she'd slipped the pages into an envelope and posted it off to him, her hands actually shaking as she'd stuck on the stamps. Five months it had felt like, until he'd phoned last Tuesday and told her he wanted to meet her, and what day would suit.

'So,' he said when coffee had been poured, 'your children's cookery book.'

She wore the blue skirt she'd bought for her fortieth, and a grey jacket over it that she'd thought made her look businesslike. Now, in the face of his denim and corduroy, she felt overdressed. She added milk to the coffee she had no intention of drinking as she waited for him to go on.

'I road-tested it on my two girls, aged eight and twelve,' he said, 'neither of whom had shown any interest in cooking. I challenged them to cook dinner one evening.'

He raised his cup and drank. With difficulty, Sarah resisted the urge to slap it from his hands. He set it back in its saucer.

'It was a disaster,' he said.

Sarah's heart plummeted.

'They fed us for a week,' he went on, straight-faced. 'My wife hardly saw the kitchen. I gained four pounds. My wife went shopping with the time on her hands and did severe damage to our bank account. It's all your fault.'

He smiled. 'I would like to offer you a publishing deal,' he said. 'I think you're onto something good here. Really good.'

Sarah was afraid to return his smile. 'Are you serious?'

'Well, not about the bank account,' he said. 'Thankfully, my wife has her own job. But yes to the rest – including, sadly, the weight gain.' Patting his stomach, which, as far as she could see, wasn't a bit bigger than it should be. 'The girls found your instructions very easy to follow, and really enjoyed the experience. Maureen, my older girl, wants the book for her birthday – but considering it's next month, I told her she might not have it on time.'

Sarah laughed delightedly. 'You mean it? You really want to publish it?'

'I certainly do. I can see why Helen was so enthusiastic about it.'

Helen, enthusiastic? She hadn't even seen the manuscript, hadn't read a word of it. Sarah decided to keep that information to herself.

He reached for his briefcase and snapped it open. 'I take it,' he said, 'that you don't have an agent.'

An agent. Sarah Flannery with an agent. Don't laugh. 'No.'

'I've drawn up a contract,' he went on, pulling out a thin sheaf of paper. 'Bring it home, have a read, see what you think.'

Because he imagined there was a possibility, did he, that she might turn down a publishing deal? She accepted the pages with what she hoped was a pleasant smile, rather than a grateful beam of such brilliance it might just blind him, and tucked them into her bag as he produced a diary from the briefcase.

'Let's talk again,' he said, 'in a week or so. If you're happy with the contract, I'd like to get moving on this, to have it on the shelves as soon as possible. I've had a few ideas about format that we'd need to discuss.'

He'd been thinking about it, he had a few ideas. He was serious about wanting to publish her recipes, and he was thinking about how best to do it. He was talking about it being *on the shelves*.

She had an urge to pull the contract out of her bag and sign it now, before he had a chance to change his mind, and possibly to accompany this with a kiss. Instead she found herself agreeing, in as normal a voice as she could manage, to let him

442

know by the end of the following week if she was happy with the contract.

Driving to Christine's to collect the children, she remembered the book she'd started several years earlier, before she and Neil had even met. She remembered the hours she'd spent working on it, choosing her characters, writing their story, changing the plot umpteen times, the years of rewriting and changing again and more rewriting that had all come to nothing.

She recalled Helen's angry letter, the hurtful things she'd said about a manuscript she hadn't even seen. Funny that she was doing the opposite now, talking up something else she hadn't read, as if they'd come full circle.

And today they'd made a new connection – Sarah had met someone who knew Helen personally, who'd seen her face to face, who knew what she sounded like, and how tall she was, and the way she moved.

Sarah must write with the news as soon as she got home. If it wasn't for Helen she wouldn't have got a publishing deal so easily, might not have got one at all. A publishing deal – the phrase made her laugh out loud, in the darkness of the car. She was going to be published. Her cookery book was going to sit on bookshelves all over the country. Someone might even buy it.

She turned slowly and carefully onto Christine's road, hugging her happiness.

1995

HELEN

On February the sixteenth, shortly before her fifty-third birthday, Frank Murphy proposed to Helen Fitzpatrick for the sixth time in five years.

'You can't be serious,' she said, pulling the duvet over her head.

'I am,' he replied, not a bit put out. 'I'm seriously asking you, once again, to be my wife. To have and to hold, and so forth. God loves a trier.'

She threw back the duvet and grabbed the fan that was sitting on the locker, and began flapping it in front of her face. '*Jesus*, I'm burning up again. I thought I'd made it abundantly clear that I'm perfectly happy the way we are.'

'And wouldn't you like to make me just as happy by wearing my ring? That's the only difference, that you'd have a nice sparkly ring on your finger.'

She continued to flap. 'God, I'm going to die, I'm going to burst into flames. Look, Frank, it's sweet of you to keep asking me, and I'm sure you'd buy me a very sparkly ring, but honestly I'd rather not. Feel free to write me into your will, if that's what's bothering you: I won't put up any

447

objections to that. Now would you be a dote and bring me up some ice?'

He sighed as he got out of bed. 'You haven't heard the last of this, woman. I'll wear you down yet.'

She watched him shamble from the room, his pyjama bottoms bagging unflatteringly around the rear. They were as comfortable with one another as any husband and wife – why was he so fixated on tying the knot?

And why, she wondered, listening to his bare feet thumping down the stairs – he couldn't be quiet if he tried – did she feel so compelled to keep refusing him? What difference would it make, as he'd pointed out, apart from a ring on her finger? He'd buy her the Hope diamond if she asked for it. And if it made him happy, shouldn't she swallow her reservations and just do it?

And still there was some instinct that stopped her from saying yes every time. Let them stay together for the rest of their lives – and she had no objection to that – but let them stay as they were, and avoid that final step.

She flapped her fan, remembering how eagerly she'd looked forward to being Cormac's wife, how she couldn't wait for them to be married. But what she had with Frank was different: it didn't have to lead to a walk down an aisle.

So they continued to live together, with her mother coming to them every week now for Sunday lunch – Frank's idea, naturally – and Alice and Jackie, still together in Cardiff, visiting periodically.

Her relationship with her mother, since her discovery of the truth, had undergone its own change. Nothing overt, nothing anyone observing them would notice, Helen was sure, but the knowledge of her parents' suffering had brought with it a sort of acceptance, a quieting of the rage and resentment that she'd carried for years.

She didn't excuse them – even if they hadn't meant to, they'd still punished her unfairly – but she found herself able to forgive, finally, and move on. She was somewhat gentler with her mother now, and more patient, and her mother, she felt, sensed it and was glad.

Frank returned, carrying a little bowl of ice and a tea towel, the newspaper and a padded envelope wedged under an arm. He set the bowl and tea towel on her locker and let the envelope drop onto the duvet – 'From your penfriend' – before climbing back into bed with the newspaper.

'Thanks.'

Helen tipped ice into the tea towel and pressed the bundle to her face, feeling the waves of heat gradually begin to ebb from it as she inhaled the frosty air. Eventually she dropped her damp bundle into the bowl and ripped open the envelope and pulled out a slim hardback book.

Party Food for Little People was written in sky blue on a bright green background, above a line drawing of two beaming children, a boy and a girl, wearing

449

aprons and chef's hats. The girl held a plate of buns iced in primary colours, each studded with a lighted candle, and the boy clutched the string of an enormous yellow balloon on which the words *Happy Birthday* were inscribed in red.

Running across the top of the page was the now familiar *Cooking is Child's Play* logo of the series, blue letters on a banner that matched the yellow of the balloon.

Helen opened the book and found a notelet paper-clipped to the first page. She detached it and began to read.

Dear Helen

Look what arrived this morning – I had to send you one straight away! I just love the colour of this one – best so far, don't you think? Paul sent a lovely note with it, saying he'd never worked with such an obliging author before – I still have to pinch myself when someone calls me an author!

And the letters just keep on coming, another pile last week! I'm so glad you suggested getting a response printed up – even though I'd love to reply to every one of them personally, there's just no way I could. I can't believe how many people take the time to write. One woman told me that she'd given her name to her local bookshop with strict instructions to notify her every time a new one comes out! And a teacher wrote that she'd recommended them to all the parents in her class as Christmas presents!

We're still getting cards from children themselves too, so cute. I'm making a scrapbook with Martha and Stephen. Sorry, I'll stop blathering on about it – but it's all thanks to you, and I want to share every step of this wonderful journey with you!

Hope you and Frank are well – I know I'd love him if I ever met him, he just sounds so sweet. WHEN are you going to agree to marry him? Really, I could shake you sometimes, Helen Fitzpatrick!

How's your mother? I hope she's over that cold. The weather's so changeable I'm not surprised she got one. Dad is hardly going outside the door these days. He's still fairly active though, for eighty-five, still driving and everything. Maybe we should get your mother and my father together!!

Hope your hot flushes are fading, they sound unpleasant (although your description of poor Frank rushing around with the ice was hilarious). It's all ahead of me! Forty-four last October – and Stephen, my baby, is seven, hard to believe. I'd still love another, but at this stage I'm afraid it will hardly happen. It won't be for want of trying, though! (Oh my God, I can't believe I wrote that – I'm blushing! Or maybe it's my first hot flush!!!)

I'd better go – Martha has a piano lesson this afternoon, and I'm driving her because it looks like it's going to rain again. Not looking forward to it, still the world's worst (and most nervous) driver.

love Sarah xx

PS Check out the dedication!

Helen laid the letter aside and picked up the book again, the fifth in the series. It had taken two, *Easy Peasy Dishes* and *C is for Cooking*, before people had begun to sit up and take notice. By the time *More Kitchen Fun* hit the shelves, the first two were being reprinted to cope with the demand, and with the publication of *The Smallest Cook in the House* last year the series was getting top billing in bookshops, with its own dedicated display units.

The idea was beautifully simple. Each book contained just ten dishes, and each recipe was presented in comic-strip form by two young chefs, Martina and Charlie, who demonstrated the steps using few words and lots of pictures. Martina, the elder, led the way, having to stop every so often to scold Charlie, who would inevitably spill or drop something, or furtively eat some of the ingredients. It was children teaching children how to cook, and it slotted perfectly into the gap that had existed.

And it was all down to Sarah, who, Helen was quite sure, bent over backwards to meet whatever rewriting deadlines Paul threw at her – no wonder he called her obliging.

'She's got such enthusiasm,' he'd told Helen. 'She's like a child herself, not an ounce of guile in her, but she sure knows her way around a recipe.'

He'd been bemused to learn that the two women had never met. 'I thought you knew her well.'

'I do, on paper. We've been penpals for years. I know things about her that she doesn't tell her own family.'

'Crikey . . . In that case, maybe you should come along next time we meet, seeing as how you're the one who brought us together.'

But Helen had declined. Not the right occasion, a business meeting not the right setting. They'd know when the perfect opportunity arose, she was sure.

She *had* reviewed each book, though.

Our newest author is a professional cook who loves her job. She also just happens to love children – her own two are arguably the most cherished in Ireland. It's the perfect recipe for a cookery book aimed at any child who's ever shown an interest in cooking – or any other child, come to that.

Easy Peasy Dishes, the first in a planned series, has ten basic recipes written in a beautifully simple style, with clearly outlined safety guidelines and a wonderfully colourful and appealing comic-strip layout – think Dr Seuss colour and fun. There's even a 'tidy-up as you go' ethos running through the book, to keep parents happy. But the genius stroke is that each recipe is presented by two child characters, perfect for your little chef to identify with.

As the books had gained in popularity, Sarah's publishers had been approached by journalists eager for information about the books' mystery author – *S. Flannery* was barely visible on the covers, and no autobiographical details were contained within – but Sarah had been reluctant to go public.

I've told Paul I'd prefer to stay in the background. The idea of seeing my photo in a magazine, or having someone writing about me and the children, gives me the shivers! Thankfully, Paul is OK with this.

Of course he was OK with it – mystery only made someone more marketable. In the end they'd settled on one publicity photo being taken, which showed Sarah standing behind a kitchen table, head bent as she stirred a mixture in a bowl, with Martha and Stephen – *the real-life inspirations for Martina and Charlie* – facing her across the table, their backs to the camera. This single photo accompanied any piece that was written about the cookery books.

With the downward tilt of her head, Sarah's features were impossible to make out. All Helen could see was the tip of her nose, the curve of her eyelash, the slant of her cheek. Since the photo was in black-and-white the colour of her hair, which looked to be cut in a short bob, remained uncertain, but it appeared to be a fairly nondescript light brown or dark blonde. She wore a full white apron, underneath which the short sleeves of a dark top emerged.

A woman she'd never met, but knew so much about. A caring, conservative, generous, self-deprecating, gullible, shy, emotional, sentimental woman. Helen knew Sarah almost as well as she knew Alice – better in some ways.

She turned the pages of the cookery book and found the dedication: *For Helen, who's always been there when I needed her.* And beneath, handwritten, *Sarah xx*

She looked at the page for several seconds before closing the book.

'Fifty injured at that match last night,' Frank said.

She turned. 'What?'

'That Ireland-England soccer match in Lansdowne Road. Fifty injured. Bloody hooligans.'

Helen continued to regard him. His hair, as usual, was in need of a cut: it seemed to grow at twice the rate of everyone else's. His reading glasses were perched halfway down his nose as he frowned at the newspaper, lips pursed. His pyjama top was frayed at the collar and faded from washing, but he refused to throw it out.

He didn't give a damn that she was a menopausal cow. He looked after her mother better than she did, and he was lovely with Alice. He'd cycle to the moon if Helen asked him. He'd never once criticised her.

He was always there when she needed him.

'Alright then,' she said. 'I will.'

He looked up. 'You will what?'

She smiled.

His eyes widened. He dropped the newspaper and opened his arms.

SARAH

My dear Alice
Congratulations! Your mother told me your good news, you must be delighted! I'm sending a card that Martha made for you – obviously it's not a patch on your gorgeous ones, but it was made with tons of enthusiasm! Martha was ten last week, and she loves art, always wants to be messing with paints and crayons. I'm sending her to piano lessons because I'd love her to be able to play, but I suspect she's really only taking them to keep me happy!

My fifth cookery book hit the shelves at the end of February, can you believe it! Time is flying!

Love to Jackie, hope you've got a big rise along with the promotion, so you and she can enjoy lots of treats!

All my best
Sarah xx

Dear Martha
My name is Alice, and I'm the one you sent

that beautiful congratulations card to – thank you so much. My friend Jackie couldn't believe you were only ten when she saw it! It's sitting on our mantelpiece now and we're showing it off to all our visitors.

I think you'll probably be an artist when you grow up, if you don't become a musician. Your mum says you're having piano lessons, and I'm really jealous. My dad was a good piano player, but he died when I was very small, and I didn't learn how to play the piano, or any instrument, and I'm really sorry now, because I'd LOVE to be able to play at parties. People who can play piano or guitar always get asked to LOADS of parties, so you're a lucky duck.

I'm sending you some dragon stickers – maybe you could share them with Stephen. I'm not sure if you're interested in dragons, but here in Wales there's lots of dragon stuff because of someone called George who was from England and who killed a fierce dragon once. Your mum probably knows the story.

Well, I'd better go, it's time to cook the dinner. I'm not a very good cook, not like your mum. You must be very proud of her for writing all those great cookbooks – I saw them when I visited my mum at Christmas. I'm sure you're the girl cook in them, even though she has a different name. And Stephen is the boy, isn't he? Bet you're secretly delighted!

Bye for now, and thanks again for the great card,

love Alice xxx

PS Your mum wrote to me when I was about your age, and sent me a present of a book, which I still have! She sounds like a lovely mum.

PPS I have a photo of you as a baby! You had only a tiny bit of hair but you were gorgeous!

Things weren't the same between them – they would probably never be the same. Something had been destroyed on that day in November more than four years ago when he'd sat across the table from her and crushed her heart, and she'd responded by smashing her fist into his face.

She didn't know if she could ever completely trust him again. But she was moving on, giving him a second chance, because she still wanted him in her life. They were a couple again, and eventually everyone had accepted it, even Christine.

They had inched their way back together. After the Christmas dinner – which had passed off more smoothly than Sarah had hoped, everyone being terribly polite – she and Neil had continued to meet just once a week, when he came to collect or return Martha and Stephen. They'd talk for a few minutes at the car, usually about the children, and then Sarah would say goodbye and that would be it.

In February she'd met Paul from the publishers, and there had been all the excitement of signing the deal, and more meetings, and making changes to the book – and inevitably, the children had told Neil.

'Congratulations,' he'd said, with as much warmth as she could have asked for. 'That's great news. You must be over the moon.'

'I am, it's all very exciting.'

And that night she'd lain in bed and imagined how it would have been if they were still married. The four of them would have gone out for a meal to celebrate, or maybe they'd have got a babysitter and gone on their own. Neil might have got her a little gift, a piece of jewellery maybe. She'd have shared each step of the journey with him.

And then at the end of April, he'd dropped the children back as usual one Sunday afternoon, and he and Sarah had exchanged the pleasantries they always did. She'd enquired after his mother's back, he'd commented on the new sitting-room curtains. She'd updated him on the book's progress.

And as she'd turned to go back into the house, he'd said, 'Sarah' – and her name on his lips, and the different tone of his voice, had caused a flush to creep into her face.

'I was wondering if you'd like to come with us to the cinema next weekend. Just if you wanted to.'

She hadn't known what to say. A family outing, like they'd had so many times before, only now they weren't a family any more.

But maybe they could be, if she had the courage to try.

'Yes,' she'd found herself saying, 'I'd like that.'

And a fortnight after the cinema – the children sitting between them in the dark, some cartoon on the screen she hadn't paid the slightest attention to – he'd suggested a trip to the wax museum, and shortly after that Stephen had wanted to go to the zoo. And with each outing, Sarah sitting beside him in the car like she'd done so many times before, it became easier to be together.

And then, when he was dropping them off one Sunday in June, Martha had said, 'Dad, why don't you stay to dinner?' She'd turned to Sarah. 'That's OK, Mum, isn't it?' And what could Sarah say, except yes?

And just like that, their reconciliation was nudged on. Neil had come in and played trains with Stephen until the chicken curry had been reheated. And during dinner he'd looked out of the window and remarked that some of the shrubs could do with pruning, and he could drop by if Sarah wanted, whenever it suited her.

And finally, as they drank tea on the garden seat one balmy August evening, after an afternoon at the cinema and a lasagne dinner, she'd told him that the publication date was September the fifteenth, and he'd told her that he still loved her, and he'd asked if there was any chance that they could try again.

And that had been nearly three years ago.

It was different; it might never be the same. It was more fragile; she felt more fragile. But he was still her husband and they were together again – and at the age of forty-four, she'd begun another baby with him.

'Congratulations,' the doctor said, sliding the box of tissues across his desk to her.

HELEN

Sarah
I had to laugh when I saw the Iron Maiden CD – yes, it did bring me back to my misspent youth, thank you very much. I think if you'd met me in my teens you'd have run a mile. I was the original enfant terrible – my poor parents had a lot to put up with. Ah well, I got my comeuppance when Alice turned out to be every bit as bad as I was. (Hasn't she turned out well, despite my terrible parenting? Maybe I got some bits right.)

I have news – don't faint. Frank proposed yet again, and this time I decided I'd run out of reasons to turn the poor man down, so we're tying the knot in a very quiet registry office ceremony on September the twentieth. It's a Friday, at two in the afternoon. Just my mother and Alice on my side – and you and Neil, if you'd like it. No fuss, a quick 'I do' and then a late lunch or early dinner or something in a decent restaurant.

Frank is, of course, insisting on footing the whole bill. He's whittled his giant guest list down to about a dozen, and is talking about us having a party for the thousand others he wanted to invite when we get home from our honeymoon. Yes, I said honeymoon. The man is unstoppable. He's booking it, and keeping the destination a secret. I've warned him I want somewhere hot, or I'm going straight to the divorce courts.

It's a bit unsettling, wearing another man's engagement ring. I never thought I would.

H x

Helen!!!

You're getting married!!! That's so wonderful!!! I'm SO thrilled for you – and yes, yes, yes, Neil and I would <u>adore to</u> be at the wedding, thank you so much for asking us. I've marked the date on the kitchen calendar, and Martha has surrounded it with red hearts! I can't believe we're finally going to meet!

I'm sending you a photo album so you can take lots of snaps and record this time – I remember how completely happy I was when Neil and I were engaged. I felt we existed in this ridiculously perfect bubble where nothing could touch us. You must feel the same now! (And I'm <u>dying</u> to see your ring – I'm sure it's gorgeous!)

On a completely different note, I have news too – I'm PREGNANT!!! I heard just the other day, and I know I should wait until the first three months are up – not till next week – and I will before I tell everyone else, but I had to tell someone besides Neil, and you were the obvious choice.

I feel like shouting it from the rooftops! Another baby, when I'd as good as given up – and I'm terrified, of course. Would you believe I'm due on my forty-fifth birthday – yikes! The doctor says forty-five isn't too old for a baby these days, especially not when I've already had one, and I'm in good health, etc. But of course he's going to keep an eye on me, with my history, and he's warned me not to exert myself (as if I would!) so I've given up cycling completely till after the baby – and I'm not going to get behind the wheel of the car either, because that would definitely play havoc with my blood pressure. I remind myself of one of those little old ladies you used to see hunched over the steering wheels of Morris Minors, holding up the line of cars behind them as they crawled to wherever they were going!

So poor Neil is driving me to and from work for the moment, but I know as soon as I tell Christine and Dad my news they'll row in and work out a rota with Neil, because it's playing havoc with his schedule. I hate being a nuisance, but I have to put the baby first. Neil, of course, is delighted with the news – he's hoping for a girl, and obviously I couldn't care less what we have!

So life is good, for both of us – I mean for you and me – isn't that wonderful? Long may it last!

Sarah xxx

PS I'll be over seven months pregnant at your wedding – I'll be HUGE!

SARAH

'You don't have to go,' Christine said. 'She's my mother-in-law – you hardly knew her.'

'Of course I'll go – I met Gráinne lots of times, I'd like to go.'

'Sarah, it's just that—'

'I know, but that's all in the past now.'

Because, of course, Noreen would be at her aunt's funeral. If Sarah went, they'd be in the church at the same time, and even if they didn't come face to face it was almost inevitable that the two of them would see one another. It would be the first time since the day of Neil's confession, so long ago now.

From the sitting room came the tinkle of piano chords. 'Listen,' Sarah said, 'he's really coming on after only five lessons. He's much more into it than Martha ever was.'

'Stop changing the subject. I really don't think it's a good idea for you to go. The doctor said you were to avoid stress.'

'But it won't be stressful,' Sarah insisted. 'I keep telling you, that's all behind us now. I'm completely over it, and I'm going, and that's that.'

The middle of August, more than six months pregnant, the curve of her growing baby very obvious now, especially when she chose clothes that accentuated her shape. She'd wear her grey jersey dress: she looked twice as big in it. What better way to show fifty-four-year-old Noreen that she and Neil were happily reunited than by making sure Noreen saw the evidence of their lovemaking?

There was no malice intended, none at all. She just wanted to make a point.

'More tea?' she asked, and Christine passed her cup across wordlessly.

HELEN

Halfway down the page the small headline caught her eye: *Former editor's wife dies.* Just two or three sentences beneath, her life and Breen's career summed up in a handful of words. Kathleen Breen, who had died aged sixty-four following a short illness. Married to Mark Breen, sixty-five, who had edited the newspaper for twenty-six years before retiring in 1987.

She turned the pages until she got to the death notices, and there it was. Removal that evening, cremation the following day. Family only, no flowers. She wondered what family he had. There'd been nobody, as far as she was aware, at his retirement party, and all it said here was 'survived by her husband Mark'. No children then, nobody but a few cousins maybe, a sibling or two.

'More toast?'

She looked up. 'No, thanks.'

Every morning he asked, and every morning she said no. You'd think he'd know by now. Was he going to ask her every day for the rest of her life, through all the years and years of breakfasts they were going to share? How long before he copped

469

that all she ever wanted first thing in the morning was one damn slice of toast?

She caught herself, and stopped. He was being attentive and solicitous, and all she could do was find fault. Moody cow, the menopause going on forever. Serve her right if he called the whole thing off. Maybe he'd wait till the day itself and leave her sitting in her finery on a chair in the registry office.

'My old editor's wife died,' she told him, to make amends. 'Sixty-four.'

'Did you know her?'

'No, never met her.' She let the silence spin out as Frank deposited the lid of his boiled egg into its empty shell. So neat, like a maiden aunt. 'She had a drink problem, and manic depression.'

He shook his head. 'Poor woman. Will we go to the funeral?'

'Family only,' she told him, smothering another dart of irritation. He wasn't butting in, he was doing the decent thing like he always did.

Breen was alone now, nobody to look after any more. She hoped there was at least one person in his family or one friend he could turn to. She hadn't laid eyes on him since the afternoon he'd bought her a brandy – four, or was it five, years ago? She remembered their conversation, how he'd opened up to her when she was practically a stranger to him.

Her new mobile phone rang. She regarded it suspiciously, the brick of squat black plastic that Frank had presented her with the week before.

'Amazingly, they don't answer themselves,' Frank said, and she made a face at him as she picked it up.

'Mum,' Alice said, 'just to let you know I've booked my flight home. Grab a pen and I'll give you the details.'

Alice loved mobile phones. Alice was twenty-four, not an ancient crone of fifty-three who wasn't at all sure she wanted to be contactable all the time, by anyone. Especially not someone who was calling from Edinburgh, and surely paying a small fortune for the privilege.

'Are you at home?'

'Yes, but—'

'I'll ring you back on the house phone,' Helen told her, and hung up before Alice could respond.

Nineteen months since she and Jackie had gone their separate ways, since she'd come home alone for Christmas, thinner and quieter and refusing to talk about it. Helen still had no idea what had happened. Alice lived in Edinburgh now, where she'd moved after the break-up – Cardiff being too small, apparently, for a separated couple to co-exist there.

'That was Alice,' she told Frank, getting up. 'She's booked her flight.'

'Won't feel it now.' He put his wedding face on, all soft and goofy.

In four weeks and three days they were getting married. Helen had bought a red dress and black patent shoes, and booked appointments for waxing and a haircut a couple of days before. That was enough; that was all that was needed. She'd had the fuss first time around: she'd worn the white dress and walked up the aisle in front of all their friends and relations, and later she'd danced in the spotlight with her husband of a few hours. This was different.

Alice had wanted her to have a hen night. 'Come on, Mum, I could do with a bit of excitement. You could fly over here, we could go to a show. Or I could have a dinner party and invite a few friends.'

After six months of waitressing in Edinburgh and knocking on doors with her portfolio she'd secured a commission to illustrate a children's book. Now she waited tables by day and drew pictures by night. Helen had been to see her studio flat, which was tiny but centrally located, bright and decently furnished.

'No hen party,' Helen had told her. 'No fuss.'

'Can I at least be bridesmaid?'

'It's a registry office. I'm not even sure I'm a bride.'

She hoped Alice was happy, and wished for her to meet someone new. As she dialled her daughter's landline number she heard Frank running water into the sink, and pictured him bringing the dishes over, clearing away the milk and butter, wiping down the table. Cleaning up more thoroughly than Helen had ever done.

She wasn't getting a husband, she was getting a wife.

SARAH

A quarter to nine. Sarah lay in bed and listened to Neil's car starting up. She waited until the sound of it had disappeared completely, and then she threw back the blankets and eased herself out of bed. She felt bad lying to him, but it was her only option. If he knew what she was planning he'd hit the roof. She was sparing them a row, that was all.

He'd been concerned, which had made her feel worse. He'd wanted to call the doctor, but Sarah had managed to persuade him that it was just tiredness after a broken night, that a few hours in bed would take care of it. 'Don't ring me,' she'd said, 'I'll probably be asleep.'

She'd told him of Gráinne's death, but hadn't made a big thing of it. She was sure the thought of her attending her sister's mother-in-law's funeral wouldn't even have occurred to him.

Of course, there was also the matter of lying to St Sebastian's, but she reasoned that in all the years of working there she'd never once taken a sick day, so she was well due one, even if it was being claimed under false pretences.

473

She slipped out of her nightdress and stood under the shower, taking more time than usual to wash and condition her hair, to apply shower gel and rinse it off. She towelled herself dry and dusted talc onto her arms and chest. She sat at the dressing-table in her underwear and regarded her clean forty-four-year-old face.

You wouldn't call it pretty. It wasn't a face that would stay with you. Christine, with her long-lashed dark blue eyes and full lips, was far more striking. Sarah had always thought of herself as the watered-down sister: hair that hovered between blonde and brown, eyes of such a pale blue they morphed to grey on colourless days – even the freckles that still dotted her cheeks, despite her having spent her teenage years trying to scrub them off with lemon juice, were a half-hearted beige. Her nose was disproportionately broad for her face, her mouth unremarkable, her teeth only so-so.

But a man had loved her enough to want to spend the rest of his life with her, and in an hour or so she would be under the same roof as the woman who had betrayed her trust, and almost put paid to all of that.

She gazed at her reflection and thought back to the innocent twenty-four-year-old woman, full of hope, who'd cycled to a job interview all those years ago, little imagining the upheaval that was waiting for her in the years ahead. The utter happiness of falling in love, the misery of losing three babies, the sharp pain of betrayal, the comfort of reconciliation, the thrill of getting published, and witnessing the success of the books – and best of all, the marvel of being pregnant again, the fervently-wanted third child on the way at last.

So much to regret, so much to be thankful for. She was older now, and hopefully wiser. Would she have done it any differently? Impossible to say. But she'd survived, she'd come through it all and she was happy, and looking forward to the future.

Today was necessary, to put the hurt of the past firmly behind her. Wasn't it?

She applied her makeup with care, patting on the loose powder she rarely bothered to use over her foundation, brushing on blusher and lipstick, stroking on two coats of mascara. She slipped her dress over her head and pulled it down, feeling it cradling her bump, anticipating Noreen's reaction when she saw it.

She dried her hair and secured her parting with the little diamond clip Neil had bought her when she'd told him he was going to be a father again. When she'd finished, she smiled at the woman in the mirror who had lost and reclaimed her husband.

'You look nice,' Christine said in the car. Brian had gone ahead with the boys, so they were alone. 'You won't be cold without a coat?'

'No.' Sarah looked out of the window as they drove past the school, imagined Martha and Stephen inside, heads bent over books. She rested a hand on the bulk of her abdomen and thought of their new brother or sister nestled within.

'How're you feeling?' Christine asked.

'Fine.'

But as they approached the church a creeping uneasiness began to unfurl within her. Maybe she shouldn't have come. What was to be gained by flaunting her pregnancy to her husband's ex-mistress? The whole notion seemed childish now: better to have left the past where it belonged.

But it was too late to change her mind, as Christine pulled up between a red Volvo and a dark blue Mini. Sarah got out and scanned the car park, and saw two green cars some distance away, either of which might belong to Noreen. Too late to back out, as they made their way with a scatter of others across the tarmac, as they passed the empty hearse outside the main door of the church.

Just before she walked inside Sarah felt the first spatters of rain – serve her right, leaving her coat at home because it would hide her condition.

The church was half full, people distributed in untidy formation through the pews. Sarah walked up the aisle beside Christine, aware that her heart had begun to thump uncomfortably. Was Noreen here? Had she already seen Sarah? What if they came face to face, what then? She looked straight ahead, conscious of heads turning to observe them, feeling as exposed as if she'd entered the church in her underwear.

Halfway up the aisle she touched Christine's arm and whispered that she wouldn't go further. Christine nodded, and Sarah slipped into a pew that was empty, apart from a bald man at the other end who was hunched into a heavy grey overcoat.

She sat, smoothing her dress over her thighs, wishing now she'd worn something a little less figure-hugging. She didn't dare look around as people kept arriving and shuffling into nearby pews. Eventually a bell was rung and everyone stood as a priest walked out onto the altar. Sarah dared a quick glance at the mourners in the seats in front of hers, and recognised nobody.

As the funeral service wore on, she began to relax. Noreen might not even be here – or if she was, there were enough other people around to easily avoid her. And, anyway, if anyone felt like remaining anonymous it should be Noreen, not her. For all Sarah knew, she was cowering in a pew hoping not to be spotted.

The service ended, the priest left the altar, and after a minute or two people began to file into the aisle, some making their way to the top to sympathise with the bereaved, others heading for the door. Sarah walked to the far end of the pew – the bald man had already disappeared – and joined the queue that was inching towards the side door. She'd wait by the car for Christine, who hopefully wouldn't be too long.

But when she reached the door she was dismayed to find that it was raining heavily. If she went outside she'd be soaked: better to sit in a corner somewhere and wait it out. She turned and made her way back against the flow into the main body of the church, murmuring apologies as she edged through.

The church was emptying. At the front, Brian and Christine were still talking with a few others. A woman broke away from the group and began walking down the side aisle, directly towards Sarah – and with a lurch of recognition she realised it was Noreen.

Her mouth went dry, her heart hammering again inside her. The blood rushed to her face as she stood frozen and watched Noreen approach, saw her expression changing, her step faltering.

They stood face to face, about ten feet apart. Sarah put her hand on the pew beside her and leant on it heavily, not sure that her quivering legs would support her. She saw Noreen's eyes dart downwards, just for an instant.

'Sarah,' she said, her voice broken, 'I'm so sorry.'

Navy jacket, grey skirt, flat black shoes, hair as dowdy as it had always been. No makeup, apart from a stripe of too-dark lipstick. Nothing to look at, this woman who had stolen Neil, this middle-aged widow who had welcomed him into her bed and turned all their lives upside-down. Alone again now, looking empty and defeated in her funeral clothes.

'If you knew,' she went on, 'how much I've regretted—'

Sarah turned abruptly into the pew and clattered through it, and made her way up the centre aisle, not daring to look back. She lowered herself into a pew a few rows from the front. Christine glanced back and looked at her questioningly, and Sarah gave a small nod, unable to summon a smile.

She felt no triumph, no sense that she'd achieved any kind of victory. Neither of them had won – they were both losers. She didn't turn around to see if Noreen had left. She closed her eyes and breathed in slowly, hands resting on her abdomen, and she realised that all she felt was shame.

'You OK?'

She opened her eyes. Christine stood in the aisle beside her.

'Did you talk to her? What did she say?'

She could see Brian ushering the boys out of the pew. She took her sister's arm and heaved herself to standing.

'Nothing,' she told her. 'She said nothing. We didn't talk.'

They walked down the aisle and out into the pouring rain.

HELEN

H er mother's hand trembled slightly as she filled their cups. How long had that been going on? Still, to be expected at eighty-four.

'So Alice arrives on Tuesday.'

'That's right.'

'And you're getting your hair cut, are you?'

Helen smiled. 'Yes, Mother, on Wednesday. And I'm getting married on Friday.'

Her mother poured cream, a tiny amount that barely coloured her coffee. 'I'm just asking, that's all. Your hair grows quickly, and it looks better with a tidy-up.'

There was a short silence. Helen sipped her coffee, welcoming its bitter strength. Her mother had always made the best coffee, ground her own beans too.

She wondered what her parents' wedding day had been like. Had her mother been happy? Had she lain in bed the night before too excited to sleep? Hard to imagine it – in their wedding album she looked mostly solemn and terrified – but her parents had loved one another, she was sure of that. And they'd lived more than half of their lives together, forty-seven years of wedded bliss. So much more than she'd got with Cormac.

'I must see your dress,' her mother said. 'Red always suited you. And what colour shoes did you say?'

She was looking forward to it, Helen realised. She wasn't being polite; she wasn't making small-talk. Maybe for the first time in her life, Helen was doing something that her mother truly approved of.

'The shoes are black,' she said. 'I'll bring them over, and the dress.'

'I was thinking,' her mother said, 'that you might like to borrow some jewellery. Just . . . if there was anything you wanted.'

'Thanks. I'll have a look.'

Every day they were leaving more and more of the past behind them. It was a comfort; it pleased her.

Helen
One week to go – you must be getting jittery! Or maybe not, maybe you're as cool as a cucumber second time round. I'm really looking forward to us coming face to face at last! We're going to get the train up; I think that's better than trying to find our way around Dublin by car. You'd never think we only lived forty miles away. We're total country bumpkins!

481

I can't wait to meet Alice too – the only photo I have of her is the baby one she sent me years ago, that hilarious one where her face is covered with ice-cream, so I have no idea what she looks like now. We'll have to take lots of snaps on the day to make up for all the ones we don't have of each other! I'm enclosing a note for Alice – you might give it to her when she gets home.

I must tell you, I went to a funeral a fortnight ago – it was Christine's husband Brian's mother – and I met Noreen. She would have been a niece of the dead woman, and I knew that she would probably be there. I went for the worst of motives: I wanted her to see that I was pregnant, to gloat, I suppose – wasn't that awful? Anyway, we did come face to face after the service, and she tried to apologise but I walked away, I just couldn't listen. She looked so dowdy and plain – and sad too – that I actually found myself feeling sorry for her, if you can believe it. I wanted to hate her, but it was Neil I felt angry at, for treating us both badly.

On a happier note, I've finally begun putting the next cookbook together, which will probably be the last in the series. The emphasis in this one will be on cooking with vegetables – Paul says it's an ongoing battle for parents to get their kids to eat them. It reminded me of the piece you wrote about

cooking for Alice when she was really young
– you said something about her not recognising a vegetable if it hit her in the face (I'm
really sorry now that I didn't keep that
article!) and I was so scandalised I sent you
a few recipes – and look what that led to!
Anyway, I'm trying to come up with a title
for this one, something along the lines of Fun
with Greens, only more snappy – all sugges-
tions will be carefully considered!

Better go – my oldest nephew Aidan is
moving all the way to Dublin in a few days
to study medicine at Trinity, and we've been
invited around for a farewell dinner this
evening. Poor Christine is really going to miss
him, even though he's not going far really.

See you soon (can't wait!)

love Sarah xx

PS Lots of baby kicking – I think he's
getting impatient!

Dear Alice
Just a quick note to say I'm really looking
forward to meeting you and your mum – you
must be very excited at the thought of the
wedding!

Hope you're enjoying life in Edinburgh. I've
never been, but I've heard it's a lovely city.

love Sarah xxx

SARAH

Neil rummaged in the fridge. 'Where are the lunchboxes?'

'On the worktop by the fridge.' Sarah was closing Stephen's duffel coat. 'Leave this on you until you get into school,' she told him. 'Not in the yard, all the way into school. Did you brush your teeth like I asked you?'

'Sort of.'

'There's a stone in my shoe,' Martha said.

'You can take it out in the car. Neil, give me that comb. Martha, do *not* take off that shoe – you don't have time. Neil, make sure you're back by half twelve at the latest. We need to leave at one for the train.'

'Yes, ma'am.'

A minute later they were gone, and Sarah was alone in the kitchen. She cut a slice of the brown bread she'd baked the previous evening, but as she was spreading it with butter she realised she didn't want it. Her stomach had been in a knot since she'd woken, which was ridiculous: if anyone should be nervous it was Helen, the star of the show today.

But it was their first meeting, after writing to

one another for the best part of twenty years. They'd never said hello, never shaken hands, never come face to face. The only photo she'd seen of Helen was the tiny one that was still used with her articles, which really didn't show her at all – and Sarah's publicity shot for the cookbooks, all Helen had to go on, was equally vague. Visually and aurally, they were strangers.

What if they didn't click? What if they found they had nothing at all to say to one another? What if Sarah came across as gauche and naïve to Helen, her nervousness making everything she said come out wrong?

She looked out of the window at a sky the colour of tinfoil. Not a hint of sun, but hopefully it would stay dry. She would be glad when they got to the restaurant after the ceremony, when everyone would be a bit more relaxed. No doubt she'd be hungry then, ready for a good meal.

She massaged her abdomen absently, the butterflies still very much alive. Another scan due in a few days, everything fine according to her doctor. Seven weeks today she was due, the day she turned forty-five. In her sixties when this one would be graduating from university, the oldest mother in town.

She wished Neil had taken the day off, instead of arranging to do a morning's work on his current project about fifteen miles away. She would have welcomed his presence now, needed something to distract her, to make the time pass faster.

She thought about going back to bed for a couple of hours, but lying there trying to sleep would be worse than mooching around the house. At ten o'clock she tidied up the kitchen and hauled herself up the stairs. She'd have a bath, paint her nails, take her time putting on her face and getting dressed.

When she'd finished, barely an hour later, she eyed herself critically in the full-length mirror on the landing. At this stage she wasn't going to look remotely glamorous – not that she'd ever looked particularly glamorous, pregnant or otherwise – but the pink empire-line dress was pretty, and didn't draw too much attention to her bump, and the blow-dry she'd had the day before was holding up well, even if it was glued together with spray. She'd have to do.

As she walked downstairs, she felt another fluttering in her gut. Great, the baby had decided it was time for some gymnastics. A few minutes later, as she was polishing the knives and forks – anything to pass the time – it came again, stronger, forcing her to drop the knife and lean against the table. Had she picked up a stomach bug? Of all days.

As the spasm subsided, she felt a strong urge to urinate. She turned wearily for the stairs – but before she'd put her foot on the first stair something gushed from her, drenching her legs and splashing onto her flat grey shoes.

HELEN

lice twisted the bottle slowly and eased the cork out with a gentle *pop*. Helen watched as she poured the champagne, wishing it was brandy to settle her stomach, which had been churning since she'd got up three hours earlier. That was the thing about curry: tasted fine at the time, made its presence felt later.

'My mother's wedding day,' Alice said, handing her a glass with a smile. 'You look beautiful, by the way.'

'I do not.'

But Helen had been pleased enough with what she'd seen in the wardrobe mirror. The red dress was far from designer – she'd never paid more than fifty pounds for a dress, usually a lot less – but it suited her dark colouring, and fell in a smooth line to just below her knee. The lines on her face, deeper every year, couldn't be helped, but Frank knew his way around them all and hadn't been put off.

'Are you nervous?'

'Not in the least.'

Her hair had been given the same trim it always

487

got from Ray, who'd repaired the hatchet job she'd given herself twenty years ago, and who'd been keeping her curls at bay ever since. 'What are we doing for the wedding?' he'd asked, when she'd made the appointment. 'Fresh flowers, veil, a little colour rinse?' When Helen had told him just the usual, he'd thrown up his hands in despair.

The new shoes that she'd forgotten to break in, higher than she normally wore, were sure to cause problems later on. She'd bring plasters, and kick them off anyway once they got to the restaurant.

'Have you spoken to Granny this morning?' Alice asked.

'No.'

'Maybe I'll give her a quick call.'

'Do if you want, but there's no need – she knows we're picking her up.'

Alice, who was insisting on calling herself the bridesmaid, wore a jersey top and skirt in a rich violet that she'd bought in an Edinburgh charity shop for seven pounds – 'You wouldn't believe what some people throw out.' She had a little black feathery hat, also second-hand, and flat black velvet pumps. She looked sweet, and too thin.

Shocked to discover that Helen hadn't given any thought to a bouquet, she'd gone out the day before and come home with two identical sprays of white rosebuds. She'd tipped out the bric-à-brac from Breen's blue bowl and filled it with iced water and left them propped in it overnight.

'Right, your dress is new and your bag is old. Have you got something borrowed?'

Helen indicated her mother's heavy gold neck chain. 'And your watch.'

'Oh yes – and something blue?'

'Certainly not – blue does nothing for me.'

'Mum, you're hopeless. You should have got a garter with blue ribbon. I could have brought one for you.'

She'd wanted to get a cake, but Helen had been adamant that none was required. Bad enough to be parading around as a newly-wed at her age; producing a wedding cake would be ridiculous.

'This is making me a bit tiddly,' Alice said. 'We'd better eat something.'

'You go ahead, I'm not hungry. There are Danish pastries in the fridge – Frank got them yesterday.'

He'd slept in his own house, determined to observe all the wedding superstitions. 'I'll see you there,' he'd told Helen the evening before. 'Don't be too late, I'll be a nervous wreck.' Kissing her on the doorstep, murmuring that she'd made him very happy, lingering so long that in the end she'd pretended a tiredness she didn't feel.

Unsettled had been how she'd felt, memories of Cormac filling her head earlier as the three of them had eaten Alice's lamb curry and sat in front of the television afterwards. More and more she'd been thinking about him lately, snatches of her first wedding day catching her unawares.

A huddle of neighbours standing at the gate,

waving her off to the church as she'd stepped into her father's car. The scratchy feel of her dress's net underskirt, the sprays of red flowers attached to the ends of the church pews, Cormac's face as he'd turned to watch her walk up the aisle.

'Are you thinking about Dad?'

She looked at Alice, who smiled at her. Alice, who'd turned out far better than Helen deserved. 'Just a bit,' she said, holding out her glass for a top-up she didn't want.

SARAH

'Hold on,' Christine said, 'hold on, dear, everything's going to be OK—' but Sarah knew that nothing about this was OK, not the frantic drive in Christine's car to the hospital, Sarah hunched over and sobbing wildly in the back seat, not the trolley she'd been lifted onto in her ruined pink dress, not this rush down the corridor now, trying to hang on to Christine's hand as her sister half ran alongside her, not the faces of the men in white uniforms who didn't speak as they raced Sarah to wherever they were going.

Something was terribly wrong, pain knifing through her body as the too-bright lights flashed by above her head, as the trolley was pushed through doorways and turned down new corridors, as something was announced over a speaker that she couldn't make out, as she cried for Neil but he didn't come.

And then more doors opening into a room, and the trolley stopping and now Christine was gone, Sarah's hand suddenly empty. New people rushed silently about, nobody at all meeting her eye,

491

and she could hear beeping and the pain came again, worse, making her cry out – and here was her doctor, the bottom of his face covered with a mask, the top part creased with worry as she begged him, weeping, to save her baby, grabbing on to his green gown and screaming again with the terror and pain of it—

And then a stinging jab into the back of her hand, just before the doctor slid with everything else into the darkness.

HELEN

As the taxi pulled away from the kerb, Helen turned to Alice. 'Bring Granny in, I'll follow you.'

Alice looked at her. 'Where are you going? Are you OK?'

'Fine, I just want a minute.'

She watched them walk up the steps of the registry office, her mother leaning on Alice's arm, smart in the navy coat and dress she'd picked up in the July sales. At the top of the steps Alice glanced back, and Helen smiled and waved, and waited until they disappeared inside.

She stood on the path as people brushed past her. She pictured Frank sitting on some chair, or pacing the floor maybe, wearing the dark grey suit he'd bought a few weeks ago, his white beard neatly trimmed. George would be there too with his matching buttonhole, the garden centre closed for the day, both partners otherwise engaged.

She thought of Sarah and her husband somewhere inside, sitting apart from the others, or maybe having already introduced themselves – yes, Sarah would be friendly, eager to make herself known to them. And she couldn't miss Frank: she'd recognise him straight away.

She checked Alice's watch and saw that it was twenty past two. The restaurant was booked for three, the guests who were meeting them there probably en route by now. Everyone's day disrupted, everyone gathering to celebrate the occasion of Frank Murphy and Helen Fitzpatrick finally getting married.

She thought of Breen, recently widowed. She looked down at the bunch of white roses she held, pictured it sitting all night in the blue bowl his hyacinths had come in . . . and she knew she couldn't go through with it.

She walked a few metres up the path and laid the bouquet on top of a litter bin. She stooped and removed her new black shoes one by one – already starting to pinch – and set them carefully side by side on the edge of the path, and she walked barefoot to the end of the street. She took her mobile phone out of her bag and scrolled through her short contact list until she found him.

Future husband, he was listed as. Already there in the phone when he'd given it to her, and for the laugh she'd left it unchanged.

He'd taken her out and bought her countless presents. He'd held umbrellas over her in the rain, and looked after her when she'd been sick. He'd filled her house with plants and been kind to her mother. Every Valentine's Day he'd given her a dozen red roses. He'd sent Alice fifty pounds when she'd moved to Edinburgh, told her to spend it on something totally frivolous.

She couldn't phone him. She couldn't talk to him, because whatever she said would come out wrong. She couldn't let him know that she was breaking his heart; he'd have to figure that out all by himself.

She replaced her phone in her bag. She turned the corner and kept on walking, ignoring the ringing when it started.

SARAH

It wasn't like before, it was a million times worse than before.

'Talk to me,' Neil begged, but she turned away.

He had a beautiful pursed little mouth and a cap of damp black hair, and perfect tiny toes and fingers. He was the size of a rabbit and he weighed nothing at all and his skin was paler than paper. He never made a sound, never opened his eyes. Never looked into his mother's face.

Christine didn't demand that she talk, just sat by Sarah's bed weeping quietly, a tissue pressed to her eyes, her free hand resting lightly in Sarah's.

They'd wrapped him in a white blanket and laid him gently on her chest, and she'd slid her hand inside the blanket to cradle the curve of his skull, and she'd lifted him up to press her lips to his soft forehead, to each of his eye sockets, to his cheeks and his chin and his throat.

His tiny fingers, his adorable little fingers, broke her heart.

'Drink the tea at least,' a nurse had urged, but Sarah had left it beside the untouched slice of toast.

He had grown cold and stiff in her arms as she'd gazed at him, memorising his blue-veined eyelids, his long dark lashes, his elfin nose, the adorable squiggles of his ears. They named him Luke, a name she'd always loved.

'I'm so terribly sorry, Sarah,' the doctor had told her, hands thrust into the pockets of his hospital gown. 'The umbilical cord had become twisted, it had interfered with the oxygen supply, and by the time we were able to get to him it was too late. It was nobody's fault, there was no warning.'

No warning. He'd died all alone inside her, the air choked out of him by the cord that joined her to him, that was supposed to keep him alive. They'd cut her open, they'd lifted him out, they'd disentangled the cord, but his heart had already stopped. They'd done all they could, but he stayed dead. Her baby was dead.

For six days she lay in bed, forcing down food to make the nurses stop asking. On the seventh day, when they let her go, she sat silently as Neil wheeled her to the car, she remained silent as he drove her home, the children blessedly absent, still at Christine's. She stood under the shower and let the hot water mingle with her tears. She climbed into bed, her hair still dripping, and closed her eyes.

And the following morning, when Neil woke her with tea she didn't want, she said, in a voice rusty with disuse, 'Let Helen know what happened.'

HELEN

Nobody understood. Everyone demanded an explanation.

'I can't believe you did that,' Alice said. 'I can't believe you just walked away. How could you?'

'I hope you're ashamed,' her mother said. 'You made a fool out of that decent man. What have you got to say for yourself?'

'I expected better of you,' George said. 'Frank worshipped you. You've destroyed him.'

But when Helen tried to explain, none of them would listen.

'What do you mean, you don't love him?' Alice asked incredulously. 'You were living together for years. You seemed perfectly happy. That makes no sense.'

'You sound like a teenager,' her mother said. 'You're fifty-three – you think your knight in shining armour is still on the way? Grow up.'

'How can you say you didn't mean to hurt him?' George asked. 'What else did you think you were doing?'

The only one who didn't look for a reason was

Frank. He didn't show up at the house: it was George who came to get his things, George who stood with his arms folded while Helen packed them up, who refused Alice's offer of coffee as he told Helen what he thought of her.

And six days later, when the house was empty of Frank's possessions, when his ring had been slipped into an envelope and handed to George, who'd accepted it wordlessly, when Alice had gone back to Edinburgh after a stiff hug for her mother at the airport, there was nothing left to do but sit alone in the living room and try to make sense of it.

But what sense was there to be made? She hadn't loved him, that was all there was to it, however much she might wish it otherwise. She hadn't loved him, and he deserved better.

And of course she'd done it badly – waited till the last possible minute before running away, made him believe that he was going to have his happy-ever-after before snatching it away from him – but in the end it had been the right thing to do, and now it was done, and she must remember that. She'd done the right thing.

In time she'd be forgiven by Alice and her mother – and possibly even by George, who'd looked at her like he hated her as he'd shoved the ring into his breast pocket. Frank was another matter. By him she might not be forgiven, and that was something she would probably never discover.

As she was climbing into bed in her ancient and much-beloved Alice Cooper T-shirt, which

Frank had for some reason christened Prudence, she thought again of Sarah and her husband – and the thought was accompanied, as it had been since the aborted wedding day, by a pang of guilt.

They hadn't introduced themselves. According to Alice, nobody had come forward to make themselves known, although Sarah must have identified the wedding party. She would surely have known it was them.

Helen pictured them sitting apart from the small gathering, wondering when she was going to appear, maybe witnessing the growing unease when Helen hadn't shown up, and wasn't answering her phone.

She imagined them watching the group leaving, and wondering what was going on. She thought of them finally deciding that they'd had a wasted journey and making their way back to Heuston station for the train to Kildare.

She recalled Sarah's delight when she and Neil had been invited to the wedding, how excited Sarah had sounded at the prospect of them finally meeting up. Helen remembered her own misgivings, particularly as the day itself approached, and her doubts about the wisdom of getting married had been growing silently. She'd regretted her impulse to invite them then, and wished it undone.

She'd write to Sarah tomorrow, she'd try to explain, and hope that Sarah would understand. She'd apologise, and maybe send something as a token of how sorry she was – and knowing Sarah, and her infinite capacity to see the best in everyone, Helen would be forgiven by her too.

But the following day an envelope arrived, stamped with the Kildare postmark. There was no return address in the corner and the handwriting wasn't Sarah's, but it rang a faint bell. She tore it open and pulled out the single sheet within.

Dear Helen

Just a note to apologise for missing your wedding last week: I'm afraid we have very sad news. Sarah went into premature labour that morning, and our son Luke was delivered by emergency Caesarean section but didn't survive. We are both devastated, as you can imagine.

May we offer you our sincere congratulations on your wedding, and wish you all the best in the future. Sarah will be in touch when she feels able.

Sincerely

Neil Flannery

Helen reread the words, trying to take them in. Not sitting in the registry office then, no wasted journey because they'd never made it to Dublin. Sarah had gone into labour too early, and their baby had died. While Helen was taking off her wedding shoes and walking away from a life with Frank, Sarah was losing her baby.

She laid the page and its envelope on the hall

table and picked up the phone and dialled Alice's number. When the answering machine came on, she listened to her daughter's voice and waited for the beep.

'It's me. Maybe you could ring me back when you get this. I have news.'

> My dear Sarah
> I simply don't know what to say. I can't imagine what you must be going through. I'm so terribly sorry.
> I'm enclosing a lavender sachet. Slip it inside your pillow case and know that I'm thinking of you.
> H xx
> PS I'm not married, long story. I'll tell you sometime, when you want to hear.

> Dear Mrs Flannery
> Mum told me what happened, and I just wanted you to know that I feel very very sad for you.
> I'm sending you some of my favourite chocolate. It's all I can think of.
> love Alice xx

SARAH

'It's only been a month,' he said. 'You're still upset. It's understandable. You don't know what you're saying.'

But she knew exactly what she was saying. 'I'm sorry,' she repeated. 'I know you don't want to hear this, but I can't go on living a lie any longer.'

Neil searched her face. 'Sarah,' he said, 'love, you're still hurting after . . . what happened—'

'Luke,' she said. 'We lost Luke, that's what happened.' Every word ripping her into pieces. The wound still raw and bleeding, the image of his tiny white coffin being lowered into the ground still obscenely vivid.

Neil flinched, his eyes closing briefly. '*Jesus* . . . Do you think I don't know what happened? Do you think I can bear it any more than you can? But turning against me won't help things: we need to support each other now.'

She shook her head, searching for the words that would hurt the least, because she didn't want to hurt him any more than she had to.

'This isn't about losing our baby, this is about me . . . changing. I've changed towards you. I've

503

fallen . . .' and here she faltered, because there was no kind way to say what had to be said.

'Sarah, don't do—'

'I don't love you any more,' she said loudly, the words trampling over his. 'I'm not in love with you, so I can't stay married to you. It would be wrong, and dishonest.'

She watched his face twisting, his forehead creasing, his head shaking from side to side. 'Don't say that, you don't mean that. You're—'

'It was wrong to get back together,' she said. 'It was wrong for me to take you back. I did it because I was lonely and I missed you, I missed being married, and I thought us being a couple again would make me happy, but it didn't – or not for long.'

'We *were* happy,' he insisted. '*You* were happy, I know you were—'

'No,' she said. 'I thought I was, I told myself I was, but I wasn't. I was happy when I found out I was pregnant. That was what I wanted, that was *all* I wanted. I didn't admit it, even to myself, but when Luke died . . .'

She stopped, struggling against the tears that still tried to pour out of her whenever she dropped her guard enough to let them. She usually managed to save them for the times she was alone – cycling to and from the nursing home, lying in the bath, waiting in the car for Stephen and Martha to come out of their joint piano lesson. Snatching a few minutes to sit in the nursing-home garden, overgrown and wild again now without Charlie or Martina to look after it.

She drew in a shaky breath and forced herself to continue. 'I went to Brian's mother's funeral,' she told him, watching his expression changing. 'I saw Noreen there. I think I knew that day, when I saw how . . . defeated she looked. I felt bad for her. I felt bad because of what you had done, to both of us. I was ashamed of what you had done.'

He nodded slowly. 'Ah,' he said, 'so that's what this is all about. You're getting your own back. I hurt you, so now you're hurting me.'

'*No*,' she said fiercely, 'it's *not* that – I'm not like that. I don't think like that, you know I don't. I *was* heartbroken when you left me, of course I was, and the fact that it was for someone I'd trusted and liked made it twice as bad. And when you came back I could see that you were genuinely sorry, and I was prepared to forgive you – I *did* forgive you. It was only when I saw her again that I realised that what you had done had . . . killed something between us.'

'That funeral was weeks ago,' he protested. 'You said nothing about it. You didn't even tell me you'd gone.'

'No, I didn't. I was prepared to stay with you because I was pregnant with your child. I thought I owed it to you, and to the baby, to stay together. But now—' She broke off, biting into her cheek.

'I'm still Stephen's father,' he said, 'and I'm as much Martha's parent as you are.'

'I know that – and you always will be. You'll be able to see them. We'll work out an arrangement. But we won't be together any more. We can't be. I can't.'

'Sarah, don't do this,' he said, his voice changing. 'I'm grieving too, you're not the only one.'

She looked at him, the man she'd once loved. 'I know you are,' she said gently, 'but it doesn't change things. I'm sorry.'

'We need each other,' he insisted. 'You do love me – you're not thinking straight now.'

She got to her feet. She took in the thick, light-brown hair that never lay straight, the little bump halfway down his nose, the squiggle of creases that fanned out from his grey eyes, the twin freckles in the centre of his right cheek. Not at all unattractive, in a roughly put-together sort of way. Good hands too: she'd always admired his hands.

'I *am* thinking straight,' she said. 'I'm telling you the truth for the first time in months. We're finished. This is finished. I'm not happy about it, I wish it could be different, but it's not, and it never will be. You need to understand that.'

But she knew nobody would understand it: they'd all think she'd lost her mind. They'd tell her it made no sense, she was acting irrationally, she'd regret it. They'd put it down to her grief. They'd say she was lashing out at the one closest to her, like people often did when they were overwrought.

But they'd be wrong. She'd never been so sure

of anything. It was the right thing to do, like it had been the right thing to do to marry him eighteen years earlier, after they'd met in the nursing home and fallen in love.

She'd managed without him once; she'd do it again, even without the help of her father who was eighty-five, and beginning to show signs of slowing down. She was heartbroken, torn in two with loneliness and anger and grief, but she'd cope. She was healthy and strong, with two beautiful children, a steady job and a successful series of books that was about to be published in the US. She'd find a way.

Later that week, after Neil had packed up and moved back to his mother's house, after Sarah had explained to the children that they were going to be living apart from now on, but that they'd see him as much as they wanted, after she'd broken the news to Christine and her father, and endured the disbelief and disapproval that she'd been expecting, she sat down to write to the one person she knew would understand.

Dear Helen

It's been over a month now since our darling son Luke was taken from us, the worst, most unbearable time of my life. Thank you for your kind note and the sachet. I love the scent of lavender, I sleep with it under my cheek. Alice wrote a sweet note too, and sent chocolate. You must be so proud of her.

507

Neil and I have split up again – my doing this time. He's back in his mother's house. I feel bad for the children, but they'll still see plenty of him, and I thought staying married for their sake would have been worse for everyone in the long run. I know I've done the right thing, even if nobody else seems to understand that. We should never have got back together, I can see that now. I did it for the wrong reason; it was another baby I wanted, not Neil.

I went back to work two weeks ago. I could have taken longer but I needed to have something to fill my days. I'm driving again too. I'm still hopeless but I'll probably be doing a fair bit of it from now on so I'd better get used to it.

You didn't marry Frank, I wonder why. I suppose, like me, you didn't feel it was right for you. Maybe we're more alike than we think, you and I. I hope you don't feel too bad about it now. I hope your family understood, and poor Frank too.

Write when you get the chance, I always love to hear from you.

Yours ever

Sarah xxx

1998

HELEN

The number was unfamiliar. 'Hello?'

'Am I speaking with Helen?' A woman's voice, calm, businesslike.

Helen sniffed the pineapple she was holding. 'Yes. Who is this?'

'I'm calling from St Regina's Hospital. We found your number in the mobile phone of an older lady who was brought in earlier—'

Helen lowered her arm. 'What lady?'

'The only identification we could find is a library card in the name of M. D'Arcy.'

M. D'Arcy. Margaret D'Arcy.

Helen dropped the pineapple and her half-filled supermarket basket, and began walking rapidly towards the exit. 'What happened? How is she?'

'May I ask if you're a relative?'

'Daughter.' She rummaged in her bag for her car keys as she strode through the doors into the chilly January evening. 'What happened?' she repeated.

'She collapsed on the street. She was brought in about an hour—'

'How is she?'

'The doctor is with her now. If you could—'

'What hospital did you say?'

'St Regina's. It's along by the—'

'I know where it is.'

She hung up and pushed her key into the car door, trying to take it in. Her mother had collapsed on the street: her elegant mother had stopped walking and crumpled onto the path, surrounded by strangers.

Someone, presumably, had phoned for an ambulance, which had taken her to St Regina's where someone else had rummaged in her handbag and scrolled through the contacts in her mobile phone – the phone Alice had given her for Christmas – and decided that *Helen*, first name only, might be able to identify her. She had no idea who else was in her mother's contact list, or which other person they might have tried before they'd got to *H*.

Alice's name was surely there, had to be one of the first listed. But Alice's number was foreign, so presumably they'd have passed it by, searching for a more local one.

She buckled her seatbelt and pushed the key into the ignition. She drove more carefully than usual through the early-evening streets, something inside her head buzzing oddly, until she pulled into the hospital car park.

She turned off the ignition and sat looking up at the three-storey red-brick building. She'd driven past St Regina's countless times – it was on her route to her mother's house, barely half a mile from it – but had never been inside. On her mother's insistence, her father had been brought to the Blackrock Clinic, a mile or two further away, when he'd had his stroke. Nobody around today to do the same for her.

Helen got out of the car and made her way towards the front of the building. She walked up the crumbling concrete steps and pushed through the white-painted double doors. The small lobby, with its long wooden bench set against the lemon-coloured wall to her left, held the plastic smell of hairspray.

'Margaret D'Arcy,' she said to the ludicrously young-looking woman – cropped blonde hair, pimples – who sat behind the reception desk. 'She was brought in earlier today.'

The woman – girl – set aside her magazine and tapped her computer keyboard. 'Second floor,' she said, her eyes not leaving the screen. 'Left down the corridor and up the stairs, or there's a lift further on. The nurses will tell you which room.'

The nurse Helen met on the second floor – sixties, harassed, baggy-eyed – showed her into an empty waiting room. 'I'll get the doctor for you,' she said, rushing off.

'Do you know how my mother is?' Helen asked – but the nurse had gone, making no sound in her rubber soles. Helen ignored the stack of magazines on the chipped coffee-table and stood at the little window, hands planted on the barely warm, dusty radiator beneath. She watched a man in a white apron cross the yard below with a big tray of something she couldn't make out. The darkening sky threatened rain for the first time in about a week.

'Helen?'

She turned. A woman in a white coat had entered the room, hand already extended as she crossed the floor.

'Jean Carmody,' she said. Her voice was soft, the kind of whispery voice you'd use in a church, or maybe a library. Her skin was ice-cold, her hand-shake loose. 'I was the doctor on duty when your mother was brought in.'

Helen waited, focusing on the lips that were bare of colour, and badly chapped.

'I'm afraid I don't have good news for you, Helen. Your mother suffered a brain haemorrhage, quite a severe one. There's nothing we can do, apart from making her as comfortable as we can.'

'She's dying,' Helen said, the words coming out sharper than she'd intended.

'I'm afraid so. It could be hours, it could be a few days, but she hasn't got long.'

Helen looked down at the doctor's hands, which were clasped tightly now, fingers knitted together, almost in prayer. A long time since Helen had prayed for anything.

'Can I see her?'

'Of course.'

The doctor led the way down the corridor.

Following her, Helen felt the echo of a walk down a similar corridor, leaning heavily on Breen's arm. A long time since he'd crossed her mind too. The wedding day probably, two years last September. Her bouquet sitting in his blue bowl the night before.

'She's drifting in and out of consciousness,' the doctor said, 'but she won't make a lot of sense if she's awake.' They came to a door and she pushed it open, then stood back to allow Helen to enter.

The tiny room, suffocatingly warm, held just one bed. A small television, perched on a shelf high on the opposite wall, was switched off. Helen's mother lay unmoving, her face almost as white as the pillowcase beneath her head, her eyes half open. At the sound of their approach she turned her head slightly.

Helen slipped into the tweed-covered green armchair by the bed and reached for the hand – looking, all of a sudden, terribly wizened – that lay unmoving on the sheet. 'It's me,' she said, stroking the papery skin, the swollen knuckles, the perfectly manicured nails that her mother had had repainted every Friday afternoon for as long as Helen could remember.

'I'm here,' she said. 'It's Helen. I'm here now.'

SARAH

It had begun, a few months earlier, with a mixed-up word. It was that simple.

'Grandpa said he went to the geography,' Stephen had told her. 'I didn't know what he was talking about. He meant the library. It was funny.'

Sarah, preoccupied with preparing a buffet-lunch menu for thirty guests to commemorate the nursing home's fiftieth year of existence, had passed it off as a moment of absentmindedness. The man had just turned eighty-seven: of course he was going to be forgetful.

But a few weeks later it had happened again.

'He couldn't remember the word "television". He kept saying, "That thing in the sitting room," and we were guessing sofa and fireplace and stuff. It was like a game, but he got cross when I laughed.'

The next time she saw him, Sarah had asked him lightly how he was feeling.

'I'm fine,' he'd said – and he appeared the same as ever to her. Slower, certainly, than he used to be, but still driving, still coming to them every Sunday to spend the afternoon and eat dinner.

'Let me know,' she'd said to twelve-year-old

516

Martha, 'if you notice anything about Grandpa – if he gets confused again, I mean, or does something a bit . . . odd.'

Nothing else had happened for several weeks. And then she'd dropped by his house one afternoon on her way home from work, and as he was putting the kettle on, Sarah had glanced out of the kitchen window and seen something on the lawn. She'd gone out and picked up his bedroom slippers, sitting neatly side by side.

She'd brought them into the house. 'Guess what I found on the grass.'

He'd looked at them blankly. 'What were they doing out there?'

'I was hoping you could tell me that,' she'd said, her heart sinking. One slipper might conceivably be a dog that had somehow got into the house and run off with it – but two, side by side, had to have been placed there.

'I found Dad's slippers in the garden,' she told Christine. 'They were just sitting out on the lawn.'

'Were they? That's a bit weird.'

'He couldn't explain it. I'd like him to get a check-up.'

'Ask him so.'

But the suggestion hadn't gone down well. 'I don't need a check-up. There's nothing wrong with me.'

'Dad,' she'd said gently, 'it's just that you're getting on, and it would do you no harm to go to the doctor and let him—'

'I'm fine,' he'd said. 'I'll go to the doctor if I'm sick.'

She'd had to bring it up, although she'd hated doing it. 'Dad, remember the slippers I found on the lawn?'

His face had hardened. 'I didn't put them out there,' he'd snapped. 'Why would I do something like that? Someone else must have.'

'Who, though?'

'I don't know, but someone must have.'

'I'm worried about Dad,' Sarah had told Neil. 'I think there's something wrong with him.'

'Is he sick?'

'He's . . . forgetful. I think it might be the start of something.'

Neil had shrugged. 'He seemed fine, last time I saw him. Maybe you're imagining it.'

She hadn't been forgiven, she knew that. Over two years since they'd separated, and he still felt bitter. He was civil when they met, and attended the children's birthday parties with his mother. But he didn't ask about Sarah's cookery books, didn't comment when she changed the front door from blue to green, didn't engage with her in any way apart from matters that concerned the children.

Sarah mourned the loss of their friendship, and hid the sadness and regret that seeing him so detached caused her. And it hurt, too, that they weren't sharing their other, deeper grief, that they never visited Luke's grave together – Neil had refused stiffly the only time she'd suggested it.

After Luke she'd abandoned the final cookbook, the one intended for reluctant vegetable eaters. 'I can't do it any more,' she'd told Paul. 'I can't summon up the energy.' But it wasn't lack of energy that stopped her: it was the thought that she'd begun it when she'd been pregnant, and it would always be too painful a reminder.

Thankfully, Paul hadn't pushed it, telling her to get in touch if she ever had an idea for a new project, but she doubted that she'd ever feel that creative again.

The other books continued to sell steadily. They'd been translated into several European languages, and two years ago the series had been published in America. Every six months a royalty cheque arrived from Paul that was always a lot more than Sarah had been expecting. The money wasn't important – they managed fine on Sarah's income and Neil's contributions – but she was quietly proud of her achievement.

Maybe she didn't need to worry about her father. Maybe it was just old age. There'd been no more strange happenings in at least a month, and today he seemed fine, sitting in front of her fire as they waited for the chicken to roast.

'I got another letter from America,' she told him. 'Someone who likes the cookbooks.'

'That's good,' he said. 'Nice of them to take the trouble.'

He was fine. She was worrying over nothing. He was old, that was all.

HELEN

'**F**reezing out there today,' she said, rubbing her hands together. 'Nice and warm in here.' She laid her coat across the arm of the chair and stood by the window. Below was a little garden, square in shape, bordered with shrubs and scattered about with wooden seats.

'When you're feeling up to it, and when the weather's a bit better we can have a walk around outside. You'd like that, wouldn't you?'

A man appeared in the garden, carrying some kind of basin or bowl in both hands. He crossed to the shrubs and swung it high, and an arc of liquid rose in the air and landed on the plants. He turned and went back inside, the empty container swinging by his side.

'I finished a piece today for the *Herald* magazine, I was telling you about it last week, how first-time buyers are coping with the rising house prices. I'll bring it in to you when it's printed.'

The sky above the window was pale blue, and quite cloudless. In the distance, towering above the rooftops, she could make out the skeletal shapes of several cranes. Dublin was being facelifted, apartment blocks popping up like dandelions along by the river and the canal, each one more ludicrously expensive than the last. Ireland was booming, its economy the envy of Europe.

'Alice sends her love. She'll come and see you as soon as she can.'

A lie, a downright lie. Helen hadn't said anything to Alice, who would, of course, feel obliged to come home. What was the point of two of them sitting by the bedside, waiting for the inevitable? Alice had enough to occupy her, still waiting on tables at the weekends, still illustrating by night, but in the process of setting up her own design studio.

From the corridor outside the room, muted sounds drifted in. The tap of footsteps, the clang of dishes, the squeak of a trolley wheel, the occasional raised voices of the cheerful women who appeared regularly with cups of dark-brown tea and plates of soft, plain biscuits.

'You know what I heard on the news last night? They've printed Princess Diana stamps in Britain. Bet the Queen's hopping mad. Must get Alice to bring home a few when she comes. I've pitched a piece to the *Herald* editor about who's made it onto Irish stamps over the years. I'm waiting for the go-ahead.'

It didn't matter what she talked about: what mattered was that she kept talking, kept feeding words into the too-warm little room. What mattered was that she didn't think beyond the next inane topic of her one-sided conversation – and when inspiration failed she turned to whatever book she'd brought along and read aloud from that.

She had no idea if her mother heard a single thing. There was no sign that any of it was registering within the crumbling brain of the woman who lay unmoving in the narrow bed, eyes half open and unfocused, the only indication that she was still alive the minuscule rise and fall of her chest with each shallow breath she took, or a gush of unintelligible words every now and again.

Helen should probably phone somebody. She should get in touch with the few friends her mother still met for lunch, or the relatives who shook hands with them at funerals, who sent cards at Christmas and visited occasionally. But she did nothing, told no one.

Instead she came to the hospital each afternoon, once she'd churned out however many words were required of her, and for the rest of the day she sat by the bed or stood by the window, filling the room with words until some nurse urged her to go home and get some sleep, they'd let her know if there was any change.

And then she went home and lay awake all night, waiting for the phone to ring.

SARAH

'It's about Dad,' Christine said. 'I called in to see him today on my way home from the library. He was still wearing his pyjama bottoms.'

Still in pyjamas didn't sound too worrying. 'Maybe he was just having a lazy day.'

'No – the top half of him was properly dressed. When I asked him about it, he couldn't explain. He got a bit defensive, actually.'

'Oh . . .'

'I wouldn't have taken too much notice except for the things you were talking about, the slippers and stuff.'

'Yes . . . and there's more,' Sarah said.

'What?'

'He rang yesterday afternoon and said he couldn't find his glasses. I put the kids in the car and drove over, and when I got there, only about ten minutes later, he couldn't remember phoning me, and his glasses were sitting on the kitchen table.'

'God . . . what should we do?'

'I don't know. He won't go to the doctor – I've asked him.'

'I'll call to see him more often – I haven't been half as good as you. And I'll get Brian to drop by too, now and again.'

But it was becoming increasingly apparent that it was going to take more than dropping by. Sarah hung up and returned to the kitchen, her thoughts far from the spinach and bacon tart that was waiting to be taken from the oven.

HELEN

At half past eight on Sunday evening, five days after a weakened blood vessel had burst open in her brain and caused her to drop unconscious to the ground, Margaret D'Arcy's eighty-seven-year-old heart pumped out its final beat. Her eyes fluttered closed, her head tilted a fraction to the right, the hands that lay palms up on the sheet tipping inward as the last breath left her body with a soft rattle.

Helen, dozing in the chair by the bed, opened her eyes at the sound. She sat unmoving for several seconds, looking into the still, white face of the woman she'd known for almost fifty-six years. Eventually the door opened and a young nurse entered the room.

'She's gone,' Helen said mildly. 'Just now.'

'Oh . . .' The nurse lifted Margaret's left wrist and held it briefly. 'I'm so sorry,' she said, laying it back gently on the sheet. 'Can I get you anything at all?' Her hand came to rest on Helen's shoulder, so lightly Helen hardly felt it. 'A cup of tea or coffee?'

The kindness in her voice caused Helen to rise

abruptly. 'No, thank you.' She pulled on her jacket and felt in her bag for her car keys. 'Is there anything I need to do – I mean, before I leave here tonight? Any . . . forms to be signed, or . . .?'

'Not right now, no. That can all be sorted later.' The nurse held the door open, her face full of sympathy. 'Go home and get a good night's sleep now for yourself, and you can drop in tomorrow whenever it suits you.'

Helen made her way along the corridor. She stood in the lift that smelt of feet as it carried her down with a soft wheeze. She stepped through the main doors, wrapping her coat tightly around her. She drove out of the car park and made her way home, negotiating the familiar streets automatically. In the car she felt bitterly cold, despite the full-blast efforts of its heater. When she got home, she was shivering violently.

The house was cold too. In the kitchen she plugged in a fan heater and boiled the kettle. She filled a pint glass a third full with whiskey and added a dessertspoonful of sugar and a lemon wedge. She topped it up with steaming water and brought it to the table where Sarah's last letter, delivered more than a week earlier, still sat.

Dear Helen
I hope all is well, and you had a good Christmas. Not much to report here. Still anxious about Dad – he's getting so terribly absentminded. I'm thinking about cutting

down on my days at the nursing home . . .
We'll see.

The children are well, thankfully. The latest
from Martha is that she wants to go to art
college after school and be an artist like Alice
– I must write and tell your daughter she's a
role model for mine! And speaking of Alice,
it sounds like she's going from strength to
strength – I wasn't a bit surprised when you
told me she was opening her own studio: she
has such an artistic gift, I knew it was only
a matter of time before it took her places. And
of course I love the name she's chosen – who
wouldn't want to do business with Wonderland
Design? If Martha does half as well, in whatever field she lands, I'll be thrilled.

Stephen is flying along with his piano
lessons. I'm sorry if I sound like a boastful
mother, but when I listen to him it literally
brings tears to my eyes! His teacher says he's
the most talented pupil she's ever had. I have
no idea where he got it from – neither Neil
nor I are remotely musical – but it's wonderful
to see it. He says he wants to be a musician,
and I know he's only ten, but I can definitely
see it happening.

Neil is fine, as far as I can see. We still don't
talk much, just what needs to be said. It's sad,
considering how close we were for years. And
of course Luke, my precious Luke, is always
in my thoughts, but I'm managing.

Isn't it chilly? I feel sorry for the nursing-home residents, frozen all the time, poor souls, despite the central heating. Dad feels the cold a lot too, and I suppose your mother is the same: the trials of getting old. Hopefully we'll get a nice summer after this cold snap.

Better go to bed, my eyes are closing.

All my best,

Sarah xx

PS Almost forgot – Paul made contact lately, out of the blue. He has an idea for a picture book featuring Martina and Charlie from the cookbooks – well, a whole series, really. My first instinct was to say no, but if I'm going to cut my working hours I'll have time . . . We'll see. Might be worth a try. He seems to think so.

Helen laid the letter aside, breathing in the whiskey fumes, grateful for the warmth that was beginning to creep back into her body. She sat at the table, listening to the muted tick of the clock that Frank had bought her a few weeks after he'd begun spending Saturday nights in the house.

'You can't have a kitchen without a clock,' he'd declared, so Helen had stuck it on a hook above the back door, and there it had hung ever since. Twenty past nine, it read now. Less than an hour since her mother had died.

As she sat there, hands wrapped around the warm glass, she flicked through the mental images of her mother that were stored in her head. Sprinkling holy water from a plastic bottle onto the little red Fiat that was Helen's first car; sitting in a blue dress with an infant Alice cradled in her arms; meeting Helen's eye across Cormac's open grave; hunched in her seat, eyes squeezed shut, as the plane to Scotland took off; placing her hand on Frank's offered arm, smiling up at him as they crossed an icy street in Troon.

And now she was gone, and Helen would never see her again.

She took a sheet of paper from the open ream on the table. She got her pen from her bag and unscrewed the top.

Sarah
Bad news, I'm afraid. On Tuesday my mother suffered a

She stopped and regarded the scatter of words. She crumpled up the sheet and threw it in the direction of the bin and drank again from the cooling whiskey before taking a fresh page.

Sarah
My mother died tonight, and I feel

For the second time she stopped. A drop of water splotched onto the page, just under the word tonight. She looked at it in surprise. She touched it with her finger and drew it through the still-wet ink, back and forth until the words were unreadable.

She slid the page away from her, blinking rapidly until the possibility of more tears had passed. She wished, all of a sudden, that she wasn't alone. If Frank was there he'd know what to say: he'd tell her it was perfectly understandable to feel sad when your mother died, even if you hadn't always got along. He'd take her to bed if that was what she wanted, hold her all night if she asked him. But she hadn't laid eyes on Frank in more than two years, and it would be beyond cruel to ring him now.

She drank again, her face warm, her head beginning to feel light. She'd ring Alice, who needed to be told what had happened. She brought her drink out to the hall and dialled her daughter's number and listened to the phone ringing in Scotland. Let her be home, let her pick it up.

She heard a click. *Hello there*, Alice said brightly. *You've reached Alice, I'm sorry I can't get to the phone right*—

Helen disconnected, and the line burred softly in her ear. She replaced the receiver and drank steadily until the glass was empty. She set it on the bottom step and walked up to her bedroom, keeping a tight hold on the banister.

SARAH

Matron sighed. 'Sarah, I won't pretend this is good news. You've been invaluable here since you started, you know that – and you'll certainly be a hard act to follow. But of course you have to do what needs to be done. Your family must come first.'

'If two days a week doesn't suit, if it would make it easier for me to give up completely, I'll understand perfectly.'

'Actually, two days might work out fine – I think Josie would be glad to do more than just the weekends. Let me talk to her.'

And Josie was spoken to, and said she'd be delighted with three more days each week. And just like that, half of Sarah's problem was solved.

They'd be fine, even with her reduced income. The cookbook royalties wouldn't go on forever but Neil's contribution was generous, and she was slowly warming to Paul's idea of a picture-book spin-off series.

'You have a ready-made market – so many children are familiar with Martina and Charlie. That's half the battle. Give it a go anyway – what have you got to lose?'

Remembering her long-ago failure as a fiction writer, Sarah had balked at the outset, but as she turned the idea around in her head, she began to have second thoughts. Maybe it was time to try again, maybe writing for children would suit her. If a new series took off, it would be a whole other income.

But whether or not it did, they'd manage – and she would have more time to give to her father.

'Good news,' she told him that afternoon. 'With what I'm still getting from the books I don't need to work full-time any more so I'm just going to do two days a week.'

'Oh.'

'I might start a new book, and I'll be able to call around here more often to see you, or you can call to us.'

He hadn't shaved. His chin was covered with grey stubble. She didn't ever remember him not shaving. He also looked as if he'd lost weight – how had she not noticed that before?

'What are you having for dinner?' she asked.

A beat passed. 'I have stuff in the fridge,' he said. 'I'm fine.'

He didn't look fine. 'Do you have any of that 3-in-1 oil?' she asked. 'Our small gate is squeaking and I can't find mine.'

When he'd gone out to the shed, she opened the fridge and found the turned remains of a pint of milk, two eggs, an untouched bowl of jelly spotted with mould and a dried-out wedge of Cheddar cheese – and sitting on the bottom shelf was a pair of neatly folded black socks.

She looked through presses and pulled out several half-packets of biscuits that had gone completely soft, three tins of soup and a plastic bag that held half a dozen decomposing tomatoes.

She replaced everything, thinking fast. When he returned, she took the oil she didn't need and put it into her bag.

'Why don't you come back with me for dinner?' she asked. 'I'm doing a chicken pie – it just has to be reheated. I'll drive you home afterwards.'

'Ah no, I have everything I need here.'

Everything he needed. Two eggs, or soup that came out of a tin: that was all that was edible in the house. But what could she say without confessing that she'd been rummaging through his kitchen? She could hardly drag him kicking and screaming into the car, or insist that he came to her house every day to be fed.

When she got home, she put the chicken pie into the oven and phoned Christine. 'We have to do something,' she said. 'He can't live on his own any more. Have you noticed how thin he's got?'

'I did think he'd lost weight . . . Have you said anything to him?'

'No – he can't see that there's anything wrong. I know he'll refuse to leave the house of his own accord.'

'What about looking for a home help, someone who'd go in for a few hours, cook him a dinner, tidy up a bit? I'm calling in to see him tomorrow, I could suggest it.'

But Sarah couldn't imagine him going for that either. He'd been independent for so long, healthy for most of his life. Why would he agree to have some stranger coming to his house every day when he didn't see any need for one? 'I'm not sure that'll work,' she said. 'Bring him something he can have for his dinner, enough for two days. Tell him it was left over. Leave the other with me for the moment.'

She remembered how good he'd been to her when Neil had gone to live with Noreen. She remembered how she'd leant on him, how he'd stepped in and kept things from collapsing around her.

She could help him now. All she had to do was convince him that she needed him again.

HELEN

He looked exactly as she remembered, except that he wasn't smiling. He wore a leather jacket she hadn't seen before.

'I'm sorry for your trouble,' he told her. 'She was a nice lady.' Shaking Helen's hand like everyone else, nodding at her as if she was no more than a casual acquaintance, not someone he'd asked to marry him six times, and who'd broken his heart in return.

'Thank you,' Helen murmured, aware of Alice's eyes on them. 'Thank you for coming.'

He moved on, and Helen saw him cupping Alice's elbow as he shook her hand. It hadn't crossed her mind that he would show up – but now that he had, she realised that it was completely in character. In the years they'd been together, he'd attended at least a funeral a week, sometimes when he hadn't even known the deceased.

'It's a good customer's mother,' he'd tell her. 'I'd feel bad not paying my respects.' Or 'I knew his brother well, we were at school together.' Or 'He was a neighbour of my aunt's – I never met him, but he used to drop the paper into her every day.'

535

Frank Murphy wasn't a man to miss a funeral – so of course he'd show up now to say goodbye to a woman he'd got on well with, even if it meant coming face to face with her daughter who'd spurned him, who'd walked away from him on his wedding day.

She'd been a fool to throw him over, she knew that. She'd had the chance of marrying a genuinely good man who'd have taken care of her and tried to make her happy and loved her till the day he died, and she'd turned her back on it all. And yet, given the opportunity again, she knew she'd do exactly the same. As much a fool at almost fifty-six as she'd been at sixteen.

There was a pitifully small attendance at the funeral. In eighty-seven years Helen's mother had remained faithful to the few friends she'd made in childhood, most of whom had predeceased her. The mourners this morning were mainly relatives, some of whom Helen hadn't laid eyes on in years, with a scatter of her mother's neighbours who introduced themselves whisperingly to Helen as they shook her hand.

She was touched by the idea of someone attending a funeral where the only person known to them was the one who had died. She would never have known the difference if the neighbours had stayed away, and it would never have crossed her mind to attend any of her neighbours' funerals – apart, she supposed, from Anna, Alice's old babysitter across the road, who was still very much alive.

She thought briefly of Malone, dying in a nursing home down the country. She wondered if any of his neighbours had seen his name in the paper and realised he was dead. She didn't read the death columns in her daily paper, would never have realised that Breen's wife had died if there hadn't been a separate mention made of it, in deference to the former editor.

Even though the weather had mellowed a little in the past few days, the cemetery, on the crest of a hill, was cold and bleak. Helen stood stiffly, her hands deep in the pockets of her coat, as her mother's remains were lowered into the same hole that had been dug for Helen's father eight years earlier.

She felt a hand slip under her arm and turned to Alice, who was crying quietly as she watched her grandmother's coffin being lowered. The tip of her nose was pink from the cold, her hair hidden beneath a red knitted beret. She made no attempt to stem her tears, which ran slowly down her face and into the purple scarf that was wrapped several times around her neck. Helen took her hand from her pocket and covered her daughter's.

The new business was going well, Alice had told her the night before. 'I've taken on a secretary – well, receptionist, secretary and marketing person rolled into one, really – and a graphic artist, just out of college.'

She was still renting the same tiny flat, but the business was run from a separate space in a nearby building, also owned by her landlord. 'He's giving me a good deal on both places,' she'd said. 'I'm not exactly making tons of money so I can't afford to give up the waitressing yet. It's a bit scary, having two people depending on you for their income – but they're great, and we had three new enquiries last week alone.'

She was also in a new relationship. 'I met her just after Christmas, through a mutual friend. It's going well, but it's early days. She's a dentist, her name is Lara. She's Scottish, from Aberdeen.'

She didn't ask if Helen had met anyone since Frank. After she'd had her say about the wedding that never was, the subject had been dropped and never revisited. Alice was probably hoping that her mother's love life was well and truly over – and, given that no man had shown the slightest interest in her in well over two years, Helen had to accept that it probably was.

To her relief, Frank hadn't come to the cemetery. The graveside was attended by the same relatives who'd shown up at the church, and just two of the neighbours: barely a dozen in all. When the short ceremony ended, Helen suggested that they accompany her and Alice to a nearby pub – better get them a drink and a bowl of soup at least – and the small gathering straggled its way down the gravel path towards the gates.

The cemetery, at noon on a chilly weekday, was mostly deserted. At the sound of the group's footsteps three small brown birds – thrushes?

sparrows? – rose in unison from the skeletal branches of a tree. A young woman in a white fur jacket walked towards them, holding the leash of a little Yorkshire terrier. She didn't acknowledge the mourners as she passed, her gaze fixed directly ahead; the dog sniffed at the ankles he encountered until she pulled him on.

Further on a lone man in a dark coat stood before one of the gravestones, his head bowed. As they approached he turned slightly to observe them and, catching Helen's eye, he nodded in recognition, his expression unchanging.

'I'll follow you,' she murmured to Alice. 'Get a round of drinks and ask what they want to eat. I'll just be a few minutes.'

She left the path without waiting for a reply and crossed the frosty grass towards him.

'Hello,' she said, the tips of her fingers stinging with the cold, making her wish for gloves. 'How are things?'

He inclined his head. 'Not bad. Was that someone close to you?'

'My mother.'

'I'm sorry.'

He'd got a little thinner; his cheekbones stood out a fraction more. His hair was greyer, but his eyes were as piercingly blue as ever. Helen glanced at the headstone in front of him and read, right at the top, *Emily Breen, beloved daughter, 1958–1966.*

Beloved daughter, eight when she'd died. She turned back to him. 'Your child?'

He nodded. 'Leukaemia.'

A dead child, a ruined marriage. An utterly sad synopsis of a life. She scanned the rest of the headstone and saw *Kathleen Breen, 1931–1995.* 'And your wife,' she said. 'I read she'd died. I'm sorry.'

'Thank you.'

A small silence fell. Helen listened to the fading sound of the mourners' footsteps. Alice would be wondering who he was.

'How've you been, O'Dowd?' he asked.

O'Dowd. 'Fine, same as ever . . .' She looked towards the gates, and saw her group had disappeared. 'I'd better go.'

'It was good,' he said then, 'seeing you.'

She met his gaze directly, like she always had. Like they always had. 'You too.'

'Say hello to Alice.'

She smiled, touched that he'd remembered her name. 'I will.'

She turned and began to walk away. After a few yards she stopped and looked back. He hadn't moved.

'Maybe,' she said, 'we could meet up sometime. For coffee, or brandy, or something.'

The ghost of a smile crossed his face. 'No law against it,' he said.

SARAH

'I know it sounds ridiculous, and I hate to ask, but I've got nobody else. And it wouldn't be for long, I'm sure.'

'It's not ridiculous at all,' he replied. 'It's natural that you'd be nervous, a woman on your own with three children.'

Three children: her heart dropped. He'd confused her with Christine, that was all. It was easily done.

'Are you sure you wouldn't mind? It would mean a lot to me.'

'Of course I don't mind. I'm happy to help.'

She felt bad, making up three break-ins in the area. Apart from the fact that she was lying, it was surely tempting Fate – what were the chances that real burglars would show up some night, just to teach her to tell the truth?

But it was working. Her father was packing a bag and moving into the spare room, and he was doing it because she'd asked him to help.

'You're a life saver,' she said. 'I don't know what I'd do without you.'

He smiled. 'That's what parents are for, love. Happy to help out, you know that.'

'And you'll be well fed.'

'I know I will.'

And I'll look after you, she promised him silently. It's your turn.

HELEN

'I don't like this any more than you do, O'Dowd.'

'Liar,' she breathed.

'There I was, minding my own business, going about my daily routine, and along you come . . . O'Dowd, are you listening to me?'

'Don't stop.'

'What's that? Didn't quite catch it. Open your eyes, O'Dowd.'

She slapped his arm, laughing. '*Bastard.*'

'You mean don't stop *this*? . . . Is this what you mean, O'Dowd?'

But she couldn't answer, because what he was doing was taking her breath away, like it always did.

At fifty-six. Downright ridiculous to be so utterly enthralled with any man at that age – let alone *this* man, who'd been the bane of her life for so long, who'd barked orders down the phone at her, who'd demanded a thousand words by the end of day or she'd be out on her ear, did she think it was a charity he was running? – and look at them now, for *Jesus*' sake.

'You like it?' he breathed, his face inches away.

'You want more?' His eyes blazing into hers, and all she could do, all she was capable of doing, since he'd reduced her to a state of quivering, almost unbearable arousal, was to grab what hair he had left and pull it towards her, hard, until he was forced to cover her mouth with his.

Fifty-six – and he was sixty-eight, for Christ's sake. Look at them, rolling around in her bed night after night like a pair of teenagers. Serve him right if he got a coronary.

If Alice only knew.

But Alice had no idea: Alice had gone back to Edinburgh two days after the funeral, before any of this nonsense had started.

'You don't mind?' she'd asked Helen. 'It's just that we've got this new job on, and I don't feel I should leave the others alone too long.'

'Of course not,' Helen had said.

'You'll be OK?'

'Of course I will.'

'I'll come back as soon as I can for a few more days.'

'That would be good.'

Frank had been mentioned. 'It was nice of him to come to the church, wasn't it?'

'Very nice,' Helen had replied, in a voice that said leave it alone, and Alice had wisely left it alone. And then she was gone, waving as she'd walked through to the departure lounge, promising to bring Lara next time.

Helen had driven home and made herself a pot

of coffee. Halfway through her second mug she'd opened her bag and found the piece of paper Breen had given her two days earlier.

It was a supermarket till receipt, dated the previous week. His cashier had been Vivienne, and he'd bought washing-up liquid, olives, bin liners, broccoli, milk, lemon curd, gin, cat food and anchovies. She'd turned it over and there was his phone number.

She'd give him a call; they'd meet and drink coffee, like she'd suggested. She felt sorry for him, with his dead child and his mentally unstable and now also dead wife. She was doing him a kindness, nothing more.

She'd picked up her phone. She'd put it down again and poured herself another refill.

'What's wrong with you?' she'd said aloud. 'It's Breen. You're meeting him for coffee.'

She'd dialled his number and listened as it rang seven times. She'd hung up and torn the receipt into tiny pieces and dropped them into the bin. Stupid idea.

Two minutes later her phone had rung. She'd started, slopping coffee onto the table. *Private number*, the display had told her.

'Hello.'

A pause. 'O'Dowd?'

She'd closed her eyes. 'Yes.'

'Did you just try to ring me?'

'Yes.'

Silence.

'You want to go for coffee?' It had blurted out of her, too suddenly. 'Would you like to?' she'd amended. God, that sounded worse, as if she was desperate to see him.

'Sure.' If he thought she sounded odd, he'd given no sign. 'Or would you prefer to go to dinner tomorrow night?'

Something had jumped inside her, around her abdomen. It was not a pleasant sensation. 'Dinner?'

'You know,' he'd said, 'the meal that comes after lunch, and before supper.'

It had completely washed away the tension. She didn't know whether to laugh or hang up. 'You're asking me out to dinner.' She watched a fly walk its way around the inside of the kitchen lampshade.

'Yes, O'Dowd. That's what I'm doing.'

Dinner with Breen. A whole meal in his company, just the two of them sitting across a table for an hour at least. He was probably sick of opening a can of beans, or a tin of anchovies. And she hadn't been taken out to dinner in almost three years.

It wouldn't kill her to say yes. It might even be a bit of a laugh.

'Yes,' she'd said, watching the fly.

He was at the restaurant before her, wearing one of his well-cut suits and the usual dazzling white shirt. He stood and pulled out her chair, and made no comment on the black dress she'd agonised over. Bastard.

He ordered pâté and sea bream, and chocolate

cake for dessert. She had a green salad and a steak, bloody, and no dessert, and she drank a bottle of red wine all by herself. He stuck to water until the plates were cleared, and then he ordered coffee and brandies without consulting her.

They talked; it was easy. He asked about her writing. She told him how Alice was doing. He described the two cats he'd inherited a month ago when his only niece had emigrated; she told him about Malone's cat. They talked about books and films and music. He hated *Casablanca*, had never got The Beatles. They both loved Chandler's stories, and The Rolling Stones, and *Death in Venice*. She refused to believe he'd never seen *It's a Wonderful Life*.

He didn't mention his wife. She didn't tell him about Cormac, or about nearly marrying Frank.

'I'll drive you home,' he said as they got up. She didn't argue, although her car was in the car park. She felt woozy from the alcohol; probably better to leave it there till the morning. He placed his hand lightly in the small of her back as they walked towards his car.

She directed him to her house. He parked and switched off the engine. They sat in silence for several seconds.

'You smell,' he said finally, with no particular inflexion in his voice, 'quite flowery.'

She turned her head towards him. 'Do you want to come in for coffee?'

'No,' he said. 'I don't want coffee.' He reached

across and ran a finger down her cheek. His touch sent a lightning bolt through her.

They barely made it into the house. When she woke in the morning, he was gone. She spent the day in Alice's dressing-gown with her head in her hands.

Breen. What had possessed her? And then she'd remember what he'd done to her, and what she'd done to him, and her face would scald with the memory.

In the evening she stood under the shower, trying to wash away the images that wouldn't leave her head. She remembered her car, still hopefully sitting in the restaurant car park. Tomorrow she'd deal with it. She wrapped her hair in a towel and put on a clean T-shirt and tracksuit bottoms. She went downstairs and made custard. As she was about to spoon it into a bowl, the doorbell rang.

'I have no idea what happened,' Breen said. 'It's all very confusing.'

He stood unsmiling on her doorstep. At the sight of him, warmth flooded outwards to the tips of her fingers, shot down to her toes, spiralled up into her towel-wrapped head.

'You want some custard?' she asked.

He looked suspiciously at her. 'Is that a trick question? Is custard a euphemism for something else?'

A euphemism. She smiled at him. 'Yes, it is.'

She held the door open and he walked in. She took his hand and led him into the sitting room and pulled him down onto the floor, and afterwards they ate cold custard out of the saucepan with two spoons. And that had been a month ago.

And over the past four weeks she had told him about Cormac.

And he had told her about his wife.

And she had told him about Frank.

And he had told her about his daughter.

And she had told him about her parents, and Sarah.

There would never be enough time for them to say all that there was to be said between them.

Breen, it would appear, was the second big love of her life.

Breen, for crying out loud.

SARAH

She heard the car pulling up at the gate. When she opened the front door, Martha and Stephen were dragging their rucksacks up the path. 'Hello there – did you have a good time?'

'Yeah,' Stephen said, dropping his rucksack to return her hug. 'We went to *Flubber*.'

'Did you now?'

'Yeah, it was *really* funny.'

'How's Grandpa?' Martha asked.

'He's fine, lovey, having a lie-down.'

She'd told her father that the children knew nothing about the break-ins. 'I didn't want to worry them,' she explained. To Martha and Stephen she'd simply said that her father's memory was getting bad, and it was better if he stayed with them for a while. 'He might forget to turn off the cooker in his house, and it could cause a fire. He'll be safer here, with us to look after him.'

If they suspected the truth they didn't say – were they still a little young, at ten and twelve, to realise the full significance? – but in the month that he'd been living with them, Sarah had witnessed his continuing decline with great sadness, and she knew it had to be only a matter of time before the real reason for his presence became clear to both of them.

The children disappeared into the house. Sarah walked to the gate. Neil was standing by the open car door.

'Hi,' she said. 'How are you?'

He'd got his hair cut since last weekend, shorter than usual. Over the past few months she'd noticed that his waist was thickening, and for the first time she saw the beginning of a double chin. If he was still living with her she'd be cutting down on the cakes, serving up more salads and fish, making porridge for his breakfast.

'How's your father?' he asked.

'Much the same . . . but he's in good enough form. What about Nuala?'

'She's fine.'

Her mother-in-law had been devastated, of course, when Neil had walked out to be with Noreen. Sarah had forced herself to lift the phone and call her, about a week after it had happened.

'I'm so glad you rang,' Nuala had wept. 'I didn't know whether you'd want to talk to me. I can't believe he's done this to you. I'm so sorry, Sarah, I had no idea about any of it – you must believe me.'

'Of course I believe you.'

And their relationship had remained intact, if temporarily shaken. Nuala had returned joyfully to Sarah's Christmas dinner table after the year she and Neil had been absent; and no one had been more pleased at the news that Sarah and Neil were to reunite.

'I prayed for this,' she'd told Sarah. 'I hoped so much you'd be able to forgive and forget. You've made me very happy.'

Hardly surprising then that the eventual dissolution of her son's marriage at Sarah's hand hadn't gone down well.

'I don't know why you're doing this to him,' she'd told Sarah stiffly. 'To hurt him like this, straight after what's just happened . . . why would you do that?' – and in the weeks and months that followed, while she continued to see her grandchildren, her manner towards her daughter-in-law remained polite but distant. What could Sarah do but accept with great sadness that their once-warm friendship was over?

She waited for Neil to get back in the car, but he remained where he was. Over the past few weeks she'd sensed a change in his attitude towards her, a small softening of the bitterness her rejection of him had caused. He asked about the new book project, enquired after her father, commented on the primroses in her window box.

For the children's sake she was glad of it, happy for them not to sense any rancour between their parents. She decided it could do no harm to let him share the occasional meal with them. Might be good for her father too, to have another male at the dinner table now and again. The two of them had always got on well, before all the upheaval. She opened her mouth to suggest it.

'Actually,' he said, 'there's something I wanted to tell you.'

'Oh?'

'I've met someone,' he said lightly. 'Well, I've actually known her a while, but we've recently . . . got close.'

Close. 'Oh,' Sarah said again. 'Well, that's good. I'm pleased for you.'

'I thought I should mention it.'

'Yes, of course . . . Thank you.'

'I'd like the children to meet her. Would that be OK?'

'Of course, yes, that's fine. That would be fine.' The words coming out in terribly polite little bursts. 'Of course it is. Absolutely.'

'Alright then. Maybe next weekend.'

He nodded and got into the car, and she stood there with what she hoped was a perfectly normal smile on her face until he'd driven off. And then she stood there some more.

They'd been apart for almost three years. She'd told him she didn't love him, that she didn't want to be married to him any more. She'd sent him away. They were living separate lives, they'd both moved on. And now he'd met someone else, and he wanted the children to meet her, which meant, which had to mean, that it was serious, or becoming serious.

It was perfectly natural for Sarah to feel a little

put out. It was human nature, wasn't it? Wanting to be wanted, even by the person you'd spurned. Wanting that door to remain ajar, to feel that there was still an infinitesimal chance that some day—

No. She turned abruptly and went back in through the gate, banging it behind her.

HELEN

'I don't suppose,' he said, two months after their first night together, 'you'd like to marry me.'

Helen stopped typing and looked across the kitchen table at him. He was eyeing her over his reading glasses, the newspaper spread open in front of him. It was the middle of the afternoon.

Although he hadn't officially moved in, he was spending most nights with her. His two inherited cats, which had taken up residence when Helen hadn't been looking, sat on the windowsill, purring out at the pathetic April sun.

'Pardon?'

He took off his glasses and laid them on the paper. 'We just seem to be heading in that direction.'

Helen smiled.

'I'll take that as a yes,' he said, reaching for his glasses again. 'Make the arrangements and let me know.'

She continued to watch him for a minute. When he turned a page, she got to her feet and walked around the table and stood beside his chair.

'Get up.'

He got up.

She looked into his eyes, their faces inches apart. 'Call that a proposal?'

His face took on a pained expression. 'O'Dowd,' he said, 'I'm no good at this. I'm good at being insensitive and blunt and sarcastic, and you would have me believe I'm rather good in bed. But I can't do sweet talk, you know that.'

'Just tell me how you feel about me. Tell me how you feel when you look at me.'

He sighed. He took off his glasses again and moved his hands up to cradle her face. 'I look at you and I feel happy. I think about you and I feel happy. I talk to you and it makes me happy. It's not a feeling I've had very often in my life, and I'd like to hang on to it. Will you please marry me, even though I can't imagine why the hell you'd want to, so I can stay feeling happy for the rest of my life?'

She tilted her head. 'Better. But you forgot the bit about love.'

'*Jesus*,' he said.

She waited.

He ran a finger along her cheek, like he'd done the first evening. 'I love you, O'Dowd, a hell of a lot more than I love myself. I have no idea how it happened, but I'm pretty sure it's entirely your fault – and frankly, it terrifies the daylights out of me. Good enough?'

She touched her lips to his. 'Yes. Yes it is, and yes I will. But we'll both make the arrangements.'

The following day she phoned Alice and told her she'd like to visit Edinburgh for a couple of days. A week later she travelled alone to Scotland, booked in to the B&B that had been arranged for her, and took Alice and Lara out to dinner. The next day she met Alice at Wonderland Design and the two of them went to lunch at a café around the corner.

'I have news,' Helen said, as soon as their food had been served.

Alice was precisely as dumbfounded as she'd expected.

'You're getting *married*? But who is he? How long have you even *known* him?' Her face changed. 'It's not Frank, is it?'

'It's not Frank,' Helen said. 'I've known him forever. It's just taken us a while to get to where we are.' She paused. 'It's Breen, my old boss.'

Alice's mouth dropped open a little wider – and then she smiled. 'Nice one, Mum. You got me. I totally believed you.'

'I'm not joking. We met up the day of Granny's funeral—'

'Granny's funeral? That's only a few weeks ago.'

'Actually, it's over two months.' Helen looked down at her spaghetti Bolognese. 'I know it seems sudden, and it took us both by surprise. After your father, I never thought I'd feel like this again. Frank was wonderful, and I tried really hard, but it just didn't happen.'

'But your old boss – you always *hated* him. I

remember how mad you'd be after he'd been on the phone.'

'I know. We had a . . . volatile working relationship.' Helen smiled. 'But I don't hate him now.'

Alice poked at her baked potato. 'And you're not going to do another runner?'

'Very funny.'

'Well, you'll never cease to amaze me,' Alice said, reaching for the salt. 'Sometimes – most times – I feel like I'm the mother.'

Helen laughed. So happy he'd made her, so unbelievably happy. 'Sorry about that.'

Alice didn't laugh back. 'I just hope you know what you're doing, Mum. Really.'

'Oh, I do.' Oh, she did.

When she got back to Ireland, she wrote to Sarah.

Are you sitting down? If not, sit down. I'll wait.

I'm in love. I'm truly, madly, deeply, laughably, ludicrously in love. (You see? It needed a chair.) What's more, I'm getting married. And here's the killer – it's Breen. Remember Breen, my main editor for years? Yes, you do remember him, because when you wrote your prissy first few letters to me you sent them care of him.

He annoyed the hell out of me, I often ranted to you about him, and the feeling was mutual. He was so bossy and crotchety – never ONCE did he say anything positive, even when I submitted something that was so bloody good he couldn't find anything to give out about. Probably annoyed him more. But we managed not to murder one another until he took early retirement, ten or eleven years ago.

And since then I've bumped into him now and again – I might have mentioned them – but I hadn't seen him for a few years, and then I met him again, in the cemetery of all places, on the day of my mother's funeral. And long story, but we ended up going out to dinner later in the week – and it just happened, it just came crashing into us, and it's blissful. I'm fifty-six and I'm head over heels in love with the last sixty-eight-year-old in the world I thought I'd end up with. You have my permission to howl with laughter.

I told Alice, I've just got back from Edinburgh. She thought I was joking, which is perfectly understandable. I hope I haven't traumatised the poor girl. I think she'll be OK when she gets over the shock.

Sorry I haven't been in touch. Blame my happy, distracted heart. Better still, blame Breen. He can take abuse, he gets plenty from me – he can still annoy the living daylights out of me. I know, it makes no sense, and I don't care.

We haven't made any wedding plans yet, but it'll probably be soon, and small and quiet, and maybe not in Ireland. I'll keep you posted.

Hope everything's well. How's your father doing? Catch me up when you get the chance. Oh, and I'm delighted to hear about your story-writing venture – I promise to offer no advice whatsoever, not that you'll need it. I have a feeling that Martina and Charlie's stories will flow out of you.

Must go – Breen is due in half an hour and my insides are melting in anticipation. If the old bitter and twisted Helen Fitzpatrick could hear me she'd slap my face.

H xx

PS Thank God I didn't marry Frank. I would have had to leave him, which would probably have destroyed him even more than my running away from the wedding. Did I tell you that he came to the church for my mother's funeral? Poor sweet doomed Frank.

PPS Breen calls me O'Dowd. Isn't that too quaint for words?

PPPS Helen Breen. Swoon.

SARAH

Dear Helen

Very surprised at your news, but also very happy for you. It sounds wonderful, and congratulations. Yes, I remember you mentioning your old editor once or twice.

Neil has met someone new too. Her name is Maria. He told me two weeks ago, and the children met her for the first time last weekend. She gave Stephen one of those Game Boys, which I imagine was Neil's suggestion, and which of course won Stephen over completely. I wasn't altogether pleased – Neil is well aware that I'd much prefer to see Stephen out and about or playing the piano than hunched over a silly electronic game, but I can hardly send it back.

Martha got a nail-salon set, so she and her friends have been painting and primping since it arrived. It seems a little grown-up for twelve-year-olds – surely they'll be using makeup long enough. But again, what can I say without sounding bitter and twisted?

Oh dear, I've just read over the last bit and

that's exactly how I sound. I suppose, if I'm honest, I'm a little jealous of Neil's new woman, although that sounds like I'm sorry we split up, and I'm not. I think it's just a case of wanting what I haven't got.

And it doesn't help that poor Dad is getting so forgetful. The other day he took all the photo albums from the press and piled them up on the garden seat. Thank goodness I discovered them before the rain came. And he forgets to put socks on, and he doesn't shave unless I remind him, and lots of other things. But at least he's with me and I can look after him.

Work is fine, but it's not like it was when I was there five days a week: now I almost feel like I'm trespassing when I go into the kitchen. I have to keep things as Josie likes, rather than the way I'd have them.

Sorry, just ignore me, I'm feeling a bit fed up. It seems like everyone else has someone except me. Feel free to tell me to pull myself together – I probably need it. But I _am_ happy for you, really I am. It's wonderful.

love Sarah xx

PS On a more positive note, I've sent in the first Martina and Charlie story to Paul and I'm waiting to hear his reaction. I enjoyed writing it, but I have no idea how good or bad it is. Time will tell.

The sitting-room door opened and Stephen walked in. 'Mum, Grandpa did a number two and never flushed the toilet.'

'Did you flush?'

'Yeah.'

'Good boy. Where's Grandpa now?'

'He's in the garden, but it's raining and he has no coat on.'

She folded the pages of the letter and slipped them into the waiting envelope. 'I'll be right out.'

This was her life now.

SARAH

'I do,' she said, becoming a wife for the second time.

It was the top of Scotland; it was the middle of October. Helen wore the same black dress she'd put on for their first dinner date eight months earlier, and a green velvet wrap borrowed from Alice, and horribly expensive flat silk pumps, to keep her an inch shorter than him. And the beautiful, beautiful necklace he'd given her the night before.

The church was tiny and ancient, ten knobbly wooden pews rubbed shiny by the elbows and rear ends of generations of mass-goers, an aisle running between them that had taken her fourteen bridal paces to cover. Its walls were thick enough to keep at bay the sharp wind that howled outside and the rain that pelted at the gorgeous little stained-glass windows, and its granite altar was slightly smaller than the average dining table.

Alice, standing on her mother's left, wore a pale grey trouser suit. Her newly blonde hair, long enough for the past few years to gather up, had been caught on top of her head with a triangular ivory clip, a style that managed to make her look both younger and older than her twenty-seven years.

The church held just three other occupants: the groom, the priest and the priest's niece Lara, whose suggestion the location had been. 'It was my local church growing up,' she'd told Helen. 'Uncle Peter has been there forever – he baptised all of us, and gave us communion and confirmation. He's a darling.'

Breen had been bemused at Helen's choice of wedding location. 'Aberdeen? In October? Could you possibly have found any place more remote?'

'It's not a bit remote – there's a direct flight from Dublin. Alice has been there with Lara, and she loved it. And I want to go away. I don't want to get married in Dublin.'

He didn't ask why. He knew why.

After the ceremony the little bridal party ran from the church through the wind and rain to the two waiting cars. They drove in convoy through the streets to the restaurant where Lara had waitressed every school holiday since she'd been old enough, and after the meal and the toasts, and the cake that Breen – *Breen!* – had insisted on, the two couples said goodbye to Uncle Peter and dashed across the road to the hotel where they were staying.

And later, lying awake in her sleeping husband's arms, Helen Breen listened to the storm that continued to rage outside the window of their room, and she recalled again her first wedding day, twenty-eight years earlier.

Another church, another man. She remembered her happiness that day, unaffected by her parents' disapproval – she hadn't cared how they felt, all she'd cared about was Cormac. She wondered what her parents would make of Breen. Probably approve: unlike Cormac, he was solvent and well educated. And when you thought about it, it was her mother who'd finally brought Helen and Breen together.

She turned her head and regarded his face, or what she could make out of it in the almost pure darkness of the room, and marvelled again that it had become so dear to her. She ran her fingertips lightly across his skin, feeling the tiny indentations of the pockmarks in his cheeks, the prickle of stubble on his chin, and he murmured and stirred, and gathered her closer to him.

And sometime during the night, the wind died down and the rain stopped and she slept, and didn't dream at all.

Sarah
It's done. Say hello to stupidly happy Helen Breen, currently honeymooning in Cornwall, as you can see from the picture on the other side. Weather mixed, beaches beautiful. We're walking and eating cream teas (he needs fattening up) and reading, and being

horribly competitive with the Independent's cryptic crossword. Home next week, when normal life will resume. Hope all's well.

H xx

SARAH

'When someone his age gets Alzheimer's, the progress is usually very rapid. I'm afraid you'll see big changes quite quickly. I'll drop by anytime I'm passing and see how it's going, but you'll need to consider putting him into full-time care sooner rather than later.'

'How soon?'

The doctor hesitated. 'Hard to be precise, but I would say we're talking weeks rather than months.'

Her father called her Dorothy, which had been his late mother's name, or Laura, his only sister, who'd died in a road accident at eighteen, years before Sarah had been born. He sat for hours without speaking, or roamed the house agitatedly – unable to tell her, when she asked, what he needed. He forgot words constantly, or used the wrong ones.

He stayed in bed each morning until she went into his room and helped him out of his pyjamas and into the tracksuit bottoms and loose sweaters that seemed most comfortable for him now. Once a week he sat in the bath while she washed him, like she'd washed Martha and Stephen as young children.

The children adapted astonishingly well. Martha, thirteen since May, read to him from the daily paper; ten-year-old Stephen sat beside him on the couch as they watched cartoons, or walked with him on milder days around the garden. Sarah marvelled at their capacity to accept what she struggled to come to terms with as she mourned the disintegration of his mind, the breakdown of the man she'd loved and depended on all her life.

He became incontinent. He wandered out of the house one day when she was preoccupied with dinner preparations, and was missing for three hours. He was finally discovered by Brian, sitting at a bus stop four miles away, and refused to return home, insisting that Brian was a stranger, until Christine arrived.

The weeks turned into months, confounding the doctor's predictions, and they continued somehow to manage his slide towards oblivion. And then one autumnal morning, when Sarah went in to get him up, she found him standing by the window in his pyjamas.

'Good morning,' she said in a voice that was too bright. 'You beat me to it.'

He turned to look at her, and the emptiness in his face frightened her.

'Are you all right?' she asked, walking towards him.

He clutched his pyjama top. 'Do I know you?' he asked.

In the afternoon she phoned the nursing home.

'I think it's time,' she said to Matron, struggling to keep her voice even.

'We'll get the room ready. He'll have the best of care, you know that.'

She did, but it broke her heart to see him there, in the very place she'd opted to spend less time in so that she could look after him. She'd look at him hunched in an armchair in his dressing-gown, other clothes having finally become redundant, and her heart would twist. More often than not, when she approached him he would look blankly at her, or ignore her completely.

The hardest thing, she wrote to Helen, *is that we're all strangers to him now. There's nobody he recognises – and I don't know if he's even aware of this, if he feels totally alone in the world, or if he's gone beyond feeling anything. It really is the cruellest illness.*

I think, Helen replied, *that it's safe to assume he knows nothing. I think the suffering is all on the part of the family members who are all too aware of the changes, and I can imagine how awful it is for you. I wish I could help, but all I can do is offer useless little fripperies, and my good wishes.*

She sent a fountain pen whose barrel was made of pale wood, and a small bottle of jade green ink.

Mum told me about your dad, Alice wrote on one of her handmade cards. *That must be so sad for you. I'm thinking of you, and hoping that you're managing.* She enclosed a slim little book called *Reflections,* a gathering together of poems by various people, some of whose names Sarah remembered from her schooldays, and a bar of the same chocolate she'd sent after Luke.

Neil and Maria visited Sarah's father once a fortnight. They brought grapes and bottles of Lucozade and sat with him in his room, or brought him outside to shuffle with them up and down the corridor.

Maria looked about thirty. Her auburn hair was cut into an asymmetrical bob, her clothes tailored, her nail varnish unchipped. She and Neil had met when she'd employed him to overhaul the garden of her parents' house. She'd moved in with him soon after Sarah had been told of her existence, and she commuted now to her PR job in Dublin.

'I got your cookbooks for my niece,' she had told Sarah, the first time they'd met. 'She loves them.'

'She has a sports car,' Stephen had reported. 'She let me put the roof down.'

'Can I get my ears pierced?' Martha had asked. 'Maria says she'll take me if you say yes.'

A month ago, Neil had asked Sarah for a divorce. She had seen no reason to refuse.

Her first Martina and Charlie story was almost ready for publication. Paul was aiming to have it on the shelves in time for the Christmas market.

'You've found your true calling,' he'd said. 'It's charming, it's simple and it's full of warmth. You'll go far as a children's writer.'

She had taken no pleasure from his words, no pleasure at all.

HELEN

It was shocking how quickly they'd fallen into the kind of routine that might be expected of a couple who'd been married for fifty years. It was slightly unnerving how much she enjoyed it.

Presented with a choice of three places to live in, they'd opted for Helen's. The three-storey red-brick terraced house Breen had shared with his wife had been put on the market, along with Helen's parents' home – for different reasons, neither dwelling had appealed to her. Breen professed himself well satisfied to live in Helen's house, although it was by far the least impressive of the three.

The neighbourhood was changing. There had been a recent influx of young professionals to the area, renovating and open-planning and attic-converting as they went. Helen wasn't altogether sure she approved of all the changes: the old shabbiness had had a character to it that she suspected was being replaced with something a lot more sterile and less interesting. She took some comfort from the fact that Cormac's house had remained as unchanged as possible in her twenty-eight-year tenure.

She and Breen had no long-term plan: time to think again if both properties sold – and with the housing market continuing to boom, there was every reason to believe they wouldn't have long to wait.

In the meantime Helen was happy to go on living in the house where Alice had grown up. The fact that Frank had also lived there for a few years, and the manner of their parting, still caused her an occasional pang of guilt: she hoped he'd met someone who deserved him.

She and Breen both worked from home, in separate rooms. She continued to write for various publications at the kitchen table; he compiled crosswords, proofread theses and copy-edited literary publications in the sitting room, with one or both of the cats normally keeping him company.

And every day Helen discovered a little more about him.

He was left-handed – how had she never noticed that? His birthday was on January the first. His grandfather's fifteen younger siblings had all emigrated. His only brother had died of septicaemia at the age of thirty after impaling his foot on a rusty nail, leaving behind a wife who'd since remarried, and an infant daughter. Both his parents had been university lecturers.

He had a sweet tooth. He was a far more accomplished cook than Helen, and desserts always featured when he was on dinner duty, which was most of the time. In three months of marriage she'd gained almost a stone.

He was allergic to penicillin and grapefruit. His only form of exercise was walking. He enjoyed classical music but despised opera. He'd had his appendix removed at ten, his tonsils at twelve. He'd never had chicken pox, mumps or measles. So far in his life he'd broken one arm, one collarbone and one ankle. His favourite season was autumn.

He'd been deflowered by an older woman, a married neighbour, when he was seventeen, and employed to mow their lawn over the summer. She'd followed him into the shed when he'd been returning the mower.

'I had no choice in the matter,' he told Helen. 'She had her knickers off before I knew where I was. I think I was a major disappointment, all over in about thirty seconds. It never happened again.'

They lived quietly, venturing out only occasionally to a play or a concert she was reviewing, or to have dinner with two couples he'd known for years. Soon after returning from honeymoon he'd organised a dinner party to introduce them to Helen.

'You want to invite some of your friends?' he'd asked.

'I have one friend,' she'd told him. 'She lives in Kildare. I told you about her.'

'That's the penfriend you've never met.'

'But we've been writing to one another for twenty years.'

'And you never felt like coming face to face?'

'We came close a couple of times, but it didn't happen. Probably not meant to be.'

Breen's inherited cats were mother and daughter, both neutered. The mother was affectionate, the daughter aloof. They slept curled together in a corner of the couch, and made ribbons of the kitchen chair legs when Helen wasn't looking.

You'll love them, she wrote to Alice. *Remember how you used to spoil Malone's cat, and beg me to let him sleep indoors? These two do, you'll be delighted to hear. Breen insists they've been brought up as house cats and it would be cruel to expect them to live outdoors. I said I bet they'd love the freedom, but I got nowhere.*

Alice and Lara had also moved in together. *We chose my flat because it's more central*, Alice wrote, *but it's very small for two, so we're on the hunt for a bigger one.*

Wonderland Design was doing well, three people working for Alice now. *Still can't think of myself as a boss. I suppose technically I'm the managing director but so far I've stuck with senior designer.*

She and Lara were going to Portugal for a week over Christmas, which meant Helen and Breen would be on their own. The first time her daughter and mother wouldn't be with her on Christmas Day – and even if they hadn't always gelled across the turkey and Brussels sprouts, she knew this year's celebration would be poignant in their absence.

'What do you want to do for Christmas?' she asked Breen. 'Looks like it's going to be just the two of us.'

'You want to go somewhere?'

She thought about booking into a hotel, eating turkey and ham surrounded by strangers in paper hats, like she and her little group had done in Troon. Or lying on a beach somewhere, having to keep reminding themselves that it was December the twenty-fifth. Neither scenario seemed right for their first Christmas together.

'I don't know,' she said. 'I'm just not sure that I want to stay here, in this house.'

'We do have two more houses,' he pointed out, but she shook her head. Not her parents', where the ghost of her mother might well still be hovering, and certainly not his house – what kind of awful Christmases must he have endured there?

'Well,' he said, 'that just leaves Connemara.'

'Connemara? You mean rent a house or something?'

'No.' He closed his crossword book, took off his glasses. 'I mean I have a house there. Just outside a village, about a mile from the sea.'

She stared. 'You have a house in Connemara? When were you planning to tell me about it?'

'Whenever it came up,' he said, and she felt the familiar urge to take him by the jacket lapels and shake him, hard.

'And now that it's come up, any other properties I should know about?'

He smiled. 'No, just this one. I bought it ten years ago. Seemed like a good idea at the time.'

Ten years ago, after he'd taken early retirement. 'What's it like?'

'It's small. It's a cottage, just two bedrooms. I

always liked Connemara, had the daft notion that I might move there eventually.'

I, not we. He hadn't planned on bringing his first wife.

'Have you gone there much?' she asked.

'I spent a bit of time there, after Kathleen died. Before that, not much.'

She imagined him, retired and newly widowed, looking out at the fields, or maybe the distant sea, and wondering what to do with the rest of his life.

'What condition is it in?'

'Actually, it's quite comfortable. I added central heating and spruced it up a bit. It's not the Ritz, but it's habitable.'

'It'll do,' she said.

It didn't really matter where they spent Christmas: what mattered was that he would be with her. But a small cottage in Connemara, with no memories to disturb either of them, seemed to her the perfect location for their first Christmas together.

We're getting away from it all, she wrote to Sarah. *We're going deep into the heart of Connemara, where it turns out my new husband owns a holiday cottage – he just mentioned it casually the other night. We'll walk by day and eat and drink in the evenings, and maybe take the odd trip into Galway for a city fix. Can't wait.*

It sounds wonderful, Sarah wrote back. *Christmas for me this year will be very different too – Neil asked if he and Maria can have the children, and since they've been with me every Christmas since we split up, I didn't feel I could refuse, so I'll work in the nursing home in the morning as usual, and then I'm going to Christine's for dinner. It'll be different, but I'm sure very enjoyable.*

Poor Sarah. Her father's last Christmas, by the sound of it, and her children gone to spend it with her ex and his new partner. Cooking turkey for the few lost souls in the nursing home, serving it up to a man who no longer recognised her. Going to her sister's house afterwards to pretend it was where she wanted to be.

There were two bits of positive news in her letter.

I just got advance copies of *Martina and Charlie Go on Holidays*, and it looks great. Paul has promised to send you a copy, so keep an eye out for it. It's due on the shelves some time in the next week, fingers crossed. And please don't feel you have to review it, honestly.

And listen to this – Stephen's music teacher has put his name forward for a public recital in the National Concert Hall! It's a fundraiser in aid of the street children of Calcutta, and it's going to feature music students from all over the country. Stephen will be the youngest performer by a mile – he's just gone eleven – and he's really looking forward to it.

My only small worry is that I'll have to drive up to Dublin that evening on my own. Neil will have Martha, it's one of his weekends, so she'll travel with him and Maria, and Stephen will be going earlier in the day with his music teacher – but I'm sure I'll cope. I've got directions from Brian, who often drives there on business, so if I give myself plenty of time I should be fine.

It's taking place on the Friday before Christmas, and if you haven't left for the west by then I'd love it if you both could come. Maybe we'll be third time lucky in meeting up!

'We're going to a concert,' Helen told Breen. 'I'll introduce you to my penfriend. Her son is playing the piano, and she'd like us to go.'

We'll be there, she wrote. *I'll be the one in the red coat, and Breen will have his cranky face on – nothing personal, just the one he normally wears going out. Meet you at the bottom of the stairs before the show.*

Friday before Christmas, just two weeks away. No reason why they shouldn't finally come face to face. After twenty years, it felt like the right time.

SARAH

'Excuse me.'

Pushing her trolley through the exit doors, Sarah stopped and turned.

'I hope you don't mind,' the balding man behind her said, 'but I think I know you.'

He didn't look familiar. 'I'm not sure—'

'Did you by any chance work in St Sebastian's nursing home a long time ago?'

'Actually, I—'

'In the kitchen? Were you the cook there?'

She became aware that they were holding up the flow of shoppers. She pulled her trolley back inside and stepped out of the doorway, and looked at him again. Most of his hair gone but face not that lined, brown eyes, about her own height. Pleasant-looking.

'I still work there,' she told him, 'but I'm just part-time now. I'm afraid I can't—'

'I wouldn't expect you to remember me,' he said. 'You must have met so many, and I was only there for an hour on a Sunday to visit Mam.'

One of the Sunday visitors, a son who'd been shown off in the common room.

'She was Celine,' he said, 'Celine O'Reilly, and I'm Kevin.' He put out his hand. 'And if I remember right, your name is Sarah.'

'Yes . . .'

Celine, who'd died within a year or two of Sarah starting work in the nursing home, who'd boasted to her friends of Kevin with his big job. Something to do with banking, wasn't it?

'You were very good to her,' he said. 'She had great time for you, said you always dropped in to see her when you weren't busy. And she couldn't say enough good things about your cooking.'

'You brought her fudge,' Sarah said, the memory leaping into her head.

He laughed. 'I can't believe you remember that. She had a weakness for it.'

'And you walked with her in the garden.'

She could see them now, him bent over to accommodate his mother's much lower height, his arm linked through hers as they made their slow way around the shrubbery, such as it was. Several years before Charlie had arrived to tidy it up.

Hard to put an age on him but he must be a bit older than her, somewhere in his fifties, she thought. She didn't remember anyone else coming to see Celine; maybe he'd been an only child.

'So you're still there,' he said. 'They're lucky to have you.'

She smiled. 'And you? Do you still work in . . . a bank, was it?'

'I was an accountant, but about ten years ago I

decided to change direction a bit, and I went back to college and studied psychotherapy.'

'Really? That's a big change.'

She looked a fright, hadn't even run a comb through her hair before coming out, hadn't put on lipstick or perfume, and the navy trousers should have gone to the charity shop a decade ago. Sometime over the past few months, she'd stopped caring.

He tipped his head towards her trolley. 'Anything in there that wouldn't keep for half an hour? I'd love to buy you a coffee, just to say thanks for looking after Mam.'

It wasn't a date. It wasn't anything like a date. He might be killing time, looking for some diversion to pass thirty minutes. Or he might be dying for a coffee himself, and wanting some company while he drank it.

But he was friendly, and he'd come to visit his mother each week. And she couldn't remember the last time a man had given her a second glance.

'That would be lovely,' she said.

HELEN

Alice

As we won't be meeting up till after Christmas, I'm sending you and Lara a little something for Portugal. Well, Breen is – he insisted. And far from advising you not to spend it all in the one place, he says feel free to do just that. I'm beginning to suspect that I married a rich man. Luckily, he's also generous.

He's got a house in Connemara. I only found out the other night. He's full of surprises. We've decided to go there for Christmas. He assures me it's habitable – if not, we're decamping to the nearest hotel.

And guess what – it looks like I'm finally going to meet Sarah. Her son is playing in the Concert Hall next Friday, and we're going along. I'll tell her you said hello.

Happy Christmas to you both. Have fun. Will be thinking of you.

Mum xxx

SARAH

In the end she chose a navy top and a cream skirt. It wasn't the most eye-catching outfit in the world, or even particularly fashionable, but top and skirt were well cut – sale bargains, both of them – and the peplum end to the top disguised the fact that her waistline wasn't as trim as it could be.

She was cycling so much less now, that was the problem. For years she'd been able to eat what she wanted: covering the fifteen-mile round trip to and from work on a bike five days a week ensured that any extra calories were well burnt up. Even after she'd begun driving the children to school she'd brought the bike in the boot and cycled on to the nursing home from there.

But now, with only two days of work, and the children needing to be driven around so much after school, she wasn't getting half enough exercise, and her sweet tooth made it hard to resist the treats she baked for Stephen and Martha.

It was time, she decided, to take it in hand. She was only forty-eight, and perfectly healthy, with years of active life left to her. Starting tomorrow, she'd get back on the bike. On the days she wasn't working she'd do a couple of hours in the morning, and when the children were with Neil she'd cycle to the nursing home to see Dad. It would be like old times.

And she'd update her wardrobe, which hadn't had much attention in the last few years. There were some lovely bright clothes out there, and she needn't spend a fortune.

It was natural to want to look good, to try to be at the right weight for your height. It had nothing whatsoever to do with Kevin O'Reilly.

'Maybe we could go out to dinner sometime,' he'd said, at the end of the almost-hour they'd spent together. Having discovered, because she'd told him, that she was in the process of getting divorced, and having let her know that he was also single – that he'd never, in fact, walked down the aisle.

'Confirmed bachelor,' he'd said, 'or never lucky enough to meet whoever I was supposed to meet, depending on your point of view. Mam used to tell me I had plenty of time.'

Sarah had laughed. 'Typical Irish mother. I don't think I can bear the thought of my son choosing another woman over me, and he's only eleven.'

It had been a while since she'd laughed. It had felt good. She'd given him her phone number, and he'd promised to call. She'd come away feeling uplifted: maybe it was something to do with his psychotherapy course – maybe he'd learnt how to make everyone he met feel better.

She pushed her feet into her old loafers, better for driving. She'd bring the heels and change when she arrived. She was dreading the drive to Dublin – after seven years of being legally entitled to sit behind the wheel of a car she still hated it, still finished every journey with her jaw aching from having clenched her teeth all the way.

And to have to do it on her own was far worse, but there was no alternative. She had to have the car to get home afterwards, with the concert ending too late for public transport. And she couldn't very well have asked Neil to let her hang on to Martha, just so she'd have company on the drive.

She supposed she could have swallowed her pride and asked if she could sit in with them – but the thought of having to make polite conversation with him and Maria all the way to Dublin and back was enough to put her off that idea.

'I'd love to come,' Christine had said, 'we both would, but Brian's Christmas work do is set in stone – there's no way we can't be there. You could bring Paddy if you like; I'm sure he wouldn't mind sitting in.'

But Paddy was fifteen and mad into sports – a three-hour concert would, she was sure, be his idea of absolute hell, and she couldn't do it to him. The other two boys were going – Aidan and Tom were both in Trinity now, and happy to turn up in support of their cousin – but they were already in Dublin, and of no help to her.

She'd manage, she'd be fine. She had Brian's very detailed directions printed out: all she had to do was follow them.

'Don't be distracted by other drivers,' he'd told her. 'If someone hoots at you, just ignore them. Don't speed up to keep someone else happy. And don't panic if you take a wrong turn, just pull into a side road when you can and turn around. You'll be fine if you keep calm.'

She'd keep calm, she'd get there. And she'd be meeting Helen in her red coat, and Mark, her new husband. She couldn't call him Breen: it sounded too impersonal. She hoped Helen would introduce him as Mark.

Funny, she was so keyed up about driving to Dublin, not to mention seeing Stephen on the stage, that she had no butterflies left to feel nervous about meeting Helen at last. They were grown women, for goodness' sake, they'd be fine. In fact, she was quite looking forward to it.

She checked her lipstick, patted her hair. Pity she hadn't looked like this when she'd bumped into Kevin. But he'd asked for her number all the same, and she'd make damn sure she looked good the next time they met.

Forty-eight, not too old at all to start again. Look at Helen, head over heels at fifty-six. Maybe it was Sarah's turn now.

She left the bedroom and went downstairs. The house always seemed too quiet without the children, and without her father now too. She slipped on her grey coat, wrapped Christine's silk scarf loosely around her neck.

'You can have a loan,' she'd said to Sarah. 'It'll help you make a good first impression.'

It was still in perfect condition, the swirls of colour just as fresh as when Sarah had seen it for the first time, lying on the wooden bridge. No harm to wear it, she supposed, with its original owner, and the traumatic circumstances of that day, just a distant memory now. And it was beautiful.

She took her car keys from their hook and left the house, closing the door with a soft click.

HELEN

'We'll have to take our seats,' Breen said, 'or they won't let us in.'

'Hang on, just another minute.'

But he was right. The lobby was practically empty, the last few patrons making their way to the auditorium. Helen checked the programme again, and Stephen Flannery was still listed as the second last performer in the first half of the concert. Sarah must be here; she must already be inside. She'd never have left it till the last minute to arrive.

The bell to call them to the performance rang again: they had to go. Walking up the stairs, Helen tried to remember what exactly she'd written. *Meet you at the bottom of the stairs before the show* – she could have sworn that was it. Maybe Sarah had forgotten, in the excitement of Stephen being part of the concert. Or maybe he'd got stage fright; maybe she'd had to go backstage to keep him calm. Yes, that was probably it.

As they took their seats on the upper level, the lights dimmed. Helen strained to look down into the stalls – Sarah and the others would surely have got seats near the front. She searched for a group that contained a teenage girl, a man and two women, but it was hard to make out much from the backs of people's heads. Maybe they weren't all sitting together, of course; maybe Neil and his new partner had got separate tickets.

There were empty seats dotted here and there, one in the very front row – but Sarah must be here. Helen sat back: nothing to do but wait for the interval and try again.

The concert got under way, a mix of choral and instrumental performances, overseen by an enthusiastic master of ceremonies who took, Helen felt, slightly too long to introduce each act. Stephen, when he finally appeared on stage – she'd noticed Breen checking his watch more than once – turned out to be slight and fair-haired, in a blue jacket and grey trousers. She watched him trotting onto the stage, looking remarkably composed for an eleven-year-old, and she imagined how his mother must be feeling.

As he played his two allotted pieces, she searched the audience again for anyone taking a particular interest in his performance, but once more she found no clues. The applause at the end was enthusiastic – partly, she guessed, to do with his age, although his performance had been surprisingly good – but nobody stood or waved or gave any indication that they had a special connection with him.

'What do you want to do?' Breen asked when the lights came up.

Helen took her coat from the back of her seat. 'I'm going to wait at the bottom of the stairs. She might have thought I said the interval.'

He looked doubtful. He'd probably decided that Sarah was her imaginary friend. 'Do we have to stay for the second half?'

'No, we don't.'

She'd be happy to leave too: there was only so much teenage prodigy you could be expected to stomach, especially when you weren't related to any of them. They walked downstairs.

'Bring me a red wine,' she instructed, and off he went, threading through the chattering crowds.

For the duration of the interval she stood among the perfumed women and suited men, and teenagers who looked as if they'd far rather be out getting drunk in a field than sitting in their best clothes listening to the talented one in the family. She held her red coat over her arm, perfectly visible to anyone who might be looking for one, but nobody gave it, or her, a second glance.

By the time Breen reappeared with their drinks the interval was almost over, and Helen had given up. Sarah had been preoccupied with her son and simply forgotten their arrangement to meet. So much for finally coming face to face, so much for a friendship that had turned out, after all, not to be worth the paper it was written on.

The bell rang for the end of the interval. The crowd began to drift back. Helen sipped her wine and found it to be undrinkable. She placed her glass on a nearby ledge.

'Let's go,' she said.

SARAH

Dear Mrs Flannery
Hope you like the Christmas card – it's one we designed for our clients and freelancers. I just wanted to wish you and your children a very happy Christmas. Mum told me about Stephen being in a music concert. You must be really happy about that. I hope things are OK with your father too. Tell Martha if she decides to become an artist, there's a job waiting for her in Edinburgh.

love Alice xx

PS We're heading off to Portugal tomorrow – Christmas in the sun!

HELEN

'Do I need to bring a hairdryer?' she called.

Nothing.

'Breen?'

'Helen, can you come in here a minute?'

She looked up. He never called her Helen. She crossed the landing and walked into the bedroom, still carrying the hairdryer.

He was standing by the bed. 'What did you say your friend's surname was?'

'What?'

His suitcase sat on the bed, half filled with clothes. The radio was on, someone was talking.

'Sarah,' he said, 'your penfriend. What's her last name?'

She frowned. 'Why on earth would you want to know that?'

'Is it Flannery?' he asked. 'Just tell me, please.'

A beat passed. Her face changed.

'I'm sorry,' he said, coming towards her. 'I'm so sorry, that accident on Fri—'

'No,' she said, her head shaking slowly from side to side. 'Don't tell me that.'

'I heard it just now on—'

'No, don't *tell* me that.'

'I'm so sorry, Helen—'

He took the hairdryer from her and laid it on the bed. She balled her hands into fists and squeezed her eyes closed as his arms went around her.

'Oh, God,' she said quietly, leaning into his embrace. 'Oh, *Jesus* Christ, you shouldn't have told me that.'

HELEN AND SARAH

She knew them all.

There in the front pew was Neil, who'd proposed to Sarah halfway up a Kerry hillside, who was useless at maths, who'd forgotten their fifth anniversary, who hated avocados and loved Jerusalem artichokes, who could make anything grow, who'd broken Sarah's heart.

There he stood, wearing a grey suit that looked a size too small, the black tie around his neck drawing attention to the double chin. It was all she could do to shake his hand, to meet the grey eyes behind the glasses for an instant.

And here was his mother Nuala beside him, the same chin, the same long nose. A wizened little woman bent into a navy coat, her arm around the fair-haired boy with the chalk-white bewildered face who'd played the piano for hundreds of people just three nights earlier, unaware that his mother was already dead.

And next to them Christine, her face swollen and blotchy with grief, blonde hair twisted into a knotted black scarf, tailored black coat belted tightly, leaning in to cradle the niece – it must be

596

Martha – who pressed, sobbing quietly, against her. Martha's features hard to make out, small-boned, dark-haired, the precious adopted daughter who wanted to be an artist, like Alice.

And in the seat behind, sitting in a mute row, were surely Sarah's three nephews: Aidan, the soon-to-be doctor; Tom, whose nose was usually stuck into a book; Paddy, mad about rugby and surfing. And beside them, in his navy suit, their father Brian, the accountant who loved his sister-in-law's tangy lemon tart, who had given Sarah driving directions to Dublin.

And surely, in the row behind, the woman in her thirties with the expensive haircut and camel coat was Neil's new partner, who'd bought Stephen's affection with a Game Boy, who'd tempted Martha with a few bottles of nail polish.

Helen knew them all.

She made her way along the front pew with the other mourners. She shook hands and said she was sorry, and she made no mention of who she was. She moved on and stood by the closed coffin that was wreathed in flowers. Propped on a side table was a copy of *Martina and Charlie Go on Holidays*, which had appeared in bookshops a fortnight earlier, and next to it a framed head-and-shoulders colour photograph of its author.

Helen studied the face of the woman she'd been writing to for two decades. Sarah wore a blue top whose V-neck was edged with lace, and a row of tiny pearls. Light-brown wavy hair, small nose,

597

blue pale-lashed eyes from which tiny lines had begun to fan, generous mouth. The kind of gentle smile that encouraged you to ask for directions, a fragility about it that told you it wouldn't take much to wipe it away.

It was an ordinary face. You wouldn't turn your head to have a second look at it, but if she smiled at you it would come from her eyes, and you'd know she meant it. She had the kind of face you felt you knew, a face you felt you might have seen before.

She'd driven into a tree, less than a mile from her home, on a road she must have used countless times before. It had happened long before she got to the motorway that she was so nervous of. No other car had been involved, no witnesses had come forward. The accident had been discovered by a young woman out walking her dog.

She'd died instantly, from a broken neck. She might have skidded on wet leaves; it might have been that.

'Are you sure you want to know?' Breen had asked.

'Find out,' Helen had told him, so he'd made phone calls and asked questions, and they'd learnt what there was to know.

Sarah was forty-eight. She was only forty-eight, and now she was dead.

In the church car park there was a yellow minibus with *St Sebastian's Nursing Home* on the side. They'd sat together in one of the side aisles, a huddle of bowed grey heads, the people Sarah had fed and nurtured and loved.

Afterwards, the ones who could walk had shuffled to the top to shake hands with the bereaved family; the rest had been wheeled by women and men wearing coats over their white uniforms. Sarah's father, Helen assumed, was not among the old men. No mourning for a daughter he no longer remembered.

They sat into the car and Breen immediately turned the heat on full. They watched as the coffin was slid into the hearse. In the knot of people still emerging from the church Helen spotted Paul, come to pay his respects to his most obliging author. They waited until the other cars had started to move off behind the hearse, and then they joined the line.

After the burial they were driving west. Their suitcases were in the boot, the Dublin house locked up until the New Year, the two cats packed off, much to their disgust, to a local cattery.

'Are you going to talk to any of them?' Breen asked. 'Are you going to introduce yourself?'

'No.'

What was the point in meeting them? They had nothing in common except Sarah, and she was gone.

They drove slowly through the winding country roads, behind a dark-green, mud-spattered Ford Escort with a Kildare number plate. The car grew warm. Helen opened the buttons on her coat and tried not to think about the space that Sarah would leave behind.

The funeral cortège turned onto a bridge, not attractive in the least. As she looked through the horrible mesh fencing at the river below, an image flitted for an instant across her mind – a falling cigarette, a bicycle – gone too quickly for her to grab hold and make sense of it.

She reached across and laid the back of her hand against Breen's thigh. He glanced over.

'OK?'

She nodded. He covered her hand with his. They reached the end of the bridge and drove off.